EDUCATING JACK

www.transworldbooks.co.uk

EDUCATING
JACK

The Alternative School Logbook 1982–1983

Jack Sheffield

BANTAM PRESS

LONDON · TORONTO · SYDNEY · AUCKLAND · JOHANNESBURG

TRANSWORLD PUBLISHERS
61–63 Uxbridge Road, London W5 5SA
A Random House Group Company
www.transworldbooks.co.uk

First published in Great Britain
in 2012 by Bantam Press
an imprint of Transworld Publishers

A CIP catalogue record for this book
is available from the British Library.

ISBN 9780593065693

Addresses for Random House Group Ltd companies outside the UK
can be found at: www.randomhouse.co.uk
The Random House Group Ltd Reg. No. 954009

The Random House Group Limited supports the Forest Stewardship
Council (FSC®), the leading international forest-certification organization.
Our books carrying the FSC label are printed on FSC®-certified paper.
FSC is the only forest-certification scheme endorsed by the leading
environmental organizations, including Greenpeace.
Our paper procurement policy can be found at
www.randomhouse.co.uk/environment.

Typeset in 11/15pt Palatino by
Kestrel Data, Exeter, Devon.
Printed and bound in Great Britain by
Clays Ltd, Bungay, Suffolk.

2 4 6 8 10 9 7 5 3 1

For Linda Evans

Contents

Acknowledgements 9

Map 11

Prologue 13

1   The Problem with Patience 17

2   A Decision for Vera 35

3   Ruby's Great Expectations 51

4   Roman Holiday 67

5   A Penny for the Guy 84

6   Flash Gordon and the Time-and-Motion Expert 102

7   Penny's Army 121

8   A Wedding in the Village 139

9   The Last Christmas Present 156

10 The Refuse Collectors' Annual Ball 173

11 Full English Breakfast 192

12 The Ragley Book Club 208

13 The Cleethorpes Clairvoyant   224
14 The Solitary Sidesman   243
15 Heathcliffe and the Dragon   257
16 Gandhi and the Rogation Walk   276
17 Lollipop Lil' and the Zebra Crossing   292
18 The Women's Institute Potato Champion   307
19 Educating Jack   322

Acknowledgements

I am indeed fortunate to have the support of a wonderful editor, the superb Linda Evans, and the excellent team at Transworld including Larry Finlay, Bill Scott-Kerr, Laura Sherlock, Lynsey Dalladay, Elizabeth Swain, Vivien Garrett, Sophie Holmes, copy-editor Brenda Updegraff, and the 'foot soldiers' – fellow 'Old Roundhegian' Martin Myers and the quiet, unassuming Mike *'Rock 'n Roll'* Edgerton.

Special thanks go to my industrious literary agent, Newcastle United supporter and Britain's leading authority on 80s Airfix Modelling Kits, Philip Patterson of Marjacq Scripts, for his encouragement, good humour and deep appreciation of Yorkshire cricket.

I am also grateful to all those who assisted in the research for this novel – in particular: Patrick Busby, Pricing Director, church organist and Harrogate Rugby Club supporter, Hampshire; Janina Bywater, neonatal nurse and lecturer in psychology, Cornwall; the Revd Ben Flenley, Rector of Bentworth, Lasham, Medstead and

Shalden, Hampshire; Tony Greenan, Yorkshire's finest headteacher (now retired), Huddersfield, Yorkshire; George and Gladys Hook, retired majors in the Salvation Army, Alton, Hampshire; Ian Jurd, churchwarden of St Andrew's Church, Medstead, and local builder, Hampshire; John Kirby, ex-policeman, expert calligrapher and Sunderland supporter, County Durham; Roy Linley, Enterprise Architect, Unilever Global Expertise Team and Leeds United supporter, Port Sunlight, Wirral; Sue Maddison, primary school teacher and expert cook, Harrogate, Yorkshire; Sue Matthews, primary school teacher and John Denver enthusiast, Wigginton, Yorkshire; Phil Parker, ex-teacher and Manchester United supporter, Holme-upon-Spalding Moor, Yorkshire; Dr Alison Rickard, General Practitioner, Alton, Hampshire; Elaine Roberts, ex-teacher and gardening expert, Haxby, Yorkshire; Caroline Stockdale, librarian, York Central Library, Yorkshire and all the terrific staff at Waterstone's Alton and Waterstone's Farnham, Hampshire, and Waterstone's York.

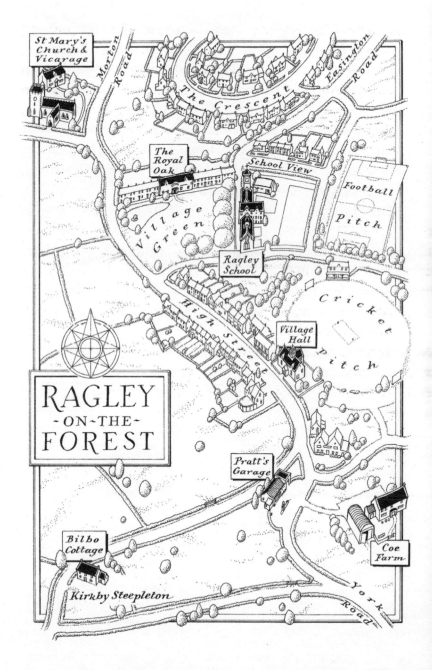

Prologue

The accident was destined to change our lives.

Like ripples on a pond after a stone has shattered the surface, all of us were affected by the reaction . . . some more than others. The tremors washed over the still surface of our thoughts and we all knew that life would never be the same again. It was time for a new direction . . . it was time for change. By the end of the academic year 1982/83 we would all be leading different lives. It was a year we would never forget, although it began quietly.

On Wednesday, 1 September 1982, I was sitting alone in the school office. All was silent apart from the ticking of the old school clock that echoed in the Victorian rafters. On this sunlit autumn day my sixth year as headmaster of Ragley-on-the-Forest Church of England Primary School in North Yorkshire was about to begin. However, the dawn of a new school year was far from my thoughts. The familiar pattern of our working lives had altered. Through the open office door in the entrance hall I could see Ruby the caretaker's galvanized bucket and mop, a reminder of times past. Vera the secretary's desk stood empty and tiny specks of dust settled on its shiny surface. Today was different: it was a morning of memories.

There are three sides to every story; at least that's how it seemed. After the car crash, Ruby the caretaker said she thought she would never see her new grandchild. Vera the secretary firmly believed the power of prayer had kept them both alive. Meanwhile, the lorry driver who caused the accident and emerged without a scratch, simply blamed the rain.

Six weeks had passed since that telephone call on the last day of the summer term. Vera's car had been hit by a skidding lorry on the rain-drenched road to York. Ruby had been the worst casualty, with a damaged pelvis and a broken leg, and was still recovering in York Hospital. The redoubtable Vera had also been badly injured, with fractured ribs and a collapsed lung. Her breastbone had been severely bruised after being crushed against the steering wheel. However, she had returned home and recovered relatively quickly. Since then, as often as she could she spent an hour by Ruby's bedside.

Now the summer holiday was almost over and the new academic year beckoned. Vera was ready to return to work and she had arranged for a temporary caretaker to do Ruby's duties. I took a deep breath and wondered what the school year had in store. It was a day of silent aspirations, a morning of fresh hope. Our familiar world had tilted a few degrees. At first it was imperceptible, but soon it became clear that our lives would change for ever. It began with small steps, but it led to a new pathway and a different journey . . . and for me, it was an education.

The clock ticked on. Outside a breeze sprang up and the branches of the horse-chestnut trees that bordered the front of the school shivered in the September sunshine. I sighed as I unlocked the bottom drawer of my desk, removed the large, leather-bound school logbook and opened it to the next clean page. Then I filled my fountain pen with black Quink ink, wrote the date and stared at the empty page.

The record of another school year was about to begin. Five years ago, the retiring headmaster, John Pruett, had told me how to fill in the official school logbook. 'Just keep it simple,' he said. 'Whatever you do, don't say what really happens, because no one will believe you!'

So the real stories were written in my 'Alternative School Logbook'. And this is it!

Chapter One

The Problem with Patience

86 children were registered on roll on the first day of the school year. Mrs Earnshaw began duties as temporary caretaker. A blocked sink in the reception class caused minor flooding in the cloakroom area.

Extract from the Ragley School Logbook:
Monday, 6 September 1982

'We've gorra problem, Mr Sheffield,' said Mrs Connie Crapper. She was standing in the school entrance hall outside the open office door.

'Have we?'

'We 'ave that. Our Patience 'as 'ad 'er ears pierced.'

'Oh, I see,' I said, glancing down at her four-year-old daughter.

Little Patience Crapper was wearing a Barbie-doll T-shirt, pink leggings, multi-coloured *Fame* leg warmers and white pixie boots. She was also sucking a stick of liquorice and she gave me a black-toothed smile.

'So what exactly is the problem?' I asked.

'Well we've given 'er a nice pair o' them little earrings jus' t'get 'er started,' said Mrs Crapper, 'an' ah don't want Mrs Grainger telling 'er t'tek 'em out.'

'Ah, I see,' I said. 'Well . . . I'm sorry to have to tell you, Mrs Crapper, but we don't encourage the wearing of jewellery.'

'Be that as it may, Mr Sheffield, but ah believe in start-ing 'em young wi' t'important things in life. It meks sense dunt it?'

We both looked down at Patience, who was picking her nose with a liquorice-coated finger. 'I suppose it depends on what's *important*,' I said and began to clean my black-framed Buddy Holly spectacles to give me thinking time. I didn't want to offend a parent or upset this little girl on her first day at Ragley.

At that moment the deputy headteacher, Anne Grainger, arrived from the store cupboard carrying a box of coloured chalks. A slim, attractive brunette, Anne had been a reassuring presence in Ragley School for more years than she cared to remember. With her professionalism and boundless patience she was a wonderful colleague and a loyal supporter. However, it was her ability to turn her class into a world of light, colour and excitement that marked her out as such an outstanding teacher and an example to us all.

Even so, Anne appeared preoccupied. There was clearly something on her mind. 'Good morning, Connie,' she said with a fixed smile and turned to me with a knowing look. 'Mrs Crapper was in my class twenty years ago, in the Sixties, Mr Sheffield. You know her mother-in-law, Elsie, who plays the organ in church.'

'Ah, yes,' I said, recalling our Valium-sedated organist and perhaps understanding for the first time why her nerves were always frayed.

Anne crouched down and took the little girl's sticky hand. 'And this must be Patience,' she said cheerfully. 'We're painting pictures today in our class.'

'Ah ain't gonna paint,' said Patience bluntly.

'Oh well,' said Anne quickly, 'we've got some lovely coloured chalks.'

'Ah ain't gonna chalk,' retorted the little girl.

Mrs Crapper beamed with pride at this response. 'She knows 'ow many beans mek five, does our Patience,' she said, which, in terms of mathematical accuracy, as we were soon to discover, was actually far from the truth.

'Oh well, there are lots of lovely new books to read,' said Anne with a reassuring smile.

'Ah ain't gonna read,' said Patience as she swallowed the last piece of liquorice and then looked up appealingly at her mother. 'Ah wanna big-shit,' she mumbled.

I looked in alarm at Mrs Crapper and then at Anne, who remained surprisingly calm.

'AH WANNA BIG-SHIT,' shouted Patience, going red in the face.

Mrs Crapper rummaged in her bag, pulled out a packet of milk chocolate digestive biscuits and gave one to Patience, who began to lick off the chocolate.

'Ah . . . a *biscuit*,' I said as realization dawned.

Anne gave me a wide-eyed look. 'Well, lots to do,' she said as she stood up and set off for her classroom. 'And Connie, when you collect her at a quarter past three,' she added, apparently as an afterthought, 'we'll have a word about the earrings.'

I breathed a sigh of relief. It was a problem solved, or at least shelved, and, not for the first time, I gave thanks for having such a superb deputy headteacher, even if she didn't quite appear to be her usual relaxed self.

As Mrs Crapper dragged Patience back to the playground, in the distance, up the Morton Road, the church bells of St Mary's chimed once to indicate the half hour and I smiled ruefully. It was exactly 8.30 a.m. on Monday, 6 September 1982, and my sixth year as headmaster of Ragley Church of England Primary School in North Yorkshire had begun.

I walked into the school office where Vera Evans, the secretary, was sitting at her immaculately tidy desk, labelling the new attendance and dinner registers, a pair for each of our four classes. Vera, a tall, elegant sixty-year-old, stood up and pressed the creases from the skirt of her smart Marks & Spencer's two-piece light-grey business suit. 'Good morning, Mr Sheffield,' she said. 'I've prepared the registers and . . .' she gave me a wry smile, 'I see you've met the Crappers.'

I sat down at my desk opposite her and smiled. 'Interesting lady,' I said.

'Just like her mother-in-law, I'm afraid,' said Vera. After over twenty years as school secretary, Vera knew every family in the village.

'And the little girl is well named . . . she'd try the patience of a saint,' I said.

'Through patience a ruler can be persuaded and a

gentle tongue can break a bone, Mr Sheffield,' recited Vera. 'Proverbs, chapter twenty-five, verse fifteen.' Vera seemed to have a quote from the Bible for every eventuality.

'Oh well, Vera, let's hope for a better year than the last one.'

She smiled wistfully and bowed her head. I noticed her beautifully permed hair was now greying at the temples. However, while the cool fingers of time had touched this remarkable lady, she showed no sign of losing enthusiasm for the job she loved. 'I agree,' she said with feeling.

'And how are you, Vera?' I asked.

She looked out of the window into the distance. 'I'm fine, thank you, Mr Sheffield,' she said reflectively. 'Fully recovered and ready to begin.' I smiled as Vera continued to call me 'Mr Sheffield'. She had always insisted this was the proper manner to address the headteacher. 'I just wish Ruby could be here as well,' she added with a hint of sadness. 'But she's making good progress and I'm going to visit her again this evening.' Vera had been a regular visitor to York Hospital and we had heard that Ruby would be home soon, although resuming her duties as caretaker would take more time.

'Well, Mrs Earnshaw seems to have settled in quickly to the temporary caretaker's job,' I said, 'so we should be fine until Ruby's return.'

'Yes, although she's had to bring her little girl in with her, I see,' added Vera with a frown.

'I think it's just for today.'

She sighed, took the cover from her electric typewriter and began to type her first letter of the school year. There was no doubt that Vera was the heartbeat of Ragley School and a wonderful secretary. Recently, we had all been thrilled that she had at last found true love. After a lifetime looking after her brother, the Revd Joseph Evans, our local vicar and chairman of the school governors, she had finally accepted a proposal of marriage from Major Rupert Forbes-Kitchener, a retired soldier and local landowner in his early sixties. Rupert's wife had died many years ago and he had found a new happiness with our school secretary.

'Also, just a thought, Mr Sheffield,' added Vera, looking up from her desk with a wry smile, 'but I wonder if I might be allowed to ring the school bell this morning. When I was in hospital it crossed my mind that I have never rung it before and it would be a way of announcing that my prayers had been answered . . . something of a symbolic gesture you understand.'

'A wonderful idea, Vera,' I said. 'You can let the whole village know that you're back where you belong . . . fit and well.'

Ragley's two other teachers suddenly walked into the office to collect their registers. Jo Hunter immediately gave Vera a hug. 'We're so pleased to have you here again safe and sound,' she said. Jo, a diminutive, athletic twenty-seven-year-old, taught the top infant class and took responsibility for physical education and science. She flicked her long black hair from her eyes and picked up her registers.

'And we were so worried,' said Sally Pringle, giving Vera's hand an affectionate squeeze. Sally was a tall, freckle-faced forty-one-year-old with bright ginger hair and a penchant for bright colours. Today she was wearing a frilly lime-green blouse, purple cords with a generous elasticated waistband and a vivid yellow waistcoat. Sally had never quite grown out of her flower-power days and, much to Vera's disapproval, loved outlandish outfits. She had also never quite regained her figure following the birth of baby Grace, now nineteen months old and leading Sally's mother a merry dance as she looked after her very mobile granddaughter. Meanwhile, Sally had returned to teaching the lower junior class, the eight- and nine-year-olds. She loved her work, especially art, music and history. 'By the way,' said Sally, 'what's up with Anne? She looks a bit preoccupied.'

'Yes,' said Jo, 'a bit out of sorts . . . not like her.'

Vera looked up as if something had just occurred to her, but then, with a shake of her head, she handed Sally her new registers. 'Anne's probably got a lot on her mind,' said Vera, 'perhaps with the new admissions.'

I glanced up at the clock on the wall. 'I think I'll go out to check on the early arrivals,' I said.

The old oak entrance door creaked on its Victorian hinges as I walked under the archway of Yorkshire stone with the date 1878 carved on its rugged lintel. The tarmac playground was bathed in September sunshine and surrounded by a low wall topped with high wrought-iron railings and decorated with fleur-de-lis. Around me, energetic children, healthy and sunburned after their summer holiday, waved in acknowledgement as I walked down the cobbled drive to the school gate. I breathed in the clear Yorkshire air and felt that familiar deep sense of contentment. There is a steady and reassuring rhythm to the life of a village headteacher. The autumn, spring and summer terms follow on in a regular pattern and the heartbeat of the seasons formed the framework of our life in this village community. It was also the job that I loved, and I smiled as I watched the children playing.

In the playground four girls from my class were enjoying the morning sunshine. Alice Baxter and Theresa Buttle were winding a skipping rope while Amanda Pickles and Sarah Louise Tait skipped like newborn lambs and chanted an old rhyme:

> *Rosy apple, lemon, pear,*
> *Bunch of roses she shall wear,*
> *Gold and silver by her side,*
> *I know who will be her bride.*

It was then that I thought of *my* bride. Just over three months ago I had married the beautiful Beth Henderson, another village-school headteacher, and, like me, in her thirties. Beth was about to begin her new academic year at Hartingdale Primary School and I prayed all would go well.

I leant my gangling six-foot-one-inch frame against one of the twin stone pillars by the wrought-iron gate and surveyed the scene. Our school was a Victorian building of weathered red brick with a steeply sloping, grey-slate roof and high arched windows. Dominating the roofline was a tall belltower waiting once more to announce the beginning of yet another school year.

Opposite the school was the village green with a

white-fronted public house, The Royal Oak, in the centre of a row of rustic cottages with tall chimneys and pantile roofs. Off to my left down the High Street, the village was coming alive. Amelia Duff was about to open the Post Office and, next door, Diane Wigglesworth was sellotaping a photograph of Toyah Willcox to the window of her Hair Salon. Nora Pratt was standing in the doorway of her Coffee Shop while the number-one record, 'Eye of the Tiger' by Survivor, was blasting out from the old juke-box. She was chatting with her brother Timothy, who was arranging a line of enamel buckets with military precision outside his Hardware Emporium. Meanwhile, Eugene Scrimshaw, supervised by his wife Peggy, was washing the front door of the village Pharmacy and Old Tommy Piercy was directing his grandson, Young Tommy, to sweep the forecourt of his Butcher's Shop. Finally, at the far end of the row of shops, Prudence Golightly was watering the colourful hanging basket that hung from the canopy over her General Stores & Newsagent. Ragley village looked a picture with its wide High Street bordered by grassy verges and the colours of early autumn, and I reflected that I had found happiness here. This gentle corner of North Yorkshire had its own sense of time and space and I was content in my world.

The peaceful scene was shattered by a screech of brakes. It was Petula Dudley-Palmer, by far the richest woman in the village. The back door of her Oxford Blue 1975 Rolls-Royce Silver Shadow opened and her two daughters, ten-year-old Elisabeth Amelia and eight-year-old Victoria

Alice, jumped out. 'Good morning, Mr Sheffield,' she said. 'Sorry, must rush into town,' and she roared off towards the York Road.

'All fur coat an' no knickers, that one, Mr Sheffield.'

I looked behind me. It was our new temporary caretaker, Mrs Earnshaw. Her daughter, Dallas Sue-Ellen, two months short of her third birthday, was running behind with the remains of a Curly Wurly bar gripped in her tight little fist and completely unaware of the two green candles of snot that adorned her chocolate-smeared face. 'Reight uppity that one,' added Mrs Earnshaw in her distinctive Barnsley accent.

'Mrs Dudley-Palmer is a good supporter of our school, Mrs Earnshaw,' I said by way of the mildest of reprimands. After all, good caretakers were hard to come by, particularly one as hardworking as this tough lady from South Yorkshire.

'Any road, Mr Sheffield,' continued Mrs Earnshaw, completely undeterred, 'ah've finished m'first shift so ah'll be back later t'put t'dining tables out. Ah've been t'see Ruby an' she's told me all about t'routine, so no need t'fret.'

'Thank you,' I said. Mrs Earnshaw had recently won an arm-wrestling competition in the taproom of The Royal Oak, so it was never a good idea to get on the wrong side of this formidable lady.

I glanced at my watch and hurried back to the entrance door. In the playground, Mrs Crapper was chatting with the mothers of the other reception class children.

'What are them then?' asked five-year-old Ted Coggins, the farmer's son, pointing down at Patience's ankles.

'Leg warmers,' said Patience bluntly.

Ted looked down at his short ankle socks and old leather sandals. 'Burrit's not cold,' said the sturdy little boy.

Patience looked at Ted and decided he would join the long list of those who would never be her friend. 'Ah don't like boys,' she said bluntly.

'Ah can whistle,' said Ted proudly.

'Ah *still* don't like boys,' replied Patience scornfully.

Ted realized he had played his trump card too early and shook his head sadly. Suddenly the church clock announced it was precisely nine o'clock, and Vera took the ancient rope in both hands and rang the school bell that had summoned children to their lessons for the last hundred years.

For this was 1982. The birth of Prince William had cheered the nation, the twenty-pence coin was in circulation and E.T., Steven Spielberg's lovable extra-terrestrial, wanted to 'phone home'. However, all was not well. Thirty thousand women protestors were destined to form a human chain around Greenham Common and unemployment was over three million. Prime Minister Margaret Thatcher, after the euphoria of victory in the Falklands, was turning her attention towards a certain Arthur Scargill, who, as President of the National Union of Mineworkers, had announced defiantly, 'We shall oppose all pit closures'. Meanwhile, the Queen had been startled to find an intruder had broken into her bedroom. The spirit of goodwill was also waning in Wales, where police in Gwent announced they were to cease their campaign of stopping drivers and giving them pens for good driving. Instead, they had decided to use unmarked cars to catch speeding motorists and simply fine them.

Roy Jenkins had become leader of the SDP and Coca-Cola introduced something called 'Diet Coke'. On the popular music scene, Barbra Streisand's *Love Songs* was the bestselling UK album of the year and a strange man called Ozzy Osbourne decided to bite the head off a bat during a live concert. The world was changing, but in the quiet North Yorkshire village of Ragley-on-the-Forest the sun was shining and eighty-six children hurried into school to begin another school year.

In my classroom, Theresa Ackroyd and Alice Baxter were waiting for me. 'Y'said me an' Alice could run t'tuck shop, Mr Sheffield,' said an insistent Theresa.

'That's right, you can,' I said. The pupils in their final year at Ragley took on extra responsibilities and shared out the monitor jobs between them. These were not to be underestimated, as they carried considerable status. So it was that Debbie Clack became register monitor, Dean Kershaw was appointed official bell ringer, Amanda Pickles was delighted to become the person who ran from class to class delivering occasional messages and Sarah Louise Tait, by virtue of *always* remembering to wash her hands, became hymn book monitor.

It was a busy morning throughout the school with the usual excitement of new exercise books, tins of Lakeland crayons and selecting reading books. In the reception class, Anne realized that, as usual, her four- and five-year-olds were already years apart in their reading and writing skills. Whereas Patience Crapper couldn't read a word and had no intention of writing a single letter, Katie Icklethwaite had written in neat printing, 'I love my Daddy. He's a bit fat now but he can still tie up my shoes.' Rufus Snodgrass had produced his longest ever sentence, 'I love my granddad because when he reads me a story he doesn't miss out bits like my mum does at bedtime.' Meanwhile, Ted Coggins, in large forceful printing that had nearly gone through the paper with the pressure of his pencil strokes, had written, 'i love my grandma because even when i've been naughty she always gives me a kiss.' Anne sighed when she looked at four-year-old Mandy Kerslake's writing. Mandy, a shy little girl, had written, 'I wasn't born I was adopted'. It was then she pondered on the lives of the children in her care, and, briefly, the problem she had been wrestling with all day was put to the back of her mind.

At morning break the children went out to play and I walked into the staff-room as the telephone rang. Vera picked up the receiver. 'It's Mrs Sheffield,' she said.

I looked up, momentarily confused. 'My mother?'

Vera raised her eyebrows and smiled. 'No, Mr Sheffield . . . your *wife*!'

'Ah, sorry,' I said with a grin. 'Still haven't got used to it.'

Beth and I had married at the end of May, a little over three months ago, and we were still getting used to her new married name. 'Good morning, *Mrs Sheffield*,' I said.

'Hello, *Mr* Sheffield,' she said cheerfully. 'Jack, Leeds University have been in touch and my first course on the M.Ed programme begins next month.' During the summer Beth had been interviewed for a place on the part-time Master of Education degree course at Leeds University. This included two years of taught modules followed by another year, supervised by a personal tutor, to complete a lengthy dissertation. Unlike me, Beth was determined to move up the career ladder.

'That's good news,' I said. 'Congratulations. I knew you'd do it.'

'Thanks . . . and are you *sure* you don't mind?' she asked, a little cautiously.

'Of course not,' I said. 'I'm thrilled for you. It's what you wanted.'

'Yes, it is,' she said. 'Well, must rush. See you tonight. There are some chops in the fridge if you're home first. Bye,' and the line went dead.

'Something to celebrate?' queried Vera.

'Beth's on that degree course in Leeds,' I said.

'She'll go far, just you wait and see,' said Vera as she heated the milk for our coffee on the single electric ring.

At lunchtime, Shirley Mapplebeck, the school cook, looked concerned. 'We've got eighty-six on roll, Mr Sheffield, an' only fifty-seven are staying f'school dinners – so, sadly, it's more packed lunches.' Since the cost of a school dinner had gone up to fifty pence our numbers had dropped and it was often the case that the children who most needed a hot meal weren't getting one.

'So we're trying t'introduce *choice*, Mr Sheffield,' said Shirley, 'to make t'meals more interestin' for t'children.'

When I queued up for my lunch Shirley's assistant,

Mrs Doreen Critchley, was serving the sweet course. The muscles in her mighty forearms bulged as she lifted another tray of jam sponge on to the counter.

'D'you want custard?' growled Mrs Critchley.

'Oh, well, er, what are my choices?' I asked hesitantly.

Mrs Critchley gave me the look that regularly caused Mr Critchley to quake in his boots. '*Yes* or *No*,' she replied bluntly. Mrs Critchley was always economical in her use of the English language.

After lunch, in the staff-room, Vera was scanning the front page of her *Daily Telegraph* and shaking her head in dismay. A sixteen-year-old girl, caned by her headteacher for smoking, had complained to the European Court of Human Rights that the punishment was 'inhuman' and therefore 'unlawful'. Also, Berkshire Education Authority had announced that Buddhism was to be taught in their schools. 'I wonder what it's all coming to,' murmured Vera to herself as she picked up her cup of Earl Grey tea.

'So what do you think of the new caretaker, Vera?' asked Sally.

Vera paused for a moment, clearly intending to choose her words carefully. 'Well, Mrs Earnshaw is definitely *different* to Ruby,' she said with a knowing look. She held up a sheet of paper covered in childlike printing. 'And I've just removed her notice from our crockery shelf.' It read:

AFTER TEA BREAK
STAFF SHOULD EMPTY POT
AND STAND UPSIDE DOWN
ON DRAINING BOARD

I grinned. 'Yes, it does seem a bit extreme, Vera.'

'Precisely, Mr Sheffield,' said Vera and dropped the notice into her wicker waste basket. 'I'll have a word, shall I?'

It was during afternoon school that Patience Crapper made her mark. While Anne was busy in the classroom, Patience blocked up the sink in the reception class cloak-room with her leg warmers and water was swimming everywhere on the tiled floor.

'Oh no!' said Anne and immediately asked Vera to con-tact Mrs Earnshaw to clear up the mess.

'And your boots and socks are soaked, Patience,' she said. 'Take them off and we'll dry them on the children's washing line.'

During afternoon break, in the staff-room, Anne was quietly fuming. 'I'll give her patience,' she muttered.

Sally looked up from her *Art & Craft* magazine. 'Patience,' she said, 'the state of endurance under difficult circumstances.'

'Too true,' said Anne through gritted teeth.

At the end of school, the parents of the children in the reception class wandered into school to collect their off-spring. While Anne was talking to Mrs Crapper, Vera saw Patience trying to put on her pixie boots.

'Come on, I'll help you,' said Vera.

After a huge struggle Vera managed to pull on both boots. 'They don't fit very well, do they?' she said, getting a little exasperated.

''Cause they're on t'wrong feet,' said Patience.

'Oh dear,' said Vera and pulled them off. Getting them on again seemed an even greater struggle. Vera was feeling exhausted.

'What about m'leg warmers?' asked Patience.

'Leg warmers?' said Vera. 'Where are they?'

'In m'boots,' said Patience.

'In your boots!' exclaimed Vera. 'Why are they in your boots?'

''Cause Miss said put 'em there t'keep 'em safe,' said Patience in a matter-of-fact tone.

'Oh no,' said Vera, pulling off the boots once again.

Eventually, fully attired with leg warmers and boots, Patience tottered off with her mother.

Back in the staff-room we all gathered to relate the events of the first day and Vera regaled us with her story of the pixie boots. Her patience had finally run out. She half closed her eyes and quoted from memory, 'Jesus might display his unlimited patience as an example for those who would believe on him and receive eternal life.'

'Point taken, Vera,' said Anne.

'First Timothy, chapter one, verse sixteen,' said Vera.

'And that's the problem, Vera . . . *eternal life.*'

'Ah,' said Vera as the penny dropped.

We all stared as, for no obvious reason, Vera suddenly put her arms round Anne and gave her a hug. 'I understand, Anne,' she said kindly. 'I've just been through the same thing, except another decade down the line. I sent you a card in the holidays.'

'Yes, thanks Vera,' said Anne, 'as you always do.'

'And without a number on it,' added Vera quietly.

There was a pause as Anne nodded.

'Ah, I see,' said Sally.

'Me too,' said Jo.

'Well, I don't,' I said.

They all gave me that 'well-he's-only-a-man' look, and shook their heads.

'Oh, Jack, haven't you worked it out yet?' said Anne. 'I loved being in my forties . . . and now I'm *bloody* fifty!'

It was then I realized that the problem with patience is that some days are better than others. It was also the first and last time I ever heard my deputy head swear.

Chapter Two

A Decision for Vera

The Revd Joseph Evans recommenced his weekly RE lesson. Major Forbes-Kitchener, school governor, visited school to discuss tomorrow's Harvest Supper. County Hall requested responses to their discussion document 'The Need for a Common Curriculum'.

Extract from the Ragley School Logbook:
Friday, 17 September 1982

Vera took her two-pint baking dish from the kitchen cupboard, propped her handwritten recipe book alongside it and then paused to look out of the vicarage kitchen window. Whispers of morning sunlight flickered through the branches of the high elms in the nearby churchyard.

It was Friday, 17 September, the day before the annual Harvest Supper in the village hall, and there was the small matter of an apple courting cake. Vera wrote a list of ingredients to purchase at Prudence Golightly's General Stores & Newsagent, called to her brother, Joseph, to

35

hurry up, checked her appearance in the hall mirror, bade a fond farewell to her three cats, Jess, Treacle and Maggie, then walked out to face a new day that she was destined never to forget.

A mile away on Ragley High Street, the queue of villagers in the General Stores was becoming restless as ten-year-old Heathcliffe Earnshaw and his nine-year-old brother Terry finally made an important decision.

Heathcliffe clutched a five-pence piece and stared intently at the glass jars of sweets, including sherbet dips, penny lollies, giant humbugs, dolly mixtures, aniseed balls, chocolate butter dainties, jelly babies and liquorice torpedoes. 'Two lic'rice bootlaces *please*, Miss Golightly,' said Heathcliffe, 'an' *please* can we 'ave three penn'th o' aniseed balls *please* in two bags, *please*.' Heathcliffe always emphasized the word *please* when he spoke to the kindly sixty-five-year-old Miss Golightly. She appreciated good manners and he gave her his best fixed smile. It was the one he had perfected over the years and also the one he had been told by his Aunt Mavis from Doncaster that, if he kept doing it, his face would stay like that.

'And here's a sherbet lemon for being such polite boys,' said Miss Golightly.

'Thank you, Miss Golightly,' said the two brothers in muffled unison as they left the shop, sucking their sweets with occasional synchronized crunching.

Next in the queue was Betty Icklethwaite with her five-year-old daughter, Katie. 'Ah want t'spend a penny,' said Katie.

'Everything on the bottom shelf is a penny,' said Miss

Golightly, pointing to the liquorice laces, gobstoppers and penny chews.

'No,' said Mrs Icklethwaite, her cheeks flushing rapidly. 'I think she actually *does* want t'spend a penny, Miss Golightly . . . if y'take m'meaning,' and she grabbed her daughter's hand and rushed out.

Finally I reached the front of the queue. 'Good morning, Miss Golightly,' I said. The diminutive lady had a set of wooden steps behind the counter and she stepped up to be on the same level as me.

Prudence knew her customers well and had already folded my copy of *The Times*. 'And good morning to you, Mr Sheffield,' she said. 'I trust *Mrs* Sheffield is well.'

'Fine thank you, Miss Golightly.' Then I looked up at Yorkshire's best-dressed teddy bear sitting on his usual shelf next to a tin of loose-leaf Lyons tea and an old advertisement for Hudson's soap and Carter's Little Liver Pills. 'And good morning, Jeremy.'

Jeremy was her lifelong friend and Prudence took great pride in making sure he was always well turned out. On this bright and busy day he was wearing a white shirt, blue bow-tie and a striped apron. Miss Golightly followed my gaze. 'Yes, we've been stocktaking this morning,' she said as she took my twenty pence and placed it in the drawer of the ancient till.

I climbed back into my Morris Minor Traveller and, as I drove past the village green towards the school gates, I pulled up and wound down my window. 'Be careful, Jimmy,' I shouted. Ten-year-old Jimmy Poole was throwing a stick into the branches of the horse-chestnut trees and at his feet a pile of glossy conkers had burst out of their spiky shells.

'Ith all right, Mithter Theffield,' lisped Jimmy. 'Ah'm juth thowing my thithter 'ow t'collect conkerth,' he shouted back cheerfully. 'Anyway ah've finithed now,' he added as he hid his special stick under a pile of leaves for another day. After all, when you're ten years old you never know when a good stick might come in useful. I smiled and drove into the car park without comment, recalling that I had done exactly the same thing thirty years ago.

The school was welcoming on this autumn morning. In the border outside Sally's classroom, chrysanthemums, red, bronze and amber, were bright in the low September sunshine and Mrs Earnshaw was sweeping the first of the autumn leaves from the stone steps leading to the entrance door.

Outside the school office our local vicar, the Revd Joseph Evans, a tall, thin figure with a clerical collar and a sharp Roman nose, was looking anxiously at his lesson notes. Joseph came in once each week to lead 'spiritual guidance' as he called it, or, to be more precise, to read Bible stories to the children with a follow-up discussion. While Joseph was calm and confident with his congregation on a Sunday morning, somehow life wasn't quite the same when he was faced with a class of young children. By morning break he was usually tearing out what was left of his grey hair.

Joseph had never married and was totally reliant on his well-organized elder sister. The two of them shared the beautifully furnished vicarage in the grounds of St

Mary's Church along with Vera's three cats. It was well known that Maggie, a sleek black cat with white paws, was named after Vera's political heroine, Margaret Thatcher. For Joseph, it was a life that filled him with contentment . . . that was, until he realized that the news of Vera's marriage would change his world for ever. So it was that, on this peaceful September morning, his lesson with Sally Pringle's class filled him with even more doubts. It had just occurred to him that his theme, 'How to Get to Heaven', might be a difficult concept for eight- and nine-year-olds.

At ten o'clock I was listening to Dean Kershaw reading his *Ginn Reading 360* story book when the ever-alert Theresa Ackroyd made an announcement. She delivered it without appearing to look up from her School Mathematics Project workcard concerning the difference between obtuse and acute angles. However, as Theresa had placed her chair strategically so that she never missed anything going on outside the classroom window, it was clear that she already possessed a meaningful and very practical understanding of angles, regardless of whatever peculiar name they were given. 'Major's posh car comin' up t'drive, Mr Sheffield,' she said with calm authority.

A large black classic Bentley purred into the car park. As usual, Major Rupert Forbes-Kitchener arrived in style from his stately home of Morton Manor and a chauffeur in a smart grey uniform and a peaked cap got out and opened the rear door. As a school governor, the major was a regular visitor, even more so now that he and Vera were engaged to be married. 'The potted plant, please,

Tomkins,' he said and the chauffeur took a beautiful orchid from the boot of the car. The major checked that every purple-white petal was perfect, walked into school and tapped on the office door.

Vera was filling the Gestetner duplicating machine with ink prior to sending out a note to parents about next month's half-term holiday and she smiled when she saw who it was. 'Rupert, what a lovely surprise.'

'For you, my dear,' he said and placed the orchid on the window ledge.

'Thank you, it's beautiful,' said Vera. She replaced the lid on the can of ink and walked over to the window to admire the beautiful plant in more detail. 'But I wasn't expecting you.'

Rupert removed his Sherlock Holmes deerstalker hat to reveal a head of close-cropped, steel-grey hair, then glanced down nervously at his size-ten brown brogues, highly polished to a military shine. 'I couldn't wait any longer, Vera,' he said. 'I simply had to speak to you. It's been on my mind all week . . . in fact, I've thought of little else since the accident.'

'Would you like a cup of tea, Rupert?' asked Vera, recognizing that this hero of distant battlefields was struggling to cope with something as yet unknown.

The major appeared grateful for the diversion. 'Yes please, quench the old fires, what?' He undid the button of his brown checked jacket and nervously fingered the immaculate knot in his East Yorkshire regimental tie, resplendent with its vivid white, gold, black and maroon stripes. Finally, he took a white handkerchief from the pocket of his cavalry twill trousers and mopped his forehead. Vera served the tea, sat back in her chair and waited until this huge bear of a man was good and ready. She was puzzled. It wasn't like Rupert to be in such a state.

Meanwhile, in Class 3, Joseph looked equally harassed. He was trying to bring his 'How to Get to Heaven' discussion to a logical conclusion and he hoped the children had finally grasped the concept.

'Now, boys and girls,' he said, 'if I sold my car and gave the money to the church, would I get to heaven?'

'No,' chorused the children.

Encouraged, Joseph pressed on. 'And if I cleaned the church and kept it tidy, would I get to heaven?'

'No,' they answered, led by nine-year-old Betsy Icklethwaite, shaking her head vigorously.

'Well done,' said Joseph enthusiastically. 'And, Betsy, why wouldn't I get to heaven?'

"Cause y'not dead yet,' said Betsy.

It was at times like this that Joseph wondered if he had chosen the right profession and, once again, he glanced at the clock as morning playtime beckoned.

In the school office Rupert had finished his tea. He put down his cup and saucer, took a deep breath and began.

'Vera,' he said quietly, 'I believe that sometimes life hangs on a moment.' He leant forward and held her hand. 'And I believe *this* is that moment, my dear.'

Vera recognized the gravitas in his words. 'What exactly is it you wish to say, Rupert?'

'It's about getting married,' he said.

Vera held up her sapphire engagement ring and

smiled. 'And of course we shall . . . next summer, as we planned.'

Rupert sighed and shook his head. 'No, Vera, the accident changed all that for me.'

The colour left Vera's cheeks. 'Rupert . . . what do you mean?'

'Don't you see?' said Rupert. 'For a moment I thought I had lost you. I couldn't bear to see you in hospital.' There was sadness in his eyes and anguish in his voice. 'Now you're well again I want to look after you . . . sooner, rather than later. I know I shouldn't have come into school to ask you this, my dear, but I couldn't wait until the Harvest Supper.'

'Oh Rupert,' said Vera, 'ask me what?'

'My dearest, let's marry at Christmas and start the new year together . . . as man and wife.'

Vera turned to stare out at the distant Hambleton hills. 'Rupert, this is so sudden and . . . I would need to talk to Joseph.'

'Of course you must, but please let me know soon.' Then he kissed her lightly on the cheek. 'I love you so very much,' he said, 'and now you know how I truly feel.'

Suddenly the bell rang for playtime and it seemed to break the spell. Vera opened the office door. 'Rupert, I need to get on. I'll talk to you tomorrow,' she said. Her mind was in a whirl.

As I arrived in the entrance hall, Rupert was standing there, clearly preoccupied.

'Good morning, Major,' I said, resisting the inclination to jump immediately to attention.

'Ah, good morning, Jack,' he said, snapping out of his reverie.

'Would you like to join us for coffee?' I asked.

He hesitated and looked at his pocket watch. 'No thanks, old chap, just called in about the . . . er . . . Harvest Supper.'

'Very well, Major, we'll see you there,' I said and he hurried off.

It was my turn for outside duty, which was a pleasure on this fine day. In the playground the nine-year-old Buttle twins, Rowena and Katrina, were winding a long skipping rope while a group of girls took turns at jumping in and out with practised ease. As they did so, they all chanted an old skipping rhyme that had been passed down from one generation of Ragley pupils to the next. In this way our heritage was sustained and renewed.

> *The big ship sails on the ally-ally-oh,*
> *The ally-ally-oh, the ally-ally-oh.*
> *Oh, the big ship sails on the ally-ally-oh*
> *On the last day of September.*

I smiled as I recalled that my mother had told me that the song had something to do with the 'big ships' that sailed on the Manchester Ship Canal, opened with great ceremony in 1894. Whatever its origin, the girls in Sally's class were word perfect.

At lunchtime I picked up a plastic tray and joined the queue behind five-year-old Rufus Snodgrass, who was casting dubious looks at the food about to be served by Shirley, our school cook.

'Do ah 'ave to eat cabbage, Mrs Mapplebeck?' asked Rufus.

'Cabbage meks yer 'air curl,' said Shirley cheerily and with absolute conviction.

'Burra don't want curly 'air,' said Rufus.

'An' it gives y'rosy cheeks,' added Shirley.

'Burra don't want rosy cheeks,' said Rufus. Shirley was running out of incentives.

'Will it mek me whistle as good as Ted Coggins?' asked Rufus.

'It might,' said Shirley.

'Go on then, ah'll 'ave some,' said Rufus, who would have eaten dead worms for just one chance to replicate the ear-shattering whistle that his new best friend had perfected.

Meanwhile in the staff-room, away from the smell of cabbage, Sally was reading her September issue of *Cosmopolitan*. An article entitled 'Futureworks' had caught her attention. It described a future society dominated by new technology.

'It says here,' she said, 'that by the year two thousand we shall all be working a twenty-five-hour week.'

'Sounds good,' said Jo.

'It also says we shall be living in a "cashless, cheque-less society",' continued Sally, '"where coins will become quaint *objets d'art*".'

'Bit far-fetched,' said Anne.

'And by then,' she continued, 'more than half of

secondary schools will have a computer and lessons will be taught on two-way videos.'

'Sounds more like *Star Trek*,' said Jo.

'Well, I'm glad I won't still be in the classroom then,' said Anne. 'I'll be collecting my pension when I'm sixty.'

Vera suddenly walked into the staff-room, sat down and stared thoughtfully out of the window.

'I see the venerable Margaret was on television again last night,' said Sally.

Vera's eyes lit up. She was a big supporter of Margaret Thatcher and, on occasion, even dressed to look like her – whereas Sally had very different political leanings.

'Mrs Thatcher's had a very busy year, what with her son, Mark, being rescued in the Sahara Desert, and then the Falklands War,' said Vera.

'Oh well,' muttered Sally, 'you can't win them all.'

Later that evening, in the vicarage kitchen, Joseph was sitting quietly at the table. He made a steeple of his long fingers, a familiar gesture and almost a precursor to prayer. An hour had passed since Vera had mentioned Rupert's hopes for a Christmas wedding.

'I'll put this button on for you, shall I, Joseph?' said Vera.

Joseph looked up and nodded, but his thoughts were elsewhere.

'I know that look,' said Vera. 'What's on your mind?'

'I just want you to be happy,' replied Joseph, 'but are you sure this is what *you* want?'

'Yes, Joseph, I believe it is,' said Vera firmly.

There was a long pause as Joseph grappled with the

enormity of the change that was soon to take place in their lives. 'But Christmas . . . it's so soon.'

'It's also to do with fulfilment, Joseph,' said Vera quietly as she opened the lid of her mother's Victorian sewing box.

'Fulfilment?' said Joseph, unsure of what this really meant.

Vera's cheeks flushed slightly as she selected a reel of navy-blue cotton and studied it thoughtfully. 'Yes, Joseph,' she said at last. *'Fulfilment,'* she repeated with emphasis. Then she tugged a length of cotton from the reel, threaded it with gimlet-eyed determination and proceeded to sew a button on Joseph's old tweed jacket.

Joseph recognized her determination and began to flick idly through his *Beginner's Guide to Wine Making*.

'Rupert asked us to share his table for the Harvest Supper,' said Vera, 'so I'm doing some baking tomorrow morning.'

Joseph's face brightened. 'And I could provide the wine,' he said.

Vera saw the eagerness in his expression and her heart softened. She couldn't find it in her heart to say no, even though his creations tasted like a mixture of decaying mushrooms and turpentine. 'A kind thought, Joseph,' she said, 'although, er, perhaps Rupert may already have that in hand.'

'Oh, it's no trouble,' said Joseph as he hurried off to the kitchen pantry. There was a rattle of bottles. 'I'll let him sample my Elderflower Glory . . . my finest creation yet.'

'Oh dear,' Vera whispered to herself.

*　　*　　*

It was later that evening, as darkness fell, that Vera found herself in a melancholy mood. She was standing by the sink in the vicarage kitchen and putting the finishing touches to her lime juice cordial.

She looked down at her hands. There were lines now as age took its toll. Then she glanced up at her reflection in the window. The face that looked back at her was no longer the young woman she had known so well. She touched the greying hair at her temples with her long fingers and smiled wistfully. A lifetime of service to the church, to the school and, of course, to Joseph . . . but now a new life awaited. Perhaps this really was *her* time.

It was Saturday morning and Beth had collected all the green tomatoes from the garden and was making chutney. She was standing by the kitchen worktop and, as she worked, her honey-blonde hair caressed her high cheekbones. Her tight blue jeans and cheesecloth blouse emphasized her slim, athletic figure and when she looked at me her green eyes twinkled with a hint of mischief.

'What is it?' she asked.

'You are so beautiful,' I said.

'I'm busy, Jack,' she said with a grin. Beth and I had settled into our married life together in Bilbo Cottage in the pretty village of Kirkby Steepleton, three miles from Ragley village. I had never been more content. 'Anyway, you said you were going into the village to buy me some ring-binders for my course.'

'I will . . . later,' I said as I wrapped my arms around her waist.

She turned round and kissed me. 'You know it's

important, Jack. I want to make a good start and then, when I've passed, I can get a larger headship and we can probably buy a bigger property,' she scanned the cramped work surfaces, 'with a *modern* kitchen.'

Her thoughts washed over me like spring rain and it was as if I was beginning to know her for the first time. Her words were soft, but there were times when her ambition struck me like an iron fist.

Four miles away in Morton Manor, Rupert's daughter, Virginia Anastasia, had just arrived back from giving lessons at her riding school and, still in her skin-tight jodhpurs, she served coffee from a silver pot.

'Can broken hearts be mended, Bunty?' asked Rupert.

Virginia Anastasia looked up in surprise. 'That's what Mummy used to call me. You've not called me that in years.'

'I know, my dear, I know,' he said quietly. 'Your mother was a wonderful woman and I miss her still.' There was a long silence, broken only by the chiming of the nearby bells of St Mary's Church. 'But I've found a new happiness with Vera, one I never expected. She really is a remarkable lady.'

Virginia sat on the arm of Rupert's chair. 'I know that, Daddy,' she said, 'and Vera is perfect for you. Life is for living, not mourning.'

'Fathers and daughters,' he muttered, leaning forward to kiss her on the forehead.

Further along the Morton Road, in the vicarage kitchen, Vera made sure all her ingredients were laid out neatly and then paused to look out of the kitchen window. Life was no longer uncertain. She had made her decision.

Vera loved baking and this was one of her specialities. As she greased an eight-inch-square, shallow cake tin she glanced again at her mother's spidery, cursive handwriting. It was a recipe she had prepared many times, except, on this occasion, it was for the special man in her life. As she began to work on her spotless kitchen surface she knew with absolute certainty that she was about to make the perfect apple courting cake . . . and Rupert would definitely understand its meaning.

That evening outside the village hall, the temperature was dropping fast. The geraniums in the hanging baskets by the entrance were dying now, blackened by the first sharp frost. Down the High Street, the bright colours of summer were just a fond memory and the first log fires were burning in Ragley village.

Inside, a dozen trestle tables had been covered with smart checked tablecloths and adorned with candles in old wine bottles. At one end of the hall six more tables had been lined up against the wall and covered with snowy white linen. The ladies of the Women's Institute had taken charge of displaying honey-roasted gammon, joints of beef and ham, bowls of potato salad, a huge mushroom quiche, fruit pies, fresh cream, freshly baked loaves and every variety of home-made jam you could imagine. At the far end of the hall Elsie Crapper was playing some harvest favourites on the old upright piano. 'Come, ye thankful people, come,' sang Elsie, 'raise the song of harvest home!'

It was a happy occasion and Rupert was in a reflective mood. 'Do you know, Jack,' he said wistfully, 'the sun never used to set on the British Empire.'

'Times change, Major,' I said.

'Exactly, my boy,' he said, 'and *time* is something that is slipping away.' He looked at Vera and she gave him a gentle smile. Meanwhile, she was reflecting on those happy days in her life, strung together like a necklace of special memories.

The festive evening was drawing to its close when Joseph found time for a private word with Vera. 'I think we should put a date in the church diary . . . for *December*,' he said simply.

Vera squeezed his hand. 'The spirit of the Lord has always been in your eyes, Joseph,' she said quietly.

'And in your soul, my dear sister,' said Joseph.

'We're moving on with our lives, Joseph,' said Vera. 'It's a new beginning – for both of us.'

It was almost midnight when Rupert was saying goodnight to Vera.

'So what do you say, my dear?' He leant forward and took her hand in his. 'Shall we get married sooner rather than later . . . at Christmas time?'

Vera bowed her head. It was time for a decision. Her youth was gone now, left on a distant shore. A new life was about to begin. She looked at the man she loved and said simply, 'Yes.'

Chapter Three

Ruby's Great Expectations

All the children sent Get Well cards to Mrs Smith. The school governors agreed to an extension of Mrs Earnshaw's contract as temporary caretaker to the end of November.
Extract from the Ragley School Logbook:
Monday, 11 October 1982

'Ah'm gonna gerra job, Miss Evans,' said Ronnie Smith, 'in t'packaging industry.' He removed his Leeds United bobble hat and nervously flattened a few wisps of greying hair.

Ronnie was Ruby the caretaker's habitually un-employed husband, whose life revolved around his racing pigeons, managing the Ragley Rovers football team, frequent visits to the bookmaker and, of course, a regular intake of Tetley's bitter.

And pigs might fly, thought Vera. She gave Ronnie a steely look. 'And what have you in mind, Ronald?' she asked evenly.

Ronnie looked down at the advertisement in the *Easington Herald & Pioneer*. 'It's a technical assistant,' he said.

'And what exactly does that mean?' asked Vera.

'Well, it's a *technical assistant*, in t'packaging industry,' he said.

'And what will you be packing, Ronald?' asked Vera with a hint of impatience.

'Well, er, Easter eggs, Miss Evans,' said Ronnie, 'an' ah need a ref'rence.'

It was 8.30 a.m. on Monday, 11 October in the school office. I closed the Yorkshire Purchasing Organization catalogue and looked up from my desk. This was definitely more interesting than ordering powder paint.

At number 7, School View, Ruby was propped up in a single bed in the front room. She had returned home from hospital and was now convalescing. This had resulted in the reorganization of the furniture and general jumble that cluttered her house. Sue Phillips, our tall blonde Chair of the Ragley Parent Teacher Association and staff nurse at the hospital in York, was in attendance.

'Ow's it lookin', Mrs Phillips?' asked Ruby, looking down at the scars on her legs.

'Fine, Ruby,' said Sue. 'They're healing well and Nurse Wojciechowski will be calling in each day to change the dressings and do some physio.'

'Ah know 'er,' said Ruby darkly. ''Er brother plays f'my Ronnie's football team. She dunt take no prisoners.'

'Well, Ruby,' said Sue with a smile, 'we all have our own bedside manner.'

'Ah know, an' 'ers is like 'Itler.' Ruby pushed a few strands of damp wavy chestnut hair away from her eyes. 'Anyway, don't worry, ah know which side m'bread's buttered an' ah'll do as ah'm told . . . it's t'only way ah'll get back t'school.'

'You need plenty of rest first, Ruby,' said Sue as she packed up her medical bag.

'Be that as it may, but ah need t'earn some money,' said Ruby disconsolately. 'We can't live on fresh air.'

Sue looked down at one of Ragley village's most popular characters and held her hand. 'Ruby, shall I make you a cup of tea before I get off to work?' Then she looked dubiously through the open kitchen door at the mountain of dirty dishes in the sink.

'No, thank you kindly,' said Ruby. 'Our Natasha should be back soon. She only does part-time at Diane's.'

'Well,' said Sue, surveying the cluttered room, 'I'll call back after work to check on you.' She picked up her bag, smoothed her smart blue uniform and paused at the front door. 'And where's Ronnie?' she asked as an afterthought.

'Out somewhere trying t'get a job,' said Ruby sadly, 'but ah'll believe it when ah see it.'

'What's the job, Ruby?'

''E sed summat abart t'packaging industry, whatever that is.'

'Well, you never know, Ruby . . . there's always a first time,' said Sue.

'This is my Ronnie we're talkin' about 'ere,' said Ruby, shaking her head. 'Y'know what they say – a tiger never changes its spots.' She looked down at her dumpy, work-red hands. 'There was a time ah 'ad great expectations, but not any more.' Sue nodded knowingly, let herself out and drove off down the High Street towards York.

Ruby was a year short of her fiftieth birthday and life was beginning to wear her down. At twenty stones and in her extra-large, bright-orange overall, she had been a familiar sight skipping round the school with her mop and galvanized bucket, singing songs from her favourite film, *The Sound of Music*. That was until the accident. Now everything had changed. Her world had become a struggle.

Ruby and Ronnie had six children. Thirty-one year-old Andy was a sergeant in the army and twenty-nine-year-old Racquel had just had a baby girl. Krystal Carrington Ruby Entwhistle was now seven weeks old and Ruby's pride and joy. The highlight of her day was when Racquel brought her rosy-cheeked daughter to visit. Ruby's other four children shared their cramped council house. Twenty-seven-year-old Duggie was an assistant to the local undertaker and his nickname 'Deadly' was appropriate. He was content to sleep in the attic with his Hornby Dublo trainset, a packet of Castella cigars and the posters of his Abba pin-up, the blonde and beautiful Agnetha Fältskog. Meanwhile, twenty-two-year-old Sharon was saving up to get married to Rodney Morgetroyd, the son of the Morton village milkman with the Duran Duran looks, and twenty-year-old Natasha worked part-time in Diane's Hair Salon. The baby of the family, nine-year-old Hazel, was a cheerful and hardworking little girl in Sally Pringle's class. As chief breadwinner it had always been a tough life for Ruby . . . never more so than now. She sat back and stared at Ronnie's spare bobble hat on top of an untidy pile of racing-pigeon magazines on the sideboard. It was then she wondered if miracles happened to ordinary folk and not just those people in the Bible that the vicar talked about. Ruby closed her tired eyes and prayed.

'Y'can 'ave a trial,' said Norman Nesbit, packaging supervisor at the local chocolate factory in York. 'We start off packagin' Easter eggs six months afore they go on sale in t'shops, so this is a busy time an' another pair o' 'ands would be, well, er, 'andy so t'speak.'

Ronnie stared at the huge conveyor belt. Chocolate eggs appeared at one end in rapid succession and a lady who resembled a Russian weightlifter wrapped foil round each one. Further along, two women, deep in conversation, put them in cardboard boxes with metronomic ease and without ever appearing to look at what they were doing. Finally they were stacked on a pallet and whisked away on a forklift truck.

'An' that'll 'ave t'go,' he added, pointing to Ronnie's bobble hat. 'It's not 'ygienic. You 'ave t'wear a special white 'at an' coat.'

Ronnie nodded but wasn't happy. He felt naked without his favourite bobble hat. Soon, looking like an advert for a Persil commercial, he sat on a high stool opposite the Russian weightlifter.

'Y'sit 'ere wi' 'Elen an' wrap t'eggs in foil as they come past, ten seconds f'each one,' said Norman. 'Ah'll go start 'er up an' come back shortly t'see 'ow y'gettin' on.'

Ronnie looked across the conveyor belt to his new colleague. 'Nah then,' he said nervously. He was unaware of Helen's charisma bypass, although he did notice that on her neck she displayed a tattoo of a love heart with the word TROY underneath. Even so, this was definitely not the woman who launched a thousand ships.

'Foil,' said Helen with a glassy-eyed stare.

'Y'what?' said Ronnie.

'Foil,' she repeated. 'We do t'foil, they do t'boxes.'

Two other women further down the conveyor belt looked at Ronnie and shook their heads in dismay. 'We've gorra reight one 'ere, Elsie,' said one of them. ''E's not 'xactly Shakin' bloody Stevens, is 'e?'

'Y'not kiddin', Doris,' replied her friend. 'Looks like summat cat's dragged in.'

With a roar the conveyor belt started up and the first chocolate egg came Ronnie's way. He picked it up clumsily and it cracked in his hand, but he wrapped it anyway just as the second arrived. This one he dropped, so he decided to eat the broken pieces as fast as he could. When the next one arrived, in panic he threw it back, where it landed on top of the next egg and both shattered. Again he scooped up the broken pieces. Helen pressed the emergency stop button and looked at Ronnie, who was eating the broken chocolate as fast as he could shove it in his mouth.

Norman wandered back, shook his head and looked at the clock. 'Guinness Book o' friggin' Records,' he said.

'Y'what?' said Ronnie.

'Y'sacked,' said Norman, 'after two minutes an' thirty-five seconds.'

Back in Ragley School, we decided to encourage all the children to send a Get Well card to Ruby. In the reception class Anne picked up a stick of chalk and in large neat letters printed 'Get well soon Mrs Smith' on the blackboard.

'Now, children,' she said, 'Mrs Smith, our caretaker, is poorly at home so I want us all to cheer her up . . . shall we do that?'

It sounded fun and everyone nodded.

Anne had distributed her new collection of safety scissors with their rounded ends and the children were soon busy cutting pieces of white card. By the end of school they had all drawn a picture with a thick pencil on the folded card, coloured it in with wax crayons and written a sentence inside. Two of her brightest five-year-olds, both sons of local farmers and fast approaching their sixth birthdays, had created wonderful messages, although they had yet to discover capital letters. Ted Coggins had written, 'get well soon and i hope you arnt all thin', and Charlie Cartwright, in scratchy lower case, had penned his own personal stream of consciousness, 'my hamster dide last week it was orfull i hope you don't di i hav a verooker luv charlie'.

Meanwhile, in the other classes, eight-year-old Ben Roberts had written, 'I hope you get well soon Mrs Smith cos my ball is stuck in that gutter outside your boiler house'. Seven-year-old Sonia Tricklebank appeared keen to give Ruby a secret present. 'Get well soon Mrs Smith,' she had written. 'My mummy gave me a Lion bar and I thort you wud like it so I have hidden it at the bottom of our mucky washing basket xx from Sonia'. And so it went on . . . sincere messages from the heart, written as only children can.

*   *   *

During lunchtime we gathered in the staff-room, collected the cards in a decorated shoebox and settled down for a welcome cup of tea. Vera was reading her *Daily Telegraph*. 'They're raising the *Mary Rose*,' she said suddenly, 'and the Prince of Wales has donned diving gear to view it. What a brave young man we have for our future king.' Vera loved the royal family.

'Fifteen forty-five,' mumbled Sally, our resident historian, from the other side of the staff-room, through a mouthful of garibaldi biscuit.

I looked up. 'Pardon?'

Sally took a sip of her tea. 'It was Henry the Eighth's great Tudor flagship, Jack, and over four hundred men died when it sank in the Solent.'

Vera made some rapid calculations. 'Four hundred and thirty-seven years,' she mused. 'Wonder what state it will be in?'

'Probably the same as him,' said Sally, nodding towards the window. A forlorn Ronnie was walking past the school entrance in the direction of The Royal Oak and I recalled Ruby's description of her work-shy husband: 'Seven stone drippin' wet an' neither use nor ornament.'

'Oh dear,' said Vera, 'doesn't look as though he got the job.'

'What job?' we all chorused.

'Something to do with the packaging industry,' said Vera, 'at the chocolate factory.'

'That reminds me,' said Sally, rummaging in her open-weave ethnic shoulder bag. She took out a brightly coloured paper bag full of assorted sweets and offered it round. 'Well, whatever happens, think on the bright side,' she said. 'There'll always be a pick 'n' mix in Woolworths.'

During afternoon school I called in to Anne's classroom to borrow her set of magnifying glasses for a science experiment. All the children were painting on large sheets of A3 paper. Little Katie Icklethwaite looked up and gave me a toothy smile. 'Ah'm painting our farm,' she said.

'It's lovely,' I said. 'I like the black pig in the garden.'

"S'norra pig, Mr Sheffield,' said Katie, 'it's a rat. We've got some reight big uns,' she added proudly.

Then Katie looked at her collection of poster paints and scratched her head. 'Ah've no blue for t'sky,' she pondered. Suddenly inspiration crept across her paint-splattered face. 'Ah know – ah'll mek it night time.' She dipped her brush in the pot of black paint and carried on cheerfully.

It was five o'clock when Vera and I walked out of school to visit Ruby. I carried the box of Get Well cards and Vera suggested we pick up a bag of grapes from the General Stores.

When we walked in, Miss Golightly was serving Elsie Crapper and her granddaughter Patience. The little girl pointed to a packet of Fruit Pastilles and Elsie searched in her purse for some change. Patience put the first pastille in her mouth and looked up at Miss Golightly on the other side of the counter. 'Ah can eat these and me teef won't break 'cause they're not plastic like me grandma's,' she said. With lips pursed, Elsie paid quickly, took the child's hand and marched swiftly out of the shop.

At the back of the queue, Betty Buttle was in conversation with Margery Ackroyd, the village gossip. Margery was eager to hear the latest on Ruby's recovery. 'Well ah've 'eard she's 'aving terrible trouble wi' 'er bowels,' whispered Betty with a knowing look. 'In fac' ah think at night she 'as t'wear them in-confidence pads.'

We bought the grapes, crossed the High Street and walked into the council estate to number 7, School View. Natasha answered the door. 'Come in, Mr Sheffield, Miss Evans, mek y'self at 'ome. Me mam's in t'front room an' ah'm mekkin' 'er tea.' She returned to the kitchen and the rich aroma of burnt bacon. Ruby was sitting up in her bed.

Vera sat on the crumpled eiderdown and held her hand. 'So how are you, Ruby?'

Ruby put on a brave smile. 'Ah'm coming on fine, Miss Evans. Ah were upset at first when ah 'eard you'd anointed a new caretaker, but ah understand and ah'll be back at work in no time.'

'There's no rush, Ruby,' I said.

'There is now, Mr Sheffield,' said Ruby firmly. 'Ah gorra new 'ealth visitor. It's that Miss Wojciechowski an' all 'er questions, questions, questions. Me brain's spinnin'. It were like t'Spanish composition.'

'Oh dear,' said Vera.

'An' she's too oighty-toighty f'me, Miss Evans,' said Ruby. 'Not *normal* like you.'

Vera looked perplexed for a moment. 'Er, well, thank you, Ruby.'

'An' my Ronnie's not 'appy,' she added darkly.

'And why is that, Ruby?' I asked.

"Is fav'rite chair 'ad to go upstairs,' said Ruby, 'an' all 'is motorcycle parts 'ad t'go back in t'garden.' The oily smears on the hearthrug bore testimony to this revelation. 'Ah don't want t'make a song 'n' dance about it,' added Ruby, 'but if my Ronnie don't get a job soon ah'll swing for 'im. A loaf o' bread 'as jus' gone up t'thirty-two pence so it's 'ard mekkin' ends meet.'

She looked out of the window as the dustbin wagon rumbled past. 'T'only good thing about being poor,' she said quietly, almost to herself, 'is that it costs nowt.' There was silence apart from the scraping of a frying pan in the kitchen. 'An' ah'm worried about our Duggie, Miss Evans,' said Ruby.

'And why is that?' asked Vera.

"E's gorra new woman-friend,' said Ruby.

'I see,' said Vera, removing her spectacles and looking thoughtful.

'So who's the new girlfriend?' I asked.

Vera frowned at me. Clearly there was more to this than met the eye.

'It's norra *girl*-friend, Mr Sheffield,' said Ruby with a sigh. 'It's more a *woman*-friend. She won't see forty again.'

'Oh dear,' said Vera, shaking her head in dismay.

"Xactly, Miss Evans, that's 'ow ah feel. 'E sez 'e likes *mature* women.'

'I'm sure he'll get over it,' said Vera with a forced smile.

'Yes, but it's that *divorced* woman from t'shoe shop in Easington, Miss Evans,' said Ruby. 'Once she's got 'er claws in, there's no lettin' go.'

'Perhaps Ronnie could have a word with him,' said Vera.

'Ah don't think so, Miss Evans,' said Ruby, "cause 'e's as much use as a choc'late fireguard. Mind you, Miss Wojciechowski said its prob'ly jus' a phrase our Duggie's going through,' said Ruby.

'A *phrase* . . . oh, yes, I see,' I said.

Vera looked at her wristwatch. 'Well, we must go now, Ruby. Eat your grapes and enjoy the children's cards and try not to worry.' I walked to the door but Vera hung back for a moment and I heard Ruby whisper, 'Ah think our Ronnie's gone t'one o' them prawnbrokers, Miss Evans. Ah can't find m'mother's locket wi' t'broken chain what ah got when ah got married. Y'know 'ow it is, Miss Evans . . . ah laugh in public an' ah cry in private.'

When we got back to the school car park Vera and I stood there for a moment. 'Poor Ruby,' I said. 'I wish I could think of a solution.'

'I might just have thought of one,' said Vera mysteriously and she climbed into her car and drove off.

Beth had an event at her school that evening, so at seven o'clock I locked up and walked across the village green to The Royal Oak for some hot food and a drink. As usual, assorted members of the Ragley Rovers football team were watching the news on the television above the bar. A man, attached by an elastic rope, had leapt from the Clifton Suspension Bridge and survived.

'That could catch on,' said Chris 'Kojak' Wojciechowski, the Bald-Headed Ball Wizard.

Ronnie was sitting on the bench seat under the dartboard with his son Duggie. They looked deep in conversation and I decided not to intervene. I glanced up at the 'Specials' blackboard. Tonight's gastronomic feast was a simple choice: corned beef hash or lamb's liver. 'I'll have the beef and a half of Chestnut Mild, please, Don.'

Don Bradshaw, the landlord and an ex-wrestler, pulled on the hand pump effortlessly and gave me a stubbly-faced grin. 'On yer own then, Mr Sheffield?'

'Yes, Don,' I said. 'And how's Sheila?' Don's wife, now in her mid-forties, still wore her Sixties miniskirts and, according to the Ragley Rovers football team, possessed the finest cleavage in North Yorkshire.

'She's gone wi' 'er mates to t'pictures,' said Don, 't'see that *E.T.*'

'What's that when it's at 'ome?' said Big Dave Robinson, the six-foot-four-inch goalkeeper, captain of Ragley Rovers and local refuse collector.

'It's that new Steven Spellbound film, Dave,' said Little Malcolm Robinson, his five-foot-four-inch cousin and fellow binman. 'Me an' Dorothy went t'see it.'

'Yeah, but what's it abart?' asked Big Dave, supping deeply on his pint of Tetley's bitter.

'Well, E.T.'s an alien from outer space an' 'e's wanderin' abart c'llectin' samples an' suchlike an' 'is spaceship buggers off an' leaves 'im be'ind,' said Little Malcolm.

"E wunt be too thrilled then, this E.T.,' said Big Dave.

'Y'reight there, Dave,' agreed Little Malcolm, 'leavin' t'poor little sod on 'is own on earth.'

Don leant over the bar and began drying a pint glass with his York City tea towel. 'So what 'appens then?' he asked.

"E gets reight poorly,' said Little Malcolm.

'So not exactly a bag o' laughs then,' pondered Big

Dave. 'Ah can't see me tekkin' my Nellie t'see it. She's more into 'Arrison Ford an' a bit of adventure.' Fenella Lovelace, or Nellie as she was known, was Big Dave's sporty girlfriend and he was immensely proud that she could recite football's offside rule word perfect.

'Same 'ere,' said Little Malcolm. 'Mind you, my Dorothy prefers a bit o' romance now an' again.'

The football team all gave Little Malcolm a knowing look. 'So we've 'eard, Malcolm,' said Don. Little Malcolm went a shade of puce and resumed staring up at the television set. The group Culture Club had been introduced and Boy George, dressed like a colour-blind Greek peasant, began to sing the new hit single 'Do You Really Want to Hurt Me'.

'Is it a woman?' asked Big Dave.

'Dunno, Dave,' said Little Malcolm.

'Ah think it's a feller,' said Don.

''E's too good lookin' for a feller,' said Big Dave.

''Is name's George,' said Don.

'Mus' be a poofter,' said Big Dave with a finality that brooked no argument.

'Y'reight there, Dave,' said Little Malcolm and they all wandered off to the taproom as Don reached up and switched off.

On Tuesday morning I peered through the leaded panes of the bedroom window at Bilbo Cottage and looked out at the October morning. The distant hills were shrouded in wolf-grey clouds and the trees in the fields looked like ghosts in the cold dawn. In the garden a scattering of fallen leaves, like a patchwork of memories, had faded and withered in the pale mist of autumn. The hedgerows were filled with the wild fruits and berries of the countryside, waiting to be collected by the nimble fingers of young children with smeared faces and purple tongues as they sampled the fruits of their labours. Soon it would be time for the autumn feast of jellies and jams and fruit pies, but for now the season was changing and bright summer had gone.

As I drove into Ragley village, Dorothy Humpleby was standing in the open doorway of Nora's Coffee Shop, swaying to the record on the juke-box, 'Starmaker' by the Kids from Fame, and hoping for a glimpse of the love of her life, Little Malcolm Robinson, the Ragley refuse collector, as he drove past in his bin wagon.

Suddenly I spotted Vera's car parked behind a shiny black hearse and I slowed down. Vera was deep in conversation with a grey-haired man in his sixties who was wearing an old-fashioned three-piece black suit, white shirt and black tie. It was Septimus Bernard Flagstaff, the local funeral director, known as Bernie to his friends and proud of his title as President of the Ragley and Morton Stag Beetle Society. It was well known in the village that he had a soft spot for the elegant Vera and was secretly heartbroken when news of her marriage to the major was announced. However, true love runs deep and there was nothing he wouldn't do for the woman of his dreams. As I drove past, he took a large brass timepiece from the pocket of his waistcoat, nodded in response to something Vera had said and gave her a nervous smile.

A few minutes later Vera walked into the school office, hung up her coat and sat at her desk. 'Good news,

Mr Sheffield,' she said. 'Ruby's husband has got a job at last.'

'Really?' I said. 'Ruby will be thrilled.'

'Yes. Mr Flagstaff needs a new assistant at the funeral parlour.'

'Ronnie . . . in the funeral parlour?'

'Yes, Mr Sheffield,' said Vera. 'Well, you'll recall, I did give him a reference.' As she took the cover from her typewriter and flicked the dust from the keys with her lace-edged handkerchief, a smile flickered across her lips.

And so it was that on that sunlit morning in the autumn of 1982, after a lifetime of broken promises and unemployment, Ronnie finally kept his word and got a job in what could loosely be described as the packaging industry . . . as a coffin polisher.

Chapter Four

Roman Holiday

School closed for the half-term holiday today and will reopen on Monday, 1 November.
Extract from the Ragley School Logbook:
Friday, 22 October 1982

It had been a journey of shadows. As we approached the wonderful city of Bath I reflected on the past few days. Beth was *different*, and I didn't know why.

It was Monday, 25 October and the half-term holiday stretched out before us. Beth and I had driven down to Bath for a short break from tired routines. We were both keen to explore the history of this wonderful Roman city, but mainly it was an opportunity to spend much-needed time together. A week ago her sister Laura had telephoned to ask if we would like to join her at her boss's house in Bath for a few days. Beth had jumped at the invitation and so we packed for two nights away from Bilbo Cottage. However, for me, it felt like the calm before the storm. The thought of meeting up with Laura again made me a little uneasy. There was history between us.

Beth had been quiet since Laura's invitation and I wondered what was on her mind. Even so, she seemed in good spirits when, on Monday morning, we packed the car and left very early. She had put aside her Masters degree assignment entitled 'The Case for Monitoring Teacher Performance' and left her books at home. It was clear she wanted a complete break from essays and schoolwork. It was also a time for us to relax. My brief relationship with Laura was in the past . . . it was history.

The hours flew by as we drove south and, on the radio, Carly Simon was singing 'Why' as we finally approached the city. Beth hummed along, seemingly in a world of her own. The Bath stone had faded with age and was now the colour of gold and honey in the late-afternoon October sunlight. Below us, in a valley surrounded by seven hills, the River Avon meandered on its timeless journey through this spectacular city. Here, over the centuries, *sanitas per aqua* or 'health through water' had attracted the infirm and the sick. However, for Beth and me, the healing waters were destined to be of a different kind.

We parked outside an elegant three-storey townhouse in Henrietta Street overlooking the park. 'This is it, Jack,' said Beth, glancing down at Laura's instructions. 'Looks very grand, doesn't it?' Then she leant over, sighed deeply and kissed me. 'A long journey. Good to relax at last.'

I smiled, climbed out of the car and found the key to open the boot. My emerald-green Morris Minor Traveller, with its ash-wood frame and shiny yellow-and-chrome AA badge, was my pride and joy and, although signs of age were beginning to show, it was reliable and had covered the long miles safely. 'I'll get the luggage,' I said, 'you ring the bell.'

'Good idea,' said Beth, although she appeared pre-occupied as I unloaded her large suitcase and my small sports bag.

Laura opened the door almost immediately. 'Hello, big sister,' she said. 'I've just got here myself – came straight from work.' Laura was a manager in the fashion department at Liberty in London. In her mid-thirties, two years younger than Beth, there was a confidence in her manner and a devil-may-care attitude to her demeanour. She was dressed in a figure-hugging, pin-striped business suit and a fashionable black leather coat. With her long brown hair piled high in stylish plaits, she looked simply stunning.

Beth gave her sister a hug. 'Thanks for inviting us,' she said. 'Super idea.'

'And how's my favourite brother-in-law?' teased Laura. She stood before me, gently smoothed my creased shirt collar and kissed me on the cheek. I could smell her perfume, Opium by Yves Saint Laurent. It was familiar and rekindled old memories.

'I'm fine, Laura,' I said. 'And how about you?'

She looked at me with questioning green eyes. 'Surviving, Jack, in a busy world.' Then she turned to Beth. 'Work seems to fill my life now.'

Above our heads, the raucous cries of screeching seagulls, perched on the tall chimney pots of the elegant terraced houses, cried, 'Go-away, go-away.' Perhaps I should have heeded their warning.

Suddenly a tall, slim woman appeared from the hallway. She had porcelain skin, a blonde pony-tail and was wearing country cord trousers and a checked baggy shirt. She looked as if she had just stepped from the cover of *Country Living* magazine. 'Welcome to Bath,' she said, giving us both a double air-kiss, 'I'm Pippa, by the way. Come on in and make yourselves at home. You must be dreadfully weary after such a long journey.'

It was over peppermint tea that we discovered Pippa Dennison was a senior figure in the Liberty fashion empire. She was around forty years old but looked much younger. She clearly thought the world of Laura.

'Pippa,' I said, 'this is a wonderful house. It's kind of you to let us stay.'

'Not a problem, Jack,' she said. 'It's actually Daddy's place and I can use it when I wish. But it was Laura's idea, so you should thank her.'

'I just thought you would enjoy the break, Beth,' added Laura a little hurriedly.

'And so we shall,' said Beth with a relaxed smile.

Conversation ebbed and flowed as Beth and Laura caught up with the latest news. 'And is there a man in your life?' asked Beth. Laura looked into her tea cup and shook her head.

'Well, it's not for the want of offers,' said Pippa with a whimsical smile.

'I've given up on men for the time being,' said Laura.

There was an awkward silence, broken eventually by Pippa saying, 'Come on, I'll show you to your rooms.' We walked into the huge carpeted hallway and collected our luggage.

'Hope you don't mind,' said Pippa, 'but I booked a table for the four of us in one of my favourite French restaurants by the river . . . absolutely super food and Daddy has an account there. So,' she glanced at the ancient grandfather clock, 'say, back down here at seven?' Rhetorical questions and swift organization seemed to be a natural part of Pippa's world and we nodded and went upstairs. It also occurred to me that, on a primary headteacher's pay, there would never come a time when I would have a restaurant account.

When we met again in the hall I immediately noticed that I was the only one who didn't appear to have changed to suit the occasion. After a welcome shower and a shave, I had dug out a clean casual polo shirt from my sports bag and put on my old herringbone sports jacket with the leather elbow patches that I had worn on the drive down. I looked down at my baggy grey trousers and old Kicker shoes and felt distinctly under-dressed for a night out with the three beautiful women who stood before me. Beth had unpacked four different outfits from her large suitcase and finally decided on a cream blouse and chocolate brown skirt, plus a neat matching waistcoat. Her beige *Cagney & Lacey* raincoat with padded shoulders and loosely tied belt was the height of fashion and emphasized her slim figure. She looked terrific.

Meanwhile Pippa, once again, had somehow managed to look both casual yet simply perfect in a DAKS country classic suit in herringbone tweed with patch pockets and leather buttons. Next to her stood Laura in a pair of skin-tight Burberry jeans, calf-length leather boots, blue denim shirt, green denim jacket and a red neckscarf tied in a knot. She had let down her long brown hair and the look was that of a confident and dynamic woman . . . except for her eyes. It was as if she had a weighty problem on her mind and her thoughts were elsewhere.

Pippa locked the door behind us and we strolled out into a cool but perfect evening and walked along Argyle Street, across Pulteney Bridge and towards the nightlife of the city. Laura led the way, deep in conversation with Beth, while I walked beside Pippa.

'You all look amazing,' I said.

Pippa grinned. 'It's nothing really. Laura and I are busy at the moment promoting the Ralph Lauren Western Collection. It's the latest casual gear.' She looked me up and down. 'And Jack, if you don't mind me saying, you *could* look really good if you put your mind to it.' She considered me as if deciding how to dress a mannequin. 'To start with, you're tall and slim, which is an advantage, and you've got naturally wavy brown hair that, if you let it grow a little longer, could look quite fashionable.'

'I haven't given it much thought,' I said, feeling as though I had been undressed and dressed in the space of a couple of sentences.

'Jack . . . there are some delightful gentlemen's shops in Bath. Not quite Oxford Street, but we girls could transform you while you're here.'

'I'm fine thanks, Pippa,' I said. Even so, I was beginning to wish I'd packed my charcoal-grey suit, the one I used for weddings, funerals and parents' evenings.

Pippa was now in full flow. 'I could see you in a rather arty sky-blue cord suit with a flamingo-pink linen shirt and a slim Eighties maroon tie and, of course, a pair of modern lightweight steel-framed spectacles with large lenses.'

I felt a little embarrassed following this assault by the fashion police and I pushed my Buddy Holly spectacles further up the bridge of my nose. 'I'm not sure *pink* has got up to Yorkshire yet,' I replied.

'Pity,' said Pippa. 'Clothes maketh the man.'

It was then I realized we were from different worlds.

The French restaurant had the feel of a London bistro, relaxed, comfortable, friendly and full of young professionals. The maître d'hôtel knew Pippa well and we were guided to a candlelit corner table.

I glanced at the menu, which was written entirely in French, apart from the prices . . . and they were extravagant. Pippa spoke fluent French and ordered for all of us. For a starter, she ordered *le sauté de grenouille persillé*, which turned out to be a sauté of frogs' legs with button mushrooms, parsley, and lemon and garlic butter. There was also a huge bowl of the local speciality for us all to share: mussels cooked in cider, shallots and cream.

I played safe for the main course and, thankful for my O-level French in the Sixties, ordered *La poitrine roulée de porc*, which turned out to be the most delicious braised organic pork belly in cider, ginger and honey, a treat for a hungry Yorkshireman after a long day's driving. Everything was perfectly cooked and I reflected that this was a long way from Sheila's *if-in-doubt-give-it-an-extra-ten-minutes* cuisine in The Royal Oak. Gradually I relaxed, and the conversation and red wine flowed in equal measure.

However, I sensed that, on occasion, behind the light laughter lay heavy thoughts. There seemed a superficiality to our conversation; what needed to be said appeared hidden. It wasn't until towards the end of the evening when we were sipping liqueurs and Pippa and Beth had slipped out to the ladies' room that Laura struck up a new conversation.

'So how's married life, Jack?' she asked. She put down her glass of cognac and looked across the table into my eyes. Her stare was challenging.

'It's fine, Laura,' I said evenly.

She dabbed her mouth with a linen napkin. 'And is my sister happy?'

'You would have to ask her yourself,' I replied.

She smiled. 'I have, Jack.' Then she leant forward. Her skin was flawless, and the scent of her perfume was both light and fragrant.

'And are *you* happy?' she asked quietly.

It seemed a curious question and the pause before my reply seemed to last an age. A private cocoon of heavy silence surrounded us as I looked into her green eyes.

'Yes, I am,' I said.

Suddenly, Beth and Pippa reappeared. 'And what are you two plotting?' asked Beth with a grin.

'Nothing, big sister,' said Laura smoothly, 'just thinking that Jack here needs pointing in the right direction.'

'Really?' said Beth.

'Yes,' said Pippa, 'to a gentleman's outfitter.'

'Poor Jack,' said Laura. 'But, sadly, I have to agree.'

'I think my dear husband is too set in his ways,' said Beth reprovingly. 'Not exactly the new-age Eighties man, are you darling?'

There was a moment when Pippa looked knowingly at Laura, who responded with a flicker of a smile. It was a brief communication that meant nothing to a mere man but, between women, spoke volumes.

It had been a long day and, back in our room, Beth switched on the television set and turned the volume low. The film was *They Call Me Mister Tibbs* and we sat on the bed together watching Sidney Poitier in his iconic role while chatting about the evening and what we might do the next day.

Later, the television was still on when I finally climbed into bed and it was almost midnight when Beth emerged from the bathroom in a nightdress I hadn't seen before. Her honey-blonde hair looked slightly tousled as she walked barefoot towards me.

'Are you *really* watching this?' she teased. The new programme was *Claire Rayner's Casebook* with a discussion dedicated to stressful marriages and divorce. I switched it off. 'I don't think it applies to us,' I said.

Beth smiled as she turned out the light. 'I agree,' she said as she climbed in next to me and we kissed. It was two hours later that we finally fell into an exhausted sleep.

*   *   *

Next morning I awoke first. I crept out of bed and peered out of the window at the view of the park and the countryside beyond. It was an eerie world of grey and ghostly images, all life blurred and featureless. Slowly, the dawn sun spread its warmth over the sleeping land and illuminated the moist vapours of mist covering the fields with a shroud of silence.

It was then that I reflected on our perfect night, and I looked back at Beth and marvelled at her naked body. Making love with this beautiful woman had always been special, a journey of ice and fire, but somehow last night had been *different*. There was an insistence about Beth, a fresh urgency and a desire that could barely be satisfied. One thing was certain . . . I would never understand women. As I hunted for my shaving kit at the bottom of my sports bag I smiled. Life was full of surprises and I wasn't complaining.

Over breakfast Beth and I were still stifling yawns, but a new day awaited us in this beautiful city and it was ours to explore.

'More coffee?' asked Pippa after a breakfast of croissants and delicious Welsh honey from Fortnum & Mason.

'Yes please,' said Beth sleepily. I watched both Beth and Laura blow on the surface of their coffee before sipping it tentatively, mirror images across the table, but clearly with different moods on this beautiful day.

'So what are your plans?' asked Pippa.

'Just a little exploring,' I said. 'Probably the Abbey and the Roman Baths.'

Pippa looked across at Laura, who seemed deep in

thought. 'Laura and I have things to do, but we could meet you for afternoon tea – say three o'clock outside the Pump Room in the Abbey courtyard.'

'Fine,' said Beth. 'Then perhaps a little shopping.'

The thought of shopping with three women filled me with horror, but I said nothing.

So it was that on a sunlit autumn morning Beth and I, hand in hand, walked the streets of Bath and marvelled together at this beautiful Palladian-style city designed by the architect John Wood.

'You look happy,' I said.

'I am,' she said simply, and there was peace in her green eyes and firmness in the way she held my hand as we strolled into the city centre. Two thousand years ago the Romans had arrived and had fallen in love with the natural thermal spas and so they built their elegant baths and temples. History touched every street and building, and I recalled that Jane Austen lived here from 1801 to 1806 and set parts of *Northanger Abbey* and *Persuasion* in the city.

We walked into Bath Abbey, known as 'the Lantern of the West'. The wonderful light that illuminated the interior explained why, and we sat on one of the pews to enjoy the mantle of peace that descended on our private haven.

'I love you,' I whispered.

'And I love you, Jack,' she said quietly, resting her head on my shoulder. 'We needed this time for the two of us.' Her words were like balm on a wounded heart and, for a fleeting moment in the sanctuary of this grand medieval cathedral, I understood the meaning of unconditional love.

Later we walked down North Parade Passage past Sally Lunn's, the oldest house in Bath and, nearby, we called into a coffee shop. We ordered filter coffee with hot milk as well as the local delicacy, a rich, round toasted brioche bun based on the famous recipe of the young French refugee, Sally Lunn.

Above the counter, in preparation for Hallowe'en, a huge orange pumpkin had been hollowed out. With a sharp knife, circular holes had been carved for the eyes, plus a triangular nose and a rectangular mouth complete with tombstone teeth. A candle flickered inside. It was a gruesome sight and we both smiled. It was good to relax together and I realized we had eased smoothly into holiday mode.

'Happy?' I asked.

Beth grinned and blew on the surface of her hot coffee. 'Perfect, Jack, simply perfect.'

A short while later we stared in wonder at the historic Roman Baths, dating from the first century AD. It seemed a pity that the city was now a spa in name only. Sadly, a few years ago the ancient pipework had revealed serious contamination and, since then, the precious hot mineral water had been simply diverted into the River Avon.

'Look at this, Jack,' said Beth, pointing to the guide book with a smile. In 1668 Samuel Pepys had written in his diary, 'Methinks it cannot be clean to go so many bodies together in the same water'. I recalled the shower

Beth and I had shared this morning but kept this precious thought to myself.

Then we continued up the hill to the Assembly Rooms and enjoyed browsing in the Bath Antiques Fair. From there we continued round the elegant curve of the Circus up to the magnificent eighteenth-century Royal Crescent, a semi-elliptical terrace of thirty grand houses, complete with over a hundred giant Ionic columns. We stopped and looked in awe. This really was a triumph of eighteenth-century geometric engineering. 'Isn't it wonderful, Jack?' said Beth, holding my hand. Above our heads a scattering of squirrels darted with quick and nimble steps along the branches of a gnarled oak tree. Her soft hair touched my cheek as I kissed her and we walked on, happy in our private world.

Finally we returned to the Abbey Churchyard outside the Pump Room where Pippa and Laura were waiting for us. Afternoon tea was a brief, simple affair as the three women planned an afternoon's shopping together which held no interest for me. Schoolwork seemed a long way off and, as we sat there, I watched the people passing by and listened to a local busker playing Paul McCartney's 'Yesterday', which really did feel so very far away.

'See you back here in a couple of hours, Jack?' said Pippa. It was another of her rhetorical questions and I smiled, grateful for the opportunity not to be involved. The three women set off shopping and I settled down with another pot of tea and a copy of the *Bath and West Evening Chronicle*. The local news seemed to be dominated by an article about two hundred members of the Wiltshire

Motor Cycle Action Group who were protesting against the wearing of helmets. It looked as though the days of the open road and wind in your hair were numbered.

After a while I decided to get some fresh air and enjoy the last of the low afternoon sunshine. The nights were drawing in now and soon it would be dark. I stood outside the Pump Room under the Colonnade, nine equal bays studded with ten classical Ionic columns, and looked at the busy shoppers in Stall Street.

To my surprise, Laura was walking towards me, carrying a variety of smart womenswear bags. As usual she turned heads in her beautifully tailored narrow skirt, a checked blouse and a fashionable Sherpa woollen quilted waistcoat. Her silk scarf matched her eyes. She looked as if she was about to be photographed for the cover of *Cosmopolitan*. 'Jack,' she said, 'we hoped you might look after these for us while you're waiting.' Her high cheekbones were flushed as the warmth left the earth and cool darkness spread its cloak.

'Yes, fine,' I said, 'I'll take them back to the tea shop and stand guard.' I glanced down at the expensive-looking bags. 'You've been busy.'

There was an awkward moment of silence and then Laura turned. 'Well, I'd better get back to the girls.'

I put my hand on her arm. 'Laura, are you OK?'

She took a deep breath and let it out slowly. 'It's just *life*, Jack. It's complicated.' She bowed her head and her long hair hung loosely around her shoulders. I knew she was right. Life had never been that simple for either of us . . . rather a maze of mistaken opportunities.

'Laura, you must know there never was anything

serious between us,' I said. 'Nothing *permanent*. And nothing really happened. We were just friends.'

'Were we?'

'I chose Beth because I loved her, Laura. You know that.'

'Love makes fools of us all, Jack.'

'And I'm happy with my life,' I said.

'That's good, but who knows where we shall come to rest,' she stepped into the shade of the Colonnade, 'in shade or in sun,' she said with an enigmatic smile and I wondered at the meaning behind these words.

'I don't understand,' I said.

Laura looked at me with sadness in her eyes. 'You will one day, Jack, and, in the end, you'll see . . . she'll hurt you.' Then she turned and I watched her slim figure stride confidently across Stall Street.

'I still don't understand,' I said, but my words were like seeds on the wind, scattered thoughts cast upon the soft breezes of the approaching night.

There had always been something about Laura that intrigued me, but I couldn't understand what it was. Then I looked around me. Above my head a huge triangular stone pediment surmounted the nine perfect archways of the Colonnade. On its face was a carving of Hygieia, the goddess of good health, and her companion was a serpent. With a wry smile I picked up the bags and walked back towards the tea shop near the Abbey.

Later, back in Henrietta Street, there was a tap on our bedroom door. Beth and I were relaxing before going out. It was Pippa. 'Bad news, I'm afraid,' she said. 'Laura's not well, so it makes sense for me to stay with her and you two can go out and enjoy your last evening in Bath.'

Beth went across the landing to see Laura and returned ten minutes later. 'She'll be fine, just a headache after overdoing it at work and then suddenly relaxing,' she said in a matter-of-fact voice. 'So where shall we go?'

'Well, we passed a cinema today, but I don't know what's on,' I said.

'Let's find out,' said Beth, grabbing her coat. She appeared full of energy again.

When we arrived outside the cinema we stared up at a large poster. It read:

Lewis Collins in *Who Dares Wins* (AA)
and
Star Trek II: The Wrath of Khan

'Well, what do you think?' I asked dubiously.

'I think I'd rather buy a bottle of wine and go back for an early night, Jack. How about you?'

It suddenly occurred to me how much I loved this beautiful woman and I couldn't recall feeling so at peace with my life. Ragley School seemed far away now and, as I held her in my arms and kissed her, the wind changed direction and a scurry of fallen leaves scattered around our feet like the wings of fragile butterflies. A turbulent past was behind us and we had relaxed in the harmony of our lives, together at last and sharing a new pathway.

'I think we should go in peace and prosper,' I said. 'At least that's what Mr Spock would say.'

'Sounds good,' said Beth with a mischievous grin and

she held my hand and led me back to the house, via the nearest wine bar. Finally, in the early hours and in each other's arms, we shared the time of the quiet mind when peaceful slumber descends like a tranquil mist.

On Wednesday morning the wind had turned in its groove and an iron-grey sky was filled with a cold rain that stung our faces as we packed the car.

Goodbyes were brief, and Laura stayed in her room as Beth said farewell to her. Pippa gave me the obligatory double air-kiss, wished us a safe journey and we were on our way through the mist. As we left the city a flock of starlings with a scattering of wings rose suddenly into the sky. In a world of white noise the sound was soothing and we both settled back with our own thoughts. It had been an eventful few days.

As the day wore on we approached the familiar countryside of Yorkshire. Ploughing had begun on the fertile plain of York, combing chocolate stripes and attracting the rooks from their lofty perches.

Finally, as darkness fell, back in Bilbo Cottage I glanced at the kitchen calendar and smiled. In a few days I would be back at school and returning to a world I could understand . . . unlike the minds of women. For me, they would always remain a mystery.

Chapter Five

A Penny for the Guy

County Hall sent the document 'Rationalization, Value for Money and a Better Life – a Vision for the Eighties for Small Schools in North Yorkshire' to all village schools in the Easington area, explaining why the high costs of maintaining small schools needed to be addressed.

Extract from the Ragley School Logbook:
Thursday, 4 November 1982

Heathcliffe Earnshaw pressed his nose against the window of Pratt's Hardware Emporium and stared in awe at the Standard Fireworks Bumper Box. The lid had been removed to reveal the treasures within. It was early morning on Thursday, 4 November and excitement was building for the children of Ragley School.

'Terry, 'ave a look,' he said to his brother, barely able to contain his excitement. 'They've got *ev'rythin'* – Cath'rine wheels, snow fountains, a Mount Vesuvius, jumping crackers, a big Roman candle, an' two big rockets.'

'An' a Fairy Rain,' said Terry, looking at the tall thin firework at the side of the box.

Heathcliffe grunted in disapproval. 'Ah'm not too fussed abart a Fairy Rain. Y'allus get one o' them, but all t'rest are brilliant.'

'But we've no money, 'Eath,' said Terry shaking his head mournfully.

However, as always, the fire of optimism burned in Heathcliffe's brave heart. 'Don't you worry, our kid,' he said. 'Ah've gorra plan.'

Terry smiled. He always had faith in his big brother and with a spring in their step the Earnshaws continued their circuitous journey towards school.

The quickthorn hedges of hips and haws flew by as I drove on the back road from Kirkby Steepleton to Ragley village. I pulled in where the York Road meets the High Street and parked on the forecourt of Pratt's Garage. Victor Pratt came out to serve me from the single pump.

I wound down my window and asked the inevitable question. 'How are you, Victor?' Our local garage owner usually had some ailment or other and the list was about to grow longer.

He unscrewed my filler cap and inserted the nozzle. 'Ah've gorra belly ache,' he said mournfully. He rubbed his tummy with a greasy hand and winced. 'Ah'm a martyr t'me stomach,' he said. 'In fac', ah'm off t'see Dr Davenport this morning. It could be one o' them sceptical ulcers, ah reckon.'

'Perhaps it is,' I replied, suppressing a smile. I guessed

that Dr Davenport might have sceptical tendencies as well.

'Nine poun' f'six gallon, Mr Sheffield,' he said. 'Keeps goin' up, dunt it? Ah blame t'government.' I gave him a ten-pound note and he shuffled off to get my change from his ancient till. 'An' ah'll see y'tonight in t'Coffee Shop. Our Nora's serving all t'locals wi' a free 'ot drink,' he said. 'Should be a good do. There'll be a load o' Pratts there.'

Meanwhile, in the flat above the Coffee Shop, Nora Pratt felt like a film star. It was the twenty-fifth anniversary of the opening of her shop and she had bought a new dress.

Nora looked in her full-length mirror and studied the reflection of the short, plump forty-five-year-old that stared back at her. Although she had 'filled out' a little in recent years, in her mind's eye she could still recall the time in 1957 on her first day in the Coffee Shop when she had a slim waist and a curvy figure. It occurred to her that, with a little luck, she could have been a famous actress. However, the fact that the furthest she climbed up the ladder of success was a non-speaking extra in *Crossroads* had nothing to do with her acting ability. Rather it was because a certain letter of the alphabet had always proved elusive for this voluble lady. She called downstairs to her assistant, Dorothy Humpleby, 'Dowothy, come an' look. Ah'm twying on one o' them top-o'-the-wange polyester cocktail dwesses . . . in bwight wed.' It was a quarter past eight and Nora's big day had begun.

*   *   *

Next door, Nora's younger brother, Timothy, was sellotaping a poster to his shop window. It read 'LIGHT UP THE SKY WITH STANDARD FIREWORKS'. Then he selected a top-of-the-range spirit level and checked the poster was exactly horizontal. Timothy liked precision and only when the bubble in the plastic transparent tube on top of the spirit level was *exactly* central did he relax. It was then that he needed to seek comfort in the familiar and he turned to his collection of screws.

In his Hardware Emporium on Ragley High Street, the pursuit of tidiness was a way of life for forty-two-year-old Timothy. However, once again, in his beautifully organized world, the realization dawned that there were customers who did not understand that, without *order*, life was not worth living. He stared in dismay at the two-inch dome-headed screw that had been picked up by a customer and replaced in the box of one-and-a-half-inch flat-headed screws. It lay there like a pork chop at a vegetarian tea party, incongruous and unwelcome. He picked it up with a sigh and replaced it in its rightful home. Then he went to arrange the boxes of light bulbs so that the labels all faced outwards and, as he did so, he smiled. He knew that in the village he was known affectionately as 'Tidy Tim' and pride filled his beating heart. For, as his mother had told him, 'Tidiness is next to godliness' and Timothy was content in his hardware heaven . . . well, almost. Some boys had obviously been pressing their noses against his window and there were smudges. He took a polishing cloth from the pocket of his spotless and neatly ironed brown overall and hurried outside to buff up his window.

Suddenly a mud-splattered Land Rover pulled up and the driver wound down his window. 'Are y'open yet, Pratt?' It was Stan Coe, local landowner, boorish bully and the most unpopular man in the village. 'Ah need a roll o' chicken wire.'

Timothy winced slightly but continued to polish the window. 'Ah open shortly, Mr Coe.'

'That's no bloody good,' shouted Stan and he lumbered over to Timothy. 'Gerra move on, 'cause ah want it now!' At sixteen stones the burly figure of the aggressive farmer was a formidable sight next to the frail shopkeeper.

''Ow much did y'want?' asked Timothy.

''Bout chest 'igh an' twenty paces,' said Stan.

'Ah get a delivery o' that size last thing this afternoon,' said Timothy. 'Ah'll put it on one side f'you t'collect.'

'Ah'll be back later then,' growled Stan. He glanced at the sign in the next-door window. It read 'JOIN NORA FOR A FREE COFFEE FROM 4.00 P.M. TODAY TO CELEBRATE 25 YEARS IN THE COFFEE SHOP'. 'An' ah'll 'ave a free 'ot drink while ah'm abart it.'

Timothy watched him drive away and shook his head. 'Some folk just 'ave no manners,' he muttered and went off to wash his hands.

It was a freezing cold morning and I sat at my desk in the school office reading a copious document from County Hall about 'Value for Money' in relation to village schools. It didn't make happy reading, and I sighed as our ancient school boiler chugged into life and the hot-water pipes creaked and groaned. The season had moved on and once again it was the time of the burning of leaves, and smoke from the gardens of Ragley village drifted into a slate-grey sky. The cold days of late autumn were here again and Ragley School flexed its ancient bones to face yet another hard winter.

At a quarter past ten the children were in good voice in morning assembly. Anne played the first few bars of 'All things bright and beautiful' and we all joined in.

'All creatures great and small,' sang eighty-six lusty voices.

'All things bright and beautiful . . . All teachers' graves are small,' sang Heathcliffe Earnshaw. I gave him a stern look from over my hymn book while trying to suppress a grin. Heathcliffe returned his innocent, glassy-eyed stare, perfected over many years of fruitless accusations.

This was followed by Jo's husband, Acting Sergeant Dan Hunter, who gave a talk on the Firework Code. Dan was our six-foot-four-inch local policeman and a popular figure at Ragley School. At the end the children repeated all the safety rules out loud before they went out to play, full of excitement as Bonfire Night drew near.

During morning break Anne was on playground duty and I was sitting with Jo near the gas fire, checking the results of the Schonell Word Recognition Test for the children in her class. Vera was shaking her head in dismay at the headline in *The Times*: 'Sunday shopping has official blessing with 58% of women working'.

'It will be a sad day when Sunday is no longer a day of rest,' she announced.

'Yes, Vera,' I murmured without conviction. Sally and Jo said nothing. Secretly they were pleased to have an extra opportunity to do their shopping, but they were wise enough not to stop Vera in full flow. Fortunately, there was even worse news.

'Oh dear, oh dear,' said Vera. 'I blame that young man, Cliff Richard. He's clearly a distraction.'

'Cliff Richard?' said Jo, who was a big fan. Lately she'd been playing *Wired for Sound* while she did the ironing on Saturday mornings.

'Yes,' said Vera. 'Sue Barker's form has slumped since she met him.' It appeared Britain's number-one lady tennis player was about to lose her top ranking to Jo Durie.

'Well, I've heard he's a very religious man,' said Sally, immersed in her *Art & Craft* magazine and an article on papier maché Easter Island face-masks.

Vera looked up. 'Oh well, perhaps he's not so bad after all . . . and his singing can't last for ever. Perhaps he'll find something better to do with his time. But in the meantime, he's definitely a *distraction.*' Fortunately she cheered up after seeing the photograph of the Queen and the Princess of Wales together after the State Opening of Parliament, and everyone settled to enjoy a welcome cup of coffee on this cold morning.

'And are you calling into Nora's Coffee Shop after school, Vera?' I asked.

'Oh yes,' said Vera, 'wouldn't miss it for the world.'

In the High Street Big Dave and Little Malcolm parked their bin wagon and walked into the Coffee Shop. To celebrate the event, Nora was featuring 1957 hit records on the juke-box and Little Richard was singing 'Lucille' when Little Malcolm arrived at the counter.

Big Dave went to sit at their usual table while Little Malcolm stared up at the love of his life. 'Y'look lovely today, Dorothy,' he said.

Dorothy Humpleby, the five-foot-eleven-inch assistant with the peroxide blonde hair, smiled down at her heart-throb. 'Ah've gone to a lot o' trouble wi' it being Nora's big day,' she said. Dorothy was wearing *Dallas* shoulder pads under her white frilly blouse, pink-leather hotpants, her favourite Wonder Woman boots and clip-on hula-hoop earrings. 'For me creamy-smooth skin ah put on me Clinique Porcelain Beige Base, then ah dab me Ivory Glow foundation under me eyes and, to finish off, ah set it wi' Transparency Loose Powder,' said Dorothy. 'It teks ages.'

'Yes, Dorothy, it's reight classy,' said Little Malcolm.

'Then ah put on me Mary Quant waterproof mascara,' continued Dorothy, barely pausing for breath.

''Urry up, lover boy,' shouted Big Dave.

'So it's two teas please, Dorothy, an'—' muttered Little Malcolm.

'An' then me Frosty Pink Blusher, o' course.'

'An' two pork pies—' said Little Malcolm.

'An' then ah use me Boots Number Seven Lip Liner,' said Dorothy.

'So it's jus' the teas an' pies, Dorothy,' said Little Malcolm, looking across to Big Dave who was becoming agitated with the long wait.

'An' then f'me *peas de insistence*, ah jus' add me Miss Selfridge Peachy Head.'

'Y'what?' said Little Malcolm, looking confused. 'Ah think Eugene Scrimshaw went there for 'is 'olidays once.'

'Where?' said Dorothy.

'Beachy 'Ead,' said Little Malcolm.

Dorothy gave him a peculiar look as she put two pork pies on a chipped plate.

Meanwhile, a new record landed on the juke-box turntable, 'Oooh, me 'eart-thwob,' said Nora from behind her Breville sandwich toaster. 'Elvis Pwesley an' "Jailhouse Wock".'

An hour later Nora hurried into Diane's Hair Salon.

'What's it t'be, Nora?' asked the phlegmatic Diane.

'Ah want t'look like Cagney,' said Nora, holding up a photograph of the new television crime-fighters.

'But she's blonde, Nora,' said Diane. ''Ow about Lacey? She's a brunette.' Nora frowned. 'An' she's t'intelligent one,' added Diane with a knowing look.

Nora pondered this for a moment. 'Mek it Lacey then, Diane.'

Diane smiled. Sometimes psychology and hairdressing went hand in hand.

Gradually, as the afternoon progressed, darkness descended on Ragley village. It was nearly 3.45 p.m. and, in my classroom, the children had put their chairs on their desks and we were saying our end-of-school prayer. After a hurried 'Amen' Heathcliffe Earnshaw looked at Jimmy Poole and winked. Jimmy understood. Tonight was 'Penny for the Guy' night and, for the first hour, it was his turn to be the guy.

*   *   *

Across the road, a diminutive figure stopped outside the bright lights of Pratt's Hardware Emporium. Lofthouse 'Lofty' Pratt looked at the sign above the door and smiled.

On this cold November afternoon, as darkness fell, Lofty didn't feel the bitter wind that swept down Ragley High Street. As the ex-Featherweight Boxing Champion of Yorkshire, he was made of sterner stuff. As they said in his hometown of Castleford, "E eats nails an' spits rust, does Lofty.' At five foot two inches tall he cut an insignificant figure in a baggy, outdated shellsuit but, as the landlord of his local Miners' Arms once said, 'Don't start owt, 'cause our Lofty'll finish it.'

Lofty had been named after Nat Lofthouse, the Bolton Wanderers and England centre forward. His father, an England fan, had always admired the tough footballer, nicknamed 'the Lion of Vienna'. Mr Pratt, one of five brothers, wanted Lofthouse to grow up to be like his famous, clean-living, honest-as-the-day-is-long namesake. However, he had to make do with a vertically challenged psychopath who could put his fist through a coalhouse door. So it was with the innate confidence of an ageing prizefighter that he walked into his cousin's shop and, appropriately, the bell above the door rang loudly as he stepped inside.

Timothy was standing behind the counter with three different-coloured pens in the top pocket of his overall.

'Nah then, our Timothy,' said Lofty.

"Ello Lofthouse,' said Timothy. 'Nora said you were coming.'

'Aye, ah wouldn't miss our Nora's special day. She's allus been a good lass.'

'An' 'ow are you getting' on?' asked Timothy.

'Ah'm fit as a flea,' he said and proceeded to give an impromptu exhibition of shadow boxing in the middle of the shop. Timothy looked alarmed. Lofty's dancing feet were dangerously near to the perfectly aligned display of his new range of *Snow White* garden gnomes and Happy was very close to being seriously disconcerted.

'Any road, our Nora said t'come 'ere fust t'get settled in like,' said Lofthouse.

'Er, yes,' said Timothy without enthusiasm. Lofthouse had never been the tidiest of guests. 'Ah've put yer in t'second bedroom wi' m'Meccano set.'

Just before five o'clock Vera and I buttoned up our coats and walked out of school to Nora's Coffee Shop. A steady stream of villagers and distant members of the Pratt family were ahead of us and Heathcliffe Earnshaw, outside the brightly lit shop window of Pratt's Hardware Emporium, was not one to miss an opportunity.

'Penny for t'guy *please*, Miss Evans, Mr Sheffield?' said Heathcliffe politely. A very realistic-looking guy in a baggy blue boiler suit, cardboard mask, Wellington boots and an incongruous pair of worn-out oven gloves was slumped in a wheelbarrow next to him. However, the guy lacked a hat, which would have hidden Jimmy Poole's distinctive head of curly ginger hair.

Vera opened her purse and put a five-pence piece in the tin offered by little Terry Earnshaw. 'Well done, boys,' she said. 'That's a wonderful guy . . . very realistic.'

I rummaged in my pocket and added a ten-pence piece. 'I thought Jimmy might be helping you,' I said.

There was a movement of black-button eyes behind the mask. "'E's busy, Mr Sheffield,' said Heathcliffe quickly . . . and, of course, truthfully.

Nora Pratt was daydreaming when Vera and I approached the counter. She was secretly in love with the television sports presenter Des Lynam, even though she had no interest in football and thought Aston Villa was a stately home. With his white jacket and a black shirt unbuttoned to reveal his hairy chest, he looked the perfect man. His moustache was the final *pièce de résistance* and Nora wondered if it tickled when you kissed him.

This was going through her mind as I approached the counter. 'Two coffees please, Nora,' I said. 'And congratulations.'

'That's weally appweciated, Mr Sheffield,' said Nora.

'You look lovely,' said Vera. 'A beautiful dress.'

'Thank you, Miss Evans,' said Nora.

A copy of *Woman* magazine was open on the counter and I glanced down at an old photograph of the elegant and beautiful film star, Grace Kelly.

'Ah feel so sowwy for 'im,' said Nora sadly.

'Who's that, Nora?' I asked.

'Pwince Wainier of Monaco,' said Nora, 'after Pwincess Gwace died. Ah saw 'er in that 'Itchcock film, *Wear Window*.' She passed over two cups of steaming froth. 'An' enjoy y'fwothy coffee . . . on the 'ouse.'

We took our drinks to a corner table and sat down. Vera attempted one cautious sip and then pushed the cup to one side. 'Oh dear,' she said and we settled back to enjoy a half hour of people-watching.

*   *   *

Nora's distant upmarket cousin from Harrogate, Veronica Pratt, had approached the counter with her usual haughty disposition.

''Ello Vewonica,' said Nora.

'Good evening, Nora,' said Veronica, known as 'Veggie-Ve' in the family.

'Ah y'still a vegetawian?' asked Nora.

'I've become a vegan,' said Veronica rather primly.

It crossed Nora's mind that it sounded like a planet in *Star Trek*. 'Well 'ave a bit o' salmon.'

'I don't eat anything with a face,' said Veronica.

Dorothy stopped rearranging the display of rock buns. 'Do fish 'ave faces?' she asked.

'Yes, they do, young lady,' said Veronica.

'Well, 'ow about some nice 'am if ah slice it reight thin?' asked Dorothy, trying to be helpful. Veggie-Ve was unimpressed and ignored the offer.

After much deliberation, she selected a mushroom omelette sprinkled with grated Wensleydale cheese and Nora went off to put it under the grill.

Milburn and Gwendolin Pratt, who ran a bed-and-breakfast in Bridlington, were sitting next to the juke-box. Both had removed their hearing aids and so were oblivious to Jerry Lee Lewis singing yet another 1957 hit, 'Whole Lotta Shakin' Goin' On', which, in Gwendolin's case, was entirely appropriate. A compulsive knitter, but sadly with little skill, she dropped stitches with reckless abandon as her shaking knitting needles clacked out an off-beat rhythm.

Timothy Pratt often recalled his first pair of knitted swimming trunks. They were multi-coloured and created from miscellaneous balls of spare wool by Gwendolin in her tiny front room. Inevitably, when they got wet they stretched horribly and hung in sodden folds around his knees. He could still remember the laughter when he emerged from the rolling waves on Bridlington beach. He had never recovered his self-esteem, and the pain of those early days remained vivid in his mind.

Meanwhile, Lofty had introduced himself to Big Dave and Little Malcolm and, along with Shane and Clint Ramsbottom, the conversation had inevitably turned to football.

'Loft'ouse, did y'say?' said Big Dave, 'Nah that were a *proper* footballer. Thirty goals in thirty-three internationals.'

'Y'reight there, Dave,' said Little Malcolm.

'Short back an' sides were Nat,' added Shane Ramsbottom, the skinhead with the letters H-A-R-D tattooed on the knuckles of his right fist. He frowned at his younger brother Clint. ''E allus tucked 'is shirt in 'is shorts . . . no long-'aired nancy boys in them days.'

'A proper old-fashioned centre forward,' said Big Dave. ''E'd be worth over a million poun' today.'

'Y'reight there, Dave,' said Little Malcolm. 'If that Trevor Francis is worth a million, then Nat Loft'ouse is worth more.'

Lofty looked at his watch. 'Ah think ah'll go an' c'llect our Timothy from next door,' he said.

"E's waiting f'Stan Coe . . . summat abart chicken wire,' said Clint.

Dorothy overheard. "E were in earlier, that Stan Coe,' she said.

'Ah've no time for 'im,' muttered Little Malcolm.

"E stirs 'is tea wi' a pencil,' said Dorothy, 'an' Nora says she doesn't want 'is sort in 'ere.'

"E's weally wude,' shouted Nora, who rarely missed snippets of conversation even from behind a cloud of hissing steam next to the coffee machine.

'Ah hope 'e gets lead poisoning,' added Dorothy darkly. 'An' 'e were givin' your Timothy a reight 'ard time by all accounts, so ah 'eard.'

Lofty looked thoughtful. 'Ah'll be back,' he said.

After he had left, Big Dave nodded in approval. 'What did y'mek o' Lofty?'

"E 'ad a wad o' money big enough t'choke a donkey,' said Shane.

'An' ah wouldn't want t'cross 'im,' added Clint.

'Y'reight there,' said Little Malcolm. 'Y'don't need t'be tall t'be tough,' he added with feeling.

Stan Coe had parked his Land Rover by the village green outside The Royal Oak and walked back to Pratt's Hardware Emporium. The bell over the door rang shrilly as he burst in. Timothy was pulling down the blinds ready to close up for the day.

'Ah'm 'ere for m'wire, Pratt,' he said gruffly.

'It's be'ind counter,' said Timothy.

'Well gerrit, y'dozey ha'porth,' shouted Stan.

Timothy passed over the roll of chicken wire and Stan

looked at the price tag. He slapped a few coins on the counter. 'That'll cover it,' he said and opened the door. The bell rang again. 'Pratt by name an' pratt by nature,' shouted Stan and he barged out into the darkness, leaving the door swinging on its hinges.

In the doorway of the Coffee Shop, still as a statue, Lofthouse Pratt, the Castleford prizefighter, controlled his anger. His eyes glittered in the moonlight.

'Penny for t'guy, Mr Coe?' said Heathcliffe. Jimmy Poole rattled the tin, as it was now Terry's turn to be the guy.

'Gerrowt o' t'way,' shouted Stan. 'It's nowt but beggin'.' With that he kicked out at the wheelbarrow, which over-turned with a clatter. Terry fell out on to the pavement and grazed his knee. Stan strode off towards the village green.

Lofty stepped out of the shadows. 'Are yer all reight, son?'

Terry looked up in surprise. 'Yes thank you, mister.'

Lofty nodded and jogged off into the darkness.

Stan Coe didn't see Lofty as he loaded the chicken wire into the back of his Land Rover. Then, as he walked under the weeping willow next to the duck pond towards the bright orange lights of the Oak, he was startled to see a little man in a shellsuit blocking his way.

'Y'forgot to give them young lads some money for t'guy,' said Lofty, looking up into the fleshy jowls of the huge pig farmer.

'Y'what?' said Stan.

'You 'eard,' whispered Lofty.

Stan pushed Lofty, to no avail. 'Gerrowt m'way.'

'Ah won't tell yer again,' said Lofty quietly and moved closer.

'Push off, shorty,' growled Stan and swung a flailing right fist.

Stan could never quite recall what came next, as it all happened so fast. Lofty jinked to the left and, as Stan's arm whistled over his head, he landed a swift one-two into Stan's solar plexus. Stan gasped for air and sat down heavily on the edge of the frozen pond.

'Now, fatty,' said Lofty quietly, 'unless y'want a cold swim, ah want yer t'walk back an' give them lads a pound note.'

'A pound note?' spluttered Stan.

'An' if y'don't ah'll give yer a second 'elping.'

'All reight, all reight,' gasped Stan. Lofty helped him to his feet and the heavyweight pig farmer tottered back down the High Street. He paused outside the Hardware Emporium and looked nervously over his shoulder, but Lofty was out of sight behind the willow tree. 'Er, ah've changed m'mind,' said Stan. He fished a pound note out of his pocket and dropped it in the tin.

'Cor, thanks Mr Coe!' said the astonished Heathcliffe.

Stan turned quickly on his heel, hurried back to his Land Rover and drove off in a spurt of gravel.

'One pound an' theventy-thix penth,' said Jimmy, counting out the last coin.

'Enough for t'fireworks . . . an' a toffee apple each on Bonfire Night,' said Heathcliffe. 'Ah told yer ah'd gorra plan.'

They stared in Timothy's shop window one final time,

feasting their eyes on the box of fireworks. 'We've done it, 'Eath,' said Terry.

Heathcliffe looked down at his little brother and smiled. 'Jump in t'barrow, our kid, an' me an' Jimmy'll wheel yer 'ome.' Terry clambered in and the boys made their way home in triumph.

In the darkness, Lofty smiled. The music blared out from the Coffee Shop as Nora, having the time of her life, had put a Chuck Berry 1957 classic on the juke-box. 'Wock and woll music,' she sang, and the villagers and assorted Pratts joined in. Then he looked at the three boys as they wandered back to the council estate chanting 'Penny for the Guy' with every squeak of the wheelbarrow's wonky wheel. After all, he thought, it's not asking much . . . a penny for the guy.

It was just that, on occasion, some people needed a little persuasion.

Chapter Six

Flash Gordon and the
Time-and-Motion Expert

*We were informed by County Hall that as part of the
'Better Life' initiative, the newly appointed North Yorkshire
adviser for Efficiency in Schools, Mr Digby Cripps, will be
visiting school to complete an Input/Output questionnaire.*
Extract from the Ragley School Logbook:
Friday, 26 November 1982

A village headteacher never knows what a new school
day will bring. Friday, 26 November was such a day.

The first harsh frosts had arrived and, as I looked out of
the bedroom window of Bilbo Cottage, the world seemed
still. Beth thought the radio was a distraction in the
morning, so the house was quiet as we moved smoothly
through our routine of showers, breakfast and, on this
freezing day, defrosting her Volkswagen Beetle so she
could leave first for work.

However, three miles away in Ragley village, life was

anything but quiet at number 7, School View. Natasha Smith had Status Quo's hit, 'Caroline', blasting out at full volume on Mike Read's Radio 1 show, while Ruby ate a Lion Bar and drank a cup of sweet tea for her breakfast. Ruby was well again and looking forward to resuming her work in December. In contrast, in her mock-Tudor home in the Crescent, Anne Grainger was swaying her hips to Barry Manilow singing 'I Wanna Do It With You' on Terry Wogan's breakfast show as she sliced a banana to go with her Weetabix. Meanwhile, in the peaceful kitchen at the vicarage, Vera was eating a slice of lightly buttered toast while listening to *Thought for the Day* on Radio 4. Sadly, it did not ease her busy mind as she stared at the calendar on the wall and the bold red circle round the date of her wedding next month. In the hallway, Joseph looked equally tense, but not because of forthcoming matrimony: he was taking school assembly this morning and it rarely turned out as expected.

As we all eased our way through our pre-school rituals, we were blissfully unaware of what was in store. This was not destined to be a usual Friday.

A car had skidded into the hedge on the back road to Ragley and I helped the driver push it back on to the road. The hazardous journey took much longer than usual, so it was almost 8.40 a.m. when I drove through the school gates and up the cobbled driveway that sparkled in the grudging daylight. George Hardisty, the local champion gardener, had put away his lawnmower for another year and the folk of Ragley-on-the-Forest nodded with under-standing: winter had begun.

Parked next to Vera's Austin A40, in front of the No Parking sign on the boiler-house doors, was a car I didn't recognize. However, as I hurried across the playground, a dejected Jimmy Poole was waiting for me with an empty shoebox in one hand and a perforated lid in the other. He clearly didn't feel the bitter cold as he stood there in his short trousers staring around him helplessly.

'What is it, Jimmy?' I asked. 'What's the matter?'

'My tortoithe ith mithing, Mithter Theffield,' said Jimmy.

'Your tortoise?'

'Yeth, Mithter Theffield . . . Flath Gordon.'

'Flash Gordon? You have a tortoise called Flash Gordon?'

'Yeth, Mithter Theffield,' said a tearful Jimmy, 'an' he'th my betht friend.'

'Oh dear. And did you bring him to school this morning?'

'Yeth, Mithter Theffield. 'E wath in thith box, an' 'e ethcaped. He'th quick for a tortoithe, ith Flath.'

'Well, I'm sorry to hear that, Jimmy.' I glanced back at the strange car and made a decision. 'Jimmy, have a good look round for him but don't go out of school. Perhaps some of your friends can help. I'll talk to you later about it . . . and I'm sure Flash will be safe.'

Jimmy wandered off looking desolate, but it was a problem I would have to solve later. As I walked into the entrance porch Mrs Earnshaw was scattering salt on the frozen steps. In her thin overall and headscarf she didn't appear to be troubled by the sub-zero temperatures and the bitter north wind. 'Ah'll tell y'summat f'nowt, Mr Sheffield,' she said.

It was clearly an offer I couldn't refuse, particularly from a tough lady from Barnsley who happened to be holding a heavy yard broom. 'And what's that, Mrs Earnshaw?'

'Ah wouldn't trust that feller from t'office as far as ah could throw 'im.'

Looking at Mrs Earnshaw's substantial biceps, it occurred to me that she could probably throw whoever-it-was quite a distance.

'And who's that, Mrs Earnshaw?' I asked.

''E thinks 'e's a proper little Shylock 'Olmes does that one,' she said, leaning on her broom and glowering towards the entrance door, 'but 'e didn't get one o'er me.'

'Who is it that you mean?'

''Im what's askin' questions an' keeps lookin' at 'is watch.'

'Oh . . . and what did he ask?'

''Bout when did ah start work.'

'And what did you say?'

'Ah told 'im straight, ah've been workin' since ah were fifteen.'

Good answer was the thought that flickered through my mind. 'Oh well, I had better see who it is.'

'An' one more thing, Mr Sheffield: one o' t'toilets in t'infants' cloakroom is all frozzed up. T'other one's fine so ah'll 'ave another go in a bit.'

Vera was sitting at her desk opening the morning mail with a brass letter-opener when I walked into the school office. She looked up sharply. 'There's a gentleman to see you, Mr Sheffield,' she glanced at her shorthand pad, 'a

Mr Cripps. Seems quite a forceful little man. I've put him in the staff-room with a cup of coffee. He says he's on official business from the office. I told him he must speak to you first.'

'Thank you, Vera,' I said, checking the time on the office clock. 'I'm glad you were here to meet him. I've been a bit held up this morning, what with icy roads and lost tortoises.' The experienced Vera never flinched at this news. When you've been a school secretary for over twenty years, nothing surprises you any more. I hung my duffel coat and threadbare college scarf on the hook on the back of the door. 'I'll see him now,' I said.

Suddenly the telephone rang. Vera automatically flicked open her spiral-bound shorthand notepad to the next clean page and selected a perfectly sharpened HB pencil from the 1977 Jubilee mug next to her wire in-tray. 'Ah, good morning Miss Barrington-Huntley,' she said. I stopped in my tracks. The Chair of the Education Committee in Northallerton rarely rang for a polite chat.

'Fine, thank you,' said Vera, 'and how's Felix?' I wondered who Felix was . . . perhaps a new friend. 'Oh dear, yes, I'm not surprised,' said Vera. 'May I suggest a flea collar? It worked beautifully for me,' she continued, from which I deduced Felix wasn't Miss High-and-Mighty's new gentleman-friend. 'Yes, he's here now. It's Miss Barrington-Huntley for you, Mr Sheffield,' said Vera.

I walked over to her desk, took the receiver from her with practised care, so that the twirly cord did not knock over the framed photograph of her three cats, and took a deep breath. 'Good morning, Miss Barrington-Huntley,' I said with forced calm.

'Jack,' there was a riffling of papers, 'how are you?'

'Fine, thank you, Miss Barrington-Huntley, and how are you?'

'Busy, Jack, very busy as per usual.' She had obviously found the memo she was looking for and began to read. 'A new temporary adviser, Mr, er . . . Digby Cripps, will be in Ragley School today as part of the county survey into "A Model of Teacher Efficiency".'

'Really,' I said, with a sinking feeling. 'That sounds interesting.'

'Yes, Jack, I'm sure it will be,' she said pointedly. 'Part of the County's "A Better Life" initiative, you understand. So please make him welcome. He's had some mixed responses so far.'

'Actually, I think he's here already,' I said.

'Yes, I've heard he's something of an early bird.'

'So, what do we need to know at this stage?' I asked.

'Nothing really, Jack. Just do what you normally do and answer his questions and – I'm sure I don't need to say this – make sure nobody on your staff wastes any time today, if you know what I mean.'

'Oh, well, of course. I'm sure that would never happen,' I said, feeling a little hurt by the suggestion.

'Jack, that didn't quite come out as I intended, but it was meant well. You'll understand when you meet him.'

'Fine, we'll do our best as always, Miss Barrington-Huntley.'

'I know you will, Jack, and,' she gave a deep sigh, 'goodbye and good luck.' There was a click at the other end of the line.

'Vera, it appears Mr Cripps is doing a survey.'

'About what, Mr Sheffield?' asked Vera.

'Into how *efficient* we are.'

'Oh dear,' said Vera. She shook her head sadly and returned her letter-opener to her top drawer in its usual place between the long-arm stapler and her box of treasury tags. 'The cheek of it,' I heard her mutter as I walked through the little corridor that led from the office to the staff-room.

Meanwhile, out in the playground, Heathcliffe Earnshaw was gathering a tortoise search-and-rescue team comprising his little brother and the Dudley-Palmer sisters.

''E's lotht,' said the distraught Jimmy. 'Flath 'ath gone.'

'Don't fret,' said Heathcliffe, taking control. 'We'll find 'im.'

''Ow fast does 'e walk?' asked Terry, looking across the school field.

'Very thlow . . . but fatht for a tortoithe,' said Jimmy.

'What does he look like?' asked Elisabeth Amelia. 'I mean, is he large or small?'

'Thort of thmallith-medium,' said Jimmy. 'My thithter put a thplath of red paint on 'ith thell,' he added mournfully, 'tho 'e thould thtand out.'

'And what does he like to eat?' asked the perceptive Victoria Alice.

'All thorth . . . grath an' fruit an' thtuff,' said Jimmy.

'We could work this out mathematically,' said Elisabeth Amelia confidently. 'If we know his speed we could draw a circle.'

'A thircle?' asked Jimmy.

'Yes,' said Elisabeth Amelia, 'and he'll be somewhere in that circle.'

'That's what ah was gonna say,' said Heathcliffe quickly, not wanting to relinquish his leadership to a girl who happened to be on a higher box of workcards in the School Mathematics Project. 'So let's get ev'ryone to 'elp,' he added.

'Good idea, Heathcliffe,' said Elisabeth Amelia, who had always admired this rough diamond from Barnsley with the spiky blond hair and a taste for adventure.

'Thanks, Lizzie,' said Heathcliffe with a grin. He looked around for little Ted Coggins and spotted him in the playground having a dramatic slow-motion fight with Charlie Cartwright with what appeared to be invisible *Star Wars* light sabres. 'Hey . . . Ted!' shouted Heathcliffe. 'Do one o' yer whistles.'

Little Ted was happy to oblige. He rammed the second finger of each hand between his teeth and produced his now-famous ear-splitting whistle. Moments later, a horde of excited children had been recruited and were searching the school field, flowerbeds and cycle shed.

In the staff-room, attracted by a whistle that sounded like a steam train, Mr Cripps was standing by the window, looking out on to the playground and wondering why all the older children seemed to be shuffling around in a huge circular conga line. It struck him as meaningless and he made a few more notes on the grid-patterned sheet of A4 paper that was attached to his grey clipboard with a large bulldog clip.

'Good morning . . . Mr Sheffield, I presume,' he said, glancing at his wristwatch. It resembled one you would use for deep-sea diving while telling the time in fifteen different countries. He wrote some neat little numbers with a black biro on his chart. 'Did you know your staff-room clock is one minute slow and your office clock is one minute fast?'

'Er, no I didn't,' I said. 'Good morning, and welcome to Ragley.'

Digby Cripps was a short, rotund, bearded man wearing thick, circular John Lennon spectacles, a dated flower-power shirt and a crumpled brown cord suit with a range of coloured pens in the top pocket. He looked as though he had just presented a 1970s Open University mathematics programme on BBC2 at two o'clock in the morning entitled 'Advanced Calculus'.

He ignored my greeting. 'I'm sure you remember this,' he said and pulled a newspaper cutting out of his brief-case. The headline read 'Value for Money? Teachers work a 22 hour week'.

'Yes,' I said, 'negative press is always disheartening.'

'Negative, maybe, Mr Sheffield,' he said, 'but is it *true* we ask ourselves?'

'I presume you're joking,' I said.

'I never joke,' he said blandly and I was beginning to believe it. He wrote another note, this time using a red biro.

'Well, what can we do to help?' I asked.

'I need to quantify the number of minutes devoted to each essential subject of the curriculum on my input–output checksheet and then extrapolate the data analysis

110

using our new dedicated computer at County Hall. So it will be necessary to observe each class.'

'Oh, I see,' I said . . . but I didn't.

'Is this your timetable?' he said, pointing with his biro towards an A2 sheet of squared paper on the noticeboard. I was proud of my neat, colour-coded chart showing the days of the week and blocks of time for English and mathematics for each class, along with physical education, assemblies, topic work, radio broadcasts and our weekly religious education lessons with Joseph. The fact that, in reality, our *actual* timetable varied according to the interests of the children or the weather was something I didn't want to share at that moment.

'Yes, it is,' I said.

'So, according to this, your first lesson begins at five minutes past nine.'

'That's correct.'

'And before that you do registration.'

'Yes, we do.'

'And the bell goes at nine a.m.'

'Er, yes.'

'Mr Sheffield, according to my watch it is now one minute past nine and my watch is correct every morning as per Greenwich Mean Time.' He began to write again on his clipboard.

'Oh no,' I said. 'Excuse me.' I rushed to the bottom of the belltower, dragged the ancient rope from the metal cleat on the wall and began to pull on it. Another school day had begun . . . sadly, later than usual.

*   *   *

Mr Cripps spent the next hour visiting all the classrooms. In Class 1, Anne was reading the wonderful *Tale of Jemima Puddle-Duck* and twenty eager faces stared up at her, following every word.

He seemed impressed, until Katie Icklethwaite asked him, "Scuse me mister, what are you doing?'

'I'm watching what you're doing and then I write it down,' said Digby.

'An' 'ave y'got a proper job as well?' asked Katie.

Digby didn't stay to hear the end of Beatrix Potter's classic tale. He moved on to Jo's class. In the corridor outside, seven-year-old Barry Ollerenshaw was queuing for the toilet. 'And why are you waiting here?' asked Digby.

'Ah were caught short in t'middle o' m'writing,' said Barry with a strained expression. 'We 'ad prunes f'breakfast.'

Mr Cripps added a note to his list and moved on to Class 3 and their Africa topic lesson. When he walked in, the children had just stopped making a list of animals and Sally had picked up her guitar and her *Okki-Tokki-Unga* songbook of action songs. She had turned to number eleven, 'The Animal Fair', and the children were singing 'The elephant sneezed and fell on his knees'. The cacophony of sound from a selection of percussion instruments added to the excitement. Mr Cripps shook his head, wrote a question mark against the title 'Topic Work' and walked across the corridor to my classroom, where Shirley the cook had just popped her head round the door. 'M'jelly's not settin', Mr Sheffield,' she said anxiously. 'When you've got a minute, can yer 'ave a quick look at t'big fridge?' I noticed that Mr Cripps selected a green biro and scribbled yet another note . . . and so it went on.

At a quarter past ten, in school assembly, Anne began to play the piano. On wild and windy mornings such as this, she always chose what she described as 'calming music' to relax the children. Joseph glanced nervously at Mr Cripps and launched into the story of the Good Samaritan, then decided to review the story with what he considered to be pertinent questions.

'Now boys and girls,' he said, 'if you saw a poor person injured and bleeding, what would you do?'

No one moved or offered an answer while they grappled with this unpleasant vision. Finally, Joseph pointed at little Ben Roberts. 'So, what would you do, Benjamin?'

'Well . . .' there was a long pause until finally Ben nodded with realization. 'Ah think ah'd be sick.'

'So would I,' said Mary Scrimshaw.

'And me too,' added Sonia Tricklebank for good measure.

This was followed by the Lord's Prayer with the usual deviation from the script. Rufus Snodgrass was chanting, 'Our Father, who art in Devon, Harold be thy name . . .' totally oblivious of any errors.

During morning break Anne was tearing up wallpaper books in order to use the paper for the afternoon painting session. Our school budget had been cut again. Meanwhile, Mr Cripps was standing in the corner of the classroom, making notes and looking anxiously at his watch . . .

*   *   *

At lunchtime, I was sitting at my desk in the school office reading a circular entitled 'History in a Common Curriculum – A Vision of the Future', and wondering how we would squeeze in the rest of the curriculum around it.

'I'm still getting used to these new twenty-pence coins,' muttered Vera from the other side of the room as she made neat little piles of late dinner money on her desk, double-checked the amount and added the figures neatly in her register. Suddenly the telephone on her desk rang. 'Mrs Sheffield for you,' she said with a smile.

'How's it going, Jack?' asked Beth in a conspiratorial whisper. 'I've just heard about the time-and-motion expert.'

'Not well,' I said. 'He's finding fault with everything.'

'Oh dear,' said Beth, 'he's coming to us next week so Miss B-H says.'

'Well good luck,' I whispered. 'Bye, darling.'

Mr Cripps suddenly appeared from the short corridor that led from the staff-room, via the staff toilets, to the school office. 'A personal call, Mr Sheffield?' he asked in an accusing tone.

'My wife,' I said.

'Ah, I see,' he said almost triumphantly and, after checking his watch, added a few more comments in red biro to the complex chart on his clipboard.

Later, in the staff-room, Vera was scanning the headlines in *The Times*. She was relieved to see a photograph of the Queen Mother, now aged eighty-two, smiling after an operation to remove a fish bone from her throat.

Then she frowned when she read that Arthur Scargill, President of the National Union of Mineworkers, had declared that industrial action was inevitable following the announcement of the proposed closure of up to sixty pits.

It was then that Mr Cripps reappeared. 'Where are the rest of the staff, please?' he asked. 'They don't appear to be working in the classrooms in preparation for afternoon school.' He glanced again at his watch and made another note.

'They're out in the playground,' said Vera coldly.

'And why is that?' he asked.

'Perhaps you should ask them for yourself,' said Vera.

'I shall,' he said and hurried outside.

I was with Anne, standing by the school gate, when Mr Cripps appeared, wrapped in a brown duffel coat and an Essex University scarf. 'Can you explain what is happening?' he said rather abruptly. 'Why are all the teachers outside the school building?'

'We're organizing a search for a missing pet,' I said.

'It's a tortoise,' explained Anne.

'A tortoise?' said Mr Cripps. 'Oh I see,' and a faraway look came into his eyes.

'It goes by the name of Flash Gordon,' I added, 'and the little boy who owns it is very upset. We need to find it before it gets dark.'

'Of course,' said Mr Cripps. 'I used to have a tortoise, so I can imagine how he feels. They're remarkable animals,' he added thoughtfully. 'Herbivores of course . . . so perhaps we should begin in the hedgerow.'

115

'You seem to have empathy for these creatures,' I said.

'Yes, I studied them as part of my degree,' he said with authority. 'Did you know, for example, that they have both an endoskeleton and an exoskeleton?'

'Well, er, not offhand, no,' I replied hesitantly.

'Yes, they are the most wonderful animals . . . quite fascinating really, particularly as they are diurnal animals with a tendency to be crepuscular.'

Anne glanced at me and raised her eyebrows. I knew she was thinking the same as me. At some time in his erudite past, this strange man had swallowed a dictionary.

'Sadly, it's time for the bell,' I said.

Mr Cripps was clearly preoccupied. 'Pity,' he said. 'We'd have a better chance with more pairs of eyes. However, I have a few ideas so I'll stay out a little longer.'

Anne gave me a wide-eyed stare but said nothing. I guessed what was on her mind. Perhaps this irritating little man really did have a heart.

At three o'clock there was a tap on my door. It was Mr Cripps and he appeared agitated. 'I need a word, Mr Sheffield . . . now, if you please.'

It sounded urgent. 'Very well, Mr Cripps,' I said and walked to the doorway.

'I think I've found Flash,' he said, his eyes suddenly wide with excitement.

'Really? Where?'

'Under my car. There's definitely something there.'

'Are you sure?' I asked. 'It's getting dark.'

'We need a torch,' he said, his voice trembling with excitement.

'Just a minute,' I said and leant round the classroom door. 'Boys and girls,' I said, 'I have to go out for a moment and I'll let Mrs Pringle know.'

There was a murmur of interest. 'And I want Jimmy to come with me, please.'

Jimmy stood up hesitantly. 'Don't worry,' I said, 'Mr Cripps thinks he might have seen your tortoise.'

'Now, boys and girls,' I announced, 'while we're out I want you to write down your thirteen times table, please.'

There were a few grumbles of discontent.

'But we only do up t'twelve, Mr Sheffield,' said Theresa Buttle plaintively.

'Well, this will be good practice,' I said confidently, with an attempt at a reassuring smile.

'But y'never buy thirteen eggs, Mr Sheffield,' said the ever-practical Joey Wilkinson.

'That's reight, Mr Sheffield,' said Dean Kershaw, 'an' my mam says thirteen's unlucky.'

'An' there's no number thirteen in our street,' said Tracy Hartley.

'So can we do twelve times, Mr Sheffield?' asked Sarah Louise Tait.

They were quick to see my hesitation and Jimmy was chomping at the bit.

'How about nine times, Mr Sheffield?' said Elisabeth Amelia Dudley-Palmer, ever the practical peacemaker. 'That's a tough one. And I think it has a pattern, because the digits always add up to nine.'

I was impressed with both her mathematical acumen and her negotiation skills and paused before answering.

"Ow d'you mean all t'digits add up t'nine?' piped up Theresa Buttle.

'Elisabeth is correct, boys and girls,' I said, 'so well done.' I took a deep breath. 'Very well, do the *nine* times table and then we'll look at the pattern Elisabeth is talking about.'

'Thank you, Mr Sheffield,' they all chorused.

'Very impressive,' said Mr Cripps. I smiled . . . it was good to feel valued.

At the end of school Jimmy Poole approached Mr Cripps and took the lid off his shoebox. Inside, Flash looked content as he munched on a lettuce leaf provided by Shirley in the kitchen.

'Excuthe me, Mr Crippth,' said Jimmy, 'but thank you for finding Flath.'

Digby had forgotten what it was like to be thanked. Ever since he had taken on his new role, he had been treated like public enemy number one and few people ever offered him a kind word. 'Well, I appreciate you telling me,' he said, looking down at Jimmy's tearful face. 'That's very polite. And I'm sure Flash will be well looked after.'

'Oh yeth thir, he'th my thpethial friend,' said Jimmy. 'Ah won't lothe 'im again, ah promith.'

Mr Cripps looked at the slight figure of Jimmy Poole clutching his cardboard box as if his life depended on it and for the first time that day he smiled.

At four o'clock we all gathered in the staff-room to hear Mr Cripps' report.

'Well, at one stage, Mr Sheffield, I have to say it was an *unsatisfactory* report,' he said, looking at his copious notes and shaking his head as if someone had just died.

'If we look at actual curriculum-driven activity, there would appear to be some shortfalls. For example, the deployment of staff wasn't entirely efficient, with your reception teacher spending seven minutes tearing up a wallpaper book and the headteacher checking for electrical faults in the kitchen. Children had to queue for the toilet during an English lesson and the lateness of the bell accounted for three times eighty-six wasted minutes . . . over *four* negative hours.'

Vera looked furious, Anne shook her head in dismay, Jo appeared puzzled and Sally was flexing her fingers as if she were about to throttle someone. I sighed. This was bad news.

'However,' said Mr Cripps, taking a deep breath, 'I've taken into account the extenuating circumstances.'

'Really?' I said.

'Yes, I have.' He checked his clipboard again. 'For example, the missing tortoise accounted for the bell being late, morning playtime overrunning, children off-task just before afternoon break and the temporary redeployment of the headteacher and teaching staff. So, *overall*, I'm happy to report that Ragley School will receive an excellent report.'

When his Morris Marina drove out into the darkness, Vera made everyone a welcome cup of tea and we all relaxed. 'An eventful day,' I said.

'So much for time-and-motion,' said Anne.

'And lost tortoises,' chuckled Jo.

'Well, never judge a book by its cover,' said Sally.

'Or a man by his clipboard,' added Vera with a wry smile.

A few days later a parcel arrived at school with a North-allerton postmark. Inside was a book entitled *How to Look After Your Tortoise.*

The dedication read: *'For the Ragley School library with happy memories of my visit to your highly efficient school, Digby Cripps'.*

Chapter Seven

Penny's Army

Roy Davidson, Education Welfare Officer, visited school today to discuss the proposed admission of six-year-old Rosie Sparrow owing to 'exceptional circumstances'. Mrs Earnshaw began her final week as temporary caretaker prior to Mrs Smith's return to full-time duty on Monday, 13 December. Class 1 completed their final rehearsal for their Nativity play which will take place on Wednesday afternoon, 8 December.

Extract from the Ragley School Logbook:
Monday, 6 December 1982

'Any change for a good cause, gentlemen?' asked the diminutive lady in the Salvation Army uniform.

The members of the Ragley Rovers football team stood up out of respect for this familiar visitor to the taproom of The Royal Oak. 'C'mon lads, dig deep f'Sally's Army,' said Big Dave. It was Sunday evening, 5 December, and Beth and I had just enjoyed one of Sheila's steak specials at the bay window table in the lounge bar. Beth had seemed a little quiet during the past week and I presumed that, like me, she was consumed with schoolwork, along with end-of-term reports and the run-up to Christmas.

Major Penny Boothroyd rattled the coins in her collection tin as she moved round the room and then approached our table. As always, she looked immaculate in her navy-blue two-piece uniform, a matching blue bonnet with a red ribbon and polished black court shoes. She wore a crisp white blouse fastened at the collar with a silver Salvation Army brooch and at its centre was a red shield to denote her officer status. At the age of fifty she was one of the most experienced members of the Citadel, the local Salvation Army church. 'Thank you, everyone,' said Penny, 'and a merry Christmas.'

Penny approached our table and Beth put a pound note in the tin. 'That's very generous, Mrs Sheffield,' said Penny and paused.

'What is it, Mrs Boothroyd?' I asked.

'I need a word, Mr Sheffield,' she said quietly. 'It's important. Can I call in to school tomorrow?'

'Yes, of course,' I said. 'We're busy with the Nativity play this week, so how about before school starts, say at half past eight?'

'I'll be there,' said Penny, 'and God bless you.'

When Beth and I got up to leave, I returned our glasses to the bar. Old Tommy Piercy was sitting on his usual stool and looked up at me curiously. He noticed my sombre mood. 'Better t'enjoy t'bright days, Mr Sheffield,' he said, 'rather than t'brood over t'dark uns.' I didn't know it then, but they were destined to be prophetic words.

*   *   *

On Monday morning the bitter sleet of a freezing December rattled against the kitchen windows of Bilbo Cottage and the old timber casements shook in protest. Winter had gripped the northern landscape in its cold fist.

For some reason Beth had got up an hour before me. 'Difficult journey today,' I said, peering through the frosted diamond panes, 'so do be careful.' She was leaning against the worktop seemingly in a world of her own. I walked over and held her in my arms. 'I'll make some tea, shall I?'

'Yes, Jack, that would be lovely . . . and don't worry, I'm not quite myself this morning. It will be fine when I get to school.' She looked a little pale but, after her hot drink, she completed her usual routine of packing her files in her smart black executive briefcase and, although she spent a little longer than usual over her make-up, all seemed well.

Her pale-blue Volkswagen Beetle was frozen solid and I went out, breathed on the key, turned it stiffly in the door lock and then started the engine. After I had scraped the ice from the windows she came out, wrapped in a warm coat and scarf, and I kissed her before she left. For a moment I thought she looked a little preoccupied as she drove steadily out of the driveway and past the cottages of Kirkby Steepleton with their smoking chimneys. It was at times like these I understood the true meaning of love. Our journey towards marriage and a life shared had been one of sunshine and storms, of calm and fury, but, in the end, we had found something very special.

When she left it was always the same: a few moments of sheer emptiness until I focused once again on Ragley School and the children in my care. Then, at night, when we were together again at the end of a busy day, it was good to relax as man and wife. It simply felt . . . right.

It was time to leave. I put on my duffel coat and scarf, locked up the cottage, threw my battered old leather satchel on the passenger seat and coaxed my Morris Minor Traveller out of the driveway. As I drove on the back road to Ragley the world around me was still and silent. The bare branches above my head were archways of frozen fingers against a sky that promised more snow. As I drove past the village green, Major Rupert Forbes-Kitchener was supervising a group of his gardeners and stable-hands as they erected the enormous Ragley Christmas tree. This was an annual gift from the major and on Wednesday evening the whole village would gather beneath its brightly coloured lights for the annual 'Carols on the Green', accompanied by the Salvation Army brass band. It was a popular event that marked the onset of the Christmas festivities. In the meantime, another busy day lay ahead, beginning with a meeting.

Penny Boothroyd arrived promptly and, in her smart uniform, she looked very purposeful. She was carrying a book with gold-blocked letters that read *Orders and Regulations for Corps Officers of the Salvation Army* and I guessed this was official business.

We shook hands and Penny saw me looking at the matching hexagonal blood-red patches on her lapels, each with a silver metal badge in the shape of a letter 'S'.

She smiled and tapped each one in turn. 'Save to serve,' she said. Then she pointed to the epaulettes sporting her major's crest in the shape of a fiery sun on which a cross had been set with seven stars underneath. 'Blood and fire, Mr Sheffield,' she said, touching the badge with reverence, 'and, of course, the seven stars,' she added quietly. 'They represent the seven sayings of Jesus on the Cross.'

I remained quiet, aware of the gravitas of her words. It was clear her uniform was full of powerful symbolism. This was a very special lady and, on cold days such as this, her army of soldiers went out to spread the word of God.

Vera came into the office and broke the silence. 'Good morning, Mr Sheffield,' said Vera. 'There's coffee in the staff-room. And good to see you, Penny.' They greeted each other like old friends . . . two ladies who had devoted their lives to a Christian way of life. There was mutual respect here.

'Not long to the big day, Vera,' said Penny. 'I'm sure you'll be very happy.'

'Thank you, I know we shall,' said Vera.

'And Rupert is a very fine man,' added Penny.

Vera paused and smiled. 'Yes he is . . . just a different sort of major.' She opened the door that led to the staff-room and beckoned us through. 'You won't be disturbed in there, Mr Sheffield.' Vera went back to her desk in the office to answer the early-morning calls while I poured two cups of coffee in the relative quiet of the staff-room. I noticed Penny looked tired and I soon understood why.

'So what can I do for you, Mrs Boothroyd?' I said.

'Do call me Penny, everyone else does,' she said with a gentle smile.

'Fine,' I said, 'and I'm Jack.'

She sat back, sipped her coffee and wrestled with her thoughts as if deciding where to begin. 'I've been up all night,' she said, 'dealing with a difficult case.' Then she put down her coffee cup and clasped her hands as if in prayer. 'There's a young woman, early twenties, not married, Maggie Sparrow from Leeds. Apparently, a week ago she moved into one of those old rented dwellings in Cold Kirkby, that tiny hamlet between here and Kirkby Steepleton and then, two nights ago, her partner abandoned her. He was fond of a drink and I think she's relieved he's gone. He tended to be violent, by all accounts.'

There was clearly more to come and I settled back in my chair as a fresh flurry of snow pattered against the window. 'She's living in dreadful conditions. One of my female officers heard about her and called in. After she reported back to me, I arranged for Maggie to stay at my house last night and I sent a team of cleaners to get the property habitable.' Penny looked me squarely in the eyes and I knew we had reached the denouement. 'The thing is, Jack, she has a six-year-old daughter, Rosie, and I was hoping you could take her in as a temporary admission.' She picked up her coffee cup and sat back. 'So, ideally, I need you to inform the Education Welfare Officer as soon as possible because, at the moment, this is one of those cases with no paperwork . . . no records. It's as if she's off the radar, so to speak.'

My mind was racing with the official ramifications.

Immediate action was essential, but I had to be mindful of the future paper trail. 'Penny, I'll contact Roy Davidson straight away,' I said. 'He's a wonderful supporter of the school and he'll know how to handle this. In the meantime, bring them in and we'll admit the child if that's what the mother wants.'

We finished our coffee and headed back to the school office. Penny put her hand on my arm. 'I'll be back at lunchtime, Jack, and, whatever the outcome, we *must* keep mother and daughter together. You'll understand when you meet them.'

It occurred to me that this was all in a day's work for Major Penny Boothroyd and I had to admire her energy and professionalism. She was used to a knock on her door by destitute wanderers and ex-prisoners, all wanting food, shelter and money. It was something she took in her stride. However, there was clearly more to this case. I was soon to find out.

At morning break Roy Davidson arrived. A tall, gaunt man in his late forties with a shock of prematurely grey hair, he had helped us many times in the past. As our local Education Welfare Officer, his knowledge of specialist educational support was second to none.

'Thanks for coming, Roy,' I said. 'I've briefed Anne Grainger so she knows the situation.'

'That's fine, Jack.' He checked his spiral notepad. 'You mentioned a six-year-old . . . Rosie Sparrow.' I nodded. 'I've already contacted the office and explained the early intervention of the Salvation Army. They want me to go out to see the mother and child and I've asked Mary

O'Neill from Social Services to check out the property in Cold Kirkby. I'll call back later today when I've got some background and we can decide where to go from there.' We shook hands and he was gone. The wheels were turning.

At twelve o'clock Penny Boothroyd was in the entrance hall with a nervous fair-haired woman in her early twenties and a small child wrapped up warm like an Eskimo. Vera showed them through to the staff-room and Penny did the introductions.

'This is Ms Maggie Sparrow and her lovely daughter, Rosie, Mr Sheffield,' said Penny. She gave me a postcard with the name 'Rosie Sparrow' printed neatly on it along with her date of birth.

'Welcome to Ragley,' I said. 'Please sit down and we can talk.'

Vera fussed around serving tea, orange juice and biscuits, then closed the door quietly.

'Thank you for seeing us, Mr Sheffield,' said Maggie. She was dressed in faded jeans, old leather boots and a knitted sweater. Her khaki coat had leather patches on the elbows and looked far too big for her. It had the appearance of a hand-me-down workman's coat. She was almost bird-like in her quick movements, but it was clear from the outset that she guarded her child with a fierce determination. 'I want to do my best for Rosie,' she said, 'my daughter.' The tiny girl was staring at the biscuits and orange juice and then looked up at her mother. 'Yes, go on poppet,' said Maggie, 'have a biscuit if you'd like one and then we must thank the kind lady.'

Penny leant forward, keen to commence the main business. 'We're here to seek a short-term solution, Mr Sheffield,' she said. 'Maggie is faced with demanding circumstances in a new home in a tiny hamlet off the beaten track where she knows no one. She wants to seek employment in the area and her current address is on the border of the catchment area of three local primary schools. Cold Kirkby is a little remote, but if I have a word with William Featherstone I'm sure he'll add it to his school coach run.'

'I understand,' I said, 'and, of course, we should be only too happy to admit Rosie . . . if that's what you want.'

The girl appeared a little dispirited, but she had the same grey eyes as her mother and she stared back at me with the innate curiosity of a six-year-old.

'She can read and write well, Mr Sheffield,' said Maggie proudly. 'I taught her myself. You see, we've travelled a lot.'

There was a tap on the staff-room door. It was Anne Grainger with six-year-old Jemima Poole. The little girl was carrying a familiar shoebox with the name 'Flash Gordon' written on the side.

'Hello, I'm Anne Grainger, the reception class teacher,' she said with a reassuring smile. 'I wondered if Rosie would like to see Jemima's tortoise.' Rosie's eyes widened with excitement.

'It's my brother's,' said Jemima.

Anne crouched down next to the little girl. 'Would you like to see where he lives in our classroom when he's in school?'

Rosie looked up at her mother. 'You go if you like,

129

Rosie,' said Maggie, 'and I'll come in a minute.'

'And I'll be your friend,' added Jemima and held out her hand. Rosie took it and the two little girls followed Anne out of the room.

It was as if a weight had been lifted from Maggie Sparrow's shoulders. 'Thank you,' she said, rubbing the tears from her eyes with the knuckles of her work-red hands. 'I appreciate the support.' There was silence for a moment as she gathered herself. 'You see, Mr Sheffield,' she took a deep breath, 'my mother deserted me and put me into foster care. I don't want that to happen to my Rosie.'

So that was it, I thought. Her sea-grey eyes were steady and there was steel in the demeanour of this young woman. Although downtrodden and 'damaged', she was not beaten and I admired her inner determination, her desire to do the best for her daughter. She had the strength of a mother.

When we walked into Anne's classroom, Rosie's coat was hanging on a peg and she was sitting at a small trapezoidal table with Jemima Poole. They were modelling Plasticine animals for the class Nativity scene and both little girls appeared relaxed, engrossed and content. Anne stood up and said quietly to Maggie, 'She's fine, no need to worry, and we can give her a school lunch if you wish.'

'Thank you so much, Mrs Grainger,' she said. 'I'm really grateful.'

We went to stand by the classroom door while Maggie said goodbye to Rosie. 'I'll be back soon, my little poppet,' she said and gave her a kiss on the forehead. Rosie gave her a smile that almost broke my heart and then happily resumed work on her model, which appeared to have morphed from a small cow to a large sheep.

Penny nodded in satisfaction. 'I've arranged for some temporary work for Maggie in the kitchens at the Citadel,' she said quietly, 'just until the new year and then she can look for something more permanent.' Penny looked at her wristwatch. 'So I thought we would go there now, if that's all right with you, and I'll call back at lunchtime.'

At twelve thirty Sally Pringle was in her classroom completing a final rehearsal before Wednesday's Nativity play and strains of 'Little Donkey' echoed through the school. I was with Jo, Anne and Vera in the staff-room and an inquisitive Jo was full of interest in our visitor.

'I don't know much about the Salvation Army,' said Jo.

'Well, it was founded by William Booth,' said Penny, sipping her Earl Grey tea.

'He was a remarkable man,' said Vera. 'He certainly helped a lot of people. I remember reading that, as a Methodist minister during Victorian times, he was appalled by the poverty around him so he decided to dedicate his life to helping the poor, particularly those in hazardous occupations such as making matches. Sadly, at the time, many of the poor women in those factories died of "Phossy Jaw".'

'Phossy Jaw?' said Jo.

'Necrosis of the bone,' explained Penny, 'caused by the toxic fumes of the phosphorus . . . a terrible death.'

'So Booth built a modern factory,' said Vera, 'with

large windows, a rest room, a canteen and a place for the workers to wash their hands.'

Jo nodded thoughtfully. 'It's quite a story,' she said.

'And we're still trying to help those in need today,' said Penny.

'Like Maggie and Rosie Sparrow,' said Anne, and Penny looked out of the window. More snow was falling and a bitter wind was blowing towards the village of Cold Kirkby.

Two miles away, Penny Boothroyd's team of volunteers had transformed Maggie Sparrow's tiny rented cottage. A morning's hard work had resulted in a clean kitchen, curtains in the single bedroom and a welcoming log fire in the lounge. Although sparsely furnished, it was now a home.

The hamlet of Cold Kirkby comprised six terraced dwellings and a few farm buildings. The nearest shops were a mile away in Kirkby Steepleton, a long walk on a winter's morning, but William Featherstone had re-routed his daily coach journey so Maggie and Rosie could now get to school and into York. Mary O'Neill, our local Social Services Officer, had telephoned to say all was well and she would monitor the situation. She asked if I could attend a hastily arranged case conference at five o'clock in their offices in Easington, our local market town.

At the end of afternoon school, Sally Pringle popped her head round Anne Grainger's door. 'Anne,' she said with a grin, 'thanks, you've done my choir a favour.'

'Really?' said Anne as she displayed a collection of

chalk snowflake patterns on black sugar paper.

'Yes,' said Sally, 'the new little girl has the voice of an angel.'

'Rosie Sparrow?'

'Yes. She's bright as well. I've given her a verse of "Away in a Manger" to sing solo.'

'Wonderful,' said Anne, and Sally hurried back to her classroom. 'Angel,' murmured Anne to herself. She picked up a wire coat-hanger and, with the experience of a teacher of small children, bent it into the shape of a halo. 'Good idea . . . now where's that silver tinsel?'

At six o'clock the case conference was over and I sat back and admired the highly professional contributions made by Mary O'Neill and Roy Davidson. The Head of Services had also questioned Penny Boothroyd, resplendent in her major's uniform, and the detailed sequence of events had been recorded. The safety of Rosie Sparrow had been secured and, following an impassioned speech by Penny, there was unanimous approval for mother and daughter remaining together. It was a job well done, and Penny and I left side by side.

We walked under the frozen trees towards the car park and on to a small stone bridge. Beneath us the dark, icy waters of the Foss flowed south towards the great River Ouse and the city of York ten miles away. 'He leads me beside still waters,' Penny said quietly as we paused on the bridge. Her words were like a caress in the darkness, a soothing gesture in a world of shadows.

I nodded in understanding. 'The Twenty-third Psalm,' I said.

She smiled and stared thoughtfully at the dark tumbling waters beneath our feet. 'Life's like that, rushing along with the current,' she said, almost to herself. 'The water that flows past is different today than yesterday. For me, Jack, it's the river of grace, leading me to the still waters where life will be restored.'

Penny was on a journey I could barely comprehend, but she had chosen her pathway. There was an inner strength at the core of her soul, and somehow she had found peace in a raging world.

On Wednesday afternoon the hall was packed with parents for one of the highlights of the school year. The children in Anne's class were presenting their Nativity play and many mothers had their hankies at the ready. Soon there wouldn't be a dry eye in the house.

Sally Pringle propped her teacher's copy of *Carol, Gaily Carol* on her music stand, picked up her guitar, put the plectrum in her mouth while she flicked through the pages, selected number three, 'Little Donkey', and began to strum. The choir included Rosie Sparrow dressed as an angel in a white tablecloth and with a circlet of silver tinsel in her hair. It was soon clear to everyone that she had the sweetest voice, a good memory and a perfect sense of rhythm.

The surprise, however, was the casting of baby Jesus. After a little cajoling from Vera, Anne had agreed that the very lively Krystal Carrington Ruby Entwhistle, now four and a half months old, could act the part of baby Jesus. Ruby's daughter, Racquel, had made sure the little girl had been fed and changed and, right on cue, between scene one and scene two, she placed her, fast asleep, in a small cot that Anne had converted into a manger.

Ruby was sitting in the front row. 'Wild 'orses wouldn't 'ave kept me away, Mr Sheffield,' she had said on arrival. 'An' it's good t'be back,' she added. Next to her was a spare seat, reserved for Vera. Since the accident they had become even greater friends. Now there was an unbreakable bond between them.

Meanwhile, Maggie Sparrow was in the back row sitting next to Penny Boothroyd, who was now out of uniform and blended in like one of the many grandmothers. Maggie leant forward as Sally strummed the introduction to 'Away in a Manger' and when little Rosie sang her solo she could no longer hold back the tears.

Fortunately it was largely a trouble-free Nativity . . . that is until the very end. The shepherds looked the part in their tea-towel headdresses, the kings delivered their gifts and Mary and Joseph remembered their lines. However, no one had thought to mention to little Ted Coggins, playing the part of Joseph, that he shouldn't actually *unwrap* the gifts that the kings had placed with great ceremony at the feet of baby Jesus. Consequently, there were a few giggles in the audience when Ted removed the shiny giftwrap to reveal not gold, frankincense and myrrh but rather a tin of spaghetti, an empty Persil packet and a box of Aqua Manda Golden Body Rub. Also, no one had explained to little Krystal that hers was a passive part. So it tended to distract from the general dignity of the occasion when she filled her nappy and the Nativity concluded on a decidedly toxic note. Vera winced slightly and held a handkerchief to her nose, clearly concerned that, while entirely understandable, it really was inappropriate behaviour for the Son of God.

At the end, Joseph Evans stood up and said a few words of thanks to Mrs Earnshaw, our temporary caretaker, whose contract had come to an end prior to Ruby's return to full-time duty next week. He presented her with a hamper of food from Prudence Golightly's General Stores on behalf of the school governors, and everyone joined in the applause. As she returned to her seat she gave Ruby a kiss on the cheek. 'Thanks, Ruby,' she whispered in her ear. 'T'money came in 'andy.'

Finally, as the crowds dispersed, little Barry Olleren- shaw was puzzled by the three iconic gifts and approached the Revd Joseph Evans. 'Ah feel sorry f'Jesus, Mr Evans,' said Barry.

'And why is that?' asked Joseph.

'Well, Jesus jus' got that gold and frankincense and t'other one . . . no *real* presents.'

And, once again, Joseph was stuck for words.

As the families returned to their homes, meals were pre- pared and thoughts returned to the events of the day.

In the Earnshaw household, Mrs Earnshaw was glow- ing with pride as she fried sausages in a large pan. 'Eric, our 'Eath an' Terry sang their 'earts out.'

'S'good, is that,' said Eric, not raising his eyes from his *Racing Post*.

The boys were at the kitchen table writing their Christmas lists. Terry was writing as if his life depended on it, whereas the economical Heathcliffe had merely written one word: 'Everything'.

'Terry,' said Mrs Earnshaw, 'why are you writing such a long list for Father Christmas?'

'Well Mam . . . it's jus' in case ah don't believe in 'im nex' year.'

Meanwhile, up the Morton Road, in her state-of-the-art kitchen, Petula Dudley-Palmer was watching the new television station, Channel 4. The first advert was for a Kenwood Gourmet 'that even makes ice cream' and Petula knew she must buy it.

Her husband, Geoffrey, a chief executive at the local chocolate factory, was also interested in this new television station. He thought he would mention at the next board meeting that, at £75 for a ten-second advertisement, this could revitalize sales of Lion Bars.

Likewise, Betty Buttle was tuned in to the same channel and considered the Co-op advertisement with interest. With Nescafé at 96 pence and ninety-nine teabags for 64 pence, she decided she might have to take her business away from Prudence Golightly's General Stores & Newsagent and into the new supermarket in York.

Predictably, the final advert for a One Parent Benefit leaflet was ignored by both Betty and Petula. However, on the council estate, single parent Daphne Cathcart quickly scribbled down the title. Then she turned to nine-year-old Michelle and asked, 'Who was that new girl in Mrs Grainger's class – t'little blonde one wi' t'lovely voice?'

'She's called Rosie, Mam,' said Michelle, through a mouthful of beans on toast. 'She's reight nice an' she's like me an' our Cathy.'

''Ow d'you mean, luv?'

'Well,' said Michelle, looking up from the television, 'she 'asn't got a dad.'

That evening at seven o'clock it seemed as if all the residents of Ragley had gathered on the village green. At the foot of the giant Christmas tree, lit up with a thousand coloured lights, was the Salvation Army brass band, conducted by Penny Boothroyd.

Penny had persuaded our postmistress, Amelia Duff, to play her flugelhorn and, with the haunting, mellow opening bars of 'Silent Night', our carol concert began. It was then that I remembered Old Tommy's adage about not brooding over the dark days but, instead, finding comfort in the bright ones. I looked down at Beth, put my arm round her shoulders and smiled as I remembered the strength in her slender body and the look of love in her green eyes. The fine thread of history had interwoven our lives, bound together in a shared destiny, and here we were, together on this perfect night.

And so it was that, under the vast purple sky over the plain of York, we huddled in our little groups and enjoyed music that stirred the soul. Christmas was coming to Ragley village and, as snow began to fall once again, we raised our voices to the heavens. It had been a day to remember and a time to reflect on the lives of others less fortunate than ourselves.

Chapter Eight

A Wedding in the Village

A presentation of a watercolour painting was made in school assembly today by Mrs Sue Phillips, Chair of the PTA, to Miss Vera Evans prior to her marriage tomorrow to Major Forbes-Kitchener.

Extract from the Ragley School Logbook:
Friday, 17 December 1982

The constant cawing of the rooks in the swaying branches of the tall elms was a familiar sound to Vera. It was the call of the countryside.

As Vera and Joseph set off in their little white Austin A40 for the last day of term and crunched down the gravel drive towards the Morton Road, Vera stared back at the vicarage. It had been her home for so many years and she wondered if she would miss these familiar scents and sounds when she was in the manicured, peacock-strutting grounds of Morton Manor. Joseph sensed her mood and gave her a nervous smile. It was Friday, 17

December 1982 and, for the school secretary of Ragley-on-the-Forest Church of England Primary School, a new world awaited . . . a new life.

Meanwhile, in Bilbo Cottage Beth appeared a little tired with her exertions as she packed her briefcase. 'I've checked your suit, Jack,' she said. 'It's back from the cleaners and looks fine.' She hung my charcoal-grey three-piece suit in our huge double wardrobe in the tiny space on the left reserved for my modest collection of clothing. 'And I've ironed the monogrammed white hanky that Vera gave you last Christmas ready for your top pocket, so we're all set for the big day.'

'Thanks Beth,' I said as I fastened the buckles on my leather satchel and put on my duffel coat and scarf. 'See you tonight and good luck for the end of term.' I kissed her as we stepped out into a frozen, silent world with a fresh dusting of snow.

Once again, she seemed preoccupied. 'I wonder how Vera's feeling,' she said. 'It's her last day as Miss Evans. *Mrs Forbes-Kitchener* will take some getting used to.' And with a gentle smile she drove off.

School was a hive of activity when I arrived. 'Morning, Mr Sheffield,' said Ruby. It was good to see the familiar face of our cheerful caretaker, finally back at work and appearing to enjoy every minute of it. She had just finished giving the hall floor a final polish and her rosy cheeks were flushed with the exertion. 'It's like Fred Karno's in there,' she said. 'And Mrs Grainger wants it jus' reight.'

When I walked into the hall Sally and Jo were carrying

the large pine table from the entrance area and Anne was following close behind with Vera's oldest and dearest friend, Joyce Davenport, the doctor's wife. Anne was unfolding a snowy-white tablecloth and Joyce was holding one of her precious vases, in which she had arranged a most beautiful winter display of poinsettias and variegated holly with bright-red berries.

'Morning, Jack,' said Anne with a smile. 'We're getting ready for Vera's presentation at the end of assembly.'

'I would have come earlier if I'd known,' I said, looking round at the music stands next to the piano and the benches where the choir would be sitting.

'Well, to be perfectly honest, Jack, we didn't think flower arranging was exactly your forte,' said Sally with a grin.

The energetic Jo Hunter pulled back the large curtain that hid the dining tables and chairs from view. 'You can help me with the chairs if you like,' said Jo, ever the peacemaker. I had learned a long time ago how to deal with determined women: don't say anything and appear to do as you're told. I picked up a stack of chairs and followed Jo.

At ten o'clock a large group of parents were sitting at the back of the hall as Anne wheeled our 'music centre' to the front on its squeaky castors. This was our wood-veneered, Contiboard trolley on which a radio and a record player had been fitted on the top shelf. A hinged lid kept the dust off the records and on the bottom shelf two bulky speakers were stored.

Anne slid her precious Harry Belafonte LP from its

sleeve, cleaned the grooves on its vinyl surface with an anti-static cloth and placed it carefully on to the circular rubber mat on the turntable. With practised ease she turned the dial to 33 revolutions per minute, clicked the start lever with her thumb, lifted the plastic arm and lowered it carefully until the sharp stylus needle settled into the black grooves at the beginning of 'Mary's Boy Child'. As usual, it had a soothing effect on those assembled, and parents, teachers and children waited for the Revd Joseph Evans to lead us in our final assembly of the autumn term.

Joseph welcomed everyone and introduced the first hymn, 'While shepherds watched their flocks by night', and Anne played the introductory bars. When Jimmy Poole, urged on by his partner-in-crime Heathcliffe Earnshaw, sang 'While theperdth wathed their thocks by night', I saw Sally give him a stern stare and he returned his attention to his hymn book.

Finally, Sarah Louise Tait stood up and in a clear confident voice led us in our school prayer:

Dear Lord,
This is our school, let peace dwell here,
Let the room be full of contentment, let love abide here,
Love of one another, love of life itself,
And love of God.
Amen.

Then Sue Phillips gave a wonderful speech on behalf of the Parent Teacher Association, describing Vera's work over the years as school secretary. Ruby Smith and

Shirley Mapplebeck were both dabbing away the tears as Sue extended our best wishes to Vera for a happy married life. With great ceremony, Theresa Ackroyd and Dean Kershaw presented Vera with a bulky parcel wrapped in lavender tissue paper. There was an awkward silence as she opened it and then smiles of delight as she held up a beautiful original watercolour painting by local artist Mary Attersthwaite. It was a spectacular painting of Ragley School in winter . . . a perfect gift for Vera and an ideal addition to the valuable collection that adorned the rooms of Morton Manor.

When the bell rang for lunchtime I called in to Anne's reception class. They were tidying up after making a special Christmas gift for their parents – curve-stitching calendars – and I marvelled at the skill of children so young.

Just outside the classroom door, I was concerned to see that nine-year-old Betsy Icklethwaite was trying to console her five-year-old sister, Katie, who was sobbing her heart out.

'What's the matter, Betsy?' I asked.

'Ben Roberts told my sister there's no Father Christmas, Mr Sheffield,' she said, 'but don't worry . . . it's sorted.' Betsy didn't suffer fools gladly.

'Really?' I said.

'Yes, Mr Sheffield,' continued the determined Betsy. 'Ah've explained to m'sister that our mam 'oovers up them pine needles reight reg'lar under t'Christmas tree, but las' year on Christmas morning there were *crumbs* on t'carpet.'

'Crumbs?'

'That's right, Mr Sheffield,' interjected tearful Katie, 'from 'is mince pie.'

'Mince pie?'

'Yes, Mr Sheffield,' said little Katie, drying her eyes and becoming more animated by the moment. 'What we leave wi' 'is glass o' milk.'

Betsy gave Katie a cuddle and then smiled up at me, secure in the knowledge that the magic of Christmas would survive another year.

It was a poignant moment when, at the end of the day, Vera tidied up her desk in the office and put the cover on her electric typewriter. We had all gathered to wish her luck.

'How will you all cope until the end of term,' said Vera, 'when I'm away next Monday and Tuesday?' The school governors had agreed to Vera's request to be absent for the last two days of term to accommodate her honeymoon. However, as she was actually marrying one of the governors, this had not been a difficult decision. 'Rupert insisted, you see,' she said, but her words fell on deaf ears.

'Don't worry,' said Anne with a smile, 'we'll manage.'

'And get a good night's rest, Vera,' said Sally, giving her a hug. 'We want you to look your beautiful best tomorrow.'

'Dan's got time off, but he's coming in his dress uniform just for you,' added Jo.

I walked out with Vera to her car, carrying her painting and holding her firmly by the elbow. 'I don't want you falling down on the icy car park, Vera,' I said. 'The major would never forgive me.'

She put the painting in the boot of her car and then looked back at the school, taking in all its detail. 'The gift was perfect, Jack,' she said softly. It was rare for her to call me by my first name and I recognized the significance. For Vera, term was over. 'And I am aware it was *your* choice . . . so thank you.' She stretched up and kissed me on the cheek. 'We've made a good team, haven't we?' she said. Then she drove away for the last time as Miss Evans.

Almost everyone in the village had been invited to the service in St Mary's Church, so on Friday evening Diane the hairdresser worked long hours to make sure the ladies of Ragley looked their best.

"Ow d'you want it, Nora?' asked Diane.

Nora Pratt produced the copy of *Smash Hits* magazine that she had borrowed from Dorothy. 'Ah'd like it like that Irene Cara in *Fame*, please, Diane,' she said, pointing to the photograph of the athletic dancer.

Diane looked in the large mirror at the reflection of the plump forty-five-year-old Nora with hair that looked like tired seaweed. 'That'll tek some doin', Nora,' she said. 'Are y'sure y'don't fancy a Carly Simon? That wouldn't tek as many rollers.'

'No thanks, Diane, ah weally want it t'go wi' me new leg wawmers.'

Life was much quieter in the vicarage. Vera and Joseph were sitting at the kitchen table drinking tea from bone-china cups. Vera's three cats were at her feet in various positions of repose. 'You'll have to learn a new routine,' said Vera almost to herself.

Joseph sipped his tea thoughtfully. 'I know,' he said. His voice was strained.

'No, not you, Joseph,' said Vera. 'You'll be fine. I'm talking to my *cats*.' Maggie, Jess and Treacle purred contentedly, completely unaware that, after Vera's honeymoon, they would be moving to Morton Manor and a whole new world of strange gardens, newly installed cat flaps and unsuspecting mice.

On Saturday the dawn came slowly on a perfect winter's morning. All was still, as if the world were holding its breath. However, a loud rat-a-tat on the front door of the vicarage shattered the silence and announced the beginning of Vera's special day.

Diane Wigglesworth had arrived early with her hairdressing equipment and Vera relaxed in her expert care. Her friend, Joyce Davenport, confidante since their schooldays, was making sure she did her matron of honour duties down to the last letter and had been at the vicarage since the crack of dawn. Joseph was nowhere to be seen. He had left early for the church. Today was different, as he had to do the jobs that were usually done by Vera.

In Bilbo Cottage Beth and I looked up at the clock on the kitchen wall. It was ten o'clock and Vera was due to be married in one hour.

'Come on, Jack,' said Beth as we stood in the hallway

together. She readjusted my tie and stood back to check my appearance one last time. I smiled at her.

'What is it?' she said.

'I was thinking back to our wedding day.'

Beth reached up to kiss me. 'No regrets?'

'None,' I said. Beth looked beautiful in a new dusky-pink two-piece suit and her honey-blonde hair hung free. I held her in my arms. 'I love you,' I said. 'Always will.'

She stared into my eyes for a long time as if there was something she wanted to say but was holding back. Her cheeks were pale and she rested her head on my shoulder. 'Oh Jack, what a journey we've been on,' she said softly. 'And, yes, I love you too.' Then she glanced in the hall mirror, picked up her leather gloves and wide-brimmed hat and we walked out to her pale-blue Volkswagen Beetle. Beth had suggested that she should drive so that I could enjoy a few beers after the wedding. As she drove cautiously on the frozen back road towards Ragley village, I peered through the windscreen at the distant Hambleton hills. Where the sky met the earth in a grey fusion, heavy snow clouds were approaching, interspersed with sharp rays of sunshine. On this momentous day, the road to St Mary's Church was lit up in sharp relief. God was in his heaven and had blessed this little corner of Yorkshire.

As we drove up the High Street many families were hurrying up the Morton Road while the church bells rang out joyously to announce that today was a special day. There was a wedding in the village.

In the vestry, Joseph opened the door of the huge oak

wardrobe and took out his cassock, a long black robe that fitted perfectly over his tall, lean frame. Then he selected a spotless white surplice and cope and put them on. Finally, round his neck he added a white stole, edged with beautiful gold crosses. It had been hand-stitched with loving care by Vera and tears of love ran down his cheeks as he kissed it gently and smiled at the memory.

Later, in the stillness of the nave, a composed Joseph greeted Rupert and his best man, Colonel Richard Carruthers, an old army colleague he had known for all of his military life. Both were dressed in formal three-piece wedding suits with their matching East Yorkshire regimental ties, while Rupert's daughter, thirty-year-old Virginia Anastasia, looking stunning in a pale-blue dress, fussed around her father like a mother hen.

Outside, the crowds were gathering. Heathcliffe Earnshaw was carefully and deliberately scuffing the shiny toecaps of his best black leather shoes against the church wall.

'Stop it, 'Eath,' said Mrs Earnshaw, giving him a clip round the ear. 'Y'ruinin' y'Sunday shoes.'

'Yeah, schtop it 'Eeef,' echoed little Dallas Sue-Ellen, who had begun to imitate her mother's reprimands, much to the disgust of both Heathcliffe and Terry. Heathcliffe reluctantly gave his shoes a final surreptitious scrape and glowered at his little sister. He gave her his menacing steely-eyed stare, faithfully copied from his *Buck Rogers in the 25th Century Annual*, and was pleased he had hidden her pink plastic potty in the coal shed that morning.

*   *   *

The pews were filling up quickly and I looked around as the congregation settled. All the school staff had arrived early and members of the governing body and Parent Teacher Association whispered in eager anticipation, while Elsie Crapper played soothing music on the organ. Also, thanks to the efforts of the ladies of the Women's Institute, the church had never looked more beautiful. As well as the huge floral displays next to the pulpit, on each of the wide ledges of the stone pillars was a tall white candle surrounded by green variegated holly with bright red berries. Refracted sunlight from the stained-glass windows lit up the ancient stone in a myriad of colours and the hint of incense touched our senses.

Beth and I were sitting next to John and Anne Grainger. Anne had added a new light-blue ribbon to the dramatic wide-brimmed navy hat that she had worn for our wedding last Easter. Behind us, Jo had bought an olive-green two-piece suit and a small hat to complement the outfit. She was holding hands with the huge figure of Acting Sergeant Dan Hunter, immaculate in his dress uniform and with a pair of white gloves tucked in his belt. Colin Pringle, in his best suit, was sucking sherbet lemons as if his life depended on it as once again he tried to give up smoking. Meanwhile, Sally had pulled out all the stops with an outrageous salmon-pink outfit and an extravagant hat that looked like an explosion in a turkey-plucking factory.

Two pews behind, Ruby was wearing her best floral dress and her favourite straw hat decorated with a ring of bright-red poinsettias. She looked out eagerly for the arrival of her dear friend, recalling that terrible day of the accident just five months ago and how, since then, their lives had taken a new direction. Next to her, Ronnie was in his best suit, sadly crumpled following a late visit to his pigeon loft to feed his new pride and joy, Genghis Khan II. The dank odour of bird droppings was now competing favourably with the smell of the furniture polish Mary Hardisty had used on the dark-mahogany Victorian pews. Close by, Shirley Mapplebeck, the school cook, was sitting next to her formidable assistant, Doreen Critchley. Both were in their best dresses with sufficient undergarments to keep out the cold.

Edith Tripps, the recently retired headteacher of Morton village school, was also in the congregation. She had never thought this day would come for Vera. 'We enjoy our freedom too much, don't we Vera?' Edith had said a few years ago. That, of course, was before Vera had met Rupert. As she picked up the elegant Order of Service, she reflected that she had never known what it must be like to be loved by a man.

Vera arrived in Rupert's classic Bentley with his chauffeur, Tomkins, at the wheel and there were cheers of approval from the ladies of the Women's Institute as the bride emerged. Although it took longer to drive the distance from the vicarage and up the gravel path to the church gate rather than simply walk the fifty yards through the churchyard, Rupert had insisted that Vera arrive in style.

In a beautiful lace-trimmed lilac dress, long-sleeved and high-buttoned, and with her mother's Victorian brooch at her throat, it was a classical look, yet with understated elegance. It was also noticeable to everyone that Vera appeared completely at ease as she smoothed her dress over her slim figure. As always, she was in complete control.

She waited for a few moments beneath the shelter of the stone porch at the entrance to the church. Next to her was a dear ecclesiastical friend, the Revd David Wainwright, a trusted colleague since college days and, like Joseph, a parish priest.

'Vera,' said David, 'you look really lovely and I'm so very proud you chose me to walk beside you down the aisle.'

She looked up at him with an enigmatic smile. 'You have always been a special friend, David, and if my brother forgets the Order of Service, I'm sure you can help him out.' Then Vera turned to face the open church doorway and took a deep breath. 'Well, I do think I'm ready . . . so, shall we go? I'm sure poor Elsie Crapper must be on the edge of her seat by now. Let's hope she's taken her Valium.' Then, with calm grace, she took his arm and, with measured, deliberate steps, walked down the aisle. As she came alongside Ruby she paused for the briefest moment, stretched out and pressed her cool fingers on the back of Ruby's dumpy hand. Tears flowed freely down Ruby's cheeks but, on this special day, they were tears of joy.

Beyond the chancel, a balustrade of low mahogany rails separated it from the candlelit altar with its beautiful hand-stitched cloth. On this cold, clear winter's day, a low sun illuminated the tall east window and the stained glass refracted the serene white light into a kaleidoscope of colours that shone down on the choir stalls. Mary

McIntyre, the leader of the choir and the most wonderful soprano, waited to lead the congregation in the first hymn, 'Love divine, all loves excelling'. When Vera was standing alongside Rupert, Joyce Davenport took the delicate bouquet of flowers from her and stepped back. Behind us we heard the closing of the ancient church door and the service began.

At the front of the chancel, alongside the pulpit, on the north side of the nave stood a brass lectern decorated with a wondrous eagle, upon whose outstretched wings a giant Bible had been placed. A long red ribbon marked the page of the reading and soon it was my turn. Vera had requested 1 Corinthians, chapter 13, verses 4–8, and I stepped up to read the selected passage: '*Love is patient and kind; love is not jealous or boastful; it is not arrogant or rude. Love does not insist on its own way; it is not irritable or resentful; it does not rejoice at wrong, but rejoices in the right. Love bears all things, believes all things, hopes all things, endures all things. Love never ends'*.

When I sat down again Beth slipped her hand into mine . . . and kept it there.

Finally, *this* was the moment. Time seemed to stand still as the congregation waited for the words we all knew so well. 'Wilt thou have this woman to thy wedded wife,' asked Joseph, '. . . and, forsaking all other, keep thee only unto her, so long as ye both shall live?'

His words flowed like a gentle breeze over a field of wheat, but there was gravitas in the question. It was a message bound in iron.

'I will,' said Rupert in a sure, clear voice.

*　　　*　　　*

Outside, the classic black Bentley, decorated with ribbons, waited, engine purring. The ladies of the Women's Institute had decorated the lychgate with garlands of holly, so this was the setting for the traditional photographs. However, Rupert, with military decisiveness, kept it brief. After all, it was a cold day and his new wife had forsaken warmth for style.

There was confetti and cheering in equal measure as the car set off up the Morton Road and then moved smoothly up the long driveway towards the turreted Yorkshire stone manor house.

Vera looked at Rupert, who seemed deep in thought. 'A penny for them, Rupert,' she said.

'I was just thinking of the service,' said Rupert.

'It went beautifully,' said Vera.

'Thanks to you, my dear,' said Rupert and he kissed her gently.

It was a wonderful afternoon, with toasts, speeches, dancing and gentle conversation. The major's daughter, the confident and curvaceous Virginia Anastasia, seemed to have inherited her father's ability to guide large groups of people through the formalities of the occasion without ever appearing to be rushed.

Vera and Rupert had decided to spend their first night together at Morton Manor before flying to the south of France for a relaxing honeymoon, so there was no rousing send-off. Instead, the guests slowly departed as the evening wore on and it was almost midnight when Vera walked into her new kitchen and opened the door of the wall cupboard she had recently rearranged with Virginia's blessing. From it she took her mother's Victorian tea caddy, then boiled some water and made a pot of tea. It was time for her usual nightcap and, as she sat in the vast kitchen, she reflected on the day . . . and thought of Joseph.

An owl hooted in the churchyard and snow began to fall again. At the kitchen window in the vicarage a solitary figure looked out at the winter scene and then closed the curtains.

Joseph walked into the hallway, checked the locks on the front door, turned out the lights and stood at the foot of the stairs. The house was quiet. Vera's coat peg was empty and he knew life would never be the same again. He missed her companionship, her very *presence*. Finally, he walked upstairs, alone.

And on that dark December night, as a fresh snowfall covered the sprinkle of confetti at the lychgate, there was no one to see his tears and no one to share his prayers.

At Morton Manor, Vera and Rupert were also standing in the hallway at the foot of the stairs.

'Vera,' said Rupert, 'thank you for this wonderful day.'

'It was the right decision, Rupert,' said Vera, 'and we shall have Christmas together as man and wife.'

Rupert looked at his brass timepiece. 'Well, my dear, I think it is time for us to retire.'

'Not *quite* yet, Rupert,' said Vera with a smile.

Rupert looked confused. 'Really?'

'Yes,' said Vera simply.

'I'm sorry, Vera,' said Rupert and he kissed her on her forehead. 'I'm being insensitive.'

'Not at all, Rupert,' said Vera. 'It's just that I *can't* come to bed yet.'

'Vera . . . I would never wish to rush you.'

Vera smiled. 'No, Rupert, I don't mind being *rushed* and I have no problem about coming to bed.'

'I don't understand,' said Rupert, still perplexed. 'What's preventing you from coming to bed *now*?'

'Because, my dearest Rupert . . . I haven't said goodnight to my cats.'

Chapter Nine

The Last Christmas Present

School closed today with 87 children on roll and will reopen for the spring term on Tuesday, 4 January 1983. All children attended this afternoon's Christmas party, supported by members of the PTA. The school choir will perform at the Crib Service in St Mary's Church on Wednesday, 22 December.

Extract from the Ragley School Logbook:
Tuesday, 21 December 1982

It was Tuesday, 21 December, the last day of the autumn term, and the school Christmas party beckoned. A busy week was in store, with the closing down of school for the holiday, Christmas shopping, a variety of church services and, finally, on Saturday, Christmas Day for Beth and myself at Bilbo Cottage. My Glaswegian mother, Margaret, and her sister May had been invited to a gathering of the Scottish clans for Christmas and Hogmanay, while Beth's parents were staying in Hampshire. So a quiet and peaceful festive season was in store for just the two of us, or so I thought.

As I drove to school for the last time in 1982, iron-grey clouds hung heavy over the Hambleton hills and a fresh fall of snow covered the distant fields. Skeletal trees, like a child's charcoal drawing, stood like silent sentinels beyond the frozen hedgerows. The countryside was held fast in the grip of winter as a grudging light crept over North Yorkshire and a new day dawned.

Ruby was locking her caretaker's cupboard when I walked into the entrance hall. 'G'morning, Mr Sheffield,' she said. 'Ah came in reight early t'day to 'ang up m'presents on t'tree for all t'kiddies.' It was a tradition that Ruby bought a small gift out of her own pocket for every child in the school and then wrapped them in North Yorkshire County Council tissue paper and hung them on our Christmas tree. Then, at the end of the party, the children took them home along with a balloon and any Christmas decorations and cards they had made for their parents.

'That's really kind of you, Ruby,' I said.

'Well they're only young once, Mr Sheffield,' she said, 'an' we 'ave t'mek Christmas special for 'em.' This good-hearted lady then fastened her headscarf, her only concession to the freezing conditions, and hurried towards the entrance door. 'An' ah'll be back to 'elp wi' t'party,' she called over her shoulder.

It was a hectic morning, particularly in Anne's reception class, where excitement was building. All the children had written their letters to Santa and posted them in the school post-box. Little Ted Coggins was sending his letter at the same time as Katie Icklethwaite.

'What y'getting' f'Christmas, Katie?' asked Ted.

'We're 'avin' a 'amster,' said five-year-old Katie.

'A 'amster?' said Ted in surprise. 'We're 'avin' a turkey.'

When the bell rang for afternoon school, eighty-seven children, all the staff and a group of willing mothers from the Parent Teacher Association filled the school hall for our end-of-term party. We began with lively and energetic games such as Statues and Musical Chairs, then moved on to a dancing competition to the accompaniment of Abba's 'Super Trouper'. The winner, surprisingly, was eight-year-old Mo Hartley, the youngest and quietest of the Hartley sisters, and, not for the first time, I realized that many children keep their talents hidden from their teachers and their peer group. As she received her prize, a bag of chocolate decimal coins, I recalled that, as teachers, we always needed to be sufficiently observant to help children reach their full potential.

At the end of school I was concerned to overhear Mrs Critchley, our dinner lady, in the entrance hall trying to persuade the vulnerable and gullible Ruby to take on yet another catalogue.

'You ought to 'ave a Grattan catalogue,' said Mrs Critchley.

'Ah dunno, Doreen,' said the hesitant Ruby.

'It's t'Winter Catalogue wi' Fashion Passion,' persisted our formidable dinner lady.

'Ah buy stuff from our Racquel's,' pleaded Ruby.

'Ah get a poun' back f'ev'ry ten poun' spent,' said Mrs Critchley. 'It's a reight money-spinner.'

'Well, er . . .'

'An' twen'y weeks no-charge credit. Y'jus' send off t'Bradford for a catalogue . . . it's dead easy.'

'Well, mebbe,' said Ruby.

It occurred to me that it would have been helpful to have been able to mention this conversation to Vera so that she could have intervened on Ruby's behalf. However, our school secretary was enjoying the scenery in the south of France and catalogue shopping was far from her mind.

On Wednesday morning bright winter sunshine lit up the countryside and I stared in wonder at the distant fields through the frosted panes of our bedroom window. I had learned to love this land with its spectacular scenery and harsh winters. Here we breathed the clean sharp air of the high moors, unsullied by the toxic car fumes of the great cities or the fetid mists of the low marshlands. It was a perfect morning for Christmas food shopping and, over breakfast, I checked Beth's long list.

'But there are only two of us,' I said. 'This would feed an army.'

Beth looked tired. She was nibbling on a digestive biscuit whereas I had just demolished a large bowl of porridge. 'Well, it's a long holiday, Jack, and if more snow comes it might be our last chance.'

It made sense and I made her a cup of tea before I left. She kissed me tenderly at the door. 'Come back safely.'

Beth's Volkswagen Beetle was on the driveway. 'Shall I put your car in the garage?' I said.

She glanced back at the hall table. Her car keys were

on top of a brown envelope. 'No, I may have to go out later.'

I guessed it was last-minute Christmas shopping, maybe for me, so I didn't enquire further.

Ragley High Street was full of Christmas shoppers and, after collecting my turkey from Old Tommy Piercy, I decided to call into Nora's Coffee Shop. Predictably, the Christmas number one was booming out for the umpteenth time. Nora clearly loved Renée and Renato singing 'Save Your Love', but she was definitely in a minority.

Little Malcolm was at the counter waiting for a mug of tea and one of Nora's festive mince pies, which only customers with strong teeth were buying.

'Ah've got you a lovely present, Malcolm,' said Dorothy.

Malcolm looked alarmed. He was intending to find a suitable gift for Dorothy on Christmas Eve at Easington market. 'Oh, er, thanks Dorothy,' he said, blushing and looking down at his boots.

'So what's it t'be, Mr Sheffield?' asked Dorothy.

'A coffee, please,' I said.

She fiddled with her huge plastic Christmas-tree earrings. 'An' we've got some crackin' mince pies.' Cracking seemed an appropriate word.

'Thanks,' I said hesitantly. The sign said HOME-MADE MINCE PIES . . . it just didn't say *when*. 'I'll try one.'

Dorothy turned to Little Malcolm. Her butterfly brain had already thought of something else. 'An' Malcolm, did y'see Princess Diana in that lovely ballgown?' she said.

'Ah don't think so,' said Little Malcolm vaguely.

'Y'know . . . when she went to see that film wi' that Indian feller wi' a bald 'ead an' sandals?' continued Dorothy.

'Gandhi,' said Little Malcolm helpfully.

Dorothy looked puzzled. 'Y'mean that little reindeer in Walt Disney whose mam got shot?'

'No, not *Bambi* . . . *Gandhi*,' said Little Malcolm. 'That Indian who wanted to be equal wi' us.'

'Never 'eard of 'im,' said Dorothy. 'Why, what's 'e been in?'

Nora looked up from shaking icing sugar through a sieve on to the plate of mince pies to give them a more appetizing appearance. "E's not *been* in owt, Dowothy,' she said. "E were a webel.'

'Like Johnny Rotten?'

'No, not that kind o' webel,' retorted Nora. "E wanted to get wid o' all t'Bwitish in 'is countwy so all t'Indians 'ad equal wights.'

'Oh, ah see,' said Dorothy. 'Well if 'e comes in 'ere *ah'm* not serving 'im.'

Escape was the only option, so I picked up the coffee and mince pie, paid quickly and retreated to the nearest table.

That afternoon Beth said she wanted to wrap some presents, so I went alone to the Crib Service at St Mary's Church. When I arrived it was already packed with children from both Ragley and Morton, many of them in costume for the traditional Nativity play. Sally, Jo and Anne were busy arranging the school choir in order of height so that their parents could see them all from the pews. I enjoyed the feeling of not being in charge and relaxed at the back next to Sue Phillips. Joseph, as always on these occasions, was on good form and all went well.

After the service Anne popped her head round the vestry door. 'Any news of Vera, Joseph?' she said quietly.

Joseph nodded and suddenly looked quite sad. 'A very brief telephone call,' he said. 'All appears well and she asked me to pass on her love to everyone.'

Then he brightened up. 'And she'll be back tomorrow. I've been invited to have Christmas dinner with them and stay overnight at the Manor.'

Anne smiled and, to Joseph's surprise, she gave him a kiss on the cheek. 'You have many friends, Joseph – never forget that.'

When the church was finally empty and all that could be heard was the ticking of the clock in the church tower, Joseph sat alone on one of the empty pews and prayed for peace on earth and goodwill to all men . . . but mainly for his sister.

That evening Beth seemed full of life again and suggested going to The Royal Oak for some hot food and a drink. The cold breath of winter froze our bones, but the bright-orange lights were welcoming and I was looking forward to a pint of Chestnut Mild and one of Sheila's gammon and egg Specials.

'Would you like a glass of white wine, Beth?' I asked.

Beth paused and thought for a moment. 'I don't think I will, Jack,' she said. 'Just a soft drink.' She found a quiet table and I waited my turn at the bar. All the familiar folk were there, enjoying an evening in the cosy warmth under the bright Christmas decorations hanging from the ancient beams.

Old Tommy Piercy was sitting on his usual stool beneath The Royal Oak's most prized possession: an autographed photograph of Geoffrey Boycott. 'How are you, Mr Piercy?' I asked.

'Fair t'middlin', thank you, young Mr Sheffield,' said Old Tommy through a haze of Old Holborn pipe tobacco. Along with the football team, he was staring intently at the television set above the taproom bar. Olivia Newton John, in a headband and skintight Lycra, was performing sexy aerobics in a gymnasium while singing her hit song 'Physical'.

'Fit as a butcher's dog,' said Derek 'Deke' Ramsbottom, local snow-plough driver, occasional farmhand, pub singer and father of Shane, Clint and Wayne. In the taproom of The Royal Oak political correctness was a far-off dream and everyone nodded. After all, in the eyes of the Ragley Rovers football team, this was the ultimate accolade any Yorkshireman could give to a woman.

'She's norra patch on your Sheila,' said Old Tommy to Don the barman.

'Y'reight there,' said Don appreciatively.

'She looks a reight ball o' fire,' said Old Tommy.

'Y'not far wrong. She were allus sex-mad, were our Sheila,' said Don. 'Ah were knackered on 'oneymoon.'

'Ah sympathize, young Donald,' said Old Tommy, sucking thoughtfully on his old briar pipe and tamping down the tobacco with his thumb. He leant forward conspiratorially. 'An' ah'll tell thee summat f'nowt. Me back's nivver been t'same since ah relieved Co-op Clara o' 'er corsets under Bridlington pier in nineteen thirty-two.'

Don looked down the bar where Sheila was serving another customer. 'An' she's got 'er John Wayne bra on tonight.'

''Ow d'you mean?' asked Deke.

'Y'know,' said Don, ''ead 'em up an' move 'em out.'

'That were *Raw'ide* wi' Clint Eastwood,' said Deke. 'We named our Clint after 'im.' Then he suddenly burst into song: *'Rollin', rollin' rollin', though they're disapprovin', keep them doggies movin', raw'ide.'* Finally he supped deeply on his pint of bitter and nodded knowingly. What Deke didn't know about cowboy songs wasn't worth bothering about.

Deke nodded towards Beth. 'Ah've got a brace o' pheasants f'your good lady, Mr Sheffield,' he said. 'Ah'll drop 'em round when ah'm passin'.'

I had come to love this village and the generosity of spirit. 'That's very kind, Deke,' I said.

'Least ah can do f'teaching my Wayne t'read,' he added with a grin. 'An' ah've gorra *cock* pheasant,' he continued. 'Ah call 'im Fritz. 'E comes roun' ev'ry morning an' eats all t'crumbs scattered round t'bird table. Mind you, ah don't actually *own* 'im, so t'speak, but as good as 'cause 'e allus comes t'my bird table first and then goes t'nex' door an' so on.'

I was unsure how to reply. 'That's interesting, Deke,' I said as Sheila arrived and served my drinks.

'Y'can't beat a game bird f'Christmas, Mr Sheffield,' said Deke.

'So ah've 'eard,' said Sheila, winking at me.

*   *   *

On Thursday I rose early and drove into York. The distant hills were a patchwork of grey, white and silver in the first rays of a cold dawn. The land was waking on this winter morning and I had to buy a present for Beth. Shopping has never been my favourite activity, more a functional necessity, so I decided to keep it short and sweet: Boots the Chemist, followed by a jeweller's in Stonegate.

In Boots, I bought a canister of Erasmic Superfoam Shaving Lather for me and some Harmony hairspray for Beth. A young woman was demonstrating a range of cosmetics behind the counter and I joined the group of interested spectators. She held up each product as if she had just discovered penicillin.

'First of all, I empty my face of shadows under the eyes,' she said, holding up a Rimmel Hide the Blemish cover-up stick. 'A bargain at sixty-four pence,' she added triumphantly. 'Then I get bright, wide eyes by putting white liner inside the lower lashes using my Boots No. 7 Two-Timer . . . it's brilliant.' She fluttered her eyelashes to give everyone the full benefit. 'And for the final flourish for a special night out, go for gold on the lips using the wet technique with Ultima II Pure Gold. Mind you, it's over a fiver so y'need to go careful.'

I bought the first two but, with memories of the Bond film *Goldfinger*, I discarded the idea of golden lips. I also bought an Estée Lauder 'Great Make-Up Organizer' and, from the jeweller's, a locket on a chain. It took forty-five minutes and, feeling very self-righteous, I drove home.

*   *   *

Meanwhile, back at Bilbo Cottage, Deke Ramsbottom, ruddy face wreathed in smiles, was in conversation with Beth. He had removed his stetson when he saw it was her that answered the door.

'Here y'are, Mrs Sheffield, summat for t'pot,' he said. 'Our Wayne were a beater at t'last shoot.'

He held up a brace of pheasants in his giant fist and Beth avoided recoiling at the sight of the lolling heads and broken wings. 'Ah, er, thank you very much, Mr Ramsbottom. Jack will be thrilled.'

'An' so 'e might be,' said Deke proudly. 'These are proper beauties, tha knaws.'

Three miles away another Christmas present was being received with similar enthusiasm. Anne heard the words that she dreaded when John walked in from the garage with his latest *Do-It-Yourself* magazine.

'Anne, I'm going to build you a dream bedroom.'

'But I'm happy with what we've got,' she said as she prepared a casserole.

John Grainger was trying to make a bedside unit using only two lengths of Contiplas white board. The instructions were difficult to say the least and resembled the assembly of a NASA space shuttle. He had also decided to use his new state-of-the-art Lutz circular saw bench with a frighteningly large saw-blade that looked as though it was a prop from the latest James Bond film. It had cost £165 and Anne did wonder if it would have been cheaper to go to the Cavendish furniture store and simply buy a set of drawers.

*   *   *

As the evening wore on, the last two customers of the day arrived in Diane's Hair Salon. This was her busiest time of the year and both chairs were occupied.

As usual, Nora Pratt wanted something special for Christmas. 'Ah wanna Carly Simon,' said Nora.

Diane frowned. 'Y'mean 'er wi' teeth like Red Rum?'

'Yeah, but 'er 'air's nice . . . sort of natural.'

Diane took a deep breath. 'Fair enough, Nora, a Carly Simon it is then.'

Amelia Duff had also called in from the Post Office for a shampoo and set. Amelia was less demanding. 'I don't mind, Diane,' she said, 'just the usual please, but I haven't got all that long. I'm seeing Postman Ted tonight.'

'No problem, Amelia,' said Diane. With her state-of-the-art accelerator, drying time for highlights had been cut considerably. Also, her range of silver-minx and deep-slate setting lotions meant she had moved into the Eighties. Even so, there was need for caution. Her customers always appreciated her *traditional* procedures. So, with the confidence of over thirty years' experience, she sprayed Yorkshire Pale Ale on Amelia's hair as a setting lotion before attaching her outsize plastic rollers.

When she had a few minutes to spare, she made Amelia and Nora a cup of coffee and sat on the bench seat in the corner. She leaned back, lit up a John Player King Size Extra Mild cigarette, took a contented puff and, out of politeness, blew the smoke towards the closed window. 'So, 'ow's that postman o' yours, Amelia? 'E seems t'be gettin' 'is feet under t'table.'

'He's a lovely man, is Ted,' said Amelia cautiously.

'Vewy wegular,' said Nora.

'So 'ah've 'eard,' chuckled Diane.

Amelia blushed furiously but said nothing.

On Christmas Eve I left Beth making preparations for our Christmas dinner and drove to Easington. It seemed as though everyone from the surrounding villages had crowded into the cobbled market square for the Christmas Fair. The tree next to the War Memorial was brightly lit and, from the loudspeaker outside Santa's Grotto, 'Orville's Song' blasted out, much to the dismay of the majority of the adults. The ventriloquist Keith Harris and his duck, Orville, were rising up the Christmas charts and the shopping public fervently wished the little green puppet would soon be able to fly . . . preferably far away.

Inside Santa's wooden hut, five-year-old Katie Icklethwaite was looking a little crestfallen. 'Hello, Santa,' she said.

'And what's your name, little girl?' said Santa.

'Katie. What's yours?'

'Oh, Kevin . . . er, I mean Santa,' he replied. Santa wasn't used to such forthright children. Kevin Bickerstaff had volunteered at the Rotary Club to be this year's Santa and, after twenty-five years as an estate agent, he was hoping to experience the feeling of being *liked* for the first time.

'And what do you want for Christmas?' asked Santa.

'Can't tell you,' said Katie.

'Why not?' asked a puzzled Santa.

'It's a secret,' said the little girl.

'But you can tell me . . . I'm Santa.'

'Well Santa,' said Katie, 'ah did want a Barbie doll, but not now.'

Santa looked surprised. 'And why don't you want it now?'

'Because I saw exactly the one I wanted at the back of the cupboard under the stairs.'

Mrs Icklethwaite, in the doorway of the grotto, muttered a quiet expletive, thanked Santa and hurried out.

Next in line was eight-year-old Ben Roberts, who had his heart set on the action bike of 1982. 'Ah'd like a Raleigh BMX Burner, please, Santa,' he said.

Santa had heard of a bunsen burner, but not this one. 'Well, er, I'll ask Rudolph,' he said guardedly.

'Why? 'As 'e got one?' asked Ben.

Kevin suddenly felt a headache coming on and, as he searched in his pocket for a bottle of aspirin, he realized what his customers must have felt like when dealing with their local estate agent.

Later, back at Bilbo Cottage, as darkness fell Beth and I sat on the sofa drinking tea and watching a wonderful animated film called *The Snowman*, based on the lovely Christmas story by Raymond Briggs. At the end, as the credits rolled, the little boy knelt beside the melted snowman. He was clutching his scarf, a present from Father Christmas, and I had a lump in my throat as I recalled the Christmases I had experienced as a child. For me it had always been magical and I regretted that, in the busy world of adulthood, this was often forgotten. When it ended I wished that I had recorded it and hoped it would be repeated, especially as I was now, at long last, an expert at using the video recorder I had purchased last year.

Christmas Day was a morning of silence and light, the dawn of a new white world. A flurry of snow had covered the distant fields and I paused to take in the beauty of the Yorkshire landscape. It was a very special time for us, our first Christmas together, and we sat in the lounge by a roaring fire and opened our gifts . . . a scene replicated in other homes.

Geoffrey Dudley-Palmer was admiring his new Philips VR2020 Video Recorder. He held up the blank cassette. 'Eight hours' recording time, Petula,' he said in a voice full of awe and admiration. He flipped over the black plastic cassette: it was the size of a paperback novel. 'Four hours on each side! Just how do they do it?'

'Yes, it's wonderful, darling,' said Petula, failing to look up from the Christmas and New Year *Radio Times*.

'It's got DTF,' added Geoffrey.

'Yes, I'm sure it has,' said Petula.

'"Dynamic Track Following",' read Geoffrey from the side of the cardboard cassette box. 'It's arrived . . . it's finally arrived.'

'What has, darling?' asked Petula, looking up at last.

'The future,' said Geoffrey.

On the council estate, Little Malcolm was staring at a present he had just unwrapped. He looked up at Big Dave. 'Dorothy bought me this f'Christmas,' he said forlornly, 'an' ah promised ah'd use it ev'ry day.'

On the box lid it read, Bullworker Super X5.

'Sez 'ere, Dave, "Power meter calibration to measure your growing strength" on side o' t'box,' said Little Malcolm.

'What's that when it's at 'ome then, Mal'?' said Big Dave.

'Ah dunno, Dave, but it sez in t'book it gives "twice the strength and fitness",' quoted Little Malcolm.

He held up a slim volume with the words 'Scientific isotonic principles developed at the Max Planck Institute in Germany, 96-page fitness training book – 14-day free trial' on the front cover.

'It sez 'ere y'can 'ave a lithe waist,' said Little Malcolm.

'Lithe? What's *lithe* when it's at 'ome?' asked Big Dave.

'Dunno . . . an' summat abart "four per cent increase ev'ry week", Dave,' said Little Malcolm.

'Four per cen' o' what?' asked Big Dave.

'Dunt say, Dave,' said Little Malcolm, 'but it mus' be summat what gets bigger.'

Big Dave looked dubiously at the telescopic steel tubes and the traction straps attached to the sides. He held each end and compressed the tubes effortlessly.

'Well,' said Little Malcolm, 'Dorothy said ah might not be all that tall but ah can 'ave a *perfec'* body . . . 'cept f'being tall.'

Beth and I exchanged gifts in our dressing gowns. She had bought me an electric drill and she seemed happy with her cosmetics and the locket.

Finally she stood up and kissed me. 'Jack, I've got one more present for you.' She took my hand and we stood by the Christmas tree. I looked under the tree. There were no presents left.

'No, Jack, not there. It's here.' On one of the branches was a small box tied with a red ribbon. Beth lifted it down carefully and placed it in my hands.

'I thought this was one of the decorations – it's so tiny,' I said.

'Open it,' she said. Her eyes were shining.

I untied the ribbon and took the lid off the box. Inside was a small card with a date that read 'July 1983'.

'Ah yes,' I said, 'you've booked a holiday.'

She shook her head. 'Jack . . . we're going to be too busy for a holiday.' She stood back and gently laid both hands on her tummy. It took a few moments for it to register.

Christmas 1982 was about to become a very special day.

'Do you mean . . . ?'

Beth looked up at me and smiled. 'Yes, I do, Jack. I'm pregnant.'

Chapter Ten

The Refuse Collectors' Annual Ball

School reopened today for the spring Term with 89 children registered on roll.

Extract from the Ragley School Logbook:
Tuesday, 4 January 1983

The vapour of discontent drifted through the village like a malodorous mist and, with every breath, icy fingers of sleet froze our bones and sank our spirits. These were hard times for the folk of Ragley and hope of spring sunshine was the stuff of dreams. It was Bank Holiday Monday, 3 January 1983, a new year stretched out before us and the villagers of North Yorkshire were enjoying a relaxing morning huddled in their homes. However, on the council estate, in Big Dave and Little Malcolm's kitchen, Ragley's favourite binmen were pondering over a problem. The highlight of their social calendar was fast approaching. The Refuse Collectors' Annual Ball was on Saturday, and it was decision time.

Big Dave and Little Malcolm were sitting at the kitchen table while Dorothy prepared large mugs of sweet tea and doorstep-sized bacon butties. Dorothy was still in her dressing gown after spending a night of passion with Little Malcolm and, fortunately, Big Dave didn't mind so long as she did the washing-up.

'So, what we doing for t'ball on Sat'day?' asked Dorothy, sitting down beside them.

Little Malcolm stared lovingly at the woman of his dreams. 'We 'ave t'go in fancy dress again,' he said, 'an' there's a prize.'

'What's t'prize?' asked Dorothy.

'A free fish-an'-chip supper in York wi' a pot o' tea thrown in,' said Little Malcolm.

'Oooh, that's lovely,' said Dorothy. 'So, what we dressin' up as?'

'We could go as Batman an' Robin,' said Big Dave, as he added a generous splash of brown sauce to his crispy bacon.

'An' ah could be Catwoman,' said Dorothy. 'Ah've gorra mask an' ah could mek pointy ears an' whiskers.'

'Can ah be Batman?' asked Little Malcolm. There was an astonished pause as six-foot-four-inch Big Dave and five-foot-eleven-inch-in-her-bare-feet Dorothy looked down at the five-foot-four-inch refuse collector. ''Cause ah'm allus t'little un.'

'Well, what about Tarzan an' Jane?' suggested Big Dave quickly.

Little Malcolm shook his head. 'Ah don't want t'be Cheetah,' he added forlornly.

'No, Dave, we can't 'ave my Malcolm in a monkey suit,' said Dorothy.

Little Malcolm smiled. He loved it when Dorothy said *my* Malcolm.

However, Big Dave wasn't captain of the Ragley Rovers football team for nothing. He could sum up the mood of his teammates quickly and, although he didn't know what it meant, he had *empathy*. 'Y'reight there, Mal', but we're all f'gettin' summat.'

"Ow d'you mean?' asked Little Malcolm.

'We're f'gettin' my Nellie,' said Big Dave.

'Y'reight there, Dave,' said Little Malcolm, appreciative of the sudden diversion.

'We need t'go as a *foursome*,' said Dorothy.

'Like t'Beatles mebbe,' suggested Little Malcolm, secretly recalling that they were all about the same height except for Ringo, and he'd always fancied himself as a drummer.

'Or t'Dave Clarke Five,' said Dorothy.

'Yeah but there's *five* o' them, Dorothy,' said Little Malcolm.

'Well mebbe that Diana Ross an' them Supremes,' suggested Dorothy. 'Ah could get me 'air done.'

'Ah don't fancy being a Supreme,' said Little Malcolm dubiously.

There was silence as they each tried to recall famous quartets. 'Ah've gorrit!' exclaimed Big Dave suddenly. "Ow abart Abba – two men an' two women? Ah could be him sittin' at t'piano; Mal' could be 'im what allus looks pleased wi' 'imself on t'guitar; Dorothy could be that blonde wi' t'nice bum and Nellie could be 'er wi' t'brown 'air what meks up t'numbers.'

Light dawned in Dorothy's eyes. She was imagining herself in a skin-tight sparkly Abba suit. Little Malcolm nodded; he was thinking of Dorothy's bum. Meanwhile Big Dave was considering that, if he put his mind to it, he could solve the Cold War and be a Middle East negotiator in his spare time.

'Crackin' idea, Dave,' said Dorothy.

'Y'reight there, Dorothy,' agreed Little Malcolm.

'Abba it is then,' said Big Dave. 'Ah'll go an' ring Nellie, an' she can collec' t'costumes in York.'

Ten miles away in her flat in York, Fenella Lovelace, or 'Nellie' as she was known to her friends, was staring in the mirror. She had realized a long time ago that she wasn't *beautiful* in the general sense of the word, but, for a young, athletic woman in her mid-thirties, she certainly had her good features. At five-foot-two-inches tall, she knew she wasn't destined to be a catwalk model, but she had lovely long wavy hair, soulful eyes and a good sense of humour.

Her boyfriend, Big Dave Robinson, had just invited her to be his partner at the Refuse Collectors' Annual Ball in York. She had never met a man like Big Dave before: tall, strong, honest-as-the-day-is-long and keen on football. They had spent many Saturday nights watching *Match of the Day* and drinking pints of Tetley's bitter. He had become the perfect companion and she was lonely when he wasn't around.

And, suddenly, the reason was obvious. She was in love.

*   *   *

Meanwhile, in the kitchen of Bilbo Cottage, Beth was sipping tea, reading her mobile-library copy of *The Perfect Pregnancy* by some obscure American psychologist while *Thought for the Day* on Radio 4 murmured away in the background. It was a relaxing morning and a time to reflect on a memorable Christmas. This had been followed by a New Year's Eve dinner and dance at Morton Manor. It had been a wonderful evening and everyone was excited by our news. Vera had already begun to knit baby clothes.

'So, how are you?' I said.

Beth looked up. 'Interesting book, Jack,' she said. 'You should read it after me.'

My mind was on other things. 'What about your Masters course in Leeds?' I said.

'No problem,' she said confidently. 'I can still do my assignments from home and it will keep my mind occupied.'

'Fine,' I said without conviction. 'And what about school and maternity leave?'

'Yes, all in hand,' she said, 'and I've already written to my chair of governors about supply cover.'

'You seem to have it all worked out,' I said.

'I'll tell you what you could do, Jack,' she said with a smile.

'And what's that?' I asked.

'You could decorate the second bedroom.'

'Aah, er, good idea,' I said. 'Pink or blue?'

She turned back to her psychological thriller. 'You choose, Jack . . . probably something *neutral*.'

'Neutral?'

Beth was reading again. 'Yes,' she murmured, 'like lemon and white.'

I smiled and wondered if it was a fact that women looked more beautiful when they were pregnant.

In Ragley village, Ruby was cooking a full English breakfast as a treat for Ronnie, Duggie, Natasha and Hazel while Radio 1 blared out throughout the house. Mike Read had just introduced Kim Wilde performing 'Kids in America' and Ruby's family, all word perfect, were singing along.

Meanwhile, on the Crescent, Anne Grainger was in her kitchen preparing porridge with a bran-flake topping for her husband, John, while listening to Terry Wogan's programme on Radio 2. David Essex was singing his new hit, 'A Winter's Tale', and she gave a deep sigh as she understood the line about 'one more love that's failed'. John was reading his latest *Do-It-Yourself* magazine, completely oblivious that Anne had now passed the serious landmark of her fiftieth birthday but still felt – and looked – a slim and attractive thirty-five.

A mile away, in the palatial lounge of Morton Manor, Vera was sitting with her three cats, listening to Vivaldi on Radio 3's *Morning Concert* and looking through her beautiful leather-bound wedding album, which had just arrived from the photographer's in York. Vera felt very much at home now and Rupert was proving the perfect husband. Even so, she doubted he would join her for the gentle, soothing experience of a Liszt piano recital to be broadcast later in the morning. As Master of Foxhounds, he had left early with the hunt, presumably with the intention of killing one of God's creatures with his pack of noisy beagles.

'Ah well,' murmured Vera to herself, 'perhaps none of us is *quite* perfect.'

That evening Big Dave Robinson was puzzled. Nellie had telephoned to say she needed to speak to him and they had agreed to meet in York in The Bay Horse public house at Monk Bar. As they each supped a welcome pint of John Smith's bitter, Big Dave looked at Nellie and said, 'So what's up?'

Nellie removed her large-lens, fashionable spectacles and began to clean them on her Barnsley football shirt. 'Well, Dave, ah've been thinking.'

'What abart?' asked Big Dave.

'We've been gettin' on all reight, 'aven't we?' she said.

Dave nodded, wondering what was coming next. 'Yes luv.'

'We both like football, don't we?'

'Yes luv.'

'An' darts. An' Tetley's.'

Big Dave held up his pint. 'An' John Smith's.'

'So ah've been thinkin' . . . p'rhaps we should get married.'

'Y'what?'

'Married, Dave . . . y'know, live t'gether an' all that. So, what d'you think?'

'It's a bit sudden, Nellie. After all,' Big Dave went a shade of puce, 'we've not 'xactly, y'know, *conjugated* t'relationship, so t'speak,' he mumbled.

179

'P'raps we ought t'do summat abart it then, Dave,' said Nellie with a searching look.

'Y'reckon?'

'Yes, Dave, ah do. So 'ow abart comin' back t'my place?'

Dave supped his pint and slammed down the glass on the table. 'Nellie, y'not 'xactly backwards in coming forwards.'

Nellie drained her glass. 'C'mon y'big lump, ah'll show yer me etchings.'

On Tuesday morning the new term began well in spite of the freezing weather. That is, until Sally brought in her Prince Charles mug with a single large ear for a handle, a Christmas present from her equally anti-monarchist husband, Colin. At morning break Vera looked at it suspiciously but poured in the hot milk anyway.

During afternoon school, my class radio broke down immediately prior to my music-lesson broadcast. I was still trying to repair it when Ruby came in to sweep my classroom at the end of the day. 'Ah'm tryin' t'finish a bit sharpish, Mr Sheffield,' she said, her face flushed with the effort of vigorous sweeping. 'My Ronnie's got a bonus f'some extra coffin polishin'. 'E sez there's more trade in t'cold weather, so we're off to t'pictures. It's a while since he's tekken me out.'

'What are you going to see, Ruby?' I asked, twiddling the knobs of Class 4's ageing ghettoblaster to no avail.

'We're goin' t'see that film abart that extra testicle,' said Ruby. 'Y'know, that alien what lands in America wi' Steven Spellbug.'

I looked up, catching her drift. 'Ah, you mean *E.T. – the Extra-terrestrial.*'

'Yes,' said Ruby, '"im what looks like Michael Foot wi'out 'is glasses – funny little bloke wi' no 'air what keeps ridin' a bike in t'sky an' mekkin' things light up.'

'Well, I hope you have a lovely time, Ruby,' I said.

She leant on her broom. 'What's matter with y'radio, Mr Sheffield?'

'It's broken, Ruby,' I said, 'and I can't fix it.'

'Y'want t'see Little Malcolm Robinson, Mr Sheffield,' said Ruby. '"E's a reight dab-'and wi' owt 'lectrical.'

'Thanks,' I said. 'I'll take it round there one night this week.'

It was after school on Wednesday and I had mounted a display of winter paintings and poems on the board in my classroom when I recalled the broken radio. I wrapped up warm in my duffel coat and scarf, locked up the school and walked round the corner to the council estate. More snow was threatening and, on School View, curtains had been drawn to shut out the cold and darkness on this bitter evening. Logs were being put on the fires and televisions switched on as Ragley village settled down for another winter's night.

In the Earnshaw household, the family had gathered for their evening meal. 'So what did y'do at school t'day?' asked Mrs Earnshaw.

'Nowt,' chorused Heathcliffe and Terry.

'Nowt,' said little Dallas, who had begun to extend her vocabulary.

'Y'must 'ave done summat,' insisted Mrs Earnshaw.

'Summat,' echoed Dallas and everyone looked at her in bemusement. Up to now, three-year-old Dallas Sue-Ellen Earnshaw had simply gurgled, laughed and cried, and the only recognizable words had been 'poo' when she had filled her nappy and 'telly' when it wasn't switched on.

'Well, Mam,' said Terry, 'we did decimals wi' Mrs Pringle.'

Heathcliffe looked up, interested. 'We did 'em again this year,' he said. 'They keep coming back, do decimals.'

Mr Earnshaw looked up from the television. 'Is m'tea ready yet?'

'Nearly, luv,' she said, giving the spaghetti hoops a final stir. ''Eath an' Terry 'ave been working 'ard at school,' she added proudly.

'What 'ave they been doin'?' he asked.

'They've been decimated or summat,' she said.

'Summat,' repeated Dallas.

'An' our Dallas 'as started saying proper words . . . anyway, c'mon it's ready.'

''Bout bloody time,' said Eric as he sat down at the table.

'Bloody-time,' repeated Dallas.

'Hey, y'reight,' said Eric, 'she's comin' on.'

I walked along School View with the ghettoblaster and stopped at Little Malcolm's garden gate. On it he had nailed a piece of plywood on which a painted sign advertised his after-work repair service. It read:

DON'T DISPAIR – I REPAIR!
no job too small – repairs garrunteed 100%
(please nock loud as bell doesn't work)

While the spelling didn't exactly fill me with confidence, I knew I would be paying for Little Malcolm's technical know-how and, as requested, I knocked loudly.

Big Dave opened the door and stood there in his vest, overalls and thick socks, a large chipped mug with '1966 World Cup Winners' emblazoned on its side gripped in his mighty fist. He seemed untroubled by the bitter cold.

'Nah then, Mr Sheffield, what can ah do f'you?'

'Hello, Dave,' I said, 'sorry to trouble you, but my classroom radio isn't working and I was wondering if Malcolm might be able to fix it for me.'

'Ah'm sure 'e can. Come on in, 'e's in t'front room,' said Dave with a smile.

Little Malcolm was trying on his Abba costume and looked embarrassed when I walked in. 'It's for t'fancy dress, Mr Sheffield,' he explained, standing behind the sofa to hide his sparkly thirty-two-inch flares.

It was the following evening that Big Dave and Little Malcolm parked their dustbin wagon outside Nora's Coffee Shop and walked in. Ben Roberts, since Christmas Day, was now the proud owner of a Raleigh BMX Burner bicycle and was practising his stunt skids on the ice patch outside, but Big Dave was too preoccupied to reprimand him. Nor did he notice the two sixteen-year-olds, Claire Bradshaw and Anita Cuthbertson, sitting at his usual table. The girls were equally preoccupied. Claire and Anita, who had been in my class when I first arrived in Ragley, were studying a picture of Bananarama, the all-girl trio, taken after their hit record 'It Ain't What You Do It's The Way That You Do It' was released, and

183

wondering who they could enlist as a third member of their new group. Also, Claire had received a Chegger's Jogger headphone radio for Christmas and was secretly in love with Keith Chegwin. Anita, of course, knew *all* her secrets. After all, that's what best girlfriends were for.

Big Dave and Little Malcolm selected a corner table, supped tea and sat in silence while Big Dave gathered his thoughts. Behind the counter, Nora began to sing along to the song that Dorothy had put on the juke-box. 'Super Twouper,' she sang contentedly as she rearranged a pile of rock buns.

Finally Big Dave took a deep breath. 'She wants t'get married, Mal',' he said. 'It'd be different f'you an' me.'

'We could still watch *Match o' t'Day* t'gether, Dave,' said Little Malcolm.

'Ah s'ppose,' said Big Dave, still unconvinced.

'An' y'won't get owt better than 'er.'

''Ow do y'mean?' asked Big Dave.

'Well she can cook,' said Little Malcolm, 'that allus comes in 'andy.'

'An' she likes football,' added Big Dave.

'An' she knows t'offside rule,' said Little Malcolm enthusiastically.

'An' she can play darts . . . in fac', nearly as good as a man,' said Big Dave, warming to the idea.

'An' she likes Tetley's,' said Little Malcolm.

Big Dave nodded. 'Y'reight, Mal' . . . ah've gorra winner.'

'But y'need t'show 'er that y'serious, Dave.'

''Ow d'you mean?'

'You'll 'ave t'buy 'er a ring.'

'Ah don't know nowt abart rings,' said Big Dave, looking anxious.

'Don't worry, Dave, women know abart these things. Ah'll ask Dorothy.'

By Friday evening Dorothy knew exactly what to do. In the meantime there was the matter of a new hair-do. As usual on a Friday, Diane was working late in her Hair Salon.

Dorothy had discovered her favourite Suzi Quatro outfit at the back of her wardrobe and wandered in clutching a photograph of Agnetha Fältskog from her Abba magazine. 'Ah want t'look like 'er, please Diane,' said Dorothy.

Diane looked at the photograph of the Swedish superstar with her long, blonde, perfectly coiffeured hair and then studied Dorothy's back-combed peroxide-blonde mop, which had the constituency of wire wool and resembled Toyah Willcox after electric-shock treatment. 'OK, Dorothy, no problem,' said Diane. She glanced at the clock and sighed. The *impossible* always took an extra ten minutes.

On Saturday morning Big Dave, Little Malcolm and Dorothy were standing outside the window of H. Samuel the Jeweller's in York.

'Does anything take y'fancy?' asked Dorothy.

'Dunno,' said Big Dave, looking perplexed at the vast array of rings on display.

'Mebbe we ought t'go in,' suggested Little Malcolm.

Dave looked terrified. 'C'mon Dave,' said Dorothy, taking him by the arm.

The manager behind the counter was immaculately dressed in a three-piece suit and a crisp white shirt, with cufflinks that sparkled like landing lights at Heathrow Airport. 'Can I be of assistance, sir?' he asked smoothly.

'We're looking for an engagement ring,' said Dorothy.

'For you, madam?' he asked.

'No,' said Dorothy. She pointed at Big Dave. 'For 'is girlfriend.'

'I see,' he said and extended a perfectly manicured finger towards the first glass-fronted cabinet. 'This is our most popular range.'

''Ow much is that one?' said Dorothy, pointing to a large, diamond-encrusted ring.

'Five hundred pounds, madam,' was the calm reply.

'Bloody 'ell!' said Big Dave.

'What were you thinking of spending, sir?' asked the shop manager with a fixed smile.

'Well, ah 'adn't thought,' said Big Dave, reflecting that the loan to his little cousin to help him buy a car wasn't such a good idea. Dorothy gave him a hard stare. 'Ah s'ppose money's no objec' when yer in love,' muttered Big Dave through gritted teeth, 'so, mebbe fifty quid.'

'Ah,' said the manager quietly.

'Y'll 'ave t'spend more than that, Dave,' said Dorothy sharply.

After considerable thought and Dorothy trying on almost every ring in the shop, a decision was made to purchase a tiny diamond solitaire in a small presentation box.

'I can alter the size if you wish,' said the manager, relieved the ordeal was over. Big Dave removed the thick elastic bands from his old leather wallet and handed over £75.

As they drove back to Ragley, Dorothy was looking pleased with herself. It had occurred to her that if Big Dave moved out to live with Nellie, then she could vacate her flat above the Coffee Shop and move in with Little Malcolm.

It was lunchtime when Little Malcolm looked up and down the High Street and, when the coast was clear, hurried into the empty pharmacy shop where Eugene Scrimshaw was standing behind the counter. His wife was in the back room sorting their new stock of baby oil.

'Ah want summat for t'weekend, so t'speak, Eugene,' said Little Malcolm quietly.

Eugene raised a forefinger, placed it on the side of his nose and winked. 'Message understood, Malcolm,' he said and slid a slim box over the counter. 'Y'certainly gettin' through these at a rate o' knots.'

'Actu'lly, Eugene,' whispered Little Malcolm, 'ah'm gettin' a bit worried.'

'What's wrong, Mal'?' asked Eugene quietly, making sure his wife couldn't overhear them.

'Ah'm gettin' 'ot an' bothered,' said Little Malcolm forlornly.

''Ow d'you mean?'

'Ah mean wi' me an' Dorothy. She's gettin' very *demandin'*, if y'get m'meaning.'

'Sounds like yer a lucky man t'me,' said Eugene. 'Even in m'Captain Kirk outfit ah don't seem t'turn on my Peggy any more. Y'should be thankful f'small mercies.'

'Mebbe so,' mumbled Little Malcolm, "xcept ah was wond'rin' if ah'd got that men-applause. Y'know, like what women get when they don't fancy y'no more.'

'Men-applause?' said Eugene. 'Oh, y'mean *menopause*. What meks y'think that?'

"Cause ah lose m'sex drive after an 'our o' two.' Little Malcolm looked heartbroken. 'An' ah'll be forty soon. Ah think ah'm goin' through that *change*.'

"Ave y'spoken to Dorothy about it?' asked Eugene.

'Y'jokin'!' said Little Malcolm.

'Well Mal',' said Eugene, putting a comforting arm round Little Malcolm's shoulders, 'ah wouldn't worry if ah were you. Compared to normal men y'sound t'be a bloody stallion.'

Little Malcolm smiled with relief. 'Thanks Eugene, yer a pal.' He put a £5 note on the counter. 'An' while ah'm 'ere, ah'll 'ave another two packets.'

The bell rang above the door as he walked out and Eugene muttered to himself wistfully, 'Go forth and prosper.'

Little Malcolm was home for a quarter past twelve and Big Dave was switching on the television for *Grandstand* with David Coleman. Five minutes later, Bob Wilson was introducing *Football Focus* when Big Dave looked across from his armchair to his very relaxed cousin. 'You look pleased wi' yerself,' he said.

Little Malcolm just smiled and settled back. After all, he thought, he might not be very tall, but life was suddenly looking up again for a vertically challenged stallion.

*   *   *

At half past six Big Dave squeezed into the passenger seat of Little Malcolm's 1250cc bright-green, two-door Deluxe 1973 Hillman Avenger and Dorothy and Nellie sat in the back. They all looked the part in their Abba outfits and it turned out to be a good night. They even won third prize in the fancy dress: namely, a can of Watney's Party Seven, which they shared before the lights dimmed for the last dance.

Little Malcolm and Dorothy walked on to the dance floor, but Big Dave held Nellie's hand tightly. 'No, let's stay 'ere for a minute,' he said. 'Ah've got summat t'show yer.'

'An' what's that, Dave?' said Nellie, disappointed they weren't enjoying swaying to Renée and Renato in the heaving throng.

He pulled a small box out of his pocket and opened it. Nellie's eyes widened at the sight of the ring. 'Ah've been thinkin' on what y'said abart gettin' married an' ah think we could get on all reight, so 'ow abart it, Nellie?'

It occurred to Nellie that Big Dave had never mentioned *love* once. 'An' what abart them three little words, Dave?'

Big Dave looked momentarily puzzled, then plucked the ring from the box and put it on the third finger of Nellie's hand. 'It were expensive,' he said.

Nellie smiled. He was daft but she loved him anyway. 'C'mon Romeo,' she said with a grin. 'You'll do f'me,' and she stretched up and gave him a kiss.

Meanwhile, on the dance floor Little Malcolm looked up at his Agnetha Fältskog lookalike. 'Dorothy,' he said quietly.

'What?' said Dorothy, chewing gum as if her life depended on it.

'D'you know what love is?'

''Ow d'you mean?'

'Y'know . . . love.'

'Like on t'pictures, y'mean?' asked Dorothy.

'Mebbe like that,' said Little Malcolm.

'Why?'

'Why what?' said Little Malcolm.

'Well, why are y'on about love?'

Little Malcolm took a deep breath. ''Cause ah'm in love.'

'Oooh, Malcolm, that's proper romantic.'

'Ah'm in love wi' you, Dorothy . . . allus 'ave, allus will.'

Dorothy went quiet and stared for a long moment at this diminutive son of Yorkshire. He was a hard worker, trustworthy and loyal. She had always imagined meeting a six-foot-two-inch version of David Essex or Shakin' Stevens, but she knew deep down that was never to be. So she leant down and kissed Little Malcolm like he'd never been kissed before. If he truly loved her, and he clearly did, then she'd settle for this little dustman with a heart of gold. 'An' ah love you, Malcolm,' she said simply. It was a moment that would live for ever in Little Malcolm's life. He stood up to his full height, pressed his cheek against her breasts and knew his life was complete.

Back in Bilbo Cottage, Beth and I were curled up on the sofa watching television. It was the wonderfully poignant film *Papillon*, with Steve McQueen and Dustin Hoffman, and I was happy in my peaceful world. Beth's head was on my shoulder and her hair brushed lightly against my cheek. It occurred to me that cuddling up next to the one you love is very precious.

As snow began to fall again over the vast plain of York, unknown to me on this cold winter night, the two bin-men of Ragley-on-the-Forest were thinking exactly the same thing.

Chapter Eleven

Full English Breakfast

County Hall requested responses to their proposal for a common geography syllabus in North Yorkshire schools with an emphasis on 'European Awareness'.

Extract from the Ragley School Logbook:
Tuesday, 1 February 1983

The silence of snow rested on the frozen earth. As I peered through the bedroom window it seemed as if all sound was muted. Under its smooth white blanket the world was still as stone. It was the first day of February and the villages of Yorkshire were held fast in the grip of winter.

However, a vision of warm days in southern France was flickering through the mind of Nora Pratt as she wrote a sign for the door of her Coffee Shop. It read:

Bonjour
CONTINENTAL BREAKFAST
7 a.m. onwards

And it seemed that early mornings in Ragley village were about to change.

It was 7 a.m. and Beth and I were in our dressing gowns, drinking tea in front of the television. We had set the alarm a little earlier than usual in order to watch the launch of the new TV-am *Good Morning Britain* programme on ITV. We sat there cuddled up on the sofa waiting for this momentous event in British television history.

The screen flickered into life. 'Hello, good morning and welcome,' said David Frost. He made it clear that he, Anna Ford, Robert Kee, Angela Rippon and Michael Parkinson would not be with us *all* the time and it occurred to me that *we* wouldn't be there either. The journey to school on this snowy morning would take longer than usual.

The programme seemed to go well, with few hitches. A young lady called in to complain about striking water men. John Cleese appeared in his pyjamas and David Philpott, the weatherman, got it just about right when he said, 'The story today is really one of wind'. We switched off, showered and dressed, then, after a bowl of porridge, we cleared the snow from our cars and drove slowly away.

Meanwhile, in the spacious kitchen of Morton Manor, Vera was enjoying a cup of Earl Grey tea to the soothing sound of Wagner and Haydn on Radio 3's *Morning Concert* and praying that her dear brother was coping without her. She was also wondering in which cupboard she should put her mother's treasured weighing scales and set of brass weights . . . *imperial* measures, of course. It was then that she heard the sound of the television in Rupert's study. 'Television,' she murmured, 'at shortly after seven in the morning. What is the world coming to?' She crossed the vast entrance hall, looked round the study door and there was Rupert, staring at his little television set, watching the weather forecast. 'Snow today, dear,' he said. Vera shook her head. She didn't need a young woman in a revealing dress to tell her what was already patently obvious. When she walked back to the hallway the sound of another television could be heard coming from Virginia's bedroom. To make matters worse, it sounded as if she was doing some form of energetic aerobics to the sound of rather vulgar music.

As Vera shut the kitchen door with some relief, it occurred to her that married life, on occasion, wasn't always sweetness and light. She turned up the volume control on the radio, picked up the tea strainer and poured herself a second cup of tea. Outside, in the high elm trees, a parliament of rooks stared down with beady eyes from their lofty perch at the commotion below. The world had suddenly become a noisier place.

BBC *Breakfast Time* had begun in mid-January and we learned that 35 per cent of all households in England had watched the first show with Frank Bough and Selina Scott. Our early-morning habits were changing and, in the living rooms of England, television had become the background wallpaper of the nation.

But not everyone had tuned in. Anne Grainger switched on her radio and looked out of her kitchen window on the Crescent. In the far distance, the leaden sky over the Hambleton hills promised more snow. On Radio 2 the hit single 'Our House' by Madness blared out and Anne reflected that living with John and his latest DIY project, namely mixer taps that didn't work, was very much like living in a madhouse.

On the way into school I eased my Morris Minor Traveller over the frozen forecourt of Victor Pratt's garage and pulled up next to the single pump. Victor wandered out, a thick, grease-stained scarf round his neck.

'Mornin', Mr Sheffield,' he said. 'Big day f'our Nora. She's goin' continental an' doin' Frenchified breakfasts.'

'And why's that, Victor?' I asked.

'Summat abart educatin' the locals she said . . . burra don't fancy it m'self, 'specially this morning. Ah gorra touch o' that bumbago.'

Fortunately I was a past master at interpreting Victor's many ailments. 'Oh dear,' I said, '*lumbago* is very painful.'

'Y'reight there, Mr Sheffield . . . speshully in y'bum,' and he limped away to get my change while rubbing his ample backside.

Meanwhile, on Ragley High Street, in the Coffee Shop, Nora Pratt was keen to give her customers a continental experience. She had read an article about Brigitte Bardot in her *Woman* magazine on the same day that she was offered a cut-price deal on a box of croissants. 'You an' me, Dowothy, aren't jus' Bwitish,' said Nora knowingly, 'but also Euwopeans.'

However, when Big Dave and Little Malcolm parked

their bin wagon outside and walked in, *entente cordiale* wasn't uppermost on their minds.

'Bloody 'ell,' said Big Dave when he spotted the tray of croissants at the front of the display cabinet. 'What's goin' on 'ere?'

''Ow d'you mean, Dave?' asked Dorothy.

'What's this, er, *cross-aunt* in aid of then?' asked Big Dave, looking at the label above the strange pastries. Big Dave had always been happy with the usual supply of pork pies and rock buns. He even turned a blind eye to the occasional cream horn purchased by the more adventurous customer, but this was different . . . and the spelling made no sense.

'It's a cwoissant,' said Nora confidently and with a passable French accent. Her pronunciation was perfect because, of course, she was blissfully unaware that this was one time in her life when the letter 'r' could be pronounced as a 'w'.

'So what is it?' asked Big Dave, none the wiser.

'Looks like, er, puff pastry t'me, Dave,' said Little Malcolm hesitantly.

'*Puff* pastry . . . *puff* pastry!' exclaimed Big Dave. 'We don't want none o' that nancy boy stuff round 'ere, Nora.'

'It's Fwench,' said Nora. 'It's what they 'ave f'bweakfast in Pawis.'

'No wonder they can't play football,' grumbled Big Dave.

'Y'reight there, Dave,' said Little Malcolm.

Nora shook her head sadly and then walked away to the juke-box where she studied the selection of records.

Dorothy returned from clearing the tables, leant over

the counter and whispered conspiratorially, 'They'll never catch on, Dave. Y'can't slice 'em like proper bread an' they go all crumbly when y'butter 'em.'

At the juke-box Nora pressed Y17, selected Sacha Distel and began to sing, 'Waindwops keep falling on my head.'

'She's been singing them French songs all morning,' said Dorothy, shaking her head, ''specially that 'unky Sasha Distillery.'

'Y'reight there, Dorothy,' said Little Malcolm.

'So . . . what's it t'be, Dave?' asked Dorothy.

'Usual please, luv,' said Big Dave while Little Malcolm stared up lovingly at the girl of his dreams.

'OK,' said Dorothy, 'two bacon butties an' two large mugs o' sweet tea coming up.'

As I drove past the village green, the school came into view, transformed in its winter coat. The belltower resembled Santa's grotto, with a perfect curve of fresh snow resting on each roof slate and icicles hanging from the eaves of the entrance porch. On the metal railings that bordered the playground, every fleur-de-lis was crowned with frozen crystals that sparkled in the low morning sunlight.

Two crates of milk for the infant classes were stacked outside the entrance and, on this freezing cold morning, the milk had frozen and forced the silver foil tops from the bottles. A desperate blue tit, perched on one of the bottles, was pecking furiously for his breakfast and fluttered away as I walked across the playground.

Ruby was spreading gritty sand from an old enamel

bucket on to the path from the driveway to the play-ground. It was clear she was back to her old self. 'It's like the bloomin' Hantarctic, Mr Sheffield,' she said. How-ever, she seemed unperturbed by the chill wind that was cutting like a knife through my old duffel coat.

'So how are you today, Ruby?' I asked.

'Fit as a flea, Mr Sheffield.'

'And how's little Krystal?'

'Startin' t'crawl now, thank you f'asking,' said Ruby. 'An', by the way, that posh lady, Mrs Dudley-Palmer, dropped 'er daughters off early so ah sent 'em in to 'elp Mrs Grainger get 'er classroom shaped up for t'little uns. 'Ope y'don't mind but they looked proper froz', poor little mites.'

'That's fine, Ruby,' I said, 'so long as they're supervised,' and I hurried in.

Behind me Terry Earnshaw was walking up the school drive sucking an icicle as if it were an ice lolly.

'A cat could have wee'd on that, Terry,' said Michelle Cathcart in mock disgust, but secretly admiring Terry's disregard for danger.

'Ah don't care,' said Terry, breaking off the end and crunching it between his teeth. However, he noticed that his icicle did appear to have a slightly yellowish tinge and, when the coast was clear, he climbed on to the school dustbins and selected a new icicle hanging from the gutter of the boiler house.

At the gate, Pauline Paxton was saying goodbye to nine-year-old Molly. 'Now work 'ard an' try y'best,' said Pauline and kissed her rosy-cheeked daughter.

'Ah allus do, Mam,' said Molly, ''xcept maths is a lot

'arder now. Yesterday we did decimals and today we're doing fractures.'

'Sounds painful luv,' said Pauline with a smile as she hurried off to catch William Featherstone's coach into York.

In the office, Vera held up a smart spiral-bound document. 'It's from County Hall, Mr Sheffield,' she said with a frown, 'and you need to respond to it.'

'What is it this time?' I asked.

'The one that wants us all to be Europeans,' she said coldly as she placed it on my desk.

'Oh dear,' I said.

'Don't worry, Mr Sheffield,' said Vera as she removed the cover of her electric typewriter. 'Mrs Thatcher will never allow it.'

It was clear throughout morning school that the children were itching to get out on to the school field to enjoy the fresh snowfall. So it was that at half past ten nearly ninety children donned boots, coats, scarves and gloves and hurried out to make snowmen, build igloos and throw snowballs. As we shivered round the gas fire in the staff-room I found it hard to remember a time when I had the same sort of fun and never felt the cold.

After morning break, in the reception class Charlie Cartwright and Ted Coggins had sopping wet feet, so Anne put their shoes and socks next to the hot-water pipes. The two little boys seemed to approve of the new freedom and wiggled their toes.

'Mrs Grainger,' said Charlie, 'ah'd like t'be a Hafrican an' 'ave bare feet.'

'An' ah'd like t'be a Hindian, Mrs Grainger,' said Ted, 'wi' bare feet *an'* feathers.'

And Anne recalled why it was that she made a choice early in her career to teach young children and smiled at the memory.

In Class 3, Sally was busy with her cities of the world project. 'Now girls and boys, Istanbul is the largest city in which country?' she asked, pointing at the large map of the world. There was a scratching of heads. This was obviously a tough one. Sally decided to offer a clue. 'We eat a lot of it at Christmas,' she added helpfully. Terry Earnshaw's hand shot up.

'Yes, Terry?' asked Sue.

'Greece, Miss,' said Terry, quick as a flash.

And Sally also recalled her decision to become a teacher and wondered if working in a bank gave the same job satisfaction.

At the end of school, the setting sun, like a fiery bronze shield, had dipped its circular rim below the Hambleton hills and the clouds were backlit with purple winter fire. Darkness was falling fast and soon the bright stars would mount their nightly vigil over the plain of York.

In Sally Pringle's classroom, Ruby was clearing up. ''Ere's an old paintbrush, Mrs Pringle,' said Ruby, 'wi' a bit o' life left in it.'

Sally looked up from mounting the children's artwork on large sheets of sugar paper. 'Thank you, Ruby, it all helps, particularly with all the cutbacks in the school budget.'

'Cutbacks – don't talk t'me about cutbacks,' said Ruby

and she stopped emptying the bin. 'We're all mekkin' cutbacks, Mrs Pringle,' she said with feeling. She took a chamois leather from the pocket of her overall and let it dangle between a calloused finger and thumb. 'Look at this. There's no *shammy* left in me leather. It's gone all limp . . . a bit like my Ronnie.'

Meanwhile, in the darkness of the council estate, Heathcliffe and Terry Earnshaw walked slowly home and said a polite but cautious hello to Mr Connelly as he walked hesitantly on the frozen footpath with his guide dog and white stick.

When he was out of earshot, Terry turned knowingly to his big brother. "Eath, ah know why Mr Connelly can't drive 'is car,' he said.

Heathcliffe wondered where this was going. 'Why not?' he asked.

"Cause they won't allow 'is dog on t'front seat wi' 'im,' said Terry.

It was Beth's night at Leeds University, so I worked late on a document for County Hall about the place for a common geography syllabus in North Yorkshire schools. The new emphasis was to be on 'European Awareness' and I realized the world was changing. By seven o'clock I had completed the report and my tummy was rumbling. The thought of hot food on the other side of the village green was hard to resist and the bright orange lights outside The Royal Oak were a welcome sight on this bitterly cold evening.

At the bar, pipe and cigarette smoke hung heavy, like

an undertaker's shroud, and my eyes smarted as I ordered my pint of Chestnut Mild. Sheila was wearing her familiar bright-pink blouse, complete with *Dallas* shoulder pads, a black leather miniskirt and enough hairspray to stop a clock at ten paces. With her Dusty Springfield mascara, she felt like a million dollars.

'Bit smoky in here tonight, Sheila,' I said.

'Goes 'and in 'and wi' drinking, Mr Sheffield,' said Sheila as she pulled on the hand pump. 'Allus 'as, allus will.'

Don looked up from the lounge bar. 'They go t'gether like fish an' chips, Mr Sheffield.'

'Or an 'orse an' carriage,' added Old Tommy Piercy from behind a cloud of Old Holborn tobacco.

'Or Cagney an' Lacey,' said Stevie 'Supersub' Cole-clough from the midst of the Ragley Rovers football team. This was immediately followed by an in-depth discussion among the footballers as to who was the more attractive of the two American detectives. The claims by Clint Ramsbottom that Lacey was more sensitive and definitely more intelligent gained little support and the blonde won hands down.

In the familiar world of the taproom, some age-old Yorkshire customs were being challenged. 'My round,' said Shane Ramsbottom. He lit up a Piccadilly King Size filter cigarette and wandered over to the bar.

'Ah'll 'ave a lager,' said his brother Clint.

There was an intake of breath from the rest of the football team.

'Lager!' said Shane in disbelief. 'Y'can't drink lager. That's a southerner's drink, y'big nancy.'

'Sorry, Shane,' said Clint hurriedly, 'mek it a bitter.' He blushed and his red cheeks clashed horribly with the orange David Bowie streaks in his hair.

'Ah should think so,' said Shane. 'Ah'm gettin' worried abart you wi' y'dyed 'air an' puffy shirts.'

'An' 'is earring,' said Big Dave.

'An' black eyeliner,' added Little Malcolm for good measure.

One thing was certain in Clint's mind. He wasn't going to order a lager again in The Royal Oak.

Don began to pull the pints, flexing his ex-wrestler's biceps. He knew his customers and smiled. It was well known that Don only ordered one nine-gallon firkin of Carlsberg lager per week for the passing trade. It wasn't a popular drink with this bastion of Yorkshire drinkers, where mild or bitter was the usual order of the day. Even so, Don had noticed an increase in lager sales as each year went by. Times were changing but, in this rural community, some old habits seemed as though they would never die and Don smiled as he heard the familiar cry from the dominoes table.

'Sheila luv, 'nother three Little Olds please,' shouted ploughman Frank Middleton from the far corner of the taproom. Don had just carried up from the cellar a crate of twenty-four bottles of very strong John Smith's beer, known as 'Little Olds', for the three brothers, Frank, Ollie and Keith Middleton, local agricultural labourers with heavy thirsts. After their day's work, they would settle down at the dominoes table and order the 'Special' from the blackboard plus the strong beer. They would each drink eight bottles while playing their fives-and-threes dominoes game. It was a ritual that never changed.

'Did y'watch it then, Dave?' asked Don the barman as he wiped a pint pot with his York City tea towel.

''E means that new brekfas' telly what started this morning,' added Sheila as she leant over the bar to give the Ragley football team a substantial glimpse of the finest cleavage in the village.

'No . . . it'll never catch on,' said Big Dave knowingly.

'Y'reight there, Dave,' added Little Malcolm, his ever-faithful supporter.

'Ah'm not so sure, Dave,' said Chris 'Kojak' Wojcie-chowski, whose broad Yorkshire accent belied his Polish ancestry. Chris, the Bald-Headed Ball Wizard, was never frightened to offer an opinion.

''Ow d'you mean?' asked Big Dave, who, as team captain, considered his word to be law.

'That Selina Scott's a bit o' 'ot stuff,' said Chris.

'Ah, well, now y'talkin',' said Big Dave, nodding in approval. 'She's loads more sexy than that Angela whats-'er-name.'

'Rippon,' added the Ball Wizard quickly.

A conversation broke out with every member of the team describing their favourite female presenter in graphic detail.

'She's got lovely legs, though, that Angela Rippon,' interjected Sheila as she walked to the far end of the bar, 'an' she can dance.'

Don gazed after his wife, an admiring look in his eyes. 'But she 'asn't got a figure like my Sheila,' he said.

'Y'reight there,' said Little Malcolm.

'It's eighth wonder o' t'world,' said Don proudly.

'So what's t'other seven then?' asked Shane.

'Well there's them 'anging gardens o' Sally Lunn,' said Clint.

'An' them pyramids what Elizabeth Taylor built in *Cleopatra*,' said Don. And that's as far as they got.

Meanwhile, I was feeling hungry and I looked up at the 'Specials' board. It had changed. Sheila's cousin, John Fotheringdale from Thirkby, was the only member of Sheila's family with any academic qualifications. So his 'C' grade in GCE Art O-level made it inevitable that he would be commissioned to paint the new bar meals menu. On a large blackboard in neat white paint it read:

Home-made Soup
Chicken & Chips (in a basket)
Gammon & Pineapple (or fried egg)
Steak & Chips
Fish & Chips
Mixed Grill
Rabbit Pie
Desperate Dan Cow Pie
Chilli con Carne

The rabbit pie came courtesy of Pete the poacher, who turned up at odd times of the day with a sack over his shoulder. Likewise, he was the main provider of the contents of the soup, occasionally a bag of carrots or a bunch of nettles, depending on the season. Usually there was a lot of light-hearted bartering between Sheila and Pete that always ended in a free pint for our local poacher before he left once again to go 'lamping' in the dark with Sniffer, his lurcher dog.

The Desperate Dan Cow Pie, a favourite of Deke Ramsbottom, was in fact a steak pie with a pastry top on which two pastry horns stood like a Viking helmet. A string of liquorice was the final embellishment for a tail.

Big Dave and Little Malcolm joined me in staring at the new menu. They didn't like change. The introduction of the television above the bar in the taproom had caused them enough concern. 'Chilli con carne!' exclaimed Big Dave, *'Chilli con carne!'*

'Y'reight there, Dave,' agreed Little Malcolm. 'It's chilli con carne all reight.'

'It's Sheila's new menu, lads,' said Don the barman, nodding sagely.

'But that's foreign muck,' said Big Dave.

'Now then, Dave, don't let my Sheila 'ear y'say that, said Don. 'We're movin' wi' t'times.'

'An' t'fish shop in Easington 'as jus' turned into a Chinese takeaway,' said Shane. 'An' this is s'pposed t'be England.'

Don looked at me apologetically. 'Don't get t'wrong idea, Mr Sheffield,' he said. 'Ah'm norra racist . . . in fac' ah quite like a curry.'

'Mebbe so, Don,' said Big Dave, 'but we're *English* an' we want proper *English* food.'

'Well they say a change is as good as a rest,' said Don, trying his best to placate the big goalkeeper.

'That's what Nora Pratt said this morning, Don,' said Big Dave darkly, 'an' she still 'asn't shifted any o' them Frenchified cross-aunts.'

I ordered the mixed grill and set off for a quiet corner table. As I passed Old Tommy Piercy he whispered in my ear, 'Y'can tell a Yorkshireman, Mr Sheffield . . . but y'can't tell 'im much.'

The next morning I was listening to the incongruous but beautifully melodious duo of David Bowie and Bing Crosby singing 'Peace on Earth' when I drove up Ragley High Street. I saw Nora Pratt sticking a new poster on the door of her Coffee Shop and smiled. It read:

Good Morning
FULL ENGLISH BREAKFAST
7 a.m. onwards

Chapter Twelve

The Ragley Book Club

*The School Library van visited today and the children and
staff changed their books. Reading workshop took place in
the school hall at 11 a.m.*

Extract from the Ragley School Logbook:
Monday, 14 February 1983

Petula Dudley-Palmer looked out of her state-of-the-art
double-glazed conservatory at the silent winter world
beyond and realized she was lonely. The new telephone
on the glass-topped cane coffee table was the latest in
design technology with a long-lead curly white flex. This
meant she could walk around the expensively tiled floor
while engaged in conversation. However, there was just
one problem: there was no one to ring.

She had just unpacked her brand-new folding exercise
bike, a Valentine's Day present from Geoffrey. However, it
occurred to her that this was yet another *solitary* occupation.
The search for a perfect body was losing its appeal. Then

she picked up her *Woman* magazine and read the headline 'Positivity for Women – are you a social success?' She shook her head sadly and read on. There were lots of hints and suggestions, but one stood out above all others and suddenly she knew what she must do. Excitement coursed through her veins. It was time to grasp the nettle – although metaphorically of course, as she realized no one in their right mind would pick up a stinging nettle with their bare hands. It was time for a new direction . . . it was time to be *positive* . . . it was time to start Ragley's first ever Book Club.

'Mutton dressed as lamb,' whispered Margery Ackroyd as Petula Dudley-Palmer walked across the playground wearing her new mahogany-stranded full length mink coat. At £995 she had convinced Geoffrey that it was money well spent.

I was emerging from the stock cupboard with a new box of white chalk when Mrs Dudley-Palmer suddenly appeared. 'Good morning, Mr Sheffield,' she said. 'I wondered if you would mind me putting this notice on the board in the entrance hall? So far I've put one outside the village hall and another in The Royal Oak. I'll probably ask all the shopkeepers as well.'

The notice read:

Join the
RAGLEY BOOK CLUB
Wednesday, 16 February 1983
7.30 p.m.
No. 38, High Street, Ragley.
Please bring a book of your choice.
Light refreshments.

'Yes, that's fine, Mrs Dudley-Palmer,' I said, scanning the poster, 'and I'm sure there will be a lot of interest.'

'I do hope so,' she said and hurried off.

Jo Hunter had just collected her dinner register from Vera and heard the conversation. She glanced at the notice in wonderment. 'Wow . . . photocopied,' she said wistfully. 'I wonder if I'll ever work in a school with a photocopier.'

At morning break Vera was making milky coffee. 'Mr Sheffield, the mobile library will be in the car park at lunchtime,' she said, 'so I'll organize the children's visits, shall I?'

'Yes, thanks, Vera,' I said.

Jo was reading the front page of Vera's *Daily Telegraph*. 'A library van would have probably made a good getaway vehicle,' she mused. 'They've not found that racehorse yet.'

Last week, a gang of six armed men had kidnapped Shergar, the world's most famous racehorse. According to his owner the Aga Khan, the horse was worth $10 million.

'I heard it was the Provisional IRA,' said Sally.

'Well, it's got to turn up,' said Jo, 'I mean to say, how can you hide a racehorse?'

Meanwhile, outside in the corridor I heard Ruby unlocking her caretaker's store cupboard. As she donned her overall she paused to read the Book Club notice and stood for a while, thinking hard.

Ruby came in each day to put out the dining tables in the school hall for our daily Reading Workshop, which began at eleven o'clock. For the period before lunchtime, parents and grandparents came in to support this event, which had proved to be very successful and had significantly increased the frequency of reading among the children. Boys and girls from all classes wandered in clutching their school reading book and a reading card. The parents listened to them read, noted any problems or words they found difficult to pronounce and jotted these down on the child's card. When they returned to class their teacher checked their card and supported the child appropriately. The workshop also provided an opportunity for parents to be involved in our day-to-day school life and further encouraged good communication. As was often the case, the regular opportunity for a two-minute conversation with a parent by the classroom door was more valuable than an end-of-term Open Evening report.

When Ruby had finished setting out the tables and chairs she tapped on the office door. "Scuse me, Miss Evans . . . ah mean Mrs Forbes-Kitchener,' she said, 'ah'd like to ask yer advice.'

'Of course, Ruby,' said Vera as she filed a letter to the school governors concerning our proposed educational visit to Flamingo Land in the summer term. 'What can I do to help?'

'Well, ah was wond'rin', do y'think this Book Club is f'likes o' me?' she asked.

Vera felt the sadness in Ruby's heart; it was almost palpable. 'I'm sure it is, Ruby,' she said. 'It's never too late to enjoy books.'

'Well,' continued Ruby, 'top an' bottom of it is,' she paused, looked down at the handle of the staff-room door and began to polish it absent-mindedly, 'ah've allus wanted t'read but ah've never 'ad time what wi' cookin' an' cleanin' and children . . . an' my Ronnie, o' course.'

Vera sighed and looked at her dear friend. 'You have talent, Ruby, and you must not let it wither like the last leaves of winter,' she said softly.

'Y'say such wonderful things,' said Ruby, looking as if she was about to burst into tears. 'An' ah 'ear what y'say, an' ah will do m'best. It's jus' ah'm a bit nervous. Rest of 'em might laugh at me.'

Vera took a deep breath and made a decision. 'Then I'll come with you, Ruby. After all, that's what friends are for.'

Meanwhile there was a hum of activity in the school hall as our Reading Workshop got under way. Sixty-five-year-old Edith Icklethwaite was sitting next to her granddaughter, five-year-old Katie. Edith had brought in some old photographs of her son's wedding to use as a talking point before listening to Katie reading her *Ginn Reading 360* graded story book.

'An' these are pictures of y'mum and dad's wedding,' said Edith.

Katie stared at the photographs of Mr and Mrs Icklethwaite on their wedding day. 'So, Katie my love, do y'understand what a wedding is now?'

'Yes, Grandma,' said Katie. 'It's when Daddy paid the vicar for Mummy to come and work for us.'

Edith sighed and wondered what children were coming to these days.

She decided on a new tack and began pointing at

different colours on the cover of the reading book. After all, as *her* mother had told her sixty years ago, it was important to learn something new every day. 'And what colour is this?' asked Edith.

'Red, Grandma.'

'And this one?'

'That's easy, blue.'

After pointing to ten different colours with Katie giving an accurate answer every time, the little girl looked a little weary.

'Grandma, maybe you should try t'work these colours out for y'self,' said little Katie, shaking her head sadly. 'After all, a grandma should know these things.'

Edith opened Katie's reading book. 'C'mon,' she said brusquely, 'let's get on wi' t'reading.' It occurred to her that it wasn't only children who learned something new every day.

At lunchtime Rosie Backhouse parked her mobile library van in the school car park and was ready for business. The children went in, a few at a time, and loved the opportunity to select from such a huge range of books, and Rosie always did her best to encourage them.

When I went in with my class I noticed Rosie had stuck a new label on the side of the tiny wooden counter. It read: IF YOU ARE NOT ABLE TO READ PLEASE TAKE A LEAFLET: IT WILL TELL YOU HOW TO GET LESSONS. I made no comment . . . after all, the left-handed Rosie had stamped so many library books it was rumoured she had a left hook like Henry Cooper.

As I left I noticed Ruby was being led into the van by

Vera. 'Excuse me, Rosie,' said Vera, 'we need a good book for Ruby. She wants to get back into reading.'

Rosie knew Ruby's background and immediately began to search through the fiction section.

Suddenly Ruby pointed to a novel. 'Mrs Back'ouse, this is what our 'Azel is reading in Mrs Pringle's class,' she said in surprise, picking up the popular Sixties paperback *A Hundred Million Francs* by Paul Berna.

Rosie gave Vera a knowing look and Vera nodded in acknowledgement. This was a children's book, but also the kind that could be enjoyed by an adult. 'A good choice, Ruby,' said Rosie. 'I'll stamp it for you.'

Ruby looked at the book as if she had won the Pools. 'Ah can read it an' then talk to our 'Azel about it,' she said full of excitement.

Both Rosie and Vera looked with some sadness as Ragley's favourite caretaker hurried off down the drive with her first ever library book. That afternoon she began to read, at first hesitantly, but gradually she got into the story, which was a French version of the great train robbery: a missing fortune in banknotes and the unsuspecting gang of children who were destined to solve the mystery. When Ruby arrived for her end-of-school shift, the novel was sticking out of her overall pocket.

She popped her head round the office door. 'Smashing story,' she said. 'Thanks ever so much . . . ah'm reight enjoying me book.'

That evening Ruby was babysitting while watching *Wish You Were Here . . . ?* on television. Judith Chalmers with her permanent suntan was enjoying the scenery in Corfu, but Ruby's thoughts were closer to home.

She looked down at her rosy-cheeked granddaughter and, as she rocked little Krystal to sleep, she whispered to the sleeping child, 'When ah get paid my love, ah'm gonna buy you a book, an' we can read it t'gether. Then when y'grow up y'can read lots o' books an' mebbe go t'one o' them universities that posh people go to. Ah don't want you t'grow up like me, cleanin' an' suchlike. Ah want a better life f'you.' And the little girl slept on, unaware of the love that was destined to fill her life.

On Tuesday morning, I looked across the breakfast table at two beautiful women, both slim, green-eyed blondes but a generation apart. Beth's mother, Diane, had come up from Hampshire to stay for a few days. Today Beth had arranged for the morning off work to go for a scan at the antenatal clinic and Diane was going to drive her there and keep her company.

'It will be fine,' said Diane. 'You'll need to drink a pint of water before going in and the radiographer will rub some cold gel on your stomach. Then you'll see an image of the baby on the screen. It's all very straightforward.'

'Yes, mother,' said Beth with a tired smile. 'I do know all this . . . but I appreciate your help,' she added quickly.

On the radio Joe Cocker and Jennifer Warnes were singing their Top Ten hit 'Up Where We Belong', quickly followed by Men at Work with 'Down Under', which somehow seemed appropriate.

*   *   *

By late that afternoon, tongues were wagging in the General Stores – none more so than Margery Ackroyd's.

'Have yer 'eard about t'eadteacher's wife?' she asked. The others in the queue were used to Margery's rhetorical questions. 'She's been for a scan in York. Betty Buttle saw 'er goin' in.'

Prudence Golightly called a halt to the conversation. 'Next please,' she said loudly. Prudence hated gossip . . . except this was *interesting* gossip. Happily, Theresa Ackroyd and her eight-year-old sister Charlotte had other things on their mind and ran home to watch *Mr Magoo* on Channel 4.

On Wednesday morning Petula Dudley-Palmer, complete with a green leotard and matching headband, had just completed her morning workout in front of the television set. Diana Moran, the 'Green Goddess', had performed her energetic routine and Petula had accompanied each stretch and gyration.

'Today's the day,' murmured Petula to herself, breathing heavily. 'Book Club day,' and she walked out of the lounge towards their new downstairs shower and wondered what she should wear for the historic inaugural meeting. It was a difficult choice: classical elegance, or the casual, understated artist with the obligatory silk scarf? As she hurried through the spacious entrance hall, she looked at the pseudo-American grandfather clock and realized she had only eleven hours to decide.

Back in school, Joseph had called in for his weekly religious education lesson today instead of on Friday, when he had to attend an ecclesiastical conference in Leeds.

He spent an hour with Sally's class on the theme of 'Prayers'. Some of the follow-up writing was interesting to say the least.

Terry Earnshaw had written, 'Dear Lord, it must be hard for you to love EVERYONE in the whole world. There's only five in our family and I find it a struggle.'

Molly Paxton's prayer was particularly poignant. 'Dear Lord, thank you for my new baby brother even though I asked you for a tortoise.'

And Rowena Buttle had written, 'Dear Lord, it's been a long time since Christmas and it's a long time to Easter when my mummy hides chocolate eggs in the bread bin. So please can we have a proper in-between holiday with presents because there's nothing good in February.'

It struck me that the older I got, the faster the months seemed to fly by. Occasionally it needed a nine-year-old to remind us that, for children, time moves at a different pace. Childhood really was a secret garden that we had left far behind, but just occasionally, if we stopped long enough to listen – really listen – we could begin to understand *their* world and try to be a part of it again.

That evening, at number 38, Petula was in her luxury home and everything was ready: drinks, nibbles and background music. She looked at her fitted kitchen, in beautiful Snowden Oak direct from Debenhams department store in Leeds, and knew it was a joy to behold. Every labour-saving device, from the electric tin-opener to the microwave oven to the latest Kenwood blender, was available to her, along with a multitude of gadgets that had since been removed to the garage, including a sodastream, a Breville sandwich toaster and a fondue set. Every cupboard was filled with Tupperware containers of all shapes and sizes and each one had been carefully labelled. It was, in fact, the perfect kitchen.

In the spacious lounge the smell of furniture polish competed with the scent of potpourri, and small bowls of olives, nuts and crisps had been placed on Portmeirion coasters. Her favourite Cliff Richard album, *Love Songs*, with twenty romantic ballads, was playing softly and she hummed along to 'We Don't Talk Anymore' and, predictably, thought of her husband Geoffrey. These days he spent less time with her and more time playing 'tennis' with his Atari 2600 video game with its woodgrain console, plastic paddles and stubby rubber joystick.

The lounge was filling up quickly with ladies from all corners of the village, most of them holding a book. Audrey Bustard was showing a well-thumbed paperback, *The Bitch* by Jackie Collins, to Betty Buttle, who had brought her favourite Mills & Boon, *Rampant Lust in the Farmyard*. On the leather sofa, Felicity Miles-Humphreys was in animated conversation with Amelia Duff about her copy of *Jonathan Livingston Seagull* by Richard Bach, while Amelia held fast to her John Fowles classic, *The French Lieutenant's Woman*. Meanwhile, Nora Pratt and Diane Wigglesworth had brought their shared copy of Jilly Cooper's *Love and Other Heartaches*, and Elsie Crapper had brought her favourite hymn book.

Julie Earnshaw and Betty Icklethwaite hadn't brought a book. Neither had Margery Ackroyd, who had merely come to check out Petula's kitchen appliances. Delia Morgetroyd, the milkman's wife from Morton, had brought her Family Album catalogue. 'Well, ah got a super 'airstyling brush and blow-dryer wi' m'first order,' said Delia. 'Y'can't lose,' she added with emphasis. 'What more can y'ask for?'

Sheila Bradshaw arrived late from The Royal Oak with *The Joy of Sex*, which was passed around with great enthusiasm during the refreshment break. Also, a small balding man with thick spectacles and wearing an immaculate three-piece suit had arrived.

'It's a man!' said Petula in surprise.

'Well, y'didn't say jus' ladies on y'poster, Petula,' said Margery, 'an' 'e looks 'armless enough.'

Bernard Edmund Hillary Brocklebank, known as 'Boring Bernard' to his workmates, was born in St James's Hospital in Leeds in 1953, just after Mount Everest was conquered. His father had hoped for a brave and adventurous son, but it wasn't to be. Bernard was a sensitive soul who hated doing anything athletic and suffered from vertigo. In fact, he had dizzy spells when looking out of the bedroom window. As an assistant to a tailor in the centre of York, he was happy cutting and stitching three-piece business suits. However, Bernard had recently taken up reading and in his spare time he had begun to study the *Encyclopædia Britannica*. Now, at the age of twenty-nine, he had reached the letter B. He carried the heavy tome under his arm and Petula tried to avoid eye contact.

It was time to bring the meeting to order. Petula picked up her favourite novel, *Love Story* by Erich Segal, and scanned the circle of book-lovers as they settled in their seats, frowning as she did so at Betty Buttle. It was a known fact in the village that Betty Buttle drank her tea from a saucer, often with much slurping, so Margery Ackroyd had reliably informed her. However, it was also common knowledge that Margery's husband, Wendell, the Rowntree's Smarties packer, ate peas off his knife, so it really was a case of the pot calling the kettle black.

'Good evening, ladies . . . and, of course, our solitary man,' said Petula.

'No man is an Iceland, as they say,' said Betty Buttle, putting down her cup and saucer with a clatter.

'And welcome to the first meeting of the Ragley Book Club,' continued Petula, undeterred. 'First of all, we need to elect a chairwoman,' she said, giving an enigmatic smile to the assembled throng and ignoring Bernard's puzzled look. This went unnoticed as the first sign of cliques began to emerge.

'I'd like to pwopose Diane,' said Nora Pratt, looking across at her hairdresser friend. 'She does a lot o' weading.'

'Ah'm not fussed,' said Diane, looking for an ashtray. ''Ow about you, Amelia?'

Amelia Duff, the timid postmistress, immediately flushed. 'I'm happy to be on a committee if there is one, but I don't want to push myself forward. How about you, Felicity?'

Felicity Miles-Humphreys, the self-appointed producer of the Ragley Amateur Dramatic Society, looked up from under her bright-red headband. 'Sorry, but I'm far too busy with my amateur dramatics,' she said with a theatrical wave of her kaftan that upset a bowl of roasted peanuts. 'So may I suggest Mrs Forbes-Kitchener?'

''Ear, 'ear,' said Ruby, who still hadn't got used to Vera's new title.

''Ear, 'ear,' echoed the throng, eager to move on.

'Well, that's kind of you, Felicity,' said Vera. She looked intently at Petula. 'But I do think it ought to be the person who thought of the idea in the first place and who is providing such wonderful hospitality this evening . . . namely, Petula.'

Petula looked suitably modest and, with a unanimous show of hands, Petula Dudley-Palmer achieved a landmark in her lonely life and became President of the Ragley Book Club.

'So what evening should we meet?' asked Petula.

An animated discussion followed that eliminated every night of the week owing to choir practice, bingo and favourite television programmes. However, a compromise was reached for the second Tuesday in every month except for July and August.

'And finally,' said Petula, 'I see most of you have brought a book along and we need to decide the first book we shall discuss at our next meeting.'

'Well, Ruby has just begun to read a lovely story about the adventures of young children in France who solve a bank robbery,' said Vera.

'That sounds a good 'un,' said Betty Buttle.

'Ah like a good adventure,' said Margery Ackroyd.

'And France is a really sexy place,' said Sheila Bradshaw.

'What's the book, Ruby?' asked Petula. 'And why did you select it?'

Ruby held up her copy of *A Hundred Million Francs* and took a deep breath. 'Well, ah jus' want t'say that ah'd f'gotten that reading can be, well . . . *different*. It were like goin' into someone else's world so t'speak. Mebbe that's what books are – sort of an 'oliday when y'f'get y'problems.' Ruby looked around, her face flushed, and Vera smiled, full of pride for her downtrodden friend. 'An' when ah've finished this,' added Ruby, 'ah'm gonna read *another* book.'

There was a silence as everyone realized something quite special had occurred. It was Petula who summed up. 'Well, Ruby, this makes it all worth while. I didn't really know what a Book Club was until this moment, but now I think I do. So thanks for sharing your thoughts with us.'

The next morning Petula Dudley-Palmer was in Reading Workshop. She sat back in her chair and stared at the next table, where Ruby was talking about her novel. Her daughter, little Hazel Smith, was loving every minute of it and, sitting next to her, nine-year-old Molly Paxton was hanging on every word.

Petula reflected that she had two intelligent and articulate daughters who were both voracious readers, but they never *shared* their stories. That afternoon she thought hard about the events of the past twenty-four hours and how it had affected her life.

So it was, for the first time in years, just before bedtime, Elisabeth Amelia and Victoria Alice snuggled up on the sofa with their mother and shared the story of *The Selfish Giant* by Oscar Wilde.

'That was lovely, Mummy,' said a sleepy Victoria Alice. 'Can we do it again tomorrow?'

Elisabeth Amelia simply gave her mother a hug. 'Thanks, Mummy,' she said. 'It's a pity Daddy couldn't hear our story.'

Our story, thought Petula . . . *our* story.

As they climbed the stairs together, she didn't feel lonely any more.

It was then that she understood.

The best Book Club begins not with a group of friends . . . but *within* the family.

Chapter Thirteen

The Cleethorpes Clairvoyant

County Hall sent out their latest 'vision statement', entitled 'School of the Future', plus a questionnaire concerning the need for a common curriculum.

Extract from the Ragley School Logbook:
Friday, 11 March 1983

It was just before 8.30 a.m. on Friday, 11 March and the conversation in the staff-room was proving livelier than usual.

'A clairvoyant!' said Sally. 'Tomorrow night in the village hall. Well, count *me* in.'

'Shall I pick you up?' asked Jo.

'Yes please,' said Sally. She stretched forward to pick up another custard cream from the tin on the staff-room table and then, when a cold shiver ran down her spine, she resisted the temptation.

'What about you, Anne?' asked Jo. 'It should be fun.'

'Well, I've seen the "Phoebe Duckworth" posters in the

High Street,' said Anne a little warily, 'and I must say I was curious, but don't you think it might be a bit, you know . . . *scary*?'

'I shouldn't think so,' said Jo. 'I heard from Margery Ackroyd that it was just an entertaining evening organized by the Village Hall Social Committee. They just wanted something *different* and apparently she offered them a reduced fee.'

'Fine,' said Anne. 'I'll come as well, but I know Vera's busy with Rupert at some high-society dinner, so she won't be there.'

'It's probably not Vera's thing anyway,' said Sally.

'And what about you, Jack?' asked Jo.

'I'm not sure,' I said. 'What exactly is a clairvoyant?'

'It means "clear vision", from seventeenth-century French,' said Sally, whose knowledge of obscure facts never ceased to amaze me. 'It's a form of extra-sensory perception – they study the paranormal.'

'I see,' I said hesitantly. 'OK, why not? It's certainly *different*.'

I returned to the morning post. County Hall's latest glossy-covered epistle, or 'vision statement' as they called it, entitled 'School of the Future', appeared as far-fetched as its predecessors. It seemed a waste of money. It occurred to me that perhaps they should have simply contacted a clairvoyant . . . and, by all accounts, Phoebe Duckworth came at a discount.

The arrival of a clairvoyant in Ragley-on-the-Forest had certainly created interest. In the High Street, out-side the village hall, Mrs Daphne Cathcart was staring with growing interest at a brightly coloured notice. It read:

Meet
Phoebe Duckworth
World-Famous Clairvoyant (from Cleethorpes)

Saturday, 5 March 1983

at 7.30 p.m.

in the Village Hall

Understand your psychic ability
Find your inner-self and that elusive sixth sense

Daphne had always known she had a sixth sense. The problem was that, on occasion, the other five didn't work all that well.

Meanwhile, across the road in Prudence Golightly's General Stores, a hint of scepticism was in the air. 'Not really my cup of tea,' said Prudence as she served Diane Wigglesworth with a pack of John Player King Size Extra Mild cigarettes.

'Mebbe we need t'keep an open mind, Prudence,' said Diane. 'Y'jus' never really know. Anyway, we're all going. You ought to come.'

'Perhaps,' said Prudence thoughtfully. 'Perhaps I will.'

Back in school, the Revd Joseph Evans was making his weekly visit. The morning had gone surprisingly well and Jo's class had hung on to every word of Joseph's rambling tale of Noah and the Ark . . . that is, until a few minutes before the end of the lesson.

'And Noah led all the animals into the ark, two by two,' said Joseph.

He was feeling confident for a change. The children in Class 2 were clearly animated by this morning's Bible story. It was almost time for the bell and Joseph asked for questions.

'Mr Evans, what did Noah eat?' asked the ever-practical Charlotte Ackroyd, '"cause 'e couldn't go shopping.'

Joseph pondered this for a moment.

'"E could collect eggs 'cause 'e 'ad 'ens,' said Barry Ollerenshaw helpfully.

'That's right. Well done, Barry,' said Joseph quickly. 'And, of course, he could have gone fishing,' he added with a burst of inspiration.

'Ah don't think so, Mr Evans,' said Sonia Trickle-bank, a serious and analytical little girl at the back of the class.

'You don't think so, Sonia? Why not?' asked Joseph, a little perplexed that his good idea had been squashed so emphatically.

'Well,' said Sonia, 'he'd 'ave only 'ad two worms.'

The bell rang and Joseph breathed a sigh of relief. He had survived another Friday morning.

At lunchtime I was on the playground talking to Daphne Cathcart, who had come to collect her daughter for a dental appointment. In the weak sunshine a group of girls were skipping. The two nine-year-olds, Michelle Cathcart and Louise Hartley, were winding the long rope and chanting:

Teddy bear, teddy bear, turn around.
Teddy bear, teddy bear, touch the ground.
Teddy bear, teddy bear, two high kicks.
Teddy bear, teddy bear, do the splits!

'Teks me back, Mr Sheffield,' said Mrs Cathcart. 'Ah used t'love skippin' when ah were young.'

'And how are you feeling today, Mrs Cathcart?' I asked. It was well known that Daphne was often depressed and my heart went out to this eccentric but steadfast single mother who would move mountains to protect her daughters. Her hair was dyed candy-floss pink and it blew in the wind.

'Not such a good day t'day, Mr Sheffield,' she said, 'but nowadays ah don't let it show . . . ah keep it to m'self.' Michelle ran to her mother and Daphne gave her a hug. They walked hand in hand down the cobbled drive and the bond of love between mother and daughter was clear to see. It was unconditional.

When I walked back into the office, the telephone rang. Vera was out returning the dinner registers so I picked up the receiver. It was Beth and she sounded a little weary.

'How are you?' I asked. 'Still tired?'

'Yes, Jack, and I've just started with backache.'

'Oh dear,' I said.

'Yes, the realities of pregnancy are just kicking in. In fact, it's hard to concentrate on the job sometimes.' There was a riffling of papers. 'So, what are you doing about this so-called *vision statement* from County Hall?'

'Just a quick response,' I said. 'It's pretty obvious they're paving the way for a nationwide common curriculum that will come sooner rather than later. I'm just going with the flow and accepting the inevitable.'

'Perhaps I could check out yours, Jack, before you send it back.'

'Fine, I'll bring it home tonight.'

'Thanks,' said Beth with a sigh.

'So I guess you won't be coming to see the world-famous clairvoyant on Saturday night then? Jo's organized a staff night out.'

Beth laughed. It was good to hear her sound cheerful again. 'Sadly no, Jack. You go and I'll use the time to finish my next assignment for the Masters course.'

She rang off and I stared out of the window. So much had happened to us since our first meeting . . . and now I was to become a father. It was a strange feeling, somewhere between elation and fear. Love was proving an uncertain companion.

At afternoon break, as a special treat, Shirley the cook had prepared a tray of piping-hot scones. With fresh butter and home-made strawberry jam, they were a veritable feast.

As we tucked in, Jo had gradually emerged as our unofficial entertainment officer. 'So we'll meet outside the village hall at seven fifteen and then go for a drink afterwards,' she said.

'The psychic Phoebe,' said Sally. 'I wonder what she's like.'

'I hope she doesn't communicate with my late Aunt Marie,' said Anne pensively.

'Why not?' asked Jo and Sally in unison.

'Well . . . when I was a teenager I broke her precious vase and blamed it on the cat,' said Anne guiltily.

'Yes, I can see your point, Anne,' said Sally, 'that *would* be embarrassing.'

'It could be worse,' said Jo with a grin.

'How?' asked Anne, surprised.

'She might talk to the cat.'

At the end of school Anne and I were in the entrance hall doing a premises check prior to the next governors' meeting when Ronnie Smith called in. He looked surprisingly smart in his best suit. Ruby was locking her caretaker's store.

'Ah've gorrit sorted, Ruby,' said Ronnie. 'We need t'go in 'alf an 'our. Big Dave sed 'e'd give us a lift in 'is wagon into York.'

'We're off t'celebrate our thirtieth wedding anniversary, Mr Sheffield,' announced Ruby.

I recalled that Andy Smith, Ruby's eldest, was thirty-one years old and Ruby telling me that 't'first an' las'' were an accident, but ah love 'em all.'

'Congratulations, Ruby,' I said. 'Enjoy your evening.'

'Where are you going, Ruby?' asked Anne.

'We're off to t'pictures in York an' then for a drink in t'Bay 'Orse at Monk Bar,' said Ruby.

'And what are you going to see?' I asked.

'We're gonna see *Tootsie*,' said Ronnie.

'Wi' 'im wi' a limp what were in *Midnight Cowboy*,' said Ruby by way of explanation.

'Ah, Dustin Hoffman?' I said.

'That's 'im, Mr Sheffield,' said Ronnie.

''E dresses up as a woman,' explained Ruby.

'But y'can tell 'e's a feller,' said Ronnie.

''Ow come?' added Ruby.

''E never gets a word in edgeways,' said Ronnie.

'Tek no notice of 'im,' said Ruby.

'Well, have a lovely time, both of you,' said Anne.

'Ah'll tell yer all about it when ah see you tomorrow night,' said Ruby.

'T'morrow night?' asked Ronnie.

'That's right, Ronnie,' said Ruby, 'we're off t'see that woman wi' sidekick powers what can talk t'dead people.'

'She wants t'come t'work wi' me then,' said Ronnie, 'she'd be spoilt f'choice.'

They walked down the cobbled drive to the school gates in animated conversation for their date with a cross-dressing superstar.

On Saturday morning, beneath the frozen earth, new life stirred. The season was changing and the bare branches of the distant forest shivered in expectation. The grip of winter had weakened at last and the folk of Ragley village felt their spirits lift. The dark days were over: spring was coming.

Hope comes in many forms. Occasionally it is found in a newspaper headline or a politician's promise. Sometimes it arrives by letter from a distant land, or perhaps in a lover's smile. More often than not it is unexpected and is the result of a simple happening. So it was for Miss Prudence Golightly when she heard a sound she had not heard for a long time. The old clock in her tiny second bedroom chimed. Curious, she stood up, adjusted the mother-of-pearl comb that held in place her tightly wound bun of grey hair and set off to investigate.

The antique English art-deco Westminster mantel clock had been her last gift from Jeremy over forty years ago. He had once been the love of her life but, as a young fighter pilot, he had been killed in the Battle of Britain in 1940. Prudence stared at the clock, mystified. It stood there just over eight inches tall in its walnut case on the mantelpiece and, for a fleeting moment, the memory of that blissful summer in a far-off Kentish village was vivid in her mind.

Later that morning she was serving her usual band of faithful customers. Vera was in animated conversation with Margery Ackroyd as I joined Betty Buttle at the back of the queue. 'Never mind the new supermarket, Margery,' she said defiantly, 'we must support Prudence in the General Stores.'

'Thank you, as always, Vera,' said Prudence quietly as she placed three tins of superior cat food on top of Vera's *Daily Telegraph*.

Vera smiled and nodded to her dear friend. 'And a tin of brown Cherry Blossom for Rupert's brogues,' said Vera as she passed over her shopping list.

'Are you coming to the village hall this evening, Vera?' asked Prudence.

'I have a dinner engagement, Prudence,' said Vera, 'but I wouldn't have gone anyway,' she added quietly. 'I don't believe in all that hocus pocus . . . as I'm sure you don't.'

Prudence smiled politely but didn't reply. She looked

up at her much-loved teddy bear, immaculately dressed in a white shirt, a small black bow-tie, black trousers and a white shopkeeper's apron. The name Jeremy was neatly stitched in royal blue cotton on the apron across his chest and she remembered happy times of long ago.

Meanwhile Mrs Buttle was telling me about her trip to the county of the red rose. 'We've jus' come back from visiting relations in Barrowford, Mr Sheffield.'

'Barrowford – in Lancashire?'

'That's t'one. Lovely place. M'sister's a cleaner at Blacko Primary School, reight nex' t'Pendle 'ill. She sez it's best school in Lancashire. Gorra lovely 'eadteacher jus' like you – y'know, normal-like, not oighty-toighty.'

'Well, er, thank you Mrs Buttle,' I said. 'Good to see you back safe and sound.'

'Mind you, Mr Sheffield, it were real 'illy over them Pennines,' she said. 'Ah felt like that Cannibal an' 'is elephants goin' over t'Alps.'

'I imagine you did, Mrs Buttle,' I said.

At seven o'clock Petula Dudley-Palmer put on her mink coat and went into the lounge to search for her handbag. Geoffrey was on his hands and knees staring at his state-of-the-art Sony CDP-101. He had plugged it in and picked up the book of instructions.

'So, what is it?' asked a bemused Petula, picking up her handbag from the sofa.

'It plays records . . . well, actually, *compact discs*,' said Geoffrey. 'It's the latest in new technology.'

'And what are these, er, compact discs?' asked Petula. 'It sounds like a back complaint.'

'Well, they're sort of *metal* records, but you don't turn them over like a normal vinyl record.'

'So what's on the other side?' asked Petula.

'Well, nothing really,' said Geoffrey a little lamely.

'So it doesn't have a B-side then?' queried Petula.

'Er, not exactly, no,' replied Geoffrey.

'Well I'm not convinced,' said Petula.

Geoffrey was still desperately pressing buttons. 'I'm sure I'll get the hang of it soon,' he said.

'It'll never catch on,' she called from the hallway and checked she had her purse.

Geoffrey glanced up and frowned. 'So where are you going?' he asked, slightly annoyed she wasn't staying to experience his brave new world of music in the Eighties.

'To see a clairvoyant,' said Petula.

'Claire who?' mumbled Geoffrey, but Petula was no longer listening. Her evening with the paranormal was about to begin.

Backstage in the village hall, Phoebe Duckworth was exercising her psychic powers. It was a case of mental manipulation, a kind of transcendental meditation she had perfected during the past year. She had a strict routine before her performances and, even though this was just a small village in a backwater of North Yorkshire, Phoebe was determined to give of her best. After all, she was a *professional*.

For Phoebe, the self-styled world-famous clairvoyant, it had begun at exactly three o'clock on 22 September 1956 when a large unidentified flying object appeared just off the Cleethorpes coast and was picked up on radar at RAF

Manby. On that long-ago afternoon when Phoebe, at the age of eight, stared at the spherical glass ball hovering in the sky, shivers ran down her spine. She later realized these were psychic pulses and from that day on her life changed. Phoebe knew she was different . . . she had one more sense than anybody else.

Phoebe was proud of her home town of Cleethorpes, a famous seaside resort with a pier and sandy beaches, close to Grimsby on the east coast. However, she had to admit it wasn't exactly the French Riviera. In fact the 'sea' that she paddled in was actually the River Humber and, at low tide, her fellow brave holiday bathers were separated from the *actual* sea by a few hundred yards of mud. Even so, Phoebe loved it.

As a young teenager she had spent most of her spare time in her bedroom analysing her dreams, which proved both plentiful and vivid. She would stack six vinyl records on her Dansette record player, set the switch to 45 r.p.m. and marvel at its auto-change facility. Then she would settle down to read her horoscope while Buddy Holly sang 'Heartbeat'. That apart, it was a normal adolescence.

Twenty years ago, in 1963, she screamed with all the other girls when the Beatles came to the Odeon in Leeds and the following year, at the age of sixteen, she left school. She got a job in the paybox at the Ritz theatre in Cleethorpes and it was there that she first met Melvin in 1967, on the evening Sandie Shaw won the Eurovision Song Contest with 'Puppet On A String'. That night Melvin introduced her to strange-smelling cigarettes, flower power and the slogan 'Make Love Not War'. The relationship lasted until Melvin met a buxom ice-cream lady and left for the delights of Grimsby without saying goodbye. Finally, many years later, the cinema closed and Phoebe joined the ranks of the unemployed. It was then that she recalled her sixth sense and decided to make use of the powers invested upon her by her encounter with an alien spacecraft.

The village hall was packed and the front rows had been filled with enthusiastic committee members, plus an agitated Ruby. Ronnie hadn't arrived. Behind her Diane Wigglesworth was chatting with Prudence Golightly and Amelia Duff, while I sat at the back with Anne, Jo and Sally. At the entrance door Margery Ackroyd was collecting tickets and feeling very important in her bright-red blouse with built-in *Dallas* shoulder pads.

The show was about to start when Ronnie rushed in. 'Where 'ave you been?' demanded Ruby.

'Ah've been workin' late,' said Ronnie breathlessly. 'Y'should 'ave let me know t'time it started.'

Ruby shook her head in dismay. 'Ah'd 'ave 'ad more chance o' contactin' someone from t'spirit world than you, y'dozey 'aporth.'

Ronnie pulled his bobble hat a little further over his ears, an automatic gesture he had developed, especially when Ruby was telling him off. 'Ah'm sorry, Ruby, ah got 'eld up,' he said plaintively. 'Ah 'ad an extra shift. Business 'as picked up – there's a lot o'people dying these days after t'cold winter.'

'Well, that should please Phoebe Duckworth,' said Ruby, looking down at the programme.

''Ow d'you mean, luv?' asked Ronnie.

'Well she'll 'ave more customers t'talk to,' said Ruby.

'Y'what?' said Ronnie.

'Well, she's one o' them wi' special powers that can talk to them what's passed away.'

'Oh 'eck,' said Ronnie. ''Ow does she do that?'

'It's summat t'do wi' an *aura*,' said Ruby mysteriously.

'A *Nora*?' said Ronnie. 'Y'mean 'er in t'Coffee Shop?'

'Shurrup Ronnie,' said Ruby. 'Y'mekkin an exhibition o' y'self, an' anyway, show's startin'.'

The lights dimmed, or to be more precise, the eight light bulbs that constituted the ceiling lights were switched off. Timothy Pratt turned on the single spotlight attached to the central beam, the curtains opened, Phoebe switched on her ghettoblaster for her big entrance and Joe Cocker and Jennifer Warnes sang their Top Ten hit 'Up Where We Belong'.

A minute later, short, skinny Phoebe, in a flower-power outfit that resembled a psychedelic tent, stepped into the spotlight and everyone clapped. 'Ladies an' gentlemen,' she said, 'ah'm pleased t'be 'ere t'use m'special psychic powers . . . an', per'aps, give a little modicum o' comfort t'those in need. Ah've got a *sixth* sense an' ah'll be using it t'night in your very midst an' before your very eyes. In t'meantime, if you 'ave a photo of a *loved-one-passed*, then please 'and it in t'Margery during t'interval an' we'll pick one out in t'second 'alf for special psychic consideration.'

Then there was a hush as Phoebe concentrated. 'The name *Arthur* is coming to me,' said Phoebe as she stared up into the spotlight, 'an' 'e's wearing a waistcoat.' She peered into the audience. 'Does anyone know an Arthur?'

Betty Buttle raised her hand. 'Ah 'ad an Uncle Arthur,' she said, 'an' 'e 'ad a waistcoat . . . well, 'e did on Sundays. 'E got knocked down by a tram in Leeds in nineteen fifty-six.'

'Well, 'e's 'ere now standing nex' t'me an' 'e says 'e didn't suffer an' 'e sends 'is love.'

'Oooh, thank you,' said Betty, reaching for her handkerchief and blowing her nose. ''E were a saint, were Uncle Arthur.'

'An' now ah 'ear a distant voice,' said Phoebe, half-closing her eyes, 'an' the name *Tim* is coming through. Does anyone know a Tim?'

'My Timothy was killed last year,' said Delia Morgetroyd.

'He says he was close to you,' said Phoebe.

'Ah loved 'im t'bits,' said Delia tearfully, 'an' ah miss 'im ev'ry day.'

'Well, when you get home,' said Phoebe, 'look at where he used to hang his coat and you will feel his presence.'

'Ah don't remember no coat,' said Delia.

'An' he says he doesn't feel any pain,' said Phoebe quickly.

'Ah'm not s'prised,' said Delia, nodding vigorously. 'Ah jus' fed 'im 'is fav'rite liver-flavoured tin o' Kitekat Supreme an' 'e ran straight outside and got flattened by a tractor, poor little sod.'

Phoebe recovered quickly. 'And he's next to me now, purring he loves you.'

'Thank you,' said Delia, overcome with the memories of her feline friend.

'That's handy,' whispered Anne in my ear.

'What is?' I asked.

'Understanding cat language.'

Suddenly Phoebe stiffened and closed her eyes. 'An' now ah can 'ear a voice but ah can't mek out t'name 'cause of a roaring noise like a big engine. Ah think it might be Jamie, or Jimmy . . . or Jeremy.'

Prudence Golightly stared and her heart began to race, but she said nothing.

'There's a clock face, and a message, but the clock has stopped,' murmured Phoebe, 'and now . . . no more, no more.'

Prudence gripped her hands together tightly. There was silence in the room and eventually Phoebe moved on.

It was an evening of light and shade. Some of her messages had a great meaning for certain individuals, whereas others fell on stony ground or, perhaps more pertinently, on deaf ears. Julie Earnshaw was told to expect a gift from an unlikely source but muttered that pigs might fly before she ever got a present. Some brave souls spoke up, notably Violet Tinkle, a septuagenarian from the Hartford Home for Retired Gentlefolk, who remarked that on occasion she felt the presence of her late husband. The articulate Violet said, 'Well, Miss Duckworth, whenever I go back to my apartment, sometimes it has a certain *ambience* about it . . . and not one I'm comfortable with.' Ruby Smith was puzzled. The ambulance she had travelled home in had comfy pillows and cotton sheets.

Daphne Cathcart asked about the future for her children and was told there were wonderful prospects in store in a world full of books. Phoebe looked out at Daphne and recognized that her words were a fragile bond but enough to give some inner peace to a troubled soul.

Finally, as the evening drew to its close, Timothy Pratt turned on the lights once again, the spell was shattered and the door to the spirit world was slammed shut. The villagers of Ragley wandered out full of their own thoughts and Phoebe Duckworth took a bow, collected her £20 and drove home to a fish-and-chip supper in her empty flat. Meanwhile, Prudence Golightly walked across the road to her General Stores and stopped outside the front door. She looked up into a starry sky and re-membered a love that was lost and a heartache that lasted for ever. As she stepped inside she thought she heard the echo of a chiming clock.

On Sunday morning Heathcliffe and Terry Earnshaw crept into their mother's bedroom and shook her sleep-ing figure gently.

'Wassamatter?' she said drowsily.

'It's Mother's Day, Mam,' said Heathcliffe.

'So we got a s'prise f'you,' said Terry.

Mrs Earnshaw smiled at her two boys. Perhaps they weren't so bad after all.

'You stay in bed, Mam,' said Heathcliffe gently.

'Y'don't need t'get up,' added little Terry.

Mrs Earnshaw gave them both a kiss on the tops of their spiky blond hair and they rushed off.

Soon she heard the clatter of pans from the kitchen and, shortly after, the delicious smell of frying bacon.

She licked her lips in anticipation and wondered if they would find the large tray under the sink and remember to bring the salt and pepper set she had won at bingo. Then it seemed to go quiet for a long while and, wondering what was happening, she got up, put on her dressing gown and tiptoed downstairs. The sight that met her eyes was not what she expected. The kitchen looked as though a bomb had hit it and, at the table, Heathcliffe and Terry were tucking into bacon, eggs and doorstep slices of burnt toast. They looked up and grinned.

'What's goin' on?' asked Mrs Earnshaw.

'This is y's'prise, Mam,' said Terry cheerfully.

'Y'what?'

'We've saved you all t'trouble o' mekkin our breakfast,' said Heathcliffe magnanimously. For these boys of Barnsley, while cooking was an elusive art, sainthood came naturally and they continued tucking into the best breakfast they'd had for weeks.

Further down the street, Daphne Cathcart was in her kitchen preparing breakfast for teenage Cathy and little Michelle. She was thinking about what Phoebe Duckworth had prophesied for her daughters in a world of books. Perhaps they would become librarians or work in a bookshop. Round her neck hung an Egyptian pendulum, a small crystal that she wore to help natural healing. She had been told it was an antidepressant crystal that increased self-worth and she stroked it and reflected on her life. It was also intended to bring good luck.

Then she had a surprise as her two girls appeared in

their dressing gowns, each holding up a home-made Mother's Day card.

'Why are you crying, Mummy?' asked Michelle.

"Cause she's 'appy,' said Cathy softly.

Daphne hugged her daughters and prayed they would grow up to have more sense than she had . . . even though she had six of them.

Prudence Golightly picked up her antique clock and stared at the face. It had stopped again at three o'clock, the time Jeremy had left all those years ago, never to return.

Then she turned it round to look at the small hinged door set into the rear of the clock and opened it carefully. There was a working key and a tiny brass pendulum . . . and something else. It was a folded sheet of paper, yellowed with age. She held it up in a bar of morning light that pierced the half-closed curtains. Hardly daring to breathe, she opened it and recognized Jeremy's distinctive neat handwriting. It was a message that had been locked away for over forty years in a dark clockwork prison and simply read 'I love you'.

Tears ran down her cheeks as memories of a youth shared filled her senses. 'And I love you,' she whispered.

It was then she recalled that there is an end to everything . . . except a love that was lost and found again.

Chapter Fourteen

The Solitary Sidesman

School closed today with 88 children on roll and will re-open for the summer term on Tuesday, 12 April. A new admission, Becky Shawcross, age 5, was admitted to commence full-time education in Class 1 next term. The school choir and orchestra are to perform at the Easter Day service at 11 a.m. in St Mary's Church on Sunday, 3 April.

Extract from the Ragley School Logbook:
Wednesday, 30 March 1983

I first met Bonnie Shawcross on Wednesday, 30 March, the last day of the spring term. She was a tall, willowy twenty-four-year-old with sea-grey eyes and long fair hair that was her crowning glory, hanging down almost to her waist and brushed until it shone. She looked nervous as she held the hand of her little daughter, Becky, a pale, fragile five-year-old but, on that morning when the scent of spring was in the air, somehow I knew they were *different*. There was something special about mother and daughter, like gold thread through calico.

It had been a long, cold winter but now, from the office window, I could see that the sticky buds on the horse-chestnut trees were cracking open and, in the flower tubs outside The Royal Oak, the first daffodils raised their bright-yellow trumpets to the sky. The spring term was almost over and the swallows had returned to their old haunts to build their nests.

Vera walked into the office. 'This is Ms Shawcross and her daughter, Mr Sheffield,' she said. Then she sat at her desk where a new admissions form had been prepared.

'Welcome to Ragley,' I said. 'Please take a seat.'

'Thank you for giving up your time to see us, Mr Sheffield. I'm Bonnie Shawcross and this is my daughter Becky. We've just moved back to Yorkshire from London and we're living with my father in his cottage on the Morton Road.'

Vera looked up from her desk. 'Which is just in our catchment area, Mr Sheffield,' she said.

'Fine,' I said. 'So how can we help?'

Bonnie Shawcross looked down at her daughter. The little girl was sitting meekly on a large chair with her legs swinging to and fro. Her eyes were alert as she scanned the old photographs on the office walls and the water-colour painting of Ragley School. 'I was hoping Becky could start school after Easter. She's five next week.'

'I can do the paperwork now if you wish,' interjected Vera with her usual efficiency.

For the first time there was a hint of anxiety. 'The only thing is, I've got a job in Banks Music Shop in York, Mr

Sheffield,' she said and then sighed. She glanced at Vera, who was scribbling on her notepad. 'I enjoy it because I've always loved music, but it means long hours and I have to get the bus back to Ragley so I'm not home until half six.'

'So who's going to collect Becky at the end of school?' I asked.

'I'm not sure just yet,' said Bonnie. 'I'll discuss it with my father, but he has a job in Easington.'

Vera looked up from her desk. 'I'm sure we can suggest something for you. There's a lot of support in Ragley.' There was a glance between the two women that meant volumes to them but nothing to me.

When they left, Vera labelled a manila folder with the name 'Becky Shawcross', followed by her date of birth, and filed it in our tall, metal four-drawer filing cabinet.

'Interesting young woman,' I said.

'Yes. Her late mother was in the Women's Institute, Mr Sheffield,' said Vera, 'so I know the background. She met her boyfriend at university in London, but it didn't work out. He left her and she's been a single parent for the past two years, so, clearly, we need to help as much as we can.' I never ceased to be amazed at the extent of Vera's local knowledge.

'Thanks, Vera,' I said. 'I'll keep it in mind.'

'And one more thing,' Vera added with a smile. 'Wait till you hear her sing . . . she has the most wonderful voice.'

The English lesson to start the day reminded me why I loved teaching. Anne and Sally had prepared a beautiful display in the entrance hall. They had covered the old pine table with a length of oatmeal hessian fabric and arranged a variety of pots and vases of spring flowers. Above it a beautiful collection of children's 'Spring' paintings had been mounted. The girls and boys in my class carried their chairs from the classroom across the hall and sat down to study the flowers.

'William Wordsworth wrote a famous poem in 1807,' I said and began to read:

> *'I wandered lonely as a cloud*
> *That floats on high o'er vales and hills,*
> *When all at once I saw a crowd,*
> *A host, of golden daffodils'*

Then we talked about the beauty of flowers and passed round some photographs I had taken of the cascades of daffodils on the grassy banks that surround York's ancient city walls. The children took turns to compile a list of words that described the daffodils along with their feelings in response to the wonders of nature. Half an hour later, the poems and pencil sketches that emerged made me realize just how creative young children can be. It also occurred to me that, while it was demanding to be a headteacher with a full-time teaching commitment, on occasions such as these it was the best job in the world.

At half past ten, in the school hall, Joseph had finished his Easter assembly and was continuing an impromptu discussion with a group of children in Sally's class.

'Well there *is* a difference between "like" and "love",' said Joseph. 'Do you know what it is, Benjamin?'

Ben Roberts nodded with the assurance of youth. 'Well, Mr Evans,' he said, 'ah *like* my mam and dad . . . but ah *love* Easter eggs.'

Joseph nodded, unsure how to respond. Occasionally the conceptual development of eight-year-olds was difficult to grasp so, as the bell rang for morning break, he decided to retreat to the staff-room.

I was on duty and enjoying the spring sunshine. In the playground the children were excited about the forthcoming Easter holiday and the promise of chocolate eggs. They were in lively spirits and a group of girls were skipping and chanting in unison:

> '*One, two, three, four, five, six, seven,*
> *All good children go to heaven.*
> *A penny on the water, twopence on the sea,*
> *Threepence on the railway and out goes she!*'

It was a busy end of term with a final rehearsal for Sally's choir and orchestra prior to the Easter Day service and the arrangements for making sure every pupil's report book found its way home to be signed by their parent. There was also the usual final clear-out from Anne's lost-property box and, at the end of school, a group of mothers rediscovered forgotten socks, Wellington boots and the occasional broken toy.

Gradually the school emptied, parents and children said their farewells, the teachers cleared their classrooms and Ruby began her famous 'holiday polish' of the hall floor. Vera was the last to leave, determined to finish her end-of-term filing.

'See you in church, Vera,' I said. 'Sally and Anne have worked wonders with the choir.'

'Yes,' she said, 'this is definitely one of my favourite services of the year, especially with the children involved.' She sounded reflective as she buttoned her coat and stared out of the window. 'To be perfectly frank, I'm not really a fan of High Church with its bells and smells, nor am I comfortable with the happy-clappy Evangelical church in Easington . . . but perhaps we should live and let live. It's just that Joseph's services are perfect for me.'

Finally, at seven o'clock, I was alone in the office completing the school logbook. The last entry of term was always a poignant moment for me and the occasional sibilant whispering of the breeze in the roof tiles was a comforting companion in the silence of the empty school.

On Good Friday morning Beth and I woke to a birdsong dawn in a land of new birth. It was the first day of April, a time of renewal, and the warm breath of spring had finally touched this cold northern land.

'I can't believe I've only got another couple of months before my maternity leave,' Beth said. 'It's a strange feeling.' She had met with the school governing body and agreed she would continue her headteacher duties until the half-term holiday at the end of May. Miss Barrington-Huntley at County Hall had appointed Simon Bartram,

Beth's deputy headteacher, to take over as Acting Headteacher at Hartingdale Primary School and he had jumped at the opportunity.

'So what shall we do today?' I asked. 'Surely you're not doing another assignment?'

Beth stood up, ran her fingers through her honey-blonde hair and stretched. 'Not today, Jack,' she said with a smile. 'It's a lovely day, so let's go to the Good Friday service and then maybe for a walk.'

Four miles away, Wilfred Noggs, the churchwarden, had arrived early at St Mary's. As he walked through the silent churchyard, he paused next to the bench on which a shiny brass plate had been fixed in memory of his late wife, Jean. The sharp pang of pain was familiar now, such was his sorrow at her recent loss. Cancer had little respect for longevity and Jean Noggs had died at the age of fifty-seven. His life seemed empty now.

Wilfred's churchwarden duties were second nature to him. He unlocked the huge oak door, turned on the lights and padded across the red carpet to the back of the church to unlock the inner vestry. Once inside the confined space, he moved with practised ease.

First, he took from the ancient Welsh dresser a beautifully laundered white cloth and the *elements*: the wine and the small circular wafers of bread. He placed these with due reverence on the pew reserved for the sidesmen, ready for their presentation at the altar during the offertory hymn. Then he put the chalice on a tray along with a small glass jug of water for washing fingers, plus a box of matches and a spill for lighting the candles.

He carried them all down the aisle and up the steps to the chancel. With military precision he arranged everything on the altar. After all, Joseph liked things to be perfect. Finally he lit the two candles on the altar and stood back to admire his work.

Back in the peaceful sanctuary of the inner vestry he nodded knowingly. Here there was a place for everything and he took the two shallow wooden collection plates from the drawer of the ancient bureau, plus a large and quite magnificent brass collection plate. He stacked the two wooden plates next to the bookcase of hymn books and service sheets, and then he remembered. Although sidesmen usually worked in pairs, only *one* plate was required. Toby Speight was on duty today and the shy young man always worked alone; he was a solitary sidesman.

Bright yellow forsythia lifted our spirits as we drove into Ragley and up the Morton Road to St Mary's Church. Outside, Beth smiled and pointed to the church noticeboard. 'Another one of Elsie's classics,' she said. Elsie Crapper's notice read: 'Don't worry yourself to an early grave – let the church help you'.

Tobias Speight had already arrived. 'Good morning, Mr Noggs,' he said quietly. The churchwarden gave him a strained smile and, like two mime artists, they continued their silent ritual.

Toby checked the pew sheet for today's hymns and mounted the thick card numbers on the heavy oak board next to the pulpit. Then he checked the huge Bible on the lectern and rested the beautiful linen markers on the correct pages for today's readings. Finally he put a bag of cough sweets out of sight in the choir stalls and, as the congregation began to arrive, he handed out the hymn books and the service sheets.

When Beth and I walked in he gave a sheepish smile. 'Good morning, Mr and Mrs Sheffield,' he said, pushing his long fair hair from his eyes with a sweep of his long, delicate fingers. He was a fresh-faced, athletic twenty-four-year-old with a charming smile and an honest face. It was after his mother died that Vera had taken him under her wing and she had related his story in the staff-room.

Tobias Whinthrop Speight was born in 1959 and, at the age of six, had begun piano lessons with the fearsome Miss Crump in Easington. At first his feet couldn't reach the pedals but later, as he grew, he would sit on a cushion on the ornate two-seater piano stool with Miss Crump perched alongside, reprimanding the slightest mistake, often with the sharp rap of a wooden ruler on the back of Toby's knuckles. Vera explained that Miss Crump was of the *old school*.

Toby had achieved Grade 1 piano at the tender age of eight and by the time he was fourteen he had passed his Grade 8 examination with flying colours. Remarkably, he was just as gifted at playing by ear as he was at sight reading. At Ampleforth College in Yorkshire the teachers gave him great support and he blossomed. As a member of the successful 1st VIII Cross Country team, he thought nothing of a seven-mile run at lunchtimes up the steep incline of the nearby Parkside Hill. Then, as a young teenager, he was invited to be the organist at

Ampleforth Church, where he soon mastered the huge number of pipes and stops and started playing regularly at weddings and funerals. Music filled his world; it was his life.

When Beth and I settled into one of the dark wood pews I looked around. There was seating for around a hundred people and the church was almost full on this special day. To my surprise, Vera was sitting in front of me with Bonnie Shawcross and little Becky, and when we stood to sing the first hymn I recalled Vera's words. Bonnie really did have a wonderful voice. It was a stunning soprano and, among the congregation, heads turned to stare in wonder.

Toby had volunteered to play the final hymn as Elsie Crapper, our regular organist, had to leave early to play at a christening service in Easington. The organ, made by Walker & Sons and installed in 1833, was showing serious signs of age and there were frequent problems; however, Toby's expertise transformed this ancient instrument. At the end of the service Vera, ever the matchmaker, introduced Bonnie to the shy and retiring Toby, whose cheeks reddened when faced with this confident woman.

'That was beautiful, Toby,' said Vera. 'We're lucky to have you standing in for Elsie.'

'Thank you,' said Toby.

'It must be wonderful to play the organ,' said Bonnie.

Toby blushed slightly. He was in awe of such a beautiful young woman. 'I've got a wedding tomorrow afternoon,' he said, 'so it's a busy weekend.'

'What pieces are you playing?' asked Bonnie.

'Well, I'm looking forward to the big finish,' he said enthusiastically. 'It's Widor's *Toccata*.'

'Oh, my favourite,' said Bonnie, 'from his Symphony for Organ, number five.'

Toby stared at her wide-eyed. 'You know it?'

'Well, I do work in a music shop,' she said with a wry smile.

The church was emptying. 'I'm afraid I'm sidesman today,' said Toby, looking a little anxious, 'so I have to count the collection and take down the hymn numbers and put the hymn books away.'

'I'll do the hymn books if you like,' said Bonnie. 'I can see where they go.' She crouched down and smiled at Becky. 'Can you help me with all the books, darling?'

'Yes, Mummy,' she said and together they wandered off to stack hymn books on the shelves at the back of the church.

Later, in the silence of the ancient church, Toby thought of the young woman who had suddenly come into his solitary life and hoped he would see her again. Until then, only the hollow footfalls remained, hanging in the air, an ellipsis of echoes to an unfinished conversation.

On Saturday morning in the hedgerow outside Bilbo Cottage there was frantic activity as birds built their nests. On the pavement, a speckled thrush with beady eyes had a snail in its beak and was beating its stubborn shell.

Beth was up early and had begun to paint our second bedroom. 'I thought I'd make a start, Jack,' she said.

Deep down I knew Beth enjoyed painting and possessed an aesthetic appreciation that I could only dream off. 'Fine,' I said, 'so I'll do the shopping.' Married life was suiting us both. However, one thing I had noticed was that Bilbo Cottage was being transformed from a functional magnolia bachelor residence, with curtains that didn't match, to a harmonious home of subtle shades that looked like something from *Country Living* magazine. I couldn't work out how Beth found the time, but whenever I was watching Saturday *Grandstand* she always seemed to be busy round the house.

In the General Stores, Prudence Golightly checked Beth's list and filled my shopping bags with loaves, vegetables and fruit. Meanwhile, I was intrigued by the headline in my *Times*: 'Thousands of hands link in CND rally'. Apparently, countless protesters had linked hands in a fourteen-mile chain from Burghfield to Greenham Common in Berkshire via the Atomic Weapons Research Establishment at Aldermaston, where research was under way for the Trident missile. Joan Ruddock, chairman of the Campaign for Nuclear Disarmament, had described the demonstration as 'a triumph' and praised the carnival atmosphere. I wondered what Vera would have made of it, as not only did it include jugglers, stilt-walkers and bands, but there was even a Punch and Judy show featuring a Margaret Thatcher puppet.

Mrs Poole and her daughter Jemima were behind me in the queue.

'We need a whistle for the dog,' said Mrs Poole.

'But Mummy,' said Jemima, 'how will he be able to

blow it?' Mrs Poole gave me a what-do-they-teach-them-at-school-these-days look as I walked out.

Beth had asked me to call into the Pharmacy to buy some vitamin tablets. However, a notice had been sello-taped to the shop door. It read: 'CLOSED DUE TO ILLNESS' and with a chuckle I returned to Prudence Golightly's as the notice in her window stated 'WE SELL EVERYTHING'.

Meanwhile, Toby Speight was playing the Widor *Toccata* at the end of a wedding ceremony to accompany the triumphal procession, although his mind was elsewhere.

Vera's mind was also elsewhere. She was busy in her kitchen making a perfect rice pudding with a distinctive dark, caramelized skin. It was Vera's own adaptation from her mother's handwritten book of cookery notes and was based on Eliza Acton's famous recipe, first published in 1845. She had quickly discovered Rupert's penchant for one of her trademark dishes. However, this was not uppermost in Vera's thoughts. At this moment her concern was young love . . . and she had a plan.

On Sunday morning dawn's pale light turned the thin mist into an amber cloak over the distant fields. Suddenly a gentle breeze sprang up and the branches stirred. The countryside was waking and the trees whispered the secrets of sycamores.

I looked at my garden where sprouting raspberry canes and the currant and gooseberry bushes were showing signs of life. The season had turned, spring was coming and four miles away up the Morton Road a young man was growing equally restive.

St Mary's Church looked a picture on this perfect Easter Day and Toby Speight was playing the opening bars of 'This Joyful Eastertide' in preparation for the service.

'Is there anything you need, Toby?' asked Vera.

'Well, you occasionally act as page-turner for me when Elsie isn't here,' said Toby.

'Don't worry,' said Vera, 'it's all in hand,' and she hurried out of church and down the path to the elegant lychgate. Bonnie Shawcross had arrived alone. Her father was at home with Becky.

'Bonnie, my dear,' said Vera, 'I wondered if you could do me a favour?'

'Of course,' said Bonnie.

'I need a page-turner,' said Vera.

Bonnie walked into church with Vera and went to sit beside Toby, who looked up and smiled.

Vera returned to her pew and sat down beside Anne and Sally.

'Bonnie may have a decision to make soon,' whispered Vera.

'What do you mean?' asked Anne.

'Toby or not Toby,' she chuckled to herself. 'Now that really is a question.'

We all smiled politely. None of us could remember Vera telling a joke before . . . perhaps it was just as well.

Chapter Fifteen

Heathcliffe and the Dragon

Children in all classes made preparations for the St George's Day celebrations on the village green on Saturday, 23 April. Mrs Pringle organized a maypole-dancing display. I responded to the latest County Hall document 'Health & Safety on Educational Visits'.

Extract from the Ragley School Logbook:
Friday, 22 April 1983

'You wouldn't think they were worth a pound, would you, Jack?' said Anne looking dubiously at one of the new pound coins.

'Dinner money will never be the same again,' said Vera, rattling her lockable metal money box. 'This is heavier for a start.' It was lunchtime on Friday, 22 April and Vera had checked the late dinner money and returned our registers.

I sat down with Anne, Sally and Jo in the staff-room while Vera served us with cups of tea.

'All set for tomorrow, Sally?' asked Vera.

'Yes,' said Sally, 'and thanks again for providing the ribbons.'

Vera smiled. She loved maypole dancing. It reminded her of days gone by when she was a little girl with flowers in her hair. 'And Rupert has arranged for a couple of his men to erect the maypole,' said Vera, 'so all we need now is good weather.'

We had volunteered to support the Ragley and Morton Women's Institute, who were organizing the St George's Day celebrations on the village green on Saturday afternoon. Warm sunny weather was forecast and the hedgerows had come alive again with green buds and new life. Outside the village hall the almond trees were in blossom and the cherry trees would soon awaken. The branches on the weeping willow next to the duck pond on the village green were heavy with a canopy of new leaves and, next to the school gates, bright-yellow forsythia lifted the spirits. We were truly blessed in this sleepy corner of God's Own Country.

Vera sounded animated. 'It promises to be a memorable day and the ladies in the Women's Institute have worked really hard. There are going to be morris dancers, a farmers' market, refreshments, Captain Fantastic's Punch and Judy, and Prudence is providing a stall with traditional sweets. Finally, of course, there's the re-enactment of St George slaying the dragon.'

'You mean Stan Coe beating some poor villager with his wooden sword, as he does every year,' said Anne.

'Sadly, yes,' said Vera. 'We put up with it partly because

it's tradition and, of course, he's done it for the last twenty-five years.'

'But mainly because he's got the complete St George costume,' added Anne.

Stan Coe, local landowner and pig farmer, was one of the most unpopular men in the village. He was a brute and a bully and had been all his life. There had been disagreements between us in the past but, in recent months, I had tended to avoid conflict and confrontation, so I kept my opinion to myself.

Jo looked up from our weekly copy of the *Times Educational Supplement*. 'Well I'm pleased we're celebrating St George's Day,' she said reflectively. 'The Scots, Welsh and Irish always make *their* patron saint day something special.'

'Cry God for Harry, England and St George,' recited Vera, recalling *Henry V*, 'and don't forget, it's Shakespeare's birthday as well,' she added proudly.

'So where does the dragon come in?' asked Jo.

Sally, our expert in obscure myths and legends, looked up from her *Woman* magazine and an article entitled 'How to achieve a film star bum in only four weeks'. 'He fought in the Crusades for Richard the Lionheart and was adopted as the patron saint of the soldiers,' she said. 'The story goes that he saved a princess from being eaten by a dragon by protecting himself with the sign of the cross and then he slaughtered the poor thing. The citizens were so thrilled with our hero that they converted to Christianity.'

'And so they should,' said Vera. 'A small price to pay for such heroism.'

'Truly a gallant Englishman,' said Jo.

'Or even a Turk,' added Sally mischievously.

'Pardon?' said Vera.

'I seem to recall St George was born in Turkey,' said Sally.

'Oh dear,' said Vera, 'that won't do. Perhaps I had better not mention that to Rupert. He's convinced he was born in Yorkshire.'

Just before lunchtime the children in my class had finished their writing about St George. Elisabeth Amelia Dudley-Palmer had done some excellent research in the school library and I asked her to come to the front of the class to read out her work.

She began in a clear, confident voice. 'St George is the patron saint of England and we celebrate his day each year on April twenty-third and fly the flag of St George, a red cross on a white background.' Elisabeth Amelia paused for dramatic effect and surveyed the class. Suddenly she knew what it must be like to be Margaret Thatcher and she determined to go into politics one day and make great speeches. She took a deep breath and proceeded. 'There is a special medal for bravery, known as the George Cross, which shows St George on horseback slaying a dragon.'

Heathcliffe Earnshaw stared open-mouthed in admiration. St George sounded like a proper Yorkshireman. He was both brave and heroic; in fact, just like Heathcliffe himself. He also liked the word 'slaying'. There was finality about it . . . better than merely stabbing with a sword.

Elisabeth Amelia was approaching the big finish with three words she had extracted from the *Encyclopædia Britannica*. 'So, in conclusion, St George was *honourable*, *courageous . . . and chivalrous.'* She smiled, gave a hesitant bow, resisted the Margaret Thatcher wave, and returned to her seat accompanied by generous applause.

Heathcliffe was impressed. 'Ah want to be hon'rable, courageous an' . . . an' shiver-rous,' he murmured to himself and ideas began to flicker through his young mind.

During lunchtime, Vera and Sally took all the girls from Class 3 and Class 4 outside to practise their maypole dancing on the village green. Sally had taught them well, but this was the first opportunity out of school and very different to dancing round a netball stand in the school hall.

In the centre of the village green, the maypole had been topped in the traditional manner with eight bell garlands and, from each one, a long coloured ribbon, provided by Vera, drifted in the light breeze. Sally turned on her battery-powered ghettoblaster and villagers from the houses on either side of The Royal Oak came out to watch. The practice went well and the onlookers applauded.

'They're a credit to you, Sally,' said Vera, 'and it will give such pleasure to so many people.'

'Thanks Vera . . . but it wouldn't have been possible without you and the major.'

Emily Cade was pushing her ninety-six-year-old mother, Ada, in a wheelchair and they had stopped to admire the performance. 'Tradition,' said Ragley's oldest inhabitant, 'y'can't beat it.'

'Emily, how's your mother?' asked Vera quietly. Everyone knew that Ada was stone deaf.

'*Her mother* is learning to lip-read,' said Ada, looking up from her wheelchair with a sly grin. 'And don't you forget it, young Vera Evans, or whatever it is y'call yourself now.'

Everyone laughed and a red-faced Emily released the brake on the wheelchair and hurried off to the chemist for Ada's weekly prescription.

At afternoon playtime I was on duty and, not for the first time, I marvelled at the inexhaustible energy young children seemed to possess. Some of the older girls had decided to take a break from maypole dancing and were enjoying a more familiar pastime. A skipping rope was whirling round while they chanted:

> *'Jelly on a plate, jelly on a plate,*
> *Wibble wobble, wibble wobble, jelly on a plate.*
> *Pickles in a jar, pickles in a jar,*
> *Ooh! Ah! Ooh! Ah! Pickles in a jar.'*

After school I settled in the office for a long haul. There was a lot of paperwork to complete, so I arranged to meet Beth in The Royal Oak at seven o'clock for a drink and a meal. Then I stared at my in-tray. Yet another document had arrived from County Hall, this time concerning health and safety, and we had been asked to respond in detail. After reading the new regulations I began to think twice about some of the more adventurous outdoor activities we had planned. With a sigh, I filled my fountain pen with Quink ink and began to write.

Meanwhile, on Ragley High Street, Deke Ramsbottom was feeling distinctly uncomfortable. He walked with an extravagant bow-legged gait that passers-by assumed was his impression of the late John Wayne heading towards a gunfight. However, at that moment Deke would have preferred a gunfight to his current ailment. Piles were the bane of his life.

Fortunately there was no one else in the Pharmacy when Deke walked up to the counter. Eugene Scrimshaw, his Captain Kirk *Star Trek* outfit carefully hidden beneath his white coat, was in a jovial mood. He'd been in his loft, converted to resemble the Starship *Enterprise*, and had just installed an old Triumph Mayflower gearstick to represent a time-warp control lever. 'What can ah do for you, Deke? Y'don't look y'self,' said Eugene.

Deke looked around furtively. 'Eugene . . . 'as tha got any arse cream?'

'Vanilla or raspberry?' replied Eugene, who loved his little jokes.

'Y'know what ah mean, y'soft ha'porth,' growled Deke.

Eugene passed over the tube of cream. 'Here y'are,' he said. 'Go forth and prosper.' He gave his Vulcan salute, *à la* Mr Spock, but there was no response from the good-hearted cowboy. 'What is it, Deke? Is there summat else?'

Deke sighed and shook his head sadly. 'It's our Wayne,' he said, ''e's grown out of t'dragon costume. Three generations o' Ramsbottoms 'ave worn that dragon outfit – an' now it's over.'

At that moment the bell rang over the shop door and Heathcliffe Earnshaw wandered in. 'Ah've come t'collec' me mam's 'scripshun,' he said confidently.

'OK, son, jus' wait there a minute,' said Eugene and began to look under the counter.

'We need a strong lad fur t'job,' continued Deke and his eyes fell upon the young, sturdy Heathcliffe with his spiky blond crewcut, barrel-chest, socks round his ankles and scuffed shoes.

'In fac', jus' like young 'Eathcliffe 'ere,' said Deke.

'Y'reight there, Deke,' said Eugene. 'Ah bet 'e'd fit perfec' into t'dragon suit.'

Deke put his hand on young Heathcliffe's shoulder. 'Now then young 'Eathcliffe, 'ow d'you fancy earnin' one o' these new pound coins?'

Later, in the Earnshaw household a lively conversation was in progress.

'What's geography, Mam?' asked Terry.

'Ask y'dad,' said Mrs Earnshaw as she put a splash of tomato sauce on Dallas Sue-Ellen's chip sandwich.

'What's geography, Dad?' repeated Terry.

'*Geography?*' replied Mr Earnshaw, not looking up from the sports page of the *Sun*. Oxford chairman Robert Maxwell wanted to merge his club with Reading to create the Thames Valley Royals and Eric Earnshaw shook his head in disbelief. 'Er . . . ask y'mam,' he said.

'Ah've asked 'er, Dad. She said t'ask you,' said Terry.

Mr Earnshaw looked at his little bristle-haired son and pondered for a moment. 'Geography, well, er, it's . . . it's *places*, lots of 'em.'

'Thanks, Dad,' said Terry and reached for the tomato ketchup.

'Mam,' said Heathcliffe, 'what's '*istory*? 'Cause we're doing George an' t'dragon.'

''*Istory?*' replied Mrs Earnshaw. 'Ask y'dad.'

'Dad, what's 'istory?' asked Heathcliffe.

'Ask y'mam,' he replied.

'She said t'ask you,' said Heathcliffe.

Eric Earnshaw looked up, chewed his mushy peas thoughtfully and stared into space. He wasn't used to being asked so many academic questions but, for the sake of his sons' education, he was willing to impart a little wisdom. "Istory . . . 'istory, well, er, jus' one thing after t'other.'

'Thanks, Dad,' said Heathcliffe. Curiosity satisfied, the boys decided to finish their meal with a mushy-pea sandwich. From the chipped plate in the centre of the table they each selected a doorstep-size slice of bread, spread it thickly with marge and, with the skill of experienced bricklayers, trowelled on a liberal filling of peas.

'An' Dad,' said Heathcliffe, 'ah'm gonna be a dragon t'morrow on t'village green f'St George's Day.'

"Ow come?'

"Cause Mr Ramsbottom said t'costume fitted perfec',' explained Heathcliffe. 'Ah'm in a pretend battle with Mr Coe.'

'Ah don't like 'im,' said Julie Earnshaw. 'Too big for 'is boots, that one.'

Eric Earnshaw looked up from a photograph of George Best in his AFC Bournemouth football shirt and closed the newspaper. 'Who wins this battle then?'

'St George does, Dad,' said Heathcliffe.

'Pity t'dragon didn't come from Barnsley,' he said with a grin.

Little Terry looked up from his sandwich. 'But *we* come from Barnsley, Dad.'

Mr Earnshaw returned to his paper with a smile. ''Xactly,' he said.

'Ooh, our 'Eath in a dragon suit,' said Mrs Earnshaw, 'we'll 'ave t'see this.'

When Beth and I walked into The Royal Oak, Big Dave, Little Malcolm and the football team were watching the news on the television above the bar. The newsreader was holding up a new pound coin.

'Ah'll miss pound notes,' said Big Dave.

'Ah will an' all, Dave,' said Little Malcolm.

'Y'felt as though yer 'ad more money in y'pocket wi' notes instead o' these little coins,' said Big Dave. 'Ah mean a pound note were allus a pound note, but look at these,' he slapped two coins on the counter, 'jus' *loose change*.'

The newsreader moved on to the next item. He explained that someone had just made the first mobile phone call in America using an automatic cellular network.

'Mobile?' said Don the barman. 'What's 'e on abart?'

''E means wi' no wires,' said Chris 'Kojak' Wojciechowski, the Bald-Headed Ball Wizard. 'Y'can walk abart wi' it like a walkie-talkie.'

'But 'ow does it work?' asked Big Dave.

'Dunno, Dave,' said Kojak.

'Meks no sense wi' no wires,' added Little Malcolm, scratching his head in puzzlement.

'World's changing,' said Don.

'An' not for t'better,' growled Old Tommy Piercy through a haze of Old Holborn tobacco. 'Switch it off,' he grumbled. 'Whatever 'appened t'*conversation*?'

Don the barman stretched up his massive ex-wrestler's

frame and switched off. 'Nah then, Mr Sheffield,' he said, 'ah saw all t'little uns doin' that pole dancing t'day.'

'They looked reight professional, Mr Sheffield,' said Sheila. Then she glowered at her husband. 'An' it's *maypole* dancing, y'daft ha'porth, not *pole* dancing. Now what's it t'be, Mr Sheffield?'

'A pint of Chestnut and a tonic water, please, Sheila,' I said, glancing up at the Specials blackboard, 'and two chicken and chips in a basket.'

'Coming up,' said Sheila. 'And 'ow's Mrs Sheffield?'

'Fine thanks,' I said. 'She'll be there tomorrow helping on one of the stalls.'

'Well she mustn't overdo it,' said Sheila knowingly. 'No 'eavy lifting.'

Don placed my frothing pint on the bar. 'That Stan Coe'll be cavortin' abart wi' 'is wooden shield an' 'is sword again,' he said.

"E's sort o' person y'like better t'less y'see of 'im, if y'tek m'meaning, Mr Sheffield,' said Sheila and hurried off to the kitchen.

On Saturday morning I looked out of the kitchen window of Bilbo Cottage. The heady scent of wallflowers filled the air, grape hyacinths bordered the path and the tight buds on the apple tree were waiting for the certainty of frost-free days before bursting from their winter cocoons.

Kenny Everett was singing his hit record 'Snot Rap' on the radio, so I turned it off. The zany comedian's ode to mucus was not exactly the best accompaniment to my morning bowl of porridge. Then Beth and I did some housework and I reflected that a pattern was developing with our domestic chores. I did the hoovering and polishing while she did the washing and ironing . . . and I wasn't complaining. It was midday when we set out for the St George's Day celebrations and Ragley village green was a hive of activity when we drove up the High Street.

Beth wanted to buy some doilies before helping out on the refreshment stall, so I pulled up outside the village hall. She jumped out, glanced at the large glass-fronted noticeboard and smiled. 'Another one of Elsie's classics, Jack,' she said. Elsie Crapper's notice read: 'WOULD THE PERSON WHO TOOK THE STEP LADDER RETURN IT IMMEDIATELY OR FURTHER STEPS WILL BE TAKEN'.

Beth hurried across the road while I drove further up the High Street and into the school car park. When I walked back to the school gates Vera was in conversation with Ruby and Old Tommy Piercy. 'She talks a lot but says nowt, Mr Sheffield,' said Ruby, pointing towards Deirdre Coe. Stan's bossy sister was shouting orders to her group of friends. Her double chin wobbled and she looked annoyed. 'Ah want a big circle o' bales,' she yelled, 'f'my Stanley's battle.'

'Dull minds an' sharp tongues allus go together,' said Old Tommy.

'Deirdre Coe's responsible for the pageant, Mr Sheffield,' said Vera, shaking her head. 'Goodness knows what that will be like.' It wasn't like Vera to offer such ungracious comments, but I understood her feelings. I really wanted to speak my mind but, as always, I was restricted by the yoke of professional correctness and I held my tongue. Deirdre was an unpopular member of the Ragley and Morton's Women's Institute and there had been rumours that her Best Bowl of Bulbs entry that won first prize in March 1973 had been purchased at Thirkby market. According to Vera, in the pecking order of deceit this was close to the top.

At that moment, Stan Coe's mud-streaked Land Rover flashed by, its engine racing in a high-pitched whine. He glowered in our direction and parked outside the parade of shops.

"Orse power were a lot safer, Mr Sheffield, when jus' 'orses 'ad it,' said Old Tommy sagely and we all nodded in agreement.

Meanwhile, across the road, life went on as usual in Diane's Hairdresser's. Petula Dudley-Palmer was reading the April issue of *Cosmopolitan* and an article entitled 'Work Out with Moi' over a photograph of Miss Piggy. In answer to the questions, 'Can you work out without creasing your clothes?' and 'Will you retain a fabulous figure?' she shook her head in dismay. It was definitely time to invest in a home gymnasium.

'What's it to be, Petula?' asked Diane.

'Same as usual, please, Diane,' said Petula. 'Something to go with my Olivia Newton John headband.'

Outside on the pavement, Terry Earnshaw looked at the half pence coin in his hand and put it in his mouth. His pockets were full of holes. So, at that moment in his young life, it seemed a perfectly logical place to keep a precious coin. It would also buy a medium-sized gobstopper from the bottom shelf of Prudence Golightly's General Stores.

However, at that moment, Stan Coe barged past and

bumped heavily into Terry. 'Gerrowt o' m'way,' yelled Stan as he hurried into the shop.

'Warra rude man,' muttered Mrs Earnshaw.

Heathcliffe glared at the red-faced farmer and vowed retribution. It was only when he looked at his little brother that he realized something was wrong. Terry's eyes were bulging and his mouth was open.

'Mam,' said Heathcliffe, 'summat's up wi' our Terry.'

'What's matter, Terry?' asked Mrs Earnshaw.

'Mam . . . when that man bumped into me summat 'appened,' mumbled Terry.

'What 'appened luv?' she asked.

'That halfpenny . . . ah swollered it.'

'Y'swollered it!' yelled Mrs Earnshaw and began smacking Terry's back furiously. She looked towards the village green anxiously. "Eath, look after y'brother while ah find Dr Davenport,' and she rushed off.

Heathcliffe was relieved Terry seemed none the worse for his experience, simply upset that he had lost his chance to buy a gobstopper. Fortunately Heathcliffe was a kindly soul and he felt sorry for his little brother, who had been Robin to his Batman for as long as he could remember. So he made a generous decision. He put his hand in his pocket, clutched *his* half pence piece and, with the skill of an apprentice magician, he pretended to take the coin from Terry's ear.

'There it is, Terry,' said Heathcliffe magnanimously. 'It's come out of yer ear.'

Terry looked in amazement. 'Cor, that's amazing, 'Eath – like magic.' He looked at Heathcliffe in awe and admiration. It was great to have a brother that could climb trees, steal rhubarb from Mr Tupham's garden *and* do proper magic. Quickly he snatched the new half pence from Heathcliffe's hand, popped it in his mouth and swallowed it. 'Go on,' said Terry, full of anticipation. 'Do it again.'

It was at that moment that Mrs Earnshaw arrived with the reassuring presence of Dr Davenport. 'Now don't worry, young man,' said the kindly doctor. 'So he swallowed a half pence piece, did he?'

'No, it were a penny,' said Heathcliffe quickly.

'Ah thought it were a half pence,' said Mrs Earnshaw.

'No, def'nitely a penny, Mam,' said Heathcliffe with a glassy-eyed stare, perfected over the years to suggest absolute innocence.

Terry was quick to assess the situation. 'Yeah, 'Eath's reight, Mam . . . it were a penny.'

On the village green all was ready. The sun shone down on the peaceful scene and the appetizing smell of Old Tommy Piercy's hog roast drifted in the air. The Scout troop raised the flag of St George on the flagpole and the brass band played 'Jerusalem'.

The morris dancers were sitting on straw bales under the weeping willow, where Don the barman had set up a barrel of beer on a wooden trestle table. They already looked well lubricated as Sheila Bradshaw, sporting a sparkly flag of St George boob tube, a bare midriff, bright-red micro-miniskirt and white stilettos, refilled their tankards.

Joseph had proudly presented two bottles of his latest home-made wine to Beth to be served in the refreshment tent. Naming it Cowslip Chateau Evans perhaps lacked a modicum of modesty, but Joseph was convinced the brew surpassed all his previous attempts. Fortunately he was not around when Old Tommy Piercy informed Dr Davenport that it had a great future in the war against disease, particularly in sheep.

The maypole dancing was a great success. Each girl wore a pretty dress and a headband of flowers and proud parents took rolls of photographs as they danced their intricate patterns. Sally held her breath as the children skipped in and out, perfectly in time, until the ribbons were neatly plaited around the pole. Then they reversed the dance and, remarkably, the ribbons were unravelled and the applause from the large crowd was well deserved.

'Well done, Sally,' said Anne. 'Simply wonderful.'

'Our 'Azel looks a picture, don't y'think, Miss Evans . . . ah mean Mrs Forbes-Kitch'ner?' said Ruby. 'Sorry, ah keep f'gettin',' she added. 'Then again, why did you 'ave t'marry a man wi' such a long name?'

They both laughed. 'You're quite right, Ruby. It takes some getting used to. Writing a cheque these days takes an age . . . and yes, young Hazel looks lovely. It reminds me of the time your Natasha was the May Queen.'

''Appy days,' said Ruby, ''appy days.'

Finally we came to the main event and the villagers formed a huge circle around the village green.

Stan Coe was dressed like a medieval knight, complete with cardboard visor, chain mail, a shield-shaped piece of plywood painted with the cross of St George and a long wooden sword. He decided to arrive in style and had saddled up Titan, an old, shaggy black-and-white horse, now long-retired. The acclaim for our hero was distinctly muted: Stan was not a popular man and a few boos and jeers accompanied the applause led by Deirdre. In the meantime, Titan's dragon-hunting days were clearly long behind him and, when Stan had dismounted, he wandered off to chew the long grass by the village pond, supplemented by a bag of carrots that Jimmy Poole had purloined from his mother's shopping bag.

Stan waddled to the middle of the circle and yelled, 'Never fear, St George is 'ere t'save all t'damsels an' such-like.'

'Hooray,' shouted Deirdre and a few of her timid friends.

'Gerron wi' it,' shouted Old Tommy Piercy, already tired of Stan's posturing.

Heathcliffe, having been dressed in the dragon costume with the assistance of his father and Deke Ramsbottom, was in the school playground. He was peering through the cardboard teeth set in the huge open jaws.

'Can y'see owt?' asked Deke.

'Yes thanks, Mr Ramsbottom,' said Heathcliffe.

'Ah told yer it were a perfec' fit,' said Deke proudly, standing back and observing Heathcliffe from his fierce head to his scaly tail.

Stan pointed his sword towards the school. 'Where is the foul-'earted dragon? Come an' show thyself, thou cowardly creature.'

Mr Earnshaw bristled. No one called his son a coward. 'Watch y'tongue, y'great lump,' shouted Eric and pushed his son into the arena.

For Heathcliffe it was like walking into the Colosseum.

A roar went up from the pupils in my class. 'Heathcliffe, Heathcliffe!' they chanted. He stood there in front of Stan and roared. He'd been practising his roar and was pleased when Stan blinked and took a pace backwards.

'Be gone, thou evil dragon!' shouted Stan, although not as confidently as before.

And the dragon roared again.

Then, in a moment of unguarded fury, Stan clanked across the green, raised his wooden sword and smacked the dragon's rump.

'Boooo! Boooo!' shouted Ruby.

'Don't stand f'that, 'Eath!' shouted Mrs Earnshaw.

'Get thtuck in!' shouted Jimmy Poole, now standing well away from Titan, who, after his substantial lunch, had just emptied his bowels.

With a shudder of muted thunder, the dragon growled again. Heathcliffe was pleased with his roar, but even more proud of his growl, a sort of cross between the Hound of the Baskervilles and a Tyrannosaurus rex with toothache. Even with his limited visibility he could see it had a significant effect on St George, who stopped in his tracks while the front row quickly made sure they were *behind* the ring of straw bales.

Finally came the moment that went down in Ragley folklore. With the power of a raging bull, Heathcliffe charged forwards and headbutted Stan, who, with the slow-motion grace of a toppled chimney, fell backwards over the straw bales, rolled gently down the slope of the pond and came to rest in a steaming pile of Yorkshire's finest and freshest horse manure, courtesy of Titan.

The crowd cheered, Deirdre Coe had an apoplectic

fit and the battle was over. To the chant of 'Cowardy, cowardy custard' by Terry Earnshaw and his friends, our noble knight limped painfully away to his Land Rover to get cleaned up. Meanwhile, Heathcliffe was quickly relieved of his dragon suit by Deke Ramsbottom, who then put his hand in his pocket and gave him a coin. 'Here y'are, you've earned it,' he said.

Heathcliffe stared at it in amazement and showed it to Terry.

'What is it, 'Eath?' asked Terry.

'It's one o' them new pound coins.'

'Can ah 'ave a look?' said Terry.

Heathcliffe shook his head. 'Not likely . . . y'might swoller it.'

'Well, what we gonna do?'

Heathcliffe looked at Prudence Golightly's stall of old-fashioned sweets and then at Elisabeth Amelia Dudley-Palmer, who was smiling at him in admiration. 'You were honourable and courageous, Heathcliffe,' she said, 'just like in the story.'

'An' shiver-rous,' added Heathcliffe for good measure. He held up his coin. 'Would y'like some 'umbugs, Lizzie?'

I was standing with Beth and Vera watching this touching scene.

'Interesting,' said Beth.

'Yes . . . what do you think, Vera?' I asked.

'Well, Mr Sheffield,' said Vera, 'I think we've just re-written history.'

Chapter Sixteen

Gandhi and the Rogation Walk

The School Governing Body and the PTA, along with parents and children, offered to support the Revd Joseph Evans and the proposed Rogation Walk around the borders of the village on Sunday afternoon, 8 May.

Extract from the Ragley School Logbook:
Friday, 6 May 1983

The Revd Joseph Evans was in animated mood as he led our school assembly. He'd had a *vision* . . . at least that's what it seemed.

'This is a time to be at one with nature,' he declared, raising his eyes to the beam of sunlight that was streaming in the high arched Victorian window. However, the problem with visions is that, occasionally, they are far from reality. It was Friday morning, 6 May, and an eventful weekend was in store that would keep tongues wagging for some time in the generally peaceful village of Ragley-on-the-Forest.

The children were in good voice as Anne rattled out one of her personal favourites on the piano:

> *'All things bright and beautiful,*
> *All creatures great and small,*
> *All things wise and wonderful,*
> *The Lord God made them all.'*

'And, boys and girls, the Lord God really *does* love them all,' said Joseph as the final echoing chord died away. The children sat cross-legged on the hall floor while our local vicar waxed lyrical about the forthcoming Rogation Walk. 'As it says in Psalm one hundred and thirty-three, "Behold, how good and how pleasant it is for brethren to dwell together in unity".'

I glanced towards Anne at the piano and she gave me a wide-eyed stare. We were clearly thinking the same thing: *would the children know what he was talking about?* However, we needn't have worried: the cavalry had arrived. Vera had propped open the doors that led from the entrance hall to the school hall and had left the office door ajar. She had heard it all and scribbled a reminder on her spiral-bound pad in neat shorthand to send a note home to every family, written in plain English, explaining what the Rogation Walk was really about.

'So,' concluded Joseph, 'let us all meet on the green at ten o'clock on Sunday morning as a united village in which we live together in peace and harmony and in the bounty of nature.' As we all filed out the staff looked as puzzled as the children.

Joseph's idea, announced at the recent governors'

meeting, to resurrect the ancient tradition of a Rogation Walk around the village seemed a good one. It was also an opportunity for Joseph to impress Henry Fodder, the recently retired Canon Emeritus from York Minster who had come to live in the village. Henry was a pleasant, cherubic man with thinning grey hair and thick spectacles and, in spite of retirement, was still powerful in the church community. Sadly, he had not been blessed with a sense of humour, which would have been useful, particularly when you were addressed as Canon Fodder.

Vera was aware that Henry was also a good friend of Bishop Neil, memories of whose visit to school eighteen months ago still made her shudder. On that day all had not gone to plan, but surely nothing could go wrong with something as simple as a walk round the village . . . or could it? After all, thought Vera, my dear brother always *means* well.

At morning break Jo was waiting for me with a list of names on a clipboard. She had volunteered to organize our staff night out and we had decided to go to the Odeon Cinema in York on Saturday evening, followed by a fish-and-chip supper.

'We're all coming, Jack,' she said enthusiastically, 'and we're taking partners, so we need to share cars.' We were going to see Richard Attenborough's epic film *Gandhi*, the memorable story of the famous little man in a loincloth who had led the remarkable non-violent revolt in the cause of freedom in India.

'It's just won eight Oscars,' enthused Sally, 'so it should be good.'

'What time are we meeting?' asked Anne, 'and do I *really* have to bring John?' Anne's husband and cultural pursuits had never been close companions.

During morning school, Theresa Buttle made an announcement. 'Mr Sheffield,' she said, 'ah asked t'vicar if ah could bring our Engelbert on t'walk an' 'e said all God's creatures can come.' Engelbert Humperdinck was the Buttles' flea-ridden Afghan hound.

'In that cathe, Mithter Theffield,' said Jimmy Poole eagerly, 'can ah bring Thcargill?'

I hesitated before replying, 'I'm not sure.' Jimmy's York-shire terrier was lively to say the least.

"Cauth Thcargill ith one o' Godth creatureth ath well,' he pleaded.

I guessed that Ted Postlethwaite, the Ragley postman, would have disagreed. 'Well, you'll have to ask Mr Evans,' I said evasively.

At lunchtime in the staff-room Vera was scanning the front page of her *Daily Telegraph* with interest. The Conservatives were pressing for an early election, possibly as soon as next month; her beloved Margaret had rejected Mr Andropov, the Soviet leader, following his refusal to reduce the number of warheads; and John Bromley, head of sport at London Weekend Television, had announced that the Football League was 'strangling itself to death' after accepting a £3 million sponsorship deal from Canon. Vera homed in on the article on Margaret Thatcher, ignored the rhetoric about nuclear weaponry and was pleased to observe that both she and the saintly Margaret had the same taste in sky-blue blouses with elaborate bows.

Jo looked up from her *Nuffield Book of Science Experiments*. 'So just remind me again, Vera, what exactly is *rogation*?' she asked.

'It's the Christian festival that takes place five weeks after Easter and just before Ascension Day,' recited Vera with confidence.

'And what exactly will we be doing on Sunday morning? And does Colin need his walking boots?' asked Sally.

'Just comfortable footwear,' said Vera. 'We're only walking on local footpaths, so it should be straightforward. Joseph has checked the route. We simply stop at places of importance, sing the occasional hymn and say a brief prayer of thanks. It's a way of showing our Christian gratitude for the village that sustains us in all its bounty. At least that's what Joseph told me this morning.'

'I'm sure it will be fine,' I muttered, returning to the Yorkshire Purchasing Organization catalogue and an order for a blackboard ruler and a trundle wheel.

I got away from school much earlier than usual, at 5.30 p.m., and when I walked into Bilbo Cottage Beth was in the kitchen preparing a shepherd's pie and watching the portable television. She had adjusted the little wire aerial on the top sufficiently to receive a grainy picture of Richard Whiteley presenting Channel 4's *Countdown*.

'How are you?' I said and kissed her neck softly.

'A little tired,' she said. Then she touched her tummy and smiled. 'But happy.' Beth was now over six and a half months pregnant and household tasks were beginning to be wearing. One of her books for her coursework at Leeds University was propped against the bread bin and I marvelled at her ability to multitask.

It was a quiet evening and after a hot meal we settled down with a pot of tea in our tiny lounge to watch television. The choices included *Are You Being Served?* with Mollie Sugden. Apparently, this week, a golf professional from the sports section of the department store was causing a flutter among the ladies. However, while I watched the opening credits to *Hawaii Five-O* and Beth bore with stoicism my impression of canoeing across the hearthrug, we then settled for *Gardeners' World* featuring Jack 'The Carrot' Simpkins with his bumper crop of vegetables. This was followed by *Cagney & Lacey* and a strange plot where the dynamic duo tried to discover the identity of a murdered down-and-out. For my part, I merely looked at Cagney and thought how similar she was to Beth . . . without the bump of course. We were too tired to watch *Cheers* on Channel 4, which Beth explained was a new popular American comedy set in a saloon bar. I couldn't see it catching on and we settled for an early night.

Saturday morning dawned bright and clear. On the Crescent, Anne was in her kitchen trying to unblock the sink while listening to Radio 2. She was pleased that Cliff Richard was in the charts again with his new record 'True Love Ways' and she swayed along to the music while secretly cursing John for using her kitchen sink to dispose of his unused tile cement.

Meanwhile, in the High Street, Saturday shopping

was in full swing. The might of the new supermarkets appearing in York had so far not diminished the activity in Prudence Golightly's General Stores. For Margery Ackroyd, saving a penny on a loaf of white bread did not compensate for the familiarity and convenience of the local shop, or the excellence of the personal service. It was also the hub of local gossip and for Margery this made it worth paying 29½ pence for a jar of Robertson's strawberry jam.

That evening Beth and I were picked up by Dan and Jo Hunter in their two-tone-green F-registered Wolseley Hornet and we drove into York. There was a long queue outside the Odeon but, as Jo had made a block booking, we went straight in and found our seats. It was good to relax, and Beth and I sat transfixed as the story unfolded against spectacular scenes of the Indian countryside. The acting was superb, with Ben Kingsley perfect in the part of Mohandas Karamchand Gandhi, ably supported by such luminaries as John Mills as Lord Chelmsford, John Gielgud as Baron Irwin and Trevor Howard as the presiding judge at Gandhi's sedition trial. Along with the three hundred thousand locals who acted as extras, it really was a film of epic proportions.

When we walked out I asked, 'So, what did you all think?'

'Wonderful,' said Beth.

'Brilliant,' said Jo.

'Crowd control was interesting,' said Acting Sergeant Dan Hunter with a grin.

'Spectacular scenery,' said Sally.

'Boring,' said reformed-smoker Colin Pringle, searching in his pocket for his last sherbet lemon.

'The construction of John Gielgud's desk was a real craftsman's job . . . all dovetailed joints,' said John Grainger enthusiastically.

'Well, Ben Kingsley was absolutely *perfect*,' added Anne hurriedly.

'And Trevor Howard, of course, is such a wonderful actor,' swooned Vera.

'Not keen to see the demise of the British Empire, what?' grumbled Rupert with a furrowed brow.

'And what did you think, Joseph?' asked Jo.

Joseph had a faraway look in his eyes. 'Well actually, I was just thinking of tomorrow's Rogation Walk with me leading the flock . . . a bit like Gandhi really . . . almost prophetic in a way.'

'Oh dear,' murmured Vera as we meandered towards High Petergate and a fish supper.

On Sunday Joseph was up early and Henry Fodder had arrived for the 8 a.m. service. All seemed well on this perfect morning, with the purple wisteria clambering up the rectory walls, the branches of cherry blossom pink and fragrant and a warm sun lapping the ancient stones of St Mary's. Only the harsh cawing of rooks in the high elms disturbed the calm of the two clerics as they walked side by side into church.

'A splendid day, Joseph,' said Henry.

'A day to be at one with Mother Nature,' replied Joseph benignly.

Inside the church there was only the peaceful ticking

of the clock, installed in 1912 to commemorate the coronation of George V the year before. The time for the Rogation Walk was approaching and Joseph was content in his world.

Beth had decided to potter in the garden rather than join the 'route march', as she called it, so I left her tying up the new growth of clematis against the fence. I drove out of Kirkby Steepleton, wound down my window and breathed in the clean Yorkshire air. It was the time of the bleating of the lambs and new life was all around me. In the woods a carpet of bluebells swayed in the dappled shade and above my head a flock of black-headed gulls speared the clear sky in sharp formation. I followed their path towards Ragley-on-the-Forest, where around forty adults, children and assorted pets had gathered in the May sunshine on the village green.

Vera and Sue Phillips were handing out the service booklets, *A Service for Rogationtide*, and soon we were ready.

'We shall begin by singing the hymn on page one,' said Joseph, 'All people that on earth do dwell, sing to the Lord with cheerful voice'.

Without music it was a disjointed rendition; even so, we all finished within a line of each other. Then Rupert, in a loud, sonorous voice reminiscent of military commands on a parade ground, began the first reading. 'Psalm one hundred and thirty-three, verses one to three,' he announced. 'Behold, how good and how pleasant it is for brethren to dwell together in unity.' It was at that moment that two angry faces appeared at the upstairs window of The Royal Oak. Don and Sheila Bradshaw had been enjoying their weekly morning of passion only to be interrupted by a commotion outside their bedroom window.

Meanwhile Joseph led us in our first prayer. 'From petty feuds and jealousies,' he said in a resonating voice, 'from grumbling and bad temper,' he continued, 'and from talking too much about our neighbours, good Lord deliver us.'

As we set off down the High Street, Joseph turned to Vera and Henry. 'Do you know, Henry,' he said with a chuckle, 'I really do feel rather like Gandhi.'

Henry nodded benignly. 'And so you should, Joseph, leading our people to live in harmony.' Then he turned round and was surprised to see Sheila Bradshaw leaning out of her bedroom window in a see-through negligée, shouting at the departing throng. He wondered fleetingly why she was so upset on this perfect day, particularly a lady who had been blessed with such a prodigious bosom.

'Look at t'mess on t'village green,' yelled Sheila. 'Litter an' dog muck. It's a bloody disgrace, that's what it is.'

Don shook his head in disbelief. 'Nobody told us abart a bloody protest meetin',' he said, putting his arm round Sheila's shoulders.

'Sitting on our benches as large as life,' complained Sheila bitterly.

'It's a bloomin' liberty,' said Don.

They caught sight of Joseph in the distance, leading his tribe like a modern-day Moses.

''E wants shootin', does that vicar,' shouted Sheila, her words echoing down the High Street, and, for the first time that day, a grain of doubt entered the uncluttered mind of Henry Fodder.

Our first stop was the pretty meadow next to the cricket field. It was a picturesque scene, with Stan Coe's herd of Friesian cattle contentedly chewing grass to their hearts' content, and we gathered under the welcome shade of sycamore and beech, oak and elm.

It was at this moment, unknown to Joseph, that Tony Ackroyd, Margery's teenage son, let go of the lead attached to Carter, their Jack Russell, who immediately scampered off to introduce himself to the cattle. Meanwhile, Joseph led his slightly distracted multitude in prayer once again. 'Blessed shall you be in the field . . . the increase of your cattle, pigs and horses and the flocks of your sheep . . . let us treat with gentleness all living creatures entrusted to our care, through Jesus Christ our Lord. Amen.' Then he led us in the hymn

> *'All creatures of our God and King,*
> *Lift up your voice and with us sing,*
> *Alleluia, alleluia!'*

On the final 'alleluia' the cattle hurtled across the hallowed cricket square and into the nearby woods, closely followed by the frantic Carter. However, Joseph, with his back to the stampede, was blissfully unaware of a scene that resembled an episode of *Rawhide*.

With a few murmurings in the ranks, we walked to the hedge that bordered Farmer Tubbs' orchard and Joseph

Gandhi and the Rogation Walk

looked around him at the fruit trees rich in colourful blossom. Once again he raised his voice to the heavens. 'Praise be to you my Lord, for our sister Mother Earth, who gives us her fruits in due season.'

Heathcliffe and Terry Earnshaw, standing at the back of the crowd, had managed to drift away from their mother and Dallas Sue-Ellen. Heathcliffe knew the value of forward planning and an idea formed in his mind. Whenever they had visited Farmer Tubbs' orchard on autumn days, when the bounty of rich ripe fruit knew no bounds, they had usually been caught because there was no means of escape apart from through the gate by which they had entered. While they had listened to the story of Beatrix Potter's *Peter Rabbit* years ago in Anne's class, they had not heeded the implicit warning. However, here was an opportunity beyond their wildest dreams.

So, while the congregation sang 'For the fruits of his creation, thanks be to God', the two brothers created a hidden escape route through the base of the thick hawthorn hedge.

The unwitting Joseph pressed on: 'For the stirring of all young life throughout the countryside; for hard work in the open that wearies and satisfies; may God preserve your going out and your coming in, now and always. Amen.'

Meanwhile, Heathcliffe and Terry carefully hid their going out and coming in escape route using twigs and broken branches and stood back to admire their handi-work. 'Perfect,' said Heathcliffe. 'Jus' think of all them apples, Terry.'

*   *   *

A little further on we stopped again, this time by a farm gate, and Jimmy Poole's terrier decided it was time to do something that came naturally. Scargill slipped his lead, ran into the farmyard and disappeared into one of the barns.

'Health and a good constitution are better than all gold,' said Joseph, raising his arms to the heavens.

Sadly, just behind Joseph and in full view of Henry, Vera, the rest of the congregation and half the residents of the Hartford Home for Retired Gentlefolk, who had come out to see what all the noise was about, the manic Yorkshire terrier burst back on to the scene.

'Bless the hands that work here,' said Joseph, 'that they may create useful and beautiful things.'

Behind him, Scargill had a dead rat in his jaws and a bloodthirsty look in his eyes. He then proceeded to rip the unfortunate rodent to shreds.

'Thcargill!' shouted Jimmy. 'Thcargill, thtop it.'

Undeterred, Joseph walked on to the Ragley allotments and stopped next to Maurice Tupham's vegetable patch. Maurice was dozing in his shed in a deckchair on this peaceful morning. We lined up on the bank of the small stream that bordered the allotments and kept them fertile. As we bowed our heads we enjoyed the gentle tinkling of the crystal-clear water as it babbled over the stony bed.

'Your gift of water brings life and freshness to the earth; it washes away our sins and brings eternal life,' said Joseph in a humble voice. Unfortunately, he was unaware of Engelbert, who had snuggled up beside Henry. To Henry's alarm and Vera's abject horror, the hound calmly cocked his leg and urinated in the stream. In sounded like Niagara Falls. As we moved on, Maurice Tupham awoke from his reverie to see the offending dog and his shouts could be heard as we tramped on to our penultimate destination: the cornfield.

It was a scene to raise the spirits. The pussy willows hung heavy above our heads as we stared out at the green swaying carpet of new-grown wheat that had brought the brown earth to life and rippled in the watery sunlight. The pattern of ploughing, sowing and reaping marked the seasons of our life on the fertile plain of York and time was measured by the changing land. So, once again we stood in silence.

'May the blessing of God protect the young corn in this field,' said Joseph. It was just as well that he didn't see, as we did, the rest of the assorted dogs in our party race into the field, leaving trampled patterns in their wake.

Finally we arrived back in the High Street outside the village hall, where Joseph thanked everyone for sharing this experience. As he did so, Deke Ramsbottom, on the roof of the hall, had just completed the repair of the weather cock on his day off.

Emily Cade was passing by, pushing her elderly mother, Ada, in her wheelchair. In a loud voice Ada shouted, 'Isn't it lovely to see the cock upright again, vicar?' and Emily, red-faced, hurried on to complete her mother's weekly constitutional.

That evening, as the sun sank to form a golden thread where the Hambleton hills met the vast purple sky, the folk of Ragley reflected on the day.

In the taproom of The Royal Oak, Sheila Bradshaw was not impressed. 'That vicar'll be the death o' me wi' 'is bloody rotation walk or whatever 'e calls it,' she said, hitching up her Cross of St George boob tube.

'Ah thought Sunday were a day o' rest,' said Don the barman. 'At least in t'mornings.'

'Pollutin' my carrots wi' 'is dogs,' grumbled Maurice Tupham.

'Ah 'eard a pack of 'em were runnin' wild in twenty-acre field,' said Old Tommy Piercy.

'An' cricket square's knackered an' all,' said Big Dave, staring disconsolately into his pint pot.

'Y'reight there, Dave,' said Little Malcolm, 'proper knackered.'

And so it went on . . . Meanwhile, in the Hartford Home for Retired Gentlefolk, the elderly residents who had witnessed the gory end to the life of an unsuspecting rat were in need of a calming cup of Ovaltine and professional counselling.

Back in the vicarage, Joseph broke the silence.

'Well, what do you think?' he asked, looking expectantly at Henry and Vera. At that moment, Concordia, the goddess of harmony, would have smiled at the scene before her.

'All is well, Joseph,' said Vera with a fixed smile.

'And God is in his heaven,' added Henry through gritted teeth.

'I've been thinking,' said Joseph.

'Yes?' said Vera and Henry simultaneously, both looking anxious.

'Perhaps we should make this an *annual* event,' said Joseph enthusiastically.

Vera took his arm. 'Joseph,' she said firmly, 'let's go to the kitchen and discuss this over a bottle of your peapod wine.'

Joseph looked surprised. Vera had never before shown any enthusiasm for his obvious expertise in the blending of superior home-made wine.

'Good idea,' said Henry, who was well aware that Joseph's vile concoctions not only numbed all nerve endings but that they also destroyed brain cells with the rapidity of Domestos on germs. He glanced at Vera, who nodded imperceptibly.

They both knew that after three glasses Joseph would have forgotten all about it.

Chapter Seventeen

Lollipop Lil' and the Zebra Crossing

Work has begun in the village on a zebra crossing at the top of the High Street. Acting Sergeant Dan Hunter called in to school assembly to talk about road safety. The members of the PTA who are supporting the school visit to Flamingo Land on Monday, 13 June met at the end of school to confirm arrangements for the group activity work.

Extract from the Ragley School Logbook:
Friday, 10 June 1983

The school run had come to Ragley. It was Friday, 10 June and our tranquil world had changed for ever. There was no doubt that the extra traffic was beginning to cause congestion outside school and the road around the village green had begun to resemble the newly built M25 on a busy morning.

It had started a few years ago with Mrs Dudley-Palmer driving to school in her Rolls-Royce and dropping off her children at the school gate. Then a few more parents followed suit, particularly those from the outlying farms. This year, more mothers than ever were getting full-time jobs in York and Northallerton and, in consequence, it was convenient to leave their children at school en route to work.

So it was that, on this beautiful summer morning, a gang of council workmen were painting Ragley's first zebra crossing. Red-and-white cones had cordoned off half of the High Street just below the village green and opposite the Post Office.

'It says here there's to be a zebra crossing and a safety barrier, Mr Sheffield,' said Vera, looking at the letter from the County Hall Works Department.

'Times are changing, Vera,' I said thoughtfully. As I looked out of the office window I saw Mrs Dudley-Palmer drop off Elisabeth Amelia and Victoria Alice. The girls waved goodbye and walked up the drive clutching their 'Animals of the World' folders. Next Monday, as part of our project work, we were going to Flamingo Land, a zoo and theme park near Malton in North Yorkshire, and the children were full of excitement.

They were followed by a middle-aged lady who strode purposefully towards the school entrance in a bright road-crossing-patrol uniform and I walked to meet her.

'G'morning, Mr Sheffield,' she said. 'Ah'm Miss Figgins from Cold 'ampton.'

Cold Hampton was a tiny hamlet near the local airfield and, from the look of the villagers I had met from there, it was appropriately named. No trace of warmth exuded from this blunt Yorkshire lady.

'Pleased to meet you,' I said and we shook hands. Her grip was like a car crusher.

'Ah'm y'new lollipop lady,' she said, 'an' ah've jus' been appointed by t'council. Ah start Monday an' ah thought ah'd let t'children see me in m'new uniform so they get used t'me.'

'That's very thoughtful of you, Miss Figgins,' I said, massaging some life back into my fingers. 'Perhaps you'd like to call into our "road safety" assembly today and introduce yourself. We've got our local policeman coming in. It starts just after nine o'clock.'

'Thank you, Mr Sheffield,' said Miss Figgins, glancing at her watch. 'Ah'll be back.'

Our morning assembly went well. Dan Hunter had become a popular figure at Ragley School and his road safety assembly was part of our annual health-and-safety programme for North Yorkshire schools. As usual he was comfortable answering the children's questions. It struck me that Dan would have made an excellent teacher but, by all accounts, he was also making his mark in the police force and promotion was in the pipeline.

The focus this morning was how to use our new zebra crossing. Dan made sure that Miss Figgins, in her glaring uniform and clutching a circular STOP sign on a long pole that resembled a giant lollipop, was the star of the show. At the end, Joseph, who had called in for his weekly religious education lesson, led the prayers and Dan hurried off to begin his duties. Lillian Figgins, however, took the opportunity to talk to Vera and so it was that a potted version of her life story wasn't far away.

'Isn't y'brother a fine man, Mrs Forbes-Kitchener?' said Lillian. 'There's not many like 'im.'

'Thank you for saying so, Miss Figgins,' said Vera, 'and I'm sure Joseph is most grateful for all your hard work in cleaning the church.'

'It's a pleasure,' said Lillian.

'Perhaps you would like a cup of tea?' said Vera.

'Well, that's reight kind,' said Lillian.

Soon they were chatting like old friends. 'Ah wonder 'ow Mr Evans is gettin' on?' said Lillian.

'I'm sure he'll be fine,' said Vera without conviction.

Joseph was summing up his latest Bible epic with Class 2. 'So God made the world.'

'What about t'universe?' asked eight-year-old Ben Roberts.

'Yes, Benjamin, he made the universe as well,' said Joseph solemnly.

'An' t'stars and t'moon?' continued the eager Ben.

'Yes he did,' said Joseph.

'That's a shame,' said Ben.

'A shame . . . and why is that?' asked a surprised Joseph.

'Well 'e got all t'stars in t'right place, but 'e slipped up badly wi' t'moon, 'cause that dunt know whether it's comin' o' goin'.'

Joseph sighed. The logic of children was still a secret garden for him, lovely to appreciate from a distance but a private world for which he had lost the key.

Meanwhile Vera was hearing the story of Miss Figgins' life. Born in Hanging Heaton, a village near Batley in

West Yorkshire, Lillian had spent her teenage years in a greasy-spoon café making bacon sandwiches the size of a small block of flats and serving strong mugs of sweet tea. Life was hard and, to earn extra money, in October 1957 she purchased a copy of *The Practical Home Money Maker* for one shilling and threepence and spent the following weeks weaving baskets for a pittance.

She first met Bernard, the diminutive bookmaker with the Brylcreem quiff, when he ordered a Batley-Belly-Buster-Breakfast. She asked him how many slices of black pudding he wanted, which was music to his ears. After serving his meal and giving the cutlery a cursory wipe on her Batley Rugby League Club apron she noticed he was staring at the headline 'How a 7-stone weakling became the world's most perfectly developed man' above a photograph of the fist-clenching muscular pose of Charles Atlas.

He paid for his meal with a £5 note, which in those days was the size of a small tea towel. When he offered her a Craven A filter-tip cigarette and a night out to see the Bachelors at the new Batley Variety Club, she thought she had just won the jackpot on Littlewoods Pools.

That evening she opened her Lennard's Mail Order catalogue to the page headed 'Go Gay in a New Frock'. For the exorbitant price of 45 shillings she purchased a floral-patterned, spun rayon dress with a ruched waist, short sleeves and a buttoned bodice. She felt like a film star.

Bernard showered her with cheap gifts and, eventually, on the back seat of his Hillman Minx, she submitted to his charms. When he finally drove off into the sunset with a leggy usherette from the local cinema, she was left with a waffle nylon blouse, a Philip Harben cookery set and a bottle of cheap perfume. It was then that she decided to seek out her distant cousin, Nora, in the Ragley village Coffee Shop, start a new life in North Yorkshire and give up men for longer than Lent.

Now, many years later, she lived in a pretty little cottage in Cold Hampton with a thatched roof, leaded diamond-paned windows and a garden full of old-fashioned flowers. As the season progressed, passers-by would stop to admire the tulips, wallflowers, lavender, Sweet Williams, vivid pinks and a riot of Victorian roses that clung to the whitewashed walls, filling them with life and colour. In spite of her tough, curmudgeonly Yorkshire exterior, deep down Lillian had a heart of gold and had earned a reputation for her voluntary work at St Mary's Church.

'Lovely t'meet you at last, Mrs Forbes-Kitchener,' she said as she left.

'Likewise,' said Vera and she sat down to complete a typed notice entitled 'Group List for Flamingo Land'.

By the time we gathered in the staff-room at morning break, Vera had prepared milky coffee and had opened the windows to let in some fresh air on this beautiful summer morning. She was also reading my copy of *The Times* with great enthusiasm.

Following yesterday's General Election, Margaret Thatcher had won a huge victory, with over 42 per cent of the vote, to start her second term of office. The head-line 'Mrs Thatcher back with a landslide' had filled Vera with joy. The new SDP Liberal Alliance had won only twenty-three seats, even though they received nearly as many votes as Labour. Michael Foot, the defeated Labour leader, described it as a tragedy for the country.

Meanwhile, Sally was looking soulfully at Vera's *Daily Telegraph*. The article 'Labour's Michael Foot and Denis Healey back in the doldrums' made her sigh and she wondered if the Labour Party would ever get back into power. She pointed to the list of election results on page 4. 'A pity,' she said. 'Michael Foot is a bright man, but some people put image first and he never came over well in that old duffel coat.'

'He looked more like a Ban the Bomb marcher,' said Vera.

'Dan voted Conservative this time,' said Jo. While Vera smiled, Sally winced visibly. It occurred to her that Maggie would need the police on her side in the years to come, but decided to keep this to herself.

'Never mind, Sally,' said Joseph. 'You're going to the zoo on Monday. That should be a lovely day out.'

Everyone smiled, none more so than Vera, who looked tenderly at her brother. 'It will be a fine day, Sally, I'm sure,' she said. 'And don't forget, Joseph, I'm coming to the vicarage this evening to make sure you have a good meal. I've seen the snacks you've been surviving on. Perhaps we ought to think about a housekeeper for you, or at least a cleaner.'

Joseph said nothing. He missed his sister every day and the vicarage had become a dusty haven for his hollow footfalls.

*   *   *

At lunchtime Victoria Alice Dudley-Palmer was standing in the dinner queue with Terry Earnshaw.

'Terry,' said Victoria Alice, 'my sister says that when she started at this school everyone used to say their prayers before school dinner. Then we all started lining up with these plastic trays. Mummy says it's like a cafeteria.'

'S'ppose so, Vicky,' said Terry, unconcerned. He had his eyes on his favourite spam fritters.

'Do *you* say prayers, Terry, before your meals at home?' continued Victoria Alice.

'No, Vicky, we don't 'ave to,' said Terry, ''cause my mam's a good cook.'

While the logic escaped Victoria, it seemed a reasonable enough explanation. As she queued up she wondered what it must be like *always* to eat without a napkin and why they never had spam fritters or purple custard at *her* home.

Meanwhile, across the High Street, Nora's Coffee Shop was doing a roaring trade, while Dorothy served the visiting workmen who had finished painting the zebra crossing.

Bonnie Tyler's recent hit, 'Total Eclipse of the Heart', was blasting out from the juke-box and Dorothy, of course, knew all the words and was singing along. I wondered whether, if someone had put the Periodic Table to music in the Sixties, I might have got a better mark in GCE Chemistry O-level . . . but that was wishful thinking.

*   *   *

During afternoon school we had our 'Activities' lesson when we all took different classes. Anne and Vera were teaching the children in Sally's class how to cross-stitch.

'In our 'ouse it's my mam what does all t'sewing an' suchlike,' said Terry Earnshaw as he struggled to thread a needle.

'But think how useful it will be when you grow up,' said the accomplished Victoria Alice. 'You can be an Eighties Man.'

'Quite right,' said Vera.

However, Terry's maths had improved recently and he did a quick calculation. 'But in ten years, when ah'm grown up, it'll be t'*Nineties*, miss.'

'I stand corrected,' said Vera with a smile.

In Anne's class I was enjoying my story time with the youngest children in Ragley School. I had just finished reading Eric Carle's *The Very Hungry Caterpillar* when, predictably, they all wanted to impart their latest news.

'My grandma and granddad are coming to stay at our house for the weekend,' said little Rosie Spittlehouse.

'And where do they live?' I asked.

'At the bus station,' she replied sweetly.

'The bus station?'

'Yes, Mr Sheffield. We go there when we want them to come an' stay and take 'em back there when my mummy says we've 'ad enough of 'em.'

Not for the first time, I recalled that conversations with reception class children were definitely *different*.

That evening I arrived home earlier than usual. Beth was in the kitchen steaming some vegetables and the appetizing smell of fish pie drifted from the oven. She had one eye on the little portable television set. Channel 4's *Countdown* was just finishing and Richard Whiteley was teasing Carol Vorderman, a shapely young woman who seemed to be good at mathematics.

In *my* eyes Beth had never looked more beautiful. Now in the thirty-third week of pregnancy, her floral smock rested against her precious bundle as she leant back against the kitchen worktop. Splashes of paint flecked her old denim jeans. 'I think it's finished now, Jack. Would you like to come and look?'

Since Beth had begun her maternity leave she had devoted her time to making our second bedroom into a perfect nursery. I followed her upstairs and as we stood in the doorway I wrapped my arms around her. 'It's wonderful; everything is just right,' I said and I kissed her neck softly. The scent of lavender was in her hair. However, sharp reality quickly spiked my dreamy thoughts when she said, 'I thought we could put a changing mat on the sofa, Jack – what do you think?'

On Saturday morning, in the back garden of Bilbo Cottage, butterflies danced with silent wings around the arched branches of the buddleia bushes and the drone of bees hung heavy in the heat haze. Beth had begun a herb garden and a new world of parsley, sage, rosemary and thyme had appeared in a raised bed next to the wooden frame of the compost heap. She was looking a little hot and bothered in her loose, knee-length, floral-patterned maternity dress as I helped her hang out the washing on this warm summer morning. When we set off for Ragley she wound down the car windows and enjoyed the welcoming breeze in her hair.

The shopping list was interesting, as Beth seemed to have discovered a new craving for food, particularly mashed potatoes and baked beans, plus the occasional bag of sherbet lemons. When we emerged from Prudence Golightly's General Stores, all the villagers seemed to be in good spirits . . . that is, until we met the sombre Deke Ramsbottom.

He raised his cowboy hat in greeting. 'G'morning Mr Sheffield, an' 'ow y'keepin', Mrs Sheffield?'

'Very well, thank you,' said Beth. 'And how are you?'

Deke pointed to his black armband. 'June eleventh, nineteen seventy-nine,' he said, 'saddest day o' my life.'

The anniversary of the death of John Wayne, Deke's favourite cowboy, was always a sad day for this local character. Predictably, his thoughts were elsewhere and later that lunchtime, when he lost at dominoes, he didn't even complain.

Outside the General Stores Ruby was chatting with her daughter Racquel. The pushchair beside them was full of shopping and Ruby was holding her granddaughter, Krystal. 'Your turn soon, Mrs Sheffield,' she said cheerfully.

'She's beautiful, Ruby,' said Beth. 'You must be very proud.'

'I am that . . . ah love 'er t'bits.'

'Shall ah tek 'er, Mam?' asked Racquel.

'No, let me 'old 'er a bit longer,' said Ruby.

'She's going to be a real beauty,' I said.

Ruby stroked the little girl's chestnut curls. 'Y'reight there, Mr Sheffield, an' ah'll tell y'summat, she'll 'ave a good life . . . better than 'er grandma.' Ruby looked up at me and her eyes were shining. 'She'll go far, this little un, Mr Sheffield. Y'know what they say – t'world's 'er 'amster.'

'Ah think it's *oyster*, Mam,' said Racquel.

But Ruby didn't hear. She was stroking Krystal's perfectly smooth hands with a work-red calloused finger.

'But ah do worry sometimes, Mr Sheffield,' continued Ruby. 'They say 'er who lives opposite to our Racquel – 'er wi' t'gammy leg and cut-price curtains – is a G-Hovis witness. Y'don't know who y'gettin' f'neighbours these days.'

'C'mon, Mam, time to get 'ome,' said Racquel.

'See y'Monday, Mr Sheffield. Let's 'ope it's another lovely day f'yer zoo trip. Our 'Azel can't wait.'

So it was that on a perfect Monday morning in bright sunshine William Featherstone's cream-and-green Reliance coach parked by the village green and the children clambered aboard. As was his way, William, in his brown coach driver's jacket, welcomed each passenger by doffing his peaked cap. Sue Phillips and four other mothers went to sit on the back seat and Sally and I shared the front seat behind the driver.

A horde of parents waved us off as if we were about to emigrate to Australia, while the children tested the springiness of their seats and wondered how soon they could eat their packed lunches.

'Nice day for t'outing, Mr Sheffield, Mrs Pringle,' said William, double de-clutching into first gear. It was a steady journey. We travelled north on the Scarborough Road and then on the A64 beyond Malton. Eventually William joined the A169 towards Pickering and Whitby, and finally turned left on the Kirby Misperton Road.

Theresa Ackroyd was reading a Flamingo Land brochure to her friends. 'It sez 'ere they've got African lions, camels, chimpanzees, a reptile 'ouse an' a bird 'ouse.'

'Ah'm not sure about reptiles,' said Michelle Cathcart nervously.

The Buttle twins were squashed on either side of her. 'Don't worry,' said Rowena.

'We'll look after you,' added Katrina.

Undeterred, Theresa pressed on. 'An' giraffes, zebras, tigers, sea lions, parrots an' peacocks.'

'What about a 'ippopotamus?' asked Dean Kershaw.

Theresa scanned the list again. 'Yes . . . a 'ippopotamus an' all. They've got ev'rything, even pink flamingos.'

Finally we pulled up in the car park. ''Ere we are, Mr Sheffield, safe an' sound,' said William.

As a teacher I found over the years that there is usually something that children remember above everything else about a school educational visit, and it isn't necessarily connected with the intention of the experience. After a trip to London to see the wonders of the Natural History Museum, a child will invariably get back to school and write about the escalators in the Underground. Likewise, a visit to the wonderful grounds of Fountains Abbey will be recalled by another as the day his best friend was sick on the coach. Our day in Flamingo Land was to prove such a day.

It began with a startled cry. 'Miss!' shouted nine-year-old Molly Paxton. 'Miss, come quick!'

Sally turned on her heel and hurried back towards Margery Ackroyd's group.

'What is it, Molly?' asked Sally.

'It's a funny zebra, miss,' said Molly.

'No, it's a *zebroid*, girls,' said Sally calmly. 'You can tell by its faint stripes.' She couldn't see what all the fuss was about. 'It's half zebra and half donkey.'

Mrs Ackroyd was looking perplexed and, surprisingly for Ragley's most vociferous gossip, she appeared quite speechless.

'But it's got *five* legs,' said Hazel Smith. Ruby's daughter's eyes were wide in amazement.

Sally stepped closer to the fenced enclosure and looked down. Her cheeks reddened instantly. Sally had certainly witnessed some sights in her life – but nothing like this. The zebroid had the biggest erection she had ever seen. It was huge and, from a certain angle, it certainly looked like a fifth leg.

Sally's whispered explanation to me on the coach home of how she handled the ensuing questions was priceless.

At the end of the school day we arrived back safely and forty-five tired children disembarked from the coach outside the school entrance. As they reminisced about their day at the zoo, Lillian Figgins had taken up her station by the side of her zebra crossing. Ruby was in the school office collecting litter from the wastepaper basket and Vera beckoned her over to the window. 'Ruby, I need to organize a cleaner for the vicarage. What do you think of Miss Figgins?'

'Lollipop Lil',' said Ruby, 'she's one o' best cleaners i'

Yorkshire. She used t'do f'that Lady Blakelock in that big 'ouse at 'Igh Sutton. In fac', she were jus' like you wi' a cloth on t'table even when y'not expectin' company, an' one o' them fancy Prussian rugs in 'er 'allway.'

'That's very interesting, Ruby,' said Vera . . . and she meant it.

The zebra crossing was clearly a novelty for the children and they waited in small groups to cross the road safely to get to the shops on the other side of the High Street.

Molly Paxton and Hazel Smith stood behind the kerb edge and looked up at Lillian. 'Miss Figgins,' shouted Molly, 'is this *your* zebra crossin'?'

Lillian smiled. 'Well ah s'ppose so, ah'm in charge o' it.' She walked to the centre of the road and held up her sign like Boadicea going into battle.

As they walked across, Molly Paxton said, 'We saw a zebra t'day, Miss Figgins.'

'Well that's lovely,' said Lillian.

'An' it 'ad *five* legs,' said Hazel.

Margery Ackroyd was next to cross with her daughters, Theresa and Charlotte.

'Well ah've 'eard it all now,' said Lillian, 'them little uns 'ave jus' said they saw a five-legged zebra t'day on t'school trip.'

Margery Ackroyd whispered in her ear.

'Really,' said Lillian, 'that long? By gum, that's enough t'mek y'eyes water,' and with a chuckle she realized she would definitely enjoy this job. In fact, she thought, you could write a book about it.

Chapter Eighteen

The Women's Institute Potato Champion

Mrs Grainger and Mrs Pringle collected a wide range of artwork from all classes to be displayed at the Ragley and Morton Agricultural Show on Saturday, 25 June. Class 1 had a teddy bears' picnic on the school field.

Extract from the Ragley School Logbook:
Friday, 24 June 1983

'What do you think, Ted?' said Miss Amelia Duff, the Ragley postmistress.

In the back yard of the post office Ted Postlethwaite, the Ragley postman, picked up an old watering can and gave Amelia's potato plant a generous drink. Back in March, at the Women's Institute, Mary Hardisty had given an even-sized tuber to all the members for their annual competition. The rules were simple: put it in a twelve-inch pot, add compost of your own choice and in June, at the Ragley and Morton Agricultural Show, the lady with the greatest weight of potatoes would be the champion.

'Well, this looks a winner t'me, Amelia,' said Ted with an encouraging smile. After he had finished his morning round he had called in for his usual cup of tea. He enjoyed doing extra little jobs for Amelia; it made him feel wanted. He could be close to the woman he loved . . . and he wondered if she knew. It was Friday, 24 June, a beautiful summer's morning, and, across the High Street, the bell rang for the beginning of another school day.

Immediately after registration, the fourteen school leavers in my class hurried down to the school gate. It was the day of their preliminary visit to Easington Comprehensive School and they climbed on to William Featherstone's Reliance coach. Most of them had now passed their eleventh birthday and they were growing up fast. Predictably, many of the girls towered over the boys, whose growth spurt would come later. I stood in the playground with the remainder of my class, the third-year juniors, and we waved them off.

'Our turn nex' year, Mr Sheffield,' said Hazel Smith as we walked back into our classroom and, once again, I reflected on the cycle of school life for a village teacher. The carousel of children simply went on while I got a year older and hopefully a little wiser. With such a small class it was a busy but quiet morning and, by breaktime, I was intrigued to see how new forceful characters had emerged now that their older classmates were absent.

Meanwhile, across the hall, Anne was in conversation with Shirley the cook, who had volunteered to help after lunch with Class 1's teddy bears' picnic on the school field. For once their conversation was uninterrupted, as this was one of the few occasions in the school day when the infant children were silent. They were all drinking their milk, sucking furiously at their bent straws and watching the level of milk drop magically in the third-of-a-pint bottles.

Jo had agreed that her children would help serve drinks and sandwiches at the picnic, which was a treat in store. However, in morning assembly they had just listened to Joseph's story of Moses and the parting of the Red Sea and all had not gone smoothly. Ben Roberts had taken some time to settle and so, when the bell went for morning break, Joseph looked down benevolently at the little boy.

'Ben,' he said, 'you were naughty this morning, but Mrs Hunter has told me you have worked hard so you *can* come to the picnic.'

Ben looked unhappy. 'Oh dear,' he said.

'I thought you would be pleased,' said Joseph.

'No, it's too late now, Mr Evans,' said Ben, clearly full of remorse.

'Why is it too late?' asked Joseph.

'I've already prayed for rain,' said Ben sadly, 'and, like y'said, Mr Evans, God is always listening.'

At morning break Vera was scanning the front page of her *Daily Telegraph* and frowning. 'That dreadful young man John McEnroe has been misbehaving again at Wimbledon,' she muttered, and then read the next article, 'and the Commons are debating whether to bring back hanging.'

'That should keep the umpires happy,' said Sally, but Vera didn't hear.

Jo was standing by the open staff-room door. She didn't look her usual relaxed and cheerful self. 'Jack, can I have a word sometime?'

'Of course,' I said, 'how about now?'

Jo shrugged her shoulders. 'I'm on duty.'

'Well, I'll come out to the yard with you,' I said.

We picked up our coffees and walked under the overhanging branches of the giant horse-chestnut trees, heavy in leaf, and leant against the stone wall in the welcome shade.

'Sadly, it's *mixed* news, Jack,' she said, sipping her coffee hesitantly.

'Yes?'

'It's Dan . . . he's got his promotion to sergeant.'

'But that's wonderful,' I said. 'We must celebrate.'

'Yes, that's the first thing he said on the phone,' she said with a smile. Then she looked up at the belltower as if seeing it for the first time and sighed. 'I've loved it here, Jack. I couldn't have wished for a better start to my career.' She sipped her coffee again. 'Dan's job will be in York at the main station and we've been offered a police house in the city.'

'But that's only ten miles away, Jo, and it's a good road out past the hospital and the Rowntree's factory.'

'I know that, Jack, but I looked in the *Times Educational Supplement* and there's a good job in York at Priory Gate Juniors to start next January, with a Scale Two responsibility post for girls' games and science.'

'Ah, I see . . . promotion,' I said. 'Well, you've got the

experience, Jo. It would be perfect for you, and you know I would give you an excellent reference.'

'Thanks, Jack. Perhaps we can meet up over the weekend and talk it through before I mention it to the others – especially Anne. She's been like a big sister to me.'

'I understand, Jo. Let's do that. Now, how do you fancy winding a skipping rope?'

Jo grinned. 'Why not?' she said. We gave our empty mugs to Louise Hartley, took over from the Buttle twins and the skipping commenced with Jo chanting out the rhyme

> *'One two buckle my shoe,*
> *Three four knock at the door,*
> *Five six pick up sticks,*
> *Seven eight lay them straight,*
> *Nine ten big fat hen.'*

My presence clearly made a difference and a few boys joined in, but not, of course, Terry Earnshaw, who shook his head in disbelief. This boy of Barnsley was brought up to believe that only *girls* skipped; but then again, if he grew up to be a middleweight boxer, who knows? . . . and he wandered off to box his own shadow against the school wall.

It was a relaxed day, one of those a teacher treasures and, after lunch, as I sat on the school field with Anne's class, I was reminded how lucky I was to do a job I loved and in such a perfect setting. All the children had brought their much-loved and occasionally threadbare teddy bears and were sitting in a large circle, being served with honey sandwiches and orange juice. Behind me in the hedgerow the incessant murmur of insects in the tall grasses was the sound of summer and I leant back and soaked up the welcome sunshine.

Before the end of the day, the school leavers returned full of excitement.

'It was brilliant, Mr Sheffield,' said Tracy Hartley. 'They've got a new lady deputy 'eadteacher an' she's dead tall an' slim an' she gave us a talk. She told us about that first American woman in space.'

I recalled that last week the NASA astronaut Sally Ride had blasted into orbit on board the space shuttle *Challenger*. 'And what did she say, Tracy?' I asked.

'She said we should follow our dreams and take our opportunities . . . but, Mr Sheffield, ah think she was looking at us girls when she said it.'

'Ah wunt mind bein' an' astronaut, Mr Sheffield,' said Dean Kershaw, 'or mebbe a footballer.'

Elisabeth Amelia was standing to one side looking thoughtful. 'And what did you think about the visit, Elisabeth?' I asked quietly.

'Not sure, Mr Sheffield,' she said. 'The school looked lovely and has a super gymnasium and a great hockey team, but Mummy has got the prospectus for the Time School for Girls in York, so I'm probably going there and I'll have to make new friends.'

'I'm sure you'll do well wherever you go,' I said and she gave me a gentle smile and continued to pack her school-bag with the mathematics homework that her mother had requested.

*   *   *

It had been a good day and Heathcliffe and Terry Earnshaw arrived home in good spirits . . . that is, until Mrs Earnshaw asked the inevitable question: 'And what did you learn at school today?'

'Nowt,' answered Heathcliffe and Terry in unison.

'Well, y'must 'ave learned summat,' insisted Mrs Earnshaw.

Grudgingly Heathcliffe glanced at his brother and nodded. 'Well ah went to t'big school for a visit, but our Terry were at school all day.'

'So what did y'do, Terry?'

'T'vicar told us about Moses,' he said.

'So what were it abart?' she asked, refusing to serve the beans on toast until she received a satisfactory answer.

'Well, God sent Moses to rescue them Israelites,' said Terry, 'an' it were reight dangerous, Mam . . . be'ind enemy lines, so t'speak.'

Mrs Earnshaw began to serve the food. 'That's int'resting.'

Terry was rising to the occasion. 'So 'e got 'em t'build a bridge to get 'em across t'Red Sea sharpish-like.'

'A bridge?' said Mrs Earnshaw, 'ah don't recall Charlton 'Eston building no bridge.'

Terry was becoming animated as the story grew in the telling. 'So they all got across and then 'e radioed 'eadquarters for t'bombers t'come.'

'Bombers?' asked the bemused Mrs Earnshaw.

'Yes, bombers, Mam,' said Terry, 'to blow t'bridge up.'

'An' that's 'ow they were saved,' said Heathcliffe.

'An' is that what t'vicar said?'

'Well not 'xactly, Mam, 'cause if y'd 'eard 'is story y'd never 'ave believed it. Isn't that reight 'Eath?'

"E's reight, Mam,' said Heathcliffe. 'We did Moses last year.'

'Well, at least y'learnin' summat useful,' said Mrs Earnshaw and gave them both an extra spoonful of beans.

That evening Vera sat on a Victorian chaise longue in one of the expansive bay windows at Morton Manor and looked out on to the magnificent lawns and neat flower-beds. The stripes on the lawns were ruler-straight and not a weed was in sight. It was perfect . . . perhaps *too* perfect, thought Vera. Suddenly a peacock strutted across the path, tail feathers erect. It was a show of fierce pride, or perhaps mere vanity, and she smiled at the brave show of confidence.

Life was different now, mused Vera. She missed her garden. The hedgerow would be a harmony of honey-suckle and hawthorn and in her kitchen garden she could have cut a cabbage or picked raspberries. She also wondered how Joseph was coping.

In the distance Rupert was hard at work organizing the erection of the giant marquees for tomorrow's Ragley and Morton Agricultural Show. It was one of the highlights of the year and the largest annual gathering of the two villages. Vera smiled when she saw the guy ropes being tightened on the Women's Institute tent. This was where the fiercest battles would be played out, in a world of sweet peas, Victoria sponges, fragrant roses, paintings and poetry, and she smiled in anticipation.

*   *   *

Saturday was a perfect midsummer morning and I was up early in order to clean my pride and joy, namely my Morris Minor Traveller, which, as each year went by, was creating more interest at the annual show. The yellow-and-chrome AA badge on the grille gleamed in the sunshine and Beth and I set off for the spacious grounds of Morton Manor. We wound down the windows and enjoyed the fresh breeze as we drove along the narrow back road to Ragley and, with cow parsley swaying in the tall grasses and Red Admiral butterflies chasing through the lush green nettles, it was a pleasure to be alive on this special day.

We called in at Victor Pratt's garage and he emerged to serve me from the single pump on his forecourt. I noticed he was limping badly and decided, with some trepidation, to ask the inevitable question. 'How are you, Victor?' Victor's ailments over the years would have filled a good-sized medical journal.

'Ah'm in agony,' he said as he unscrewed my filler cap.

'Oh dear,' I said, 'and why is that?'

'It's me leg, Mr Sheffield,' he said, gently tapping his right leg with his free hand. 'It's gone t'sleep. Ah've no feeling.'

'I'm sorry to hear that, Victor,' I said with sympathy.

'An' it's worse at neight,' he added, with the look of a martyr in torment.

'Is it?' I replied. 'And why is that?'

'Well that's when it wakes up, jus' when t'rest o' me wants t'go t'sleep. Ah don't know if ah'm coming or going. An' ah've started t'get that room-tism in me elbow,' he added, rubbing his arm sorrowfully.

'Perhaps it's tennis elbow,' I said.

'Nah, that's jus' f'posh folks, not likes o' me,' said Victor. 'An' talkin' abart posh folks, Mr an' Mrs Sheffield, t'major 'as done a reight good job on t'show field. It looks a picture.'

We parked in one of the huge fields close to the tractors and horseboxes and alongside a Mini Clubman Estate. We stood and peered through the window at the state-of-the-art instrument panel behind the steering wheel instead of in the middle of the dashboard. 'Wouldn't you prefer one of these, Jack?' said Beth, more in hope than expectation. 'It would bring you into the Eighties.' As usual I affected a determined insouciance. After all, love for a woman is one thing, but love for a car is quite another.

The show was a magnificent affair, with large marquees surrounding the show-jumping arena where Virginia Anastasia Forbes-Kitchener was creating the usual interest among the local menfolk. Beth and I headed for the refreshment tent for a cool drink and, in Beth's case, a chance to sit down.

One end of the marquee was devoted to cream teas and the other seemed to be populated by beer drinkers. Don Bradshaw was behind one of the trestle tables talking to Big Dave and Little Malcolm, while Sheila was serving Old Tommy Piercy with a pint of Tetley's bitter from a large barrel.

'Now then, Mr Sheffield,' said Don, nodding towards

Beth, who was sitting at one of the tables, 'an' 'ow's your good lady?'

'Fine thanks, Don,' I said. 'She just fancied a cool orange juice.'

"Ow long 'as she t'go now, Mr Sheffield?' asked Sheila, as she served Old Tommy with a frothing pint.

'Just another month,' I said, 'so this hot weather doesn't help her.'

'It were t'same f'me wi' our Claire, Mr Sheffield,' said Sheila. 'Ah were sweatin' cobs in t'las' few weeks. So, what are y'drinkin'?'

'A half of bitter, please, Sheila,' I said.

Behind the bar, Clint Ramsbottom had set up a rudimentary disco and Simon and Garfunkel were singing 'Bridge Over Troubled Water'.

'Ah'll give 'em troubled water,' said Old Tommy scornfully as he supped his pint.

'How d'you mean, Mr Piercy?' I asked.

'Them Yanks,' he muttered with disdain.

'Oh you mean . . .' I said, nodding towards the jukebox.

'Yes, that Simon an' Carbuncle. Norra patch on Bing Crosby.'

'I agree,' I said. It seemed the right thing to say.

'Ah can allus tell a sensible chap, Mr Sheffield,' said Old Tommy. ''E thinks same as ah do.'

Big Dave and Little Malcolm nodded in agreement, finished their pints and peered out at the shimmering marquees. 'Any road, ah'm off to t'Bowling for a Pig stall,' said Big Dave.

'More like bowlin' for a runt,' said Old Tommy Piercy bluntly. 'It's only a little un.' Then he glanced across at Little Malcolm. 'No offence intended, young Malcolm,' he added hurriedly.

'None tekken, Mr Piercy,' said Little Malcolm with a frown, and the two binmen of Ragley went out to seek their fortune.

Vera and her friend Joyce Davenport, resplendent in her president's green sash, were in the Women's Institute marquee and looking at the various competition entries, from a posy in an egg-cup to a single rose.

It was hot and sticky in the tent and Dorothy Humpleby's conversation with Diane the hairdresser naturally turned to body odour.

'Well, Dorothy,' said Diane, 'ah use that Arrid Extra Dry. It sez on t'cannister it gives y'that *certain feeling.*'

'What d'you mean, that *certain feeling*?'

'Y'll know when yer older, Dorothy,' said Diane knowingly, and they walked off to join Nora, who had entered the Garden in a Shoebox competition.

Later Beth and I joined Vera at a wrought-iron garden table outside the Women's Institute tent for afternoon tea and scones with home-made strawberry jam and fresh cream. We sat on wickerwork chairs in speckled sunshine beneath the branches of a magnificent copper beech tree, its leaves like burnished gold under a fiery sun.

'Isn't this the most perfect day?' said Beth, pushing back her wide-brimmed straw hat. 'I do love summer,' she patted her tummy, 'although this tends to make it hot work.'

'You look radiant, dear,' said Vera. 'Simply glowing.'

Beth laughed. 'You say the nicest things, Vera. And what about you? How do you feel now?'

'I really am very happy – fully recovered and content, although I will be happier when Joseph is more settled. Fortunately, I've got Miss Figgins to go in to the vicarage to clean for him and prepare the occasional meal. So we're getting there slowly.' She looked at her watch. 'Well, it's almost time for the results of the potato competition and Deirdre Coe insists she's the favourite . . . so let's hope someone can put her in her place.'

When we walked into the Women's Institute tent the crowds were gathering in front of a sign that read:

Women's Institute Potato Growing Competition
Judging at 3 p.m.

George Hardisty, Ragley's champion gardener and a retired North Yorkshire Moors sheep farmer, was approaching his seventieth birthday but still looked remarkably fit and healthy after a lifetime of outdoor work. His wife, Mary, had wisely opted out of this competition, as George's famous liquid compost, including his 'secret ingredient', would have meant she would surely win. So it was that she wrote down the name of each competitor and the weight of their potato crop.

George had done this many times. He cut off the tall straggly haulm with his razor-sharp penknife, emptied the contents of each pot on to a table, carefully removed each precious potato and checked for scab and worm.

319

It was a close-run thing, but finally Joyce Davenport walked up to the rickety microphone, blew in it twice to confirm it was working and made the announcement. 'Ladies and gentlemen, first of all, thank you to Mr and Mrs Hardisty for being so thorough in their judging, and can we show our appreciation?' There was a ripple of applause and Amelia Duff bit her bottom lip in anticipation. Standing alongside was the faithful Ted Postlethwaite, who had finished his morning post round that day in record time. Joyce scanned the crowd of faces in front of her. 'I'm pleased to announce that, with a magnificent total weight of two pounds and twelve ounces from a single tuber, the winner of the Wilfred Grubb trophy and the Women's Institute Potato Champion for 1983 is . . . Miss Amelia Duff.'

Ted cheered, Amelia looked as if she would burst into tears, Deirdre Coe walked out in a huff and Vera led the applause from the crowd.

Gradually the crowds dispersed and Ted carried Amelia's trophy back to his car.

It was a perfect evening. The setting sun over the distant hills was a disc of polished bronze and the sky was on fire with backlit clouds. In the back yard of the Ragley Post Office Amelia and Ted were sitting at her little picnic table and enjoying a fish-and-chip supper and a pot of tea.

Ted had never been happier. 'Congratulations, Amelia,' he said, raising his cup of sweet tea.

'I've never won anything like this before,' she said.

Ted picked up the trophy from the table. 'It says 'ere you're a *champion*, Amelia,' he said softly.

'I've never been a champion,' she said.

Ted sighed. 'You'll always be a champion t'me . . . always.'

Amelia looked down and sipped her tea and she knew, after all these years, he was the one.

Chapter Nineteen

Educating Jack

14 4th-year juniors left today and will commence full-time education at Easington Comprehensive School in September. 92 children were registered on roll on the last day of the school year.

Extract from the Ragley School Logbook:
Friday, 22 July 1983

It had been an uncomfortable night. The heat was stifling and, in Bilbo Cottage, we had opened the bedroom windows to seek some relief. A summer storm was building in the far distance and occasional flashes of lightning lit up the Hambleton hills. Fortunately, the boom of thunder was far off and, for tonight at least, heaven's army was passing us by. But our turn was coming and we knew it would be soon.

Beth had tossed and turned and neither of us had snatched much sleep. It was Friday, 22 July, the last day of the school year, and I breakfasted earlier than usual in order to get to school in time to prepare for our Leavers' Assembly. Beth was at the sink filling the kettle and I wrapped my arms around her. 'How do you feel?' I asked.

'Just a little . . . well, you know, *uncomfortable*,' she said.

The truth was I didn't *know*; I could only guess. The best I could do was to offer to make a cup of tea. Having babies was a bit like my O-level Chemistry exam: I knew the theory but, sadly, that's where it ended. 'Hey, our baby moved!' I said in alarm.

Beth smiled wearily and sat down heavily on one of the old pine chairs. Her cheeks were flushed and her hair seemed to have a mind of its own; damp, wavy blonde strands framed her face. 'I'll be glad when it's all over,' she said with a brave smile. 'Shouldn't be too long now.'

When I drove into Ragley, life was going on as usual and the sights and sounds were familiar. Outside the village hall, honeysuckle clambered over the entrance porch where Joyce Davenport put up a Women's Institute notice advertising a 'Cream Teas, Crumpets and Curd Tarts' afternoon at Morton Manor. In the General Stores, Prudence Golightly was selling pink sugar mice with tails of thin white string to the Hartley sisters and, next door, Young Tommy Piercy, supervised by his grandfather, was arranging neat matching pairs of pigs' trotters in the front window of the Butcher's Shop. Meanwhile, outside the village Pharmacy, Eugene Scrimshaw, the *Star Trek* fan, was being reprimanded by his wife for swearing in Klingon. In the doorway of Pratt's Hardware Emporium, Timothy Pratt was polishing his doorbell with Brasso while Dorothy Humpleby was standing outside Nora's

Coffee Shop and humming along to the recent Police number one on the juke-box, 'Every Breath You Take'. In the window of her Hair Salon, Diane Wigglesworth was putting up a photograph of Joan Collins next to one of Kevin Keegan, as both were sporting the same hairstyle. Meanwhile, outside the Post Office, Miss Amelia Duff was blushing slightly as the postman, Ted Postlethwaite, had just asked her to go with him to the Odeon Cinema.

On the village green the ancient oak tree was heavy in leaf and acorn, and beside its massive trunk a few Ragley folk were chatting about life and the price of bread. By the village pond, under the graceful branches of the weeping willow tree, two retired farmers sat puffing happily on their briar pipes, watching the village wake up on this still, breathless morning. Outside school the horse-chestnut trees provided welcome shade to the front of the playground and a group of school leavers had gathered there to talk about their last day at Ragley School and the seemingly endless summer holiday that stretched in front of them.

When I walked into the entrance hall, Ruby was carrying a box of paper towels and singing 'Climb Every Mountain'.

'And how are you feeling, Ruby?' I asked.

'Reight champion, thank you,' said Ruby. 'An' 'ow's Mrs Sheffield?'

'Not enjoying this hot weather,' I said. 'I think she'll be relieved when the baby finally arrives.'

'Well, give 'er our love, Mr Sheffield, an' tell 'er our little Krystal is comin' on a treat,' and she hurried off to the staff cloakroom, singing to her heart's content.

*　　　*　　　*

At a quarter past ten our school hall was full of children, staff, parents, governors . . . and *expectation*. It was our annual Leavers' Assembly, when we said an official farewell to the children in their final year at Ragley. Joseph led the hymns and prayers and, at the end, Major Rupert Forbes-Kitchener presented a book to every school leaver. Each pupil came up in turn to receive their leaving gift, purchased by the Parent Teacher Association, while their parents, in the back row, clapped and, as always, some of the mothers shed a tear. They knew this was a 'coming of age' occasion, when their children said goodbye to primary school and moved on to the bigger world of secondary education. Their babies had grown up and they wondered where the years had gone.

I watched them walk out to the front of the hall one by one: Theresa Ackroyd, Alice Baxter, Theresa Buttle, Debbie Clack, Heathcliffe Earnshaw, Dean Kershaw, Amanda Pickles and so on. The books had been selected with care by Sue Phillips, Chair of the Parent Teacher Association. Elisabeth Amelia Dudley-Palmer was delighted to receive a large colourful copy of *Caring for Your Pony*, while Sarah Louise Tait, our best reader, was thrilled to be given the classic tale *Wind in the Willows*. It was a poignant moment when I stood up and thanked everyone for their support throughout the year, including Mrs Earnshaw as temporary caretaker. However, the biggest cheer of all went to Vera and Ruby, who had overcome adversity and returned to give their best to Ragley School. It was the major who led the standing ovation and Vera had to forsake yet another of her lace-edged handkerchiefs so that Ruby could wipe away the tears.

*   *   *

At lunchtime I walked out in to the playground and looked at the school leavers, who had gathered together in a private huddle on the school field. The time for fare-wells had finally arrived.

How do you say goodbye to a group of children, to a generation? They had been with me for six years, from 1977, and I had been their headteacher for almost their entire primary school career. It was a strange feeling, a mixture of sadness and satisfaction. I knew I had done my best for them and hoped that it would be good enough to prepare them for the next stage in their lives. A whole new world of acne and adolescence, tests and timetables, friends and foes awaited them, along with their journey towards the world of work in the distant Nineties. I had done my best to start them on their pathway through life. They were literate and numerate, but, more than that, I hoped they understood the importance of consideration towards others and, of course, a love of learning.

When the bell rang for afternoon classes I walked into school and Heathcliffe Earnshaw caught up with me. 'Thanks for everything, Mr Sheffield,' he said. 'Ah'll be sorry t'go, but ah'm lookin' forward t'big school.'

'And so you should, Heathcliffe,' I said. 'I hope you work hard and make the most of your opportunity.'

'They 'ave proper woodwork benches up there, Mr Sheffield, an' ah've 'eard they do metalwork an' 'ow engines work an' suchlike.' He hurried into class for his final afternoon at Ragley School, then suddenly stopped and stared as if for the first time at the displays on the walls: the paintings and the stories; the posters of the solar system and the map of the world; the little carpeted book corner and the 'wet area' next to the sink with the jam jars full of bristle brushes and clay-modelling tools. For a moment there was a flicker of sadness. It was as if he had realized he had finally grown out of his favourite pair of football boots. Then he grinned, sat at his desk and winked at Elisabeth Amelia, who blushed and picked up her reading book. It occurred to me that eleven-year-olds grew up quickly these days.

When the bell rang for the end of school I went into the office and sat at my desk. Vera was doing some end-of-year filing. I opened the bottom left-hand drawer of my desk and took out the huge leather-bound school logbook. It would be my last entry for the academic year 1982/83.

I had just written, '*14 4th-year juniors left today and will commence full-time education at Easington Comprehensive School in September*' when Vera, who was standing by the office window, said quietly, 'Jack . . . Jack, come and look at this.' She had called me Jack and it took me by surprise. It appeared that, as the school year was now officially over, the old conformities no longer applied.

'What is it, Vera?' I asked, walking over to join her.

She pointed out of the window. Heathcliffe and Elisabeth Amelia were at the back of the group of school leavers walking out of the gate for the last time as pupils of Ragley School. Then they paused, looked back and waved.

Life is a collection of moments. Some sear the soul like burning rain. Others lift the spirit and stir the imagination, captured in the stillness of a perfect memory. Like a ship in a bottle, frozen in a timeless vacuum, so many years later, the image of Heathcliffe and Elisabeth Amelia remains in my mind.

They stood at the gate talking. Elisabeth Amelia had always admired the rough-and-ready Heathcliffe with his rugged good looks and confidence in all he did. He was different to the boys she met at dancing class and piano lessons. Likewise, Heathcliffe was attracted to the positive, articulate Elisabeth Amelia . . . but, at the age of eleven, he didn't understand why.

Neither knew it then, but this was destined to be their last conversation until they finally met up again in 2008 at the Ragley School twenty-five-year reunion.

Theirs was a poignant story. Heathcliffe left Easington Comprehensive School at the age of sixteen. After an apprenticeship as a carpenter, he acquired many of the skills of the building trade and, with the ever-faithful Terry, launched the successful Earnshaw Brothers, Builders. Heathcliffe would marry the petite beauty, Mo Hartley, a girl of whom he was completely unaware during his schooldays at Ragley, and they had three sons. His brother Terry never married and was happy to follow in Heathcliffe's footsteps, working from dawn till dusk as one of Yorkshire's finest bricklayers, never far from his brother's side.

Elisabeth Amelia, after gaining four A-levels at the Time School for Girls, York's finest private school, followed by a first-class honours degree at Cambridge, became a London-based barrister with a reputation for her analytical mind and driving ambition. By the age of thirty-five she had two failed marriages behind her and a client list of the rich and famous.

But on that long-ago day in the springtime of their lives, these two children of Ragley village were still immersed in the cocoon of childhood, an innocent world of here and now. For Heathcliffe and Elisabeth Amelia, *experience* would come later . . . that was a distant doorway. Through it were different pathways and, sadly, only one of them led to true happiness.

As had become the tradition, the hall was filling up with staff, governors and a few members of the Parent Teacher Association for the end-of-year party – or, to be more precise, tea and cakes and gentle conversation. The major looked formal as always in a smart three-piece suit, while Joseph had donned his cream linen jacket, baggy white flannels and a Panama hat. Joseph had insisted that he would collect Beth from Kirkby Steepleton to save her the drive and they arrived together. Happily, Beth looked calm and unflustered, almost serene, as she perched on the comfortable height of the piano stool and listened to Sally Pringle's tale of childbirth.

Sue Phillips was chatting with Anne Grainger and Jo Hunter about her plans for the summer holiday, while Ruby was telling Vera about the party she had arranged for tomorrow afternoon to celebrate the first birthday of her granddaughter. In cross-stitch class Ruby had made a beautiful canvas place mat with the name 'Krystal Carrington Ruby Entwhistle' neatly embroidered across the centre.

'It's beautiful, Ruby,' said Vera.

'An' ah made this f'you, Mrs F,' said Ruby, who had finally adopted a shortened version of Vera's married name. For Ruby, the progression from *Miss E* to *Mrs F* had a certain alphabetical consistency. 'Jus' t'say thank you for everything you've done f'me since t'accident. It's almost a year to t'day.' Ruby handed over a small piece of white cloth set in a small white picture frame. In neat stitches was the single word 'FRIENDSHIP'.

Vera looked close to tears and gave Ruby a hug. 'My dear Ruby, I'll treasure it for the rest of my life' . . . and, of course, she did.

The squeaking wheels of the kitchen trolley and the rattle of cups and saucers announced the arrival of Shirley and Doreen with the Baby Burco boiler steaming away merrily. Sally and Jo had arranged a wonderful buffet on two of the dining tables and, as usual, the centrepiece was a large plateful of Vera's incomparable scones, competing for attention alongside another of Doreen Critchley's formidable apple tarts.

It was a happy occasion, relaxed and carefree. Another year had gone by and we had all moved on with our lives. Eventually everyone drifted off in twos and threes, and Beth went out to the car to wait for me there. Finally, Anne and I did our usual routine of checking windows and doors and I locked away the school logbook in my desk for another year. I turned the key in the giant entrance door and Anne and I looked at each other. 'Well, Jack, we've survived another year,' she said with a tired smile.

'Thanks for everything, Anne,' I said.

'I do enjoy working with you, Jack,' she said pensively, 'but for the first time I'm beginning to feel *tired* . . . *really* tired.' She sighed. 'And when this new curriculum starts, as it surely must now, I'm not sure I'll cope. Education is changing.'

'That's for another day,' I said. 'Go and enjoy a well-earned break and we'll all come back refreshed in September.'

Anne looked across the car park and waved at Beth. 'In the meantime, Jack, you need to get Beth home. She needs a rest more than I do . . . and good luck,' and she kissed me on the cheek. Moments later we both drove out of school and left the academic year 1982/83 behind us.

Saturday morning dawned heavy and oppressive. A dull purple haze etched the unfocused line where the sky met the distant hills. Beneath the iron-grey clouds lay the troubled land and the fields shimmered in the haze.

Beth's spirits seemed to lift as the day wore on and we both did a little more work in the newly decorated nursery. There was a little cot, a present from Beth's parents, a freshly painted bookcase and a bright new sofa. 'Let's go into York,' said Beth after lunch. 'We need a few more baby things.'

I smiled. Our home had been transformed into a warehouse of nappies, vests and tiny white bootees, but I guessed there was always room for a few more. In the hallway we skirted round a shiny new pram, a gift from my mother, picked up a shopping basket and drove into York, where we parked in Goodramgate.

We were in Marks & Spencer's in Parliament Street when Beth suddenly said, 'Jack, I need the loo.' The sign at the foot of the escalator indicated there was one on the first floor. By the time we got there, Beth was panting heavily. The notice on the door read: 'TOILET OUT OF ORDER, PLEASE USE FLOOR BELOW'. 'Oh dear,' said Beth with a taut smile. 'I may have to take that literally, Jack, if we don't get a move on,' but I could see she was in discomfort.

It was as we came down the stairs that it all happened.

'Oh, Jack . . . Jack!' Beth suddenly leant forward and I thought she was going to topple over. I grabbed her round the waist and we hurried through a staring crowd.

A helpful lady appeared at our side. 'Let me help,' she said and led us towards a chair next to the information desk.

Beth gripped my hand. 'Jack, I think we ought to go to Fulton . . . now.'

The young woman behind the counter summed up the situation quickly as we hurried out.

'I'll ring them to say you're on your way,' she shouted after us.

As I drove out towards Fulton Hospital, the skies darkened and there was a rumble of thunder. It was the sound of the oncoming storm and, over the distant hills, dark heavy cumulus clouds had spread dragons' wings over the horizon. Heaven's marching forces were coming and we were its battlefield. I put my foot down and coaxed my Morris Minor Traveller to go a little faster. The weather was closing in like a mighty maelstrom and we raced ahead of the raging clouds. The hospital gates appeared and I breathed a sigh of relief. As we pulled up outside the entrance the first splashes of rain hit the windscreen, large droplets, precursors of the fury to come. Beth was strangely quiet as we stepped out into the humid vortex of the gathering darkness, into the stillness before the storm.

She squeezed my hand and whispered, 'Oh, Jack . . . stay with me.' It worried me to see her so pale; gone was the vitality I knew so well. She was poised on the edge of change, between excitement and sheer exhaustion. Her green eyes were bright with expectation and she breathed deeply, summoning inner strength.

Fulton Maternity Hospital had seen better days. It was an old Victorian building dominated by a large chimney and had once been an army camp. It was about to be replaced by a new maternity wing at York Hospital, but, in spite of its crumbling walls, the doctors and nurses brought life and hope and high professionalism to their caring role. Two nurses in starched white aprons met us on the steps and spoke quickly to Beth in hushed tones: they were calm and efficient, no wasted words. A minute later, Beth, on a trolley bed, was being whisked through the entrance hall, down a corridor with cream-and-green walls and past a large sign that read DELIVERY ROOMS. I hurried along behind, feeling helpless.

An experienced midwife in a turquoise-blue uniform with a wide, dark-blue belt ushered me outside into the corridor. 'Mr Sheffield,' she said quietly, 'there's nothing you can do here for the present. Your wife is asking for her overnight bag, so why don't you go home for that and we'll talk again when you return. Nothing will happen for a good while yet.' She sounded reassuring and my heartbeat began to slow again. An auxiliary nurse was standing beside us hanging on every word. 'Jean here will take you back to the entrance.'

I nodded, although I didn't want to leave Beth. 'I understand,' I said, 'and I'll be back as soon as I can.'

Outside the heavens had opened and rained lashed down. The return journey to Kirkby Steepleton was both difficult and dangerous and I was relieved that Beth was safe in hospital. When I returned later I was offered tea and sandwiches and asked to sit in a small waiting room off the main corridor. I wanted to be with Beth, but for some reason they were keeping me at arm's length. I telephoned Beth's parents and they asked if I could ring the moment I had any news.

Time ticked by and in the early hours of Sunday morning I peered through the window. On this stormy night the secret land was bound in shadow; only the creatures of the woodland moved with effortless ease. Eventually the rain stopped and the pre-dawn touched the fields with ghostly fingers of grey light. I looked up, attracted by a sound. A metronomic click of heels on the polished tiled floor echoed down the corridor.

A doctor arrived, smart in a collar and tie and casual brown cord trousers. His white coat flapped carelessly as he strode towards me and his stethoscope bounced against his chest. It was a purposeful walk and, to my surprise, he paused and took my arm. 'Mr Sheffield,' he said, 'perhaps we can have a word.' He was about my age, tall with a square jaw and grey eyes. He beckoned me towards one of the chairs. 'Please,' he said quietly, 'do sit down. I'm here to tell you not to worry but, for the time being, we would like you to wait here.'

'Is everything . . . all right?' I asked.

His gaze was steady and unwavering and there was a deafening silence as he appeared to search for the right words. 'Just a few complications,' he said quietly, 'but nothing to worry about.'

'*Complications?*' I said.

'Yes, but nothing we can't handle.'

I looked at him, trying to gauge his mood. He appeared fond of the double negative, but he also seemed perfectly calm and utterly competent.

'I'd like to be with my wife,' I said.

'I understand, Mr Sheffield,' he said, 'but that might not be helpful right now.' The knot in my stomach tightened. He stood up and put his hand on my shoulder. 'The baby was in the breech position and we're concerned about foetal distress, so Mrs Sheffield is now in theatre. We need to do a Caesarean section,' he said. 'So please wait here and we'll let you know very soon.'

Back in the operating theatre the midwife, plus a student midwife along with an obstetrician and the duty anaesthetist, had moved smoothly into action. It felt like the longest night of my life, but finally the midwife arrived. She smiled and sat down next to me. 'Congratulations, Mr Sheffield,' she said, 'your wife is in recovery and you have a son. We think the baby will be OK, but we need to monitor his progress very carefully and he will be in an incubator for the next few hours.'

I could barely breathe, never mind reply. 'Thank you,' I muttered, 'thank you . . . can I see my wife?'

'Yes, if you'll come with me and then we'll arrange for both of you to see the baby later.'

Beth was in bed looking tired but happy.

'I love you,' I whispered in her ear.

'Jack . . . I love you . . . and we have a son.'

I held her hand and kissed her gently. 'He'll be fine,' I said, 'the midwife explained . . . apparently this is normal procedure after a difficult birth.'

Time passed by and we talked quietly about our hopes and fears, but at last the midwife and a smiling student nurse helped Beth into a wheelchair and we were taken into another room. Our baby was in an incubator, lying on his back on a cellular blanket. He had been washed clean and wore a little nappy, and the tag on his wrist showed he weighed 8lb 2oz.

Beth looked at our son with the pride of a mother. He had big, innocent eyes, fair hair, little fingers and toes . . . a tiny scrap of humanity . . . he was perfect.

Then Beth put her hand through the sleeve fixed in the side of the incubator and gently touched his face and stroked each tiny hand. I fixed the scene in my mind, never to be forgotten. The past year had changed us all; this was the end of one journey and the start of a new one.

It felt like an age, but eventually Beth looked at me and said, 'Your turn.'

I reached in and pushed my arm through the sleeve.

Then came the moment: my son reached out and gripped my finger. It was the birth of an unbreakable bond, the beginning of a life shared.

Life really was an education.

And in a heartbeat, my world seemed complete.

Advanced Bookkeeping
Level 3
Advanced Diploma in
Accounting
Question Bank
For assessments from
September 2017

Third edition 2017

ISBN 9781 5097 1257 1

British Library Cataloguing-in-Publication Data
A catalogue record for this book is available
from the British Library

Published by

BPP Learning Media Ltd
BPP House, Aldine Place
142-144 Uxbridge Road
London W12 8AA

www.bpp.com/learningmedia

Printed in the United Kingdom

Your learning materials, published by
BPP Learning Media Ltd, are printed on
paper obtained from traceable
sustainable sources.

We are grateful to the AAT for permission to reproduce
the sample assessment(s). The answers to the sample
assessment(s) have been published by the AAT. All other
answers have been prepared by BPP Learning Media Ltd.

BPP Learning Media is grateful to the IASB for
permission to reproduce extracts from the International
Financial Reporting Standards including all
International Accounting Standards, SIC and IFRIC
Interpretations (the Standards). The Standards together
with their accompanying documents are issued by:

The International Accounting Standards Board (IASB)
30 Cannon Street, London, EC4M 6XH, United
Kingdom. Email: info@ifrs.org Web: www.ifrs.org

Disclaimer: The IASB, the International Financial
Reporting Standards (IFRS) Foundation, the authors and
the publishers do not accept responsibility for any loss
caused by acting or refraining from acting in reliance
on the material in this publication, whether such loss is
caused by negligence or otherwise to the maximum
extent permitted by law.

BPP
LEARNING MEDIA

Contents

		Page
Introduction		iv

Question and answer bank

Chapter tasks		**Questions**	**Answers**
Chapter 1	Bookkeeping transactions	3	113
Chapter 2	Accounting principles	8	118
Chapter 3	Purchase of non-current assets	19	129
Chapter 4	Depreciation of non-current assets	27	136
Chapter 5	Disposal of non-current assets	35	143
Chapter 6	Accruals and prepayments	53	156
Chapter 7	Inventories	65	163
Chapter 8	Irrecoverable and doubtful debts	71	168
Chapter 9	Bank reconciliations	77	174
Chapter 10	Control account reconciliations	82	178
Chapter 11	The trial balance, errors and the suspense account	91	185
Chapter 12	The extended trial balance	105	195
AAT AQ2016 sample assessment 1		203	221
AAT AQ2016 sample assessment 2		233	
BPP practice assessment 1		237	257
BPP practice assessment 2		271	287
BPP practice assessment 3		299	315
BPP practice assessment 4		327	343

Introduction

This is BPP Learning Media's AAT Question Bank for *Advanced Bookkeeping*. It is part of a suite of ground-breaking resources produced by BPP Learning Media for AAT assessments.

This Question Bank has been written in conjunction with the BPP Course Book, and has been carefully designed to enable students to practise all of the learning outcomes and assessment criteria for *Advanced Bookkeeping*. It is fully up to date as at June 2017 and reflects both the AAT's qualification specification and the sample assessment provided by the AAT.

This Question Bank contains these key features:

- Tasks corresponding to each chapter of the Course Book. Some tasks are designed for learning purposes, others are of assessment standard

- AAT's AQ2016 sample assessments 1 and 2 for *Advanced Bookkeeping* with answers and further BPP practice assessments

The emphasis in all tasks and assessments is on the practical application of the skills acquired.

VAT

You may find tasks throughout this Question Bank that need you to calculate or be aware of a rate of VAT. This is stated at 20% in these examples and questions.

In some assessments, written or complex tasks may be human marked. In this case you are given a blank space or table to enter your answer into. You are told in the assessments which tasks these are (note: may be none if all answers are marked by the computer).

If these involve calculations, it is a good idea to decide in advance how you are going to lay out your answers to such tasks by practising answering them on a word document, and certainly you should try all such tasks in this Question Bank and in the AAT's environment using the sample assessment.

When asked to fill in tables, or gaps, never leave any blank even if you are unsure of the answer. Fill in your best estimate.

Note that for some assessments where there is a lot of scenario information or tables of data provided (eg tax tables), you may need to access these via 'pop-ups'. Instructions will be provided on how you can bring up the necessary data during the assessment.

Finally, take note of any task specific instructions once you are in the assessment. For example you may be asked to enter a date in a certain format or to enter a number to a certain number of decimal places.

Approaching the assessment

When you sit the assessment it is very important that you follow the on screen instructions. This means you need to carefully read the instructions, both on the introduction screens and during specific tasks.

When you access the assessment you should be presented with an introductory screen with information similar to that shown below (taken from the introductory screen from the AAT's AQ2016 sample assessments for *Advanced Bookkeeping*).

We have provided this **sample assessment** to help you familiarise yourself with our e-assessment environment. It is designed to demonstrate as many as possible of the question types that you may find in a live assessment. It is not designed to be used on its own to determine whether you are ready for a live assessment.

Assessment information:

You have **2 hours** to complete this sample assessment.

This assessment contains **5 tasks** and you should attempt to complete **every** task.
Each task is independent. You will not need to refer to your answers to previous tasks.
Read every task carefully to make sure you understand what is required.

The standard rate of VAT is 20%.

Where the date is relevant, it is given in the task data.
Both minus signs and brackets can be used to indicate negative numbers **unless** task instructions say otherwise.

You must use a full stop to indicate a decimal point. For example, write 100.57 NOT 100,57 or 100 57
You may use a comma to indicate a number in the thousands, but you don't have to. For example 10000 and 10,000 are both acceptable.

The actual instructions will vary depending on the subject you are studying for. It is very important you read the instructions on the introductory screen and apply them in the assessment. You don't want to lose marks when you know the correct answer just because you have not entered it in the right format.

In general, the rules set out in the AAT sample assessments for the subject you are studying for will apply in the real assessment, but you should carefully read the information on this screen again in the real assessment, just to make sure. This screen may also confirm the VAT rate used if applicable.

A full stop is needed to indicate a decimal point. We would recommend using minus signs to indicate negative numbers and leaving out the comma signs to indicate thousands, as this results in a lower number of key strokes and less margin for error when working under time pressure. Having said that, you can use whatever is easiest for you as long as you operate within the rules set out for your particular assessment.

You have to show competence throughout the assessment and you should therefore complete all of the tasks. Don't leave questions unanswered.

Grading

To achieve the qualification and to be awarded a grade, you must pass all the mandatory unit assessments, all optional unit assessments (where applicable) and the synoptic assessment.

The AAT Level 3 Advanced Diploma in Accounting will be awarded a grade. This grade will be based on performance across the qualification. Unit assessments and synoptic assessments are not individually graded. These assessments are given a mark that is used in calculating the overall grade.

How overall grade is determined

You will be awarded an overall qualification grade (Distinction, Merit, and Pass). If you do not achieve the qualification you will not receive a qualification certificate, and the grade will be shown as unclassified.

The marks of each assessment will be converted into a percentage mark and rounded up or down to the nearest whole number. This percentage mark is then weighted according to the weighting of the unit assessment or synoptic assessment within the qualification. The resulting weighted assessment percentages are combined to arrive at a percentage mark for the whole qualification.

Grade definition	Percentage threshold
Distinction	90–100%
Merit	80–89%
Pass	70–79%
Unclassified	0–69% Or failure to pass one or more assessment/s

Re-sits

Some AAT qualifications such as the AAT Advanced Diploma in Accounting have restrictions in place for how many times you are able to re-sit assessments. Please refer to the AAT website for further details.

You should only be entered for an assessment when you are well prepared and you expect to pass the assessment.

AAT qualifications

The material in this book may support the following AAT qualifications:

AAT Advanced Diploma in Accounting Level 3, AAT Advanced Diploma in Accounting at SCQF Level 6 and Further Education and Training Certificate: Accounting Technician (Level 4 AATSA).

Supplements

From time to time we may need to publish supplementary materials to one of our titles. This can be for a variety of reasons, including minor changes to the AAT unit guidance or new legislation coming into effect between editions.

You should check our supplements page regularly for anything that may affect your learning materials. All supplements are available free of charge on our supplements page on our website at:

www.bpp.com/learning-media/about/students

Improving material and removing errors

There is a constant need to update and enhance our study materials in line with both regulatory changes and new insights into the assessments.

From our team of authors BPP appoints a subject expert to update and improve these materials for each new edition.

Their updated draft is subsequently technically checked by another author and from time to time non-technically checked by a proof reader.

We are very keen to remove as many numerical errors and narrative typos as we can but given the volume of detailed information being changed in a short space of time we know that a few errors will sometimes get through our net.

We apologise in advance for any inconvenience that an error might cause. We continue to look for new ways to improve these study materials and would welcome your suggestions. If you have any comments about this book, please email nisarahmed@bpp.com or write to Nisar Ahmed, AAT Head of Programme, BPP Learning Media Ltd, BPP House, Aldine Place, London W12 8AA.

Question Bank

Chapter 1 – Bookkeeping transactions

Task 1.1

Compete the sentences below by selecting the appropriate option from the picklist.

The sales returns day book lists	▼
The purchases day book lists	▼
The purchases returns day book lists	▼
The sales day book lists	▼

Picklist:

invoices sent to customers
credit notes sent to customers
invoices received from suppliers
credit notes received from suppliers

....

Task 1.2

Record the double entry for each of the following transactions of a business:

(a) **Payment of £15,000 into a business bank account by the owner in order to start up the business.**

Account		Debit £	Credit £
	▼		
	▼		

(b) **Payment by cheque of £2,000 for the rent of a business property.**

Account		Debit £	Credit £
	▼		
	▼		

(c) **Payment by cheque of £6,200 for the purchase of goods for resale.**

Account		Debit £	Credit £
	▼		
	▼		

(d) **Payment by cheque of £150 for electricity.**

Account		Debit £	Credit £
	▼		
	▼		

Picklist:

Balance b/d
Balance c/d
Bank
Capital
Electricity
Purchases
Purchases ledger control account
Rent

....

Task 1.3

A new business has the following transactions:

(1) Receipt of £20,000 capital into the bank account from the owner
(2) Payment by cheque of £2,100 for goods for resale
(3) Sold goods for £870 cash
(4) Purchase of goods for resale on credit for £2,800
(5) Sale of goods on credit for £3,400
(6) Payment by cheque of £1,500 to credit suppliers
(7) Receipt of cheque from credit customer of £1,600

Enter the transactions into the accounts below. Balance off the accounts. As appropriate, show clearly the:

- **Balance to be carried down and brought down; or**
- **Balance to be transferred to the profit or loss account.**

Bank

	£			£
▼			▼	
▼			▼	
▼			▼	
▼			▼	

Capital

	£			£
▼			▼	
▼			▼	

Purchases

	£			£
▼			▼	
▼			▼	

Purchases ledger control account

	£			£
▼			▼	
▼			▼	
▼			▼	

Sales

	£			£
▼			▼	
▼			▼	

Sales ledger control account

	£			£
▼			▼	
▼			▼	
▼			▼	

Picklist:

Balance b/d
Balance c/d
Bank
Capital
Profit or loss account
Purchases
Purchases ledger control account
Sales
Sales ledger control account

Task 1.4

Complete the initial trial balance by entering the balances in the debit or credit columns, as appropriate. Total the trial balance.

Trial balance	Amount £	Debit £	Credit £
Bank (positive balance)	11,000		
Capital	14,000		
Electricity	2,000		
Purchases	4,500		
Purchases ledger control account	3,000		
Rent (expense)	2,500		
Sales	9,000		
Sales ledger control account	12,000		
VAT control account (due to HMRC)	6,000		

Task 1.5

The following items are included in the VAT control account.

(a) **Show whether the balances will be debit or credit items on the VAT control account.**

Ledger account	Amount £	Debit ✓	Credit ✓
Sales	13,000		
Sales returns	1,000		
Purchases	8,000		
Purchases returns	2,000		
Bank	3,500		

(b) **Calculate the amount owed to or due from HMRC at the end of the period. From the perspective of the business, indicate whether it is an asset or liability.**

Amount owed at the end of the period: £	
Asset or liability	▼

Picklist:

Asset
Liability

....

Task 2.4

Complete the sentence below by selecting the most appropriate option.

A credit balance on a general ledger account indicates

	✓
an asset, capital or an expense	
a liability or an expense	
an amount owing to the organisation	
a liability, capital or income	

Task 2.5

The scenarios take place within an accounting practice.

Identify the fundamental principle which is relevant to the scenarios below.

Both scenarios should be considered separately.

Scenarios	Fundamental principle
Employees who may receive a bonus depending on the financial performance of the accounting practice do not prepare the accounting practice's financial statements.	▼
The new trainee accounting technician is supervised by her manager and receives the necessary training.	▼

Picklist:

Confidentiality
Integrity
Objectivity
Professional behaviour
Professional competence and due care

Task 2.6

Wilson and Sons is a manufacturing business which holds a significant quantity of high value inventory.

Which organisational procedure will be used to safeguard the inventory?

Control procedures	✓
Physical controls	
Segregation of duties	
Authorisation of transactions	
Written record of procedures	

Task 2.7

Why does a business need to establish and follow organisational policies and procedures in relation to its accounting function?

Select ONE option.

	✓
To ensure that the accounting policies selected maximise the business's profits	
To ensure the accounting records truly reflect the transactions and financial results of the business	
To ensure that the business acts in the owner's best interests	
To minimise the tax payable on the business's profits	

Task 2.8

Campbell is a retailer with a number of high street stores. The business's owner suspects the checkout operator in one particular store of possible theft as the cash takings in that store are much lower than in all of the others.

Which type of organisational policy would be the most appropriate to put in place to detect missing cash in the store?

Select ONE option.

	✓
Review of budgeted to actual information	
Written record of procedures	
Physical controls	
Authorisation of transactions	

Task 2.9

Hill sells cutting edge technological products such as the latest tablets, laptops and smartphones. Inventory is stored in a central warehouse before being distributed to retail outlets or direct to customers who have ordered online.

Hill maintains computerised accounting records. You are the accounts supervisor. The junior bookkeeper has asked you why the accounting records are password protected and only the members of the accounts department and the business's owner have access to that password.

Which of the following can you use in your explanation to him?
Select ONE option for each row.

	Acceptable reason ✓	Not acceptable reason ✓
The business has high value desirable inventory, making the risk of theft high, which could be covered up by unauthorised alteration of accounting records.		
Only the accounts department are likely to have the necessary skills and knowledge to maintain the accounting records.		
The password will prevent anyone in the accounts department deliberately manipulating accounting records.		
The password will prevent theft of inventory and cash from the business.		

Task 2.10

You are working on the accounting records of a client for the year ended 30 June 20X6. The proprietor of the business has proposed that the following four adjustments be made before the accounts are finalised.

Which of the following adjustments appears genuine and should be included in the final accounts for the year ended 30 June 20X6?
Select ONE option.

	✓
A write down of a line of inventory at the year end from cost to NRV is it was sold at a loss in July 20X6	
A decrease in the allowance for doubtful debts because of a rise in the average number of days credit customers are taking to pay	
An increase in the useful life of plant and machinery to reduce the depreciation charge	
Posting a cash payment to the suspense account	

Task 2.11

You are a trainee accounting technician reporting to a managing partner in an accounting practice. You are working on the accounting records of a client.

In which circumstance would it be appropriate to disclose information about your client without breaching the fundamental principle of confidentiality from the AAT's *Code of Professional Ethics*?

Select ONE option for each row.

	Appropriate ✓	Not appropriate ✓
Allowing the manager partner to review the year end accounts that you have prepared		
Emailing the accounts to your friend who is thinking of applying for a job with the client		
Allowing the client's bank to access the accounts with the proprietor's permission		
Allowing a credit supplier of your client access to the accounts when deciding whether or not to increase credit terms without authorisation from the proprietor		

Task 2.12

You work in an accounting practice and are preparing the year end accounts for a client. The client owns a very small business and prepares his own accounting records as he has completed Levels 1, 2 and 3 of his AAT studies.

When you are preparing the year end accounts, you notice that the proprietor of the business has taken £5,000 out of the business for his own personal use and has recorded the amount as an expense.

Which of the following statements are valid in respect of the above transaction?

Select ONE option for each row.

	Valid ✓	Not valid ✓
The accounting treatment is correct so there has been no breach of the AAT's *Code of Professional Ethics*.		
If this treatment was deliberate, there has been a breach of the fundamental principle of integrity.		
If this treatment was a genuine error, there has been a breach of the fundamental principle of professional competence and due care.		
There is a clear breach of confidentiality here requiring your firm to resign as accountants for this client.		

Task 2.13

You are a trainee accounting technician reporting to the managing partner in an accounting practice. You are working on the accounts of a business. The client is a longstanding friend of the managing partner and is godfather to the managing partner's youngest child.

Which of the threats to the AAT's *Code of Professional Ethics* is most relevant here?

Select ONE option.

	✓
Self-interest	
Self-review	
Advocacy	
Familiarity	
Intimidation	

Task 2.14

The following is a list of the business's assets and liabilities at the year end.

	£
Property, plant and equipment	120,000
Inventories	43,000
Trade receivables	65,000
Bank (positive balance)	16,400
Trade payables	57,100
Bank loan	32,000

What is the business's capital at the year end?

£ 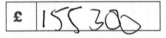 155 300

Task 2.15

At 1 January 20X6, a business had capital of £250,000. During the year ended 31 December 20X6, the following occurred:

- The business made a profit of £37,500
- The owner withdrew cash of £4,700 for his own personal use
- The owner injected new capital of £12,000 into the business

What was the amount of the business's net assets at 31 December 20X6?

£ 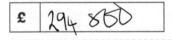 294 850

Task 2.16

Which ONE of the following statements about the accounting equation is true?

	✓
Capital – Liabilities = Assets	
Double entry bookkeeping is based on the accounting equation	✓
All elements of the accounting equation can be found in the statement of profit or loss	
Closing capital = Opening capital – Profit + Drawings	

Task 2.17

A business makes a sale of £672 on credit to a long standing customer.

How will the elements of the accounting equation be affected by recording this transaction?

	Increase ✓	Decrease ✓	No change ✓
Assets	✓		
Liabilities			✓
Capital	✓		

Task 2.18

As an accounting technician, what is the most important reason for following organisational policies and procedures?

Choose ONE:

	✓
To ensure that you understand your responsibilities	
To ensure that the company meets all of its legal responsibilities	
To make it easy for you to complete your day-to-day tasks	
To improve your technical knowledge	

Task 2.19

Which ONE of these would be acceptable professional behaviour if actioned by you?

	✓
You have been asked to account for a provision but you are unsure how to do this, so you make a guess at the appropriate treatment.	
A client has given you tickets to a high profile football match. The next day they ask you to ignore the liquidation of a customer that owes the client a substantial amount of money.	
Your firm needs to meet its deadline in preparing the accounts. Your supervisor tells you to save time by just repeating the depreciation entry from last year, rather than recalculating it.	
The bank statement for your firm shows that an insurance bill covering the next accounting period has been paid in the current accounting period. Your manager asks you to make a prepayment for the cost of the insurance.	

Chapter 3 – Purchase of non-current assets

Task 3.1

A business has a policy of capitalising expenditure over £300. Ignore VAT.

In each of the following circumstances, determine how much capital expenditure has been incurred and how much revenue expenditure has been incurred by the business.

Expenditure	Capital expenditure £	Revenue expenditure £
A machine has been purchased at a cost of £12,000. The delivery charge was £400.		
A building has been purchased at a cost of £120,000. The building is subsequently redecorated at a cost of £13,000.		
A new main server has been purchased at a cost of £10,000. Professional fees of £200 were also incurred, as a result of this expenditure.		

Task 3.2

A business has a policy of capitalising expenditure over £500. The business is not registered for VAT.

The business acquires computer equipment for £48,000 (including VAT at 20%).

At what amount should the computer equipment be capitalised?

£

Task 3.3

Match the descriptions to the relevant funding method by selecting from the picklist.

Description	Method
The vending machines in a business's premises were financed by paying an initial deposit to the finance company followed by a fixed number of instalments. After all instalments have been paid, the vending machines will be owned by the business.	▼
When a business purchases a new motor vehicle, the old vehicle is given to the dealer to cover part of the cost of the new vehicle.	▼
Factory equipment is acquired as part of a major refurbishment. The bank provides the funding, which is then paid back in instalments over an agreed period of time, together with interest.	▼

Picklist:

Cash purchase
Finance lease
Hire purchase
Loan
Part-exchange

Task 3.4

A business has a policy of capitalising expenditure over £500. You may ignore VAT in this task.

The following is an extract from a purchase invoice received by LBC Trading relating to new equipment for its head office.

To: LBC Trading 14 High Street, Hill Gate, HI2 4DN	Invoice 3728 Hugo & Sons 68 Arne Grove South Mines SM3 9MF	Date: 01 June 20X4
Item	**Details**	**£**
Boardroom table	HF405	10,500.00
Boardroom table fittings	HF405	2,600.00
Delivery costs	HF405	450.00
Boardroom chairs (5 items)	PN2948	300.00
Net total		13,850.00

The acquisition has been made under a finance lease agreement.

In respect of the item(s) to be capitalised, complete the table below. Use the DD/MM/YY format for any dates. Show your numeric answers to TWO decimal places.

Leave any unused rows blank.

Details	Acquisition date	Cost £	Funding method
▼			▼
▼			▼

Picklist:

Cash
Finance lease
HF405
Hire purchase
Loan
Part-exchange
PN2948

··

Task 3.5

A business has a policy of capitalising expenditure over £500. The business is not registered for VAT. The standard rate of VAT is 20%.

A business acquires a machine at a cost of £16,000, excluding VAT. This was paid from the bank.

Show the journal to record the acquisition of the machine.

Account	Debit £	Credit £
▼		
▼		

Picklist:

Bank
Machine at cost
Profit or loss account

··

Task 3.6

A business has a policy of capitalising expenditure over £500. The business is registered for VAT.

A machine was purchased for £13,500 excluding VAT. It was paid for by cheque.

Entries have already been made in the accounting records for existing items.

Make the entries in the accounts below to record the acquisition of the machine. On each account, show clearly the balance to be carried down.

Machine at cost

	£			£
Balance b/d	24,500		▼	
▼			▼	

Bank

	£			£
Balance b/d	32,000		▼	
▼			▼	
▼			▼	

VAT control account

	£			£
▼		Balance b/d		5,000
▼			▼	

Picklist:

Balance c/d
Bank
Machine at cost
Profit or loss account
VAT control account

Task 3.7

Which ONE of the following best explains what is meant by 'capital expenditure'?

Capital expenditure is expenditure:

	✓
On non-current assets, including repairs and maintenance	
On expensive assets	
Relating to the acquisition or improvement of non-current assets	

Task 3.8

Select the terms which correctly reflect the descriptions.

Description	Term
Expenditure for the trade of the business or to repair, maintain and service non-current assets.	▼
Expenditure for the acquisition, replacement or improvement of non-current assets.	▼

Picklist:

Capital expenditure
Revenue expenditure

Task 3.9

A business has a policy of capitalising expenditure over £300. The business's year end is 30 June 20X7.

On 1 July 20X6, the business buys a new property for £500,000 on which it has to pay stamp duty of £15,000. The business also pays the conveyancing solicitor £2,300 for his work on the property purchase.

On 31 December 20X6, the business has to carry out some repairs on the property at a cost of £8,700.

You may ignore VAT in this task.

The business will credit the bank general ledger account for the £526,000 spent on the year.

Ignoring depreciation, what is the impact of recording the debit side of the above transactions on the business's statement of financial position and statement of profit or loss for the year ended 30 June 20X7?

Description	Impact	Amount £
Statement of financial position	▼	
Statement of profit or loss	▼	

Picklist:

Increase current assets
Increase current liabilities
Increase non-current assets
Increase non-current liabilities
Increase profit
No impact
Reduce profit

Task 3.10

Complete the following sentences.

It is important to obtain prior authority for capital expenditure in order to ensure that:

| ▼ |

The business's solicitor  ▼ be the most

appropriate person to give this authority.

Picklist:

the assets are necessary to the business and are purchased at the best price
the assets are recorded in the non-current assets register
the assets are recorded in the general ledger

would
would not

Task 3.11

A business is looking to buy a non-current asset for £100,000. The business currently has a positive cash balance of £750. It wishes to become the legal owner of the asset with immediate effect from the date of purchase.

Which would be the most appropriate funding method for this business to purchase this new non-current asset?

	✓
Bank loan	
Cash purchase	
Finance lease	
Hire purchase	

Task 3.12

A business takes out a bank loan for £10,000 in order the finance the purchase of a motor vehicle. The business then purchases the motor vehicle for £9,800.

You may ignore VAT in this task.

Show the journal to record the receipt of the bank loan.

Account		Amount £	Debit ✓	Credit ✓
	▼			
	▼			

Show the journal to record the purchase of the motor vehicle.

Account		Amount £	Debit ✓	Credit ✓
	▼			
	▼			

Picklist:

Bank
Finance lease liability
Hire purchase liability
Loan
Motor vehicles accumulated depreciation
Motor vehicles at cost
Motor vehicles running expenses
Purchases ledger control account

Chapter 4 – Depreciation of non-current assets

Task 4.1

What is the purpose of accounting for depreciation in financial statements?

	✓
To spread the cost of a non-current asset over its useful life in order to match the cost of the asset with the consumption of the asset's economic benefits	
To ensure that funds are available for the eventual replacement of the asset	
To reduce the cost of the asset to its estimated market value	
To recognise the fact that assets lose their value over time	

Task 4.2

Complete the following sentence.

Depreciation is an application of the [▼] basis of accounting.

Picklist:

accruals
capital
cash
revenue

Task 4.3

A business has a policy of capitalising expenditure over £500. You may ignore VAT in this task.

Machines are depreciated on a straight line basis. A full year's depreciation is applied in the year of acquisition.

For each non-current asset, for the year ended 31 December 20X8, calculate the:

- **Depreciation charge**
- **Carrying amount of each asset**

(a) Machine purchased for £17,400 on 1 January 20X6 with a useful life of five years and no residual value

Depreciation charge £	Carrying amount £

(b) Machine purchased for £12,800 on 1 January 20X7 with a useful life of four years and a residual value of £2,000

Depreciation charge £	Carrying amount £

(c) Machine purchased for £4,600 on 1 January 20X8 with a useful life of three years and an a residual value of £700

Depreciation charge £	Carrying amount £

Task 4.4

A business has a policy of capitalising expenditure over £500. You may ignore VAT in this task.

Motor vehicles are depreciated on a diminishing balance basis. A full year's depreciation is applied in the year of acquisition.

For each non-current asset, for the year ended 31 March 20X9, calculate the:

- **Depreciation charge**
- **Carrying amount of each asset**

(a) Motor vehicle costing £24,600 purchased on 1 April 20X8 which is to be depreciated at 20% on the diminishing balance basis

Depreciation charge £	Carrying amount £

(b) **Motor vehicle costing £3,800 purchased on 1 November 20X7 which is to be depreciated at 20% on the diminishing balance basis**

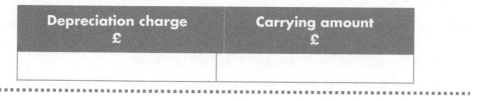

Depreciation charge £	Carrying amount £

Task 4.5

A business has a policy of capitalising expenditure over £500. You may ignore VAT in this task.

Motor vehicles are depreciated on a diminishing balance basis. A full year's depreciation is applied in the year of acquisition.

For each non-current asset, for the year ended 31 March 20X9, calculate the:

- **Depreciation charge**
- **Accumulated depreciation**

(a) **Motor vehicle costing £24,000 purchased on 1 April 20X8 which is to be depreciated at 30% on the diminishing balance basis**

Depreciation charge £	Accumulated depreciation £

(b) **Motor vehicle costing £18,700 purchased on 1 August 20X7 which is to be depreciated at 30% on the diminishing balance basis**

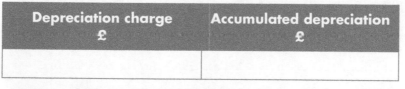

Depreciation charge £	Accumulated depreciation £

Task 4.6

A business has a policy of capitalising expenditure over £500. You may ignore VAT in this task.

Computer equipment is depreciated on straight line basis assuming no residual value. Depreciation is calculated on an annual basis and charged in equal instalments for each full month an asset is owned in the year.

For each non-current asset, for the year ended 31 December 20X8, calculate the:

- **Depreciation charge**
- **Carrying amount of each asset**

(a)   **Machine purchased on 1 May 20X8 for £15,000. This is to be depreciated at the rate of 20% per annum on the straight line basis**

Depreciation charge £	Carrying amount £

(b)   **Computer purchased on 31 October 20X8 for £4,200. This is to be depreciated at the rate of 40% per annum on the straight line basis**

Depreciation charge £	Carrying amount £

Task 4.7

A manufacturing company purchased a new item of plant and machinery for £120,000. The expected number of units to be produced over its useful economic life is 300,000.

Over the last three years it has produced the number of units shown below.

In respect of the asset, calculate the carrying amount b/d, the depreciation charges, the accumulated depreciation, and the carrying amount c/d for the first three years.

Year	Number of units produced	Carrying amount b/d £	Depreciation charges £	Accumulated depreciation £	Carrying amount c/d £
1	90,000				
2	72,000				
3	30,000				

Task 4.8

What is the double entry to record depreciation charges on vehicles in the accounts?

	Account
Debit	▼
Credit	▼

Picklist:

Bank
Depreciation charges
Profit or loss account
Vehicles at cost
Vehicles accumulated depreciation

Task 4.9

A business has a policy of capitalising expenditure over £500. You may ignore VAT in this task.

- You are working on the accounting records of a business for the year ended 31 December 20X5.
- A new vehicle was acquired on 1 April 20X5. It is estimated it will be used for four years.
- The cost was £8,200; this was paid from the bank.
- The business plans to sell the vehicle after four years when its residual value is expected to be £2,000.
- Vehicles are depreciated on a straight line basis. A full year's depreciation is applied in the year of acquisition.
- Entries have already been made in the accounting records for existing items.

Make entries in the accounts below for:

- **The acquisition of the new vehicle**
- **The depreciation charges on the new vehicle**

On each account, show clearly the balance to be carried down or transferred to the profit or loss account, as appropriate.

Vehicles at cost

	£			£
Balance b/d	50,600		▼	
	▼			▼	

Depreciation charges

	£			£
Balance b/d	12,300		▼	
	▼			▼	

Vehicles accumulated depreciation

	£			£
	▼		Balance b/d	24,400
	▼		▼	

Picklist:

Balance c/d
Bank
Depreciation charges
Profit or loss account
Vehicles accumulated depreciation
Vehicles at cost

***

Task 4.10

A business buys a machine. The business expects the units of production to vary year on year according to demand for the inventory that the machine will make.

(a) Which would be the most appropriate depreciation method?

Depreciation method	✓
Diminishing balance method	
Straight line method	
Units of production method	

The business buys a new table for its office. The business expects the asset's economic benefits to be consumed evenly over 10 years.

(b) Which would be the most appropriate depreciation method?

Depreciation method	✓
Diminishing balance method	
Straight line method	
Units of production method	

The business then purchases a computer. The computer is expected to slow down and become less efficient as it ages.

(c)   Which would be the most appropriate depreciation method?

Depreciation method	✓
Diminishing balance method	
Straight line method	
Units of production method	

Task 4.11

A business buys a property with an expected useful life of 50 years. The business wishes to apply the straight line method of depreciation.

What is the appropriate percentage to apply and what should the percentage be applied to?

Percentage: [   ] %

Apply to: [▼]

Picklist:

Accumulated depreciation
Carrying amount
Cost

Chapter 5 – Disposal of non-current assets

Task 5.1

A business has a policy of capitalising expenditure over £500. You may ignore VAT in this task.

- You are working on the accounting records of a business for the year ended 31 March 20X9.

- A machine was acquired on 1 April 20X6.

- The cost was £12,500; this was paid from the bank.

- Machines are depreciated at 30% per annum on the diminishing balance basis, with a full year's charge in the year of acquisition and none in the year of disposal.

- On 30 September 20X8 the asset was sold for £6,000.

Calculate the gain or loss on disposal of the machine. Place a tick in the relevant box to denote whether the amount is a gain or a loss.

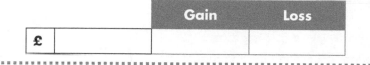

	Gain	Loss
£		

Task 5.2

This task is about the disposal of non-current assets. You may ignore VAT in this task.

- You are working on the accounting records of a business for the year ended 31 March 20X7.

- A motor vehicle was purchased on 1 October 20X4 for £13,800.

- It is being depreciated on the diminishing balance basis at a rate of 40% per annum.

- It was sold on 30 June 20X6 for £5,100.

- A full year's depreciation is applied in the year of acquisition and none in the year of disposal.

Calculate the gain or loss on disposal of the vehicle. Place a tick in the relevant box to denote whether the amount is a gain or a loss.

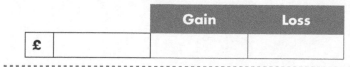

	Gain	Loss
£		

Task 5.3

Complete the following sentences.

	Answer
The gain or loss arising on disposal of a non-current asset is recorded in the	▼
In the business's accounts, the carrying amount of non-current assets is entered in the	▼
The carrying amount of a non-current asset is calculated as the cost of the asset less the	▼

Picklist:

accumulated depreciation
statement of financial position
statement of profit or loss

Task 5.4

This task is about ledger accounting for non-current assets. You may ignore VAT in this task.

- You are working on the accounting records of a business for the year ended 31 December 20X5.

- A machine was acquired on 1 January 20X3. It is estimated it will be used for five years.

- The cost was £25,000.

- Machines are depreciated on a straight line basis assuming no residual value. A full year's depreciation is applied in the year of acquisition and none in the year of disposal.

- The asset was sold on 31 December 20X5 for £12,000.

(a) Calculate the accumulated depreciation for this asset at 31 December 20X4.

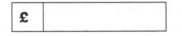

£	

(b) For the year ended 31 December 20X5, make entries in the accounts below to reflect the disposal of the machine.

On each account, show clearly the balance to be carried down or transferred to the statement of profit or loss, as appropriate.

Machine at cost

	£			£
Balance b/d	60,000		▼	
▼			▼	

Bank

	£			£
Balance b/d	22,000		▼	
▼			▼	

Machine accumulated depreciation

	£			£
▼		Balance b/d		26,000
▼			▼	

Disposals

	£			£
▼			▼	
▼			▼	
▼			▼	

(c) **Has the business made a gain or loss on disposal of the machine?**

The business has made a [▼] on disposal of the machine.

Task 5.5

A business sold an item of office equipment which originally cost £20,000. The proceeds of £4,500 were paid into the bank:

(a) **Show the journal entries to record the proceeds.**

Account		Amount £	Debit ✓	Credit ✓
	▼			
	▼			

(b) **Show the journal entries required to remove the original cost of the equipment from the general ledger.**

Account		Amount £	Debit	Credit
	▼			
	▼			

Picklist:

Bank
Depreciation charges
Disposals
Office equipment accumulated depreciation
Office equipment at cost
Profit and loss account

Task 5.6

This task is about ledger accounting for non-current assets.

- You are working on the accounting records of a business for the year ended 31 December 20X8.

- A machine was purchased on 1 July 20X6 for £15,600.

- The depreciation policy is to depreciate machines at a rate of 25% per annum on a straight line basis.

- Depreciation is calculated on an annual basis and charged in equal instalments for each full month an asset is owned in the year.

- On 30 November 20X8 the machine was sold for £6,000.

For the year ended 31 December 20X8, make entries in the account below to reflect the disposal of the machine.

Show clearly the balance to be transferred to the statement of profit or loss.

Disposal account

	£			£
▼			▼	
▼			▼	
▼			▼	

Picklist:

Bank
Depreciation charges
Machine accumulated depreciation
Machine at cost
Profit or loss account

Task 5.7

Most businesses maintain a non-current assets register.

Which of the following statements best describes the purpose of the non-current assets register?

Select ONE.

	✓
To record non-current assets in the general ledger	
To assist in the physical verification of non-current assets and check the accuracy of the general ledger entries relating to tangible non-current assets	
To list all intangible non-current assets of the business	
To authorise capital expenditure	

Task 5.8

You are working on the accounting records of a business known as LKJ Trading.

LKJ Trading is registered for VAT and has a financial year end of 30 June.

The following is an extract from a purchase invoice received by LKJ Trading:

To: LKJ Trading Unit 6, West End Trading Estate Northgate NG15 6SR	SWF Trading Ltd Stonham Way Whitford WH4 2PO		Date: 01 April 20X6 Invoice 54687
Description	Item number	Quantity	£
Plant	PM672	1	3,000.00
Testing – customer premises	For PM672	1	300.00
Maintenance contract – 24 months	For PM672	1	550.00
Net total			3,850.00
VAT at 20%			770.00
Total			4,620.00

The acquisition has been paid for from the business's bank account.

- LKJ Trading has a policy of capitalising expenditure over £400.

- Plant is depreciated over five years on a straight line basis assuming no residual value.

- Depreciation is calculated on an annual basis and charged in equal instalments for each month the asset is owned.

For the year ended 30 June 20X6, record the following in the extract from the non-current assets register below:

- **The acquisition of the new plant purchased in the year**
- **The depreciation charge on the new plant**
- **The carrying amount**

Show your numerical answers to TWO decimal places

Use the DD/MM/YY format for any dates.

Note. **Not every cell will require an entry.**

Extract from non-current assets register

Description	Acquisition date	Cost £	Depreciation charges £	Carrying amount £	Funding method	Disposal proceeds £	Disposal date
Plant and machinery							
▼					▼		
Year end 30/06/X6							

Picklist for description:

Accumulated depreciation
Bank
Depreciation charges
Office equipment OF218
Plant PM672

Picklist for funding method:

Cash
Finance lease
Hire purchase
Loan
Part exchange

Task 5.9

You are working on the accounting records of a business known as AM Trading.

You may ignore VAT in this task.

The following information relates to the sale of an item of office equipment no longer used by the business:

Item description	Head office desk DSK452
Date of sale	30 September 20X7
Selling price	£800.00

- AM Trading has a policy of capitalising expenditure over £500.00.

- Office equipment is depreciated at 25% per year on a diminishing balance basis.

- A full year's depreciation is charged in the year of acquisition and none in the year of disposal.

For the year ended 31 December 20X7, update the extract from the non-current assets register for the disposal of the head office desk. Record the:

- **Depreciation charges**
- **Carrying amount**
- **Disposal proceeds**
- **Disposal date**

Show your numerical answers to TWO decimal places.

Use the DD/MM/YY format for any dates.

Note. **Not every cell will require an entry.**

Extract from the non-current assets register

Description	Acquisition date	Cost £	Depreciation charges £	Carrying amount £	Funding method	Disposal proceeds £	Disposal date
Office equipment							
Desk DSK452	01/06/X5	2,500.00			Loan		
Year end 31/12/X5			625.00	1,875.00			
Year end 31/12/X6			468.75	1,406.25			
Year end 31/12/X7			▼	▼			

Picklist for depreciation charges:

0.00
87.89
351.56

Picklist for carrying amount:

0.00
1,054.69
1,318.36

....

Task 5.10

You are working on the accounting records of a business known as Grimmett.

You may ignore VAT in this task.

Grimmett purchased a computer on 1 April 20X1 for £5,700 (reference COM987).

The current year end is 31 March 20X4.

- Grimmett has a policy of capitalising expenditure over £1,000.

- Grimmett depreciates computers at 20% per year on a straight line basis.

- Depreciation is calculated on an annual basis and charged in equal instalments for each full month the asset is owned in the year.

- On 1 January 20X4, Grimmett sold the computer for £1,300.

For the year ended 31 March 20X4, update the extract from the non-current assets register for the disposal of the computer. Record the:

- **Depreciation charges**
- **Carrying amount**
- **Disposal proceeds**
- **Disposal date**

Show your numerical answers to TWO decimal places.

Use the DD/MM/YY format for any dates.

Note. **Not every cell will require an entry.**

Extract from the non-current assets register

Description	Acquisition date	Cost £	Depreciation charges £	Carrying amount £	Funding method	Disposal proceeds £	Disposal date
Office equipment							
Computer COM987	01/04/X1	5,700.00			Part exchange		
Year end 31/03/X2			1,140.00	4,560.00			
Year end 31/03/X3			1,140.00	3,420.00			
Year end 31/03/X4			▼	▼			

Picklist for depreciation charges:

0.00
855.00
1,140.00

Picklist for carrying amount:

0.00
2,565.00
3,135.00

Task 5.11

This task is about the non-current assets register for a business known as CDE Trading. CDE Trading has a financial year end of 31 March.

The following is a purchase invoice received by CDE Trading relating to some items to be used in its office:

To: CDE Trading Unit 6, East End Trading Estate Southgrove HS14 6PW	Refurb & Co 82 Maryland Street Bishops Moat SH34 9TT		Date: 24 June 20 X6 Invoice RE2391
Item	Details	Quantity	£
Refurbished operator chairs	3 × Ergo 803 and 3 × Ergo 697 @ £60 each	6	360.00
Oak boardroom table	2 metres × 1 metre	1	850.00
Delivery and assembly of oak table		1	75.00
Oak maintenance and repair kit		1	60.00
Total			1,345.00
Delivery date: 24/06/X6			

CDE Trading paid the invoice in full on 31 July 20X6 using a £1,345.00 bank loan.

This amount is to be repaid over 12 months.

The following information relates to the sale of a motor vehicle no longer required by the business:

Description	1.6 litre car – AF05 LKR
Date of sale	23 September 20X6
Selling price	£5,340.00

- VAT can be ignored.

- CDE Trading has a policy of capitalising expenditure over £350.

- Furniture and fittings are depreciated at 15% per year on a straight line basis assuming no residual value.

- Motor vehicles are depreciated at 25% per year on a diminishing balance basis.
- A full year's depreciation is applied in the year of acquisition and none in the year of disposal.

For the year ended 31 March 20X7, record the following in the extract from the non-current assets register below:

- **Any acquisitions of non-current assets**
- **Any disposals of non-current assets**
- **Depreciation**

Show your answers to 2 decimal places.

Use the DD/MM/YY format for any dates.

Note. **Not every cell will require an entry, and not all cells will accept entries.**

Extract from non-current assets register

Description/ Serial number	Acquisition date	Cost £	Depreciation charges £	Carrying amount £	Funding method	Disposal proceeds £	Disposal date
Furniture and fittings							
Filling racks	31/10/X5	832.60			Cash		
Year end 31/03/X6			124.89	707.71			
Year end 31/03/X7							
▼					▼		
Year end 31/03/X7							
Motor vehicles							
1.6 litre car AF05 LKR	01/09/X4	10,600.00			Part-exchange		
Year end 31/03/X5			2,650.00	7,950.00			
Year end 31/03/X6			1,987.50	5,962.50			
Year end 31/03/X7			▼	▼			

Description/ Serial number	Acquisition date	Cost £	Depreciation charges £	Carrying amount £	Funding method	Disposal proceeds £	Disposal date
1.8 litre van AD05 ACT	01/09/X5	10,400.00			Part-exchange		
Year end 31/03/X5			2,600.00	7,800.00			
Year end 31/03/X6			1,950.00	5,850.00			
Year end 31/03/X7							

Picklist for description:

1.6 litre car AF05 LKR
1.8 litre van AD05 ACT
Boardroom table and chairs
Oak boardroom table

Picklist for funding method:

Cash
Part-exchange and cash
Loan

Picklist for depreciation charge:

0.00
496.88
1,490.63
1,987.50

Picklist for carrying amount:

0.00
3,975.00
4,471.87
5,465.62

Task 5.12

This task is about the non-current assets register for a business known as QW Trading. QW Trading is registered for VAT and has a financial year end of 31 March.

The following is a purchase invoice received by QW Trading relating to some items to be used in its factory:

To: QW Trading Unit 6, East End Trading Estate Southgrove HS14 6PW	PX Trading Ltd Watchet Way Marston BT23 4RR		Date: 01 April X6 Invoice 23953 VAT 203 9613 01GB £
Power lathe PM892	Delivery 01 April X6	1	9,930.00
Maintenance contract – 24 months	01/04/X6 – 31/03/X8	1	625.00
Testing – customer premises	2 hrs @ £129.90	2	259.80
Net total			10,814.80
VAT @ 20%			2,162.96
Total			12,977.76

This invoice is to be settled by a hire purchase agreement.
10% deposit is due on the delivery date.

The following information relates to the sale of an item of office equipment no longer needed by the business:

Item description	Reception desk – FaradyR
Date of sale	30 September 20X6
Selling price excluding VAT	£600.00

- QW Trading has a policy of capitalising expenditure over £1,000.

- Machinery is depreciated at 25% per year on a diminishing balance basis.

- Office equipment is depreciated over eight years on a straight line basis assuming no residual value.

- Depreciation is calculated on an annual basis and charged in equal instalments for each full month an asset is owned in the year.

For the year ended 31 March 20X7, record the following in the extract from the non-current assets register:

- Any acquisitions of non-current assets
- Any disposals of non-current assets
- Depreciation

Show your answers to TWO decimal places.

Use the DD/MM/YY format for any dates.

Note. Not every cell will require an entry, and not all cells will accept entries.

Extract from non-current assets register

Description/ Serial number	Acquisition date	Cost £	Depreciation charges £	Carrying amount £	Funding method	Disposal Proceeds £	Disposal date
Office equipment							
Copier 4	01/04/X5	3,200.00			Finance lease		
Year end 31/03/X6			400.00	2,800.00			
Year end 31/03/X7							
Reception desk – FaradyR	01/01/X5	1,200.00			Cash		
Year end 31/03/X5			37.50	1,162.50			
Year end 31/03/X6			150.00	1,012.50			
Year end 31/03/X7			▼	▼			

Description/ Serial number	Acquisition date	Cost £	Depreciation charges £	Carrying amount £	Funding method	Disposal Proceeds £	Disposal date
Machinery							
CNC machine CNC3491	01/04/X4	16,400.00			Part-exchange		
Year end 31/03/X5			4,100.00	12,300.00			
Year end 31/03/X6			3,075.00	9,225.00			
Year end 31/03/X7							
▼					▼		
Year end 31/03/X7							

Picklist for description:

CNC Machine CNC 3491
Power lathe PM892
Reception desk – FaradyR
Copier 4

Picklist for depreciation charge:

0.00
75.00
112.50
150.00

Picklist for carrying amount:

0.00
862.50
900.00
937.50

Picklist for funding method:

Cash
Hire purchase
Part-exchange

Task 5.13

This task is about ledger accounting for non-current assets.

You are working on the accounts of a business which is not registered for VAT. The business's year end is 31 July 20X6.

- An item of machinery was part exchanged for a newer model on 1 August 20X5.

- The original machinery cost £3,500 on 1 January 20X3.

- The business's depreciation policy for machinery is 15% using the diminishing balance method.

- A full year's depreciation is applied in the year of acquisition and none in the year of disposal.

- A part exchange allowance of £575 was given.

- £2,150 was paid from the bank to complete the purchase of the new machine.

(a) **Complete the following tasks relating to the original item of machinery:**

  (i) **Calculate the accumulated depreciation (to the nearest whole £).**

£	

  (ii) **Complete the disposals account. Show clearly the balance to be carried down or transferred to the statement of profit or loss, as appropriate.**

  Disposals

	£		£
▼		▼	
▼		▼	
▼		▼	

  Picklist:

  Bank
  Machinery accumulated depreciation
  Machinery at cost
  Profit or loss account

(b) **Complete the tasks below:**

(i) **Calculate the total cost of the new machinery from the information above.**

£	

Before the part-exchange entries were posted, the balance on the machinery at cost account was £25,820.

The entries have now been correctly made.

(ii) **Complete the sentence:**

The machinery at cost account will have a final balance carried down

of £ [   ] when the ledger accounts are closed

for the year.

Chapter 6 – Accruals and prepayments

Task 6.1

This task is about ledger accounting for accruals and prepayments.

- During the year ended 31 March 20X6, a business has paid £845 of telephone bills.

- The bill for February and March 20X6 has not been received as at the year end but it is expected to be approximately £170.

> **Business policy: accounting accruals and prepayments**
>
> An entry is made into the income or expense account and an opposite entry into the relevant asset or liability account. In the following period, this entry is removed.

(a) **Write up the following ledger account to reflect the telephone expenses for the year showing the transfer to the statement of profit or loss for the year.**

Telephone expenses

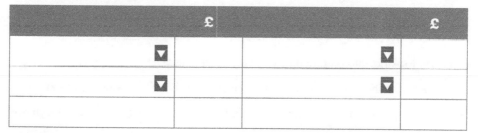

	£			£
▼			▼	
▼			▼	

Picklist:

Accrued expenses
Accrued income
Balance b/d
Balance c/d
Bank
Prepaid expenses
Prepaid income
Profit or loss account
Statement of financial position

At the beginning of the next accounting period the accrual for telephone expenses will need to be reversed.

(b)   Complete the following statements:

The reversal of this accrual is dated [▼] .

The reversal is on the [▼] side of the telephone expenses account.

Picklist:

31 March 20X6
1 April 20X6
1 April 20X7

credit
debit

Task 6.2

This task is about ledger accounting for accruals and prepayments.

You are working on the accounting records of a business for the year ended 30 June 20X1.

You are looking into electricity expenses for the year.

- At 30 June 20X0, there was an accrual of £370 for electricity expenses.

- The cash book for the year ended 30 June 20X1 shows payments for electricity of £2,300.

- An invoice for £900 for electricity for the period of 1 May 20X1 to 31 July 20X1 was received and paid on 10 August 20X1.

Update the electricity expense and accrued expenses ledger accounts. Show clearly:

- **The reversal of the opening accrual**

- **The cash book figure**

- **The year end adjustment**

- **The balance carried down or the transfer to the statement of profit or loss for the year as appropriate**

Electricity expense (SPL)

	£			£
▼		▼		
▼		▼		

Accrued expenses (SOFP)

	£			£
▼		Balance b/d		370
▼			▼	

Picklist:

Accrued expenses
Accrued expenses (reversal)
Accrued income
Accrued income (reversal)
Balance b/d
Balance c/d
Bank
Electricity expense
Prepaid expenses
Prepaid expenses (reversal)
Prepaid income
Prepaid income (reversal)
Profit or loss account
Statement of financial position

Task 6.3

This task is about ledger accounting for accruals and prepayments.

You are working on the accounting records of a business for the year ended 31 May 20X8.

You are looking into insurance expenses for the year.

- There was a prepayment for insurance of £180 at 31 May 20X7.

- The cash book – credit side shows that in the year ended 31 May 20X8 £2,300 was paid for insurance.

- However this includes £250 for the year ending 31 May 20X9.

Update the insurance expense account for the year ended 31 May 20X8. Show clearly:

- **The reversal of the opening prepayment**
- **The cash book figure**
- **The year end adjustment**
- **The transfer to the statement of profit or loss for the year**

Insurance expense

	£			£
▼		▼		
▼		▼		

Picklist:

Accrued expenses
Accrued expenses (reversal)
Accrued income
Accrued income (reversal)
Balance b/d
Balance c/d
Bank
Prepaid expenses
Prepaid expenses (reversal)
Prepaid income
Prepaid income (reversal)
Profit or loss account

Task 6.4

This task is about ledger accounting for accruals and prepayments.

You are working on the accounting records of a business for the year ended 30 June 20X5.

You are looking into rent expenses for the year.

- At 30 June 20X4, there was a prepayment for rent expenses of £300.
- The cash book for the year shows payments for rent of £4,500.
- This amount includes £800 for the 6 months ended 30 September 20X5.

Update the prepaid expenses account. Show clearly:

- **The reversal of the opening prepayment**
- **The year end adjustment**
- **The balance carried down**

Prepaid expenses

	£			£
Balance b/d	300		▼	
	▼		▼	

Picklist:

Accrued expenses
Accrued expenses (reversal)
Accrued income
Accrued income (reversal)
Balance b/d
Balance c/d
Bank
Prepaid expenses
Prepaid expenses (reversal)
Prepaid income
Prepaid income (reversal)
Profit or loss account
Rent expense
Rental income

Task 6.5

This task is about accounting for accruals and prepayments.

You are working on the accounting records of a business for the year ended 30 June 20X3.

You are looking into rental income for the year.

- There is accrued rental income of £490 at 30 June 20X2.

- The cash book for the year shows receipts in respect of rental income of £5,600.

- On 10 September 20X3, rental income of £1,500 for the period 1 June 20X3 to 31 August 20X3 was received into the bank.

(a) Calculate the rental income for the year ended 30 June 20X3.

£	

Your junior colleague asks you why you are considering the receipt dated 10 September 20X3.

They are confused as the financial year ended on 30 June 20X3.

(b) Which of the following can you use in your explanation to them?

You must choose ONE answer for each row.

Reason for considering the receipt dated 10 September 20X3	Acceptable reason ✓	Not acceptable reason ✓
The accruals concept requires income to be recorded in the financial statements in the period in which it is earned.		
The proprietor of the business has asked you to increase the profit for the year to maximise his chances of increasing the business' overdraft limit.		
The transaction results in a current liability at 30 June 20X3.		

Task 6.6

An accrual for electricity expenses of £375 was treated as a prepayment in preparing a business's statement of profit or loss for the year ended 31 December 20X4.

What was the resulting effect on the electricity expense of the business for the year? Select ONE.

	✓
Overstated by £375	
Overstated by £750	
Understated by £375	
Understated by £750	

Task 6.7

Cleverley Ltd started in business on 1 January 20X0, preparing accounts to 31 December 20X0. The electricity bills received were as follows.

		£
30 April 20X0	For 4 months to 30 April 20X0	7,279.47
31 July 20X0	For 3 months to 31 July 20X0	4,663.80
31 October 20X0	For 3 months to 31 October 20X0	4,117.28
31 January 20X1	For 3 months to 31 January 20X1	6,491.52

What should the electricity charge be for the year ended 31 December 20X0 (show your answer to 2 decimal places)?

£

Task 6.8

At 31 December 20X0 the accounts of a business show accrued rent payable of £250. During 20X1 the business pays rent bills totalling £1,275, including one bill for £375 in respect of the quarter ending 31 January 20X2.

What is the statement of profit or loss charge for the rent expense for the year ended 31 December 20X1?

£ [   ]

Task 6.9

During the year £5,000 commission income was received. At the beginning of the year the business was owed £1,000 and at the end of the year the business was owed £500.

What was the commission income figure in the year's statement of profit or loss? Select ONE.

	✓
£4,000	
£4,500	
£5,000	
£5,500	

Task 6.10

This task is about accounting for accruals and prepayments.

You are working on the accounting records of a business for the year ended 31 December 20X4.

You are looking into maintenance services income for the year.

- At 31 December 20X3, there was prepaid income in relation to maintenance services of £850.

(a) **Show the journal entry to reverse the opening prepaid income.**

Account		Amount £	Debit ✓	Credit ✓
	▼			
	▼			

Picklist:

Accrued expenses
Accrued income
Balance b/d
Balance c/d
Bank
Maintenance services expense
Maintenance services income
Prepaid expenses
Prepaid income
Profit or loss account

- During the year, the cash book included receipts for maintenance services of £12,750.

- This amount includes £3,000 for the year ended 30 June 20X5.

(b) **Update the maintenance services income account for the year ended 31 December 20X4. Show clearly:**

- **The reversal of the opening prepaid income**
- **The cash book figure**
- **The year end adjustment**
- **The transfer to the statement of profit or loss for the year**

Maintenance services income

		£			£
	▼			▼	
	▼			▼	

Picklist:

Accrued expenses
Accrued income
Balance b/d
Balance c/d
Bank
Maintenance services expense
Maintenance services income
Prepaid expenses
Prepaid expenses (reversal)
Prepaid income
Prepaid income (reversal)
Profit or loss account

Task 6.11

This task is about ledger accounting, including accruals and prepayments.

You are working on the final accounts of a business for the year ended 31 March 20X6. In this task, you can ignore VAT.

Business policy: accounting for accruals and prepayments

An entry is made into the income or expense account and an opposite entry into the relevant asset or liability account. In the following period, this entry is removed.

You are looking at service income:

The cash book for the year shows receipts of service income of £1,680. Service income of £185 is still due for March 20X6 at the year end.

(a) Update the service income account. Show clearly:

- **The cash book figure**
- **The year end adjustment**
- **The transfer to the statement of profit or loss for the year**

Service income

	£		▼	£
Accrued income (reversal)	210			
▼			▼	

Picklist:

Accrued expenses
Accrued income
Balance b/d
Balance c/d
Bank
Service income
Prepaid expenses
Prepaid income
Profit or loss account
Sales
Sales ledger control account

(b) **Answer the following regarding the accrued income reversal of £210 in the service income account above.**

(i) **How were the elements of the accounting equation affected by this transaction?**

Tick ONE box for each row.

	Increase ✓	Decrease ✓	No change ✓
Assets			
Liabilities			
Equity			

(ii) **Which ONE of the following dates should be entered for this transaction in the ledger account?**

	✓
1 April 20X5	
31 March 20X5	
31 March 20X6	

You are now looking at insurance expenses for the year.

There was an accrual of £78 on 31 March 20X5. This has been reversed.

The cash book for the year shows payments for insurance of £670, including in March 20X6, £15 paid for insurance covering April 20X6.

(c) **Complete the following statement:**

The administration expenses account needs an adjustment for

| | of | £ | | dated | |

Picklist:

Description:
Accrued expenses
Insurance expenses
Amount:
£798
£48
Date:
31 March 20X5
1 April 20X6

(d) **Taking into account all the information you have, calculate the insurance expense for the year ended 31 March 20X6.**

£ [   ]

BPP
LEARNING MEDIA

Chapter 7 – Inventories

Task 7.1

A business has 125 units of a product in inventory which cost £24.60 per unit plus £0.50 per unit of delivery costs. These goods can be sold for £25.80 per unit although in order to do this selling costs of £1.00 per unit must be incurred.

(a)   What is the cost of these units?

£   25·10

(b)   What is their net realisable value?

£   24·80

(c)   At what value will the 125 units of the product be included in the extended trial balance?

£   3,100·00

Task 7.2

Indicate which TWO of the following can be included as part of the cost of inventory in the accounts.

	✓
Selling costs	
Cost of purchase, including delivery	✓
Storage costs of finished goods	✗
Costs of conversion, including direct labour	✓

NRV.   Cost.

Task 7.3

In relation to inventory, what is meant by net realisable value?

	✓
The expected selling price of the inventory	
The expected selling price of the inventory less costs to completion and selling costs	✓
The replacement cost of the inventory	
The market price of the inventory	

Task 7.4

Accounting for inventory is governed by IAS 2 *Inventories*.

Complete the following sentence.

The rule for inventory is that it should be valued at the | *lower* ▼ |

of | *Cost* ▼ | and | *NRV.* ▼ | .

Picklist:

cost
higher
lower
net realisable value

Task 7.5

A business has five lines of inventory.

Complete the table below.

(a) **Show the:**

- **Net realisable value of each line of inventory**

- **Value PER UNIT of each line of the inventory, for accounting purposes**

- **The total value to appear in the business accounts for each line of inventory**

(b) **On the final row, show the total value of inventory lines A to E to be included in the accounts.**

Inventory line	Quantity (units)	Cost	Selling price	Selling costs	Net realisable value	Value per unit	Total value
		£	£	£	£	£	£
A	180	12.50	20.40	0.50	19·90	12·50	
B	240	10.90	12.60	1.80	10·80	10·80	
C	300	15.40	22.70	1.20	21·50	15·40	
D	80	16.50	17.80	1.50	16·30	16·30	
E	130	10.60	18.00	1.00	17·00	10·60	
Total							

Task 7.6

(a) **Match the descriptions to the relevant method of estimating cost by selecting from the picklist.**

Description	Method of estimating cost
Under this method a simple average cost can be calculated whereby the cost of all purchases/production during the year is divided by the total number of units purchased.	*Average cost* ▼
Under this method it is assumed that the last goods to be purchased/produced will be the first to be sold.	*LIFO* ▼
Under this method it is assumed that the first goods purchased/produced will be the first to be sold.	*FIFO* ▼

Picklist:

Average cost
First in first out
Last in first out

(b) **Answer the following question.**

Question	Answer
Is LIFO permitted by International Financial Reporting Standards?	*No* ▼

Picklist:

Yes
No

....

Task 7.7

A business has closing inventory of £20,000.

Show the journal entries to record closing inventory in the general ledger.

Account		Debit £	Credit £
	▼		
	▼		

Picklist:

Closing inventory (SOFP)
Closing inventory (SPL)
Opening inventory
Purchases

Task 7.8

In the business accounts, closing inventory is included in both the statement of financial position and the statement of profit or loss.

Select the terms which best reflect the relationship between inventory and the business accounts.

Statement	Term
Closing inventory in the statement of financial position is best described as	▼
Closing inventory in the statement of profit or loss is best described as	▼

Picklist:

a liability
a reduction in expenses
a reduction in income
an asset
an increase in expenses
an increase in income
capital

Task 7.9

Show whether the following statements are true or false.

Statement	True or false
In the statement of profit or loss, carriage inwards must be included within cost of goods sold.	▼
In the statement of profit or loss, carriage outwards must be included within cost of goods sold.	▼

Task 7.10

Show whether the following statements are true or false.

Statement	True or false
The main purpose of an inventory count is to value inventory at the end of the accounting period.	▼
On a regular basis an inventory reconciliation should be performed, comparing the warehouse's record of the quantity of each item held with the actual quantity counted.	▼

Picklist:

True
False

Task 7.11

Complete the following sentence.

Accounting for inventory as a deduction from cost of goods sold in the statement profit or loss is an application of the [▼   ] basis of accounting.

Picklist:

accruals
cash
international

Task 7.12

A business that is registered for VAT, sells an item of inventory to customers for £12,000 inclusive of VAT.

Included within the selling price is a profit of £4,000.

What is the cost of this item of inventory?

£ [   ]

Chapter 8 – Irrecoverable and doubtful debts

In this chapter, VAT should be ignored (learning outcome 4.2).

Task 8.1

A business has a balance on its sales ledger control account at 31 December 20X1 of £60,000. As part of its year-end procedures, it has reviewed its customer files and realised that one customer, SH, which owes £4,500 has severe financial difficulties and is unlikely to be able to pay its debt.

Show the journal entries to write off the debt in the general ledger.

Account		Debit £	Credit £
	▼		
	▼		

Picklist:

Bank
Irrecoverable debts
Sales
Sales ledger control account

....

Task 8.2

A business WH has a balance on its sales ledger control account at 31 March 20X2 of £45,000. As part of its year-end procedures, it has reviewed its customer files and realised that one customer, ZX, which owes £6,900 has severe financial difficulties and is unlikely to be able to pay its debt.

(a)   Show the journal entries to write off the debt in the general ledger.

Account		Debit £	Credit £
	▼		
	▼		

(b) Update the sales ledger control account and the irrecoverable debts account to record this information.

As appropriate, on each account show clearly the:

- Balance to be carried down; or
- Balance transferred to the profit or loss account.

Sales ledger control account

	£			£
Balance b/d	45,000		▼	
	▼			▼	

Irrecoverable debts

	£			£
	▼			▼	

(c) Write up ZX's subsidiary sales ledger account in the books of WH. Record the irrecoverable debt. Total the sales ledger account (you do not need to enter a balance c/d if it comes to zero).

ZX – Sales ledger account

	£			£
Balance b/d	6,900		▼	
	▼			▼	

Picklist:

Balance b/d
Balance c/d
Bank
Irrecoverable debts
Sales
Sales ledger control account
Profit or loss account

Task 8.3

A business has a balance on its sales ledger control account at 31 December 20X3 of £70,000. In November 20X3, the business unexpectedly receives £9,500 from a customer. This relates to an amount written off in the previous financial period.

Show the journal entries to record the recovery of this irrecoverable debt previously written off in the general ledger.

Account		Debit £	Credit £
	▼		
	▼		

Picklist:

Bank
Irrecoverable debts
Sales
Sales ledger control account
Profit or loss account

Task 8.4

RN Trading has a balance on its sales ledger control account at 31 August 20X7 of £86,000.

At 31 August 20X6, the allowance for doubtful debts was £1,160. At 31 August 20X7, the allowance for doubtful debts will be 2% of the outstanding trade receivables.

(a) **What is the allowance for doubtful debts at 31 August 20X7?**

£ [   ]

(b) **What is the allowance for doubtful debts – adjustment for the year ended 31 August 20X7? Select whether it results in an increase or decrease in expenses.**

£ [   ] [▼]

Picklist:

Increase in expenses
Decrease in expenses

Task 8.5

WP Trading has a balance on its sales ledger control account at 31 December 20X6 of £90,000. Included within this balance is £4,400 of irrecoverable debts to write off and a specific allowance to be made of £1,300.

At 31 December 20X5, the allowance for doubtful debts was £1,600. At 31 December 20X6, the allowance for doubtful debts will be 4% of the outstanding trade receivables.

Update the following accounts to show this information:

- **Sales ledger control account**
- **Irrecoverable debts**
- **Allowance for doubtful debts (SOFP)**
- **Allowance for doubtful debts – adjustments (SPL)**

As appropriate, on each account show clearly the:

- **Balance carried down; or**
- **Balance transferred to the profit or loss account.**

Sales ledger control account

	£		£
Balance b/d	90,000	▼	
▼		▼	

Irrecoverable debts

	£		£
▼		▼	

Allowance for doubtful debts

	£		£
▼		Balance b/d	1,600
▼		▼	

Allowance for doubtful debts – adjustments

	£			£
	▼		▼	

Picklist:

Allowance for doubtful debts
Allowance for doubtful debts – adjustments
Balance b/d
Balance c/d
Bank
Irrecoverable debts
Sales ledger control account
Profit or loss account

Task 8.6

GY Trading has a balance on its sales ledger control account at 31 December 20X6 of £200,000. Included within this balance is £16,000 of irrecoverable debts to write off and a specific allowance to be made of £3,000.

At 31 December 20X5, the allowance for doubtful debts was £7,600. At 31 December 20X6, the allowance for doubtful debts will be 2% of the outstanding trade receivables.

Complete the trial balance extract by entering the figures in the correct places.

Trial balance (extract)

	Ledger balance	
Ledger account	Debit £	Credit £
Sales ledger control account		
Irrecoverable debts		
Allowance for doubtful debts		
Allowance for doubtful debts – adjustments		

Task 8.7

An allowance for doubtful debts is an example of which basis of accounting?

	✓
Depreciation	
Inventory	
Accruals	
Prudence	

Chapter 9 – Bank reconciliations

Task 9.1

Complete the following sentences.

	Answer
A credit balance on the bank statement indicates a	▼
A credit balance on the cash book indicates a	▼

Picklist:

negative cash balance
positive cash balance

....

Task 9.2

Complete the following sentences.

A positive cash balance is a [▼] entry in the cash book.

A negative cash balance is shown on the bank statement as a [▼] entry.

Picklist:

debit
credit

....

Task 9.3

Murray's Office Supplies' received the following bank statement for July 20X2.

Date 20X2	Details	Paid out £	Paid in £	Balance £	
01 July	Balance b/d			8,751	C
03 July	Counter credit – LKI		2,875	11,626	C
11 July	Cheque 103122	1,100		10,526	C
13 July	Direct debit – Gas	4,895		5,631	C
14 July	BACS ABW		6,351	11,982	C
18 July	Cheque – 103123	158		11,824	C
27 July	Cheque – 103125	7,565		4,259	C
28 July	Counter credit – OKM		8,590	12,849	C
	D = Debit, C = Credit				

(a) **Check the items on the bank statement against the items in the cash book below.**

(b) **Enter any items into the cash book as needed.**

(c) **Total the cash book and clearly show the balance carried down at 31 July AND brought down at 1 August.**

Cash book as at 31 July

Date 20X2	Details	Bank £	Date 20X2	Cheque number	Details	Bank £
01 July	Balance b/d	8,751	11 July	103122	ENG	1,100
03 July	LKI	2,875	18 July	103123	JHP	158
14 July	ABW	6,351	27 July	103125	MWY	7,565
17 July	WNY	3,560	29 July	103126	YMN	4,320

(d) Identify the **TWO** transactions that are included in the cash book but missing from the bank statement and complete the bank reconciliation statement below as at 31 July.

Bank reconciliation statement		£
Balance per bank statement		
	▼	
Total to add		
	▼	
Total to subtract		
Balance as per cash book		

Picklist:

Balance b/d
Balance c/d
ABW
Direct debit – Gas
ENG
JHP
LKI
MWY
OKM
WNY
YMN

Task 9.4

The balance showing on the bank statement is a debit of £778 and the balance in the cash book is a debit of £3,851.

The bank statement has been compared to the cash book and the following differences identified:

(1) Bank charges of £25 are included on the bank statement but have not been entered in the cash book.

(2) Cash receipts totalling £1,738 have been entered in the cash book but are not yet banked.

(3) An automated receipt from a credit customer for £743 has been incorrectly entered in the cash book as £734. It is correct on the bank statement.

(4) A BACS payment of £2,827 has not been entered in the cash book.

(5) A cheque sent to a supplier for £452 has been entered in the cash book but has not yet cleared the bank statement.

(6) The bank made an error and duplicated the payment of a standing order for £500.

Use the following table to show the THREE adjustments you need to make to the cash book.

Adjustment		Amount £	Debit ✓	Credit ✓
	▼			
	▼			
	▼		·	

Picklist:

Adjustment (1)
Adjustment (2)
Adjustment (3)
Adjustment (4)
Adjustment (5)
Adjustment (6)

....

Task 9.5

The balance showing on the bank statement is a credit of £7,377 and the balance in the cash book is a debit of £11,442.

The bank statement has been compared to the cash book and the following differences identified:

(1) A cheque sent to a supplier for £990 has been entered in the cash book but has not yet cleared the bank statement.

(2) Cash receipts totalling £3,560 have been entered in the cash book but are not yet banked.

(3) An BACS receipt from a credit customer for £996 has cleared the bank statement but has not yet been entered in the cash book.

(4) A faster payment of £2,827 for the purchase of a non-current asset has cleared the bank statement but has not been entered in the cash book.

(5) A cheque sent to a supplier for £776 has been entered in the cash book but has not yet cleared the bank statement

(6) Bank charges paid of £440 were not entered in the cash book.

Use the following table to show the THREE adjustments you need to make to the cash book.

Adjustment		Amount £	Debit ✓	Credit ✓
	▼			
	▼			
	▼			

Picklist:

Adjustment (1)
Adjustment (2)
Adjustment (3)
Adjustment (4)
Adjustment (5)
Adjustment (6)

Chapter 10 – Control account reconciliations

Task 10.1

Given below are summaries of transactions with receivables for the month of February for a business. The balance on the sales ledger control account at 1 February was £4,268.

	£
Goods sold on credit	15,487
Goods returned by credit customers	995
Irrecoverable debts	210
Money received from credit customers	13,486
Discounts allowed	408
Contra entries	150

Enter the items above in the sales ledger control account (including the balance b/d at the start of the month). Show the balance c/d at the end of the month.

Sales ledger control account

	£		£
▼		▼	
▼		▼	
▼		▼	
▼		▼	
▼		▼	
▼		▼	

Picklist:

Balance b/d
Balance c/d
Bank
Discounts allowed
Irrecoverable debts
Purchases ledger control account
Sales
Sales returns

Task 10.2

The balance on the purchases ledger control account for a business at 1 February was £3,299. The transactions with payables for the month of February are summarised below:

	£
Credit purchases	12,376
Cheques to payables	10,379
Returns to credit suppliers	1,074
Discounts received	302
Contra entry	230

Enter the items above in the purchases ledger control account (including the balance b/d at the start of the month). Show the balance c/d at the end of the month.

Purchases ledger control account

	£			£
▼			▼	
▼			▼	
▼			▼	
▼			▼	
▼			▼	

Picklist:

Balance b/d
Balance c/d
Bank
Discounts received
Purchases
Purchases returns
Sales ledger control account

Task 10.3

At 31 March the balance on a business's sales ledger control account was £7,380 but the total of the list of balances from the sales ledger was £6,310. The following errors were discovered:

(1) A customer account with a credit balance of £460 was omitted from the total of the subsidiary sales ledger account balances.

(2) A contra entry for £250 has been made in the sales ledger control account but not in the subsidiary ledger.

(3) A cash book – debit side total of £1,650 has been posted to the wrong side of the sales ledger control account.

(4) A total of the sales day book has been undercast by £1,000.

(5) A credit note to a customer for £680 has been entered on the wrong side of the customer's account in the sales ledger.

(6) A total of the discounts allowed book of £840 has been omitted from the sales ledger control account.

Use the following table to show the THREE adjustments required to the sales ledger control account.

Adjustment		Amount £	Debit ✓	Credit ✓
▼				
▼				
▼				

Picklist:

Adjustment (1)
Adjustment (2)
Adjustment (3)
Adjustment (4)
Adjustment (5)
Adjustment (6)

Task 10.4

At 31 December the balance on a business's sales ledger control account was £11,840 but the total of the list of balances from the sales ledger was £6,100. The following errors were discovered:

(1)   The subsidiary sales ledger account of G Hargreaves was understated by £100.

(2)   A total in the sales returns day book was undercast by £3,000.

(3)   A total in the sales day book of £2,400 was duplicated in the sales ledger control account.

(4)   A sales invoice of £570 was incorrectly posted to the wrong side of the sales ledger account. It was entered correctly in the sales day book.

(5)   A credit note to a customer for £680 has been entered on the wrong side of the customer's account in the sales ledger.

(6)   A contra entry for £460 has been entered in the subsidiary sales ledger but was not posted to the sales ledger control account.

Use the following table to show the THREE adjustments required to the listing of subsidiary sales ledger balances.

Adjustment		Amount £	Debit ✓	Credit ✓
	▼			
	▼			
	▼			

Picklist:

Adjustment (1)
Adjustment (2)
Adjustment (3)
Adjustment (4)
Adjustment (5)
Adjustment (6)

Task 10.5

The balance on a business's purchases ledger control account at 31 January was £3,450 but the total of the list of balances from the purchases ledger was £2,219 at the same date. The following errors were discovered:

(1) A credit note of £160 to R Milne was incorrectly entered in the subsidiary ledger account of J Roberts.

(2) A page in the purchases day book had been overcast by £850.

(3) A total in the purchases returns day book of £791 was entered in the general ledger as £719.

(4) A contra entry of £214 was included in the purchases ledger control account but has been omitted from the relevant subsidiary purchases ledger accounts.

(5) A purchases credit note of £403 was recorded as a credit entry in the purchases ledger. It is correctly entered in the purchases day book.

(6) A total in the cash book – credit side of £1,329 has been omitted from the purchases ledger control account.

Use the following table to show the adjustments you need to make to the purchases ledger control account.

Adjustment		Amount £	Debit ✓	Credit ✓
	▼			
	▼			
	▼			

Picklist:

Adjustment (1)
Adjustment (2)
Adjustment (3)
Adjustment (4)
Adjustment (5)
Adjustment (6)

Task 10.6

The balance on a business's purchases ledger control account at 31 January was £5,248 but the total of the list of balances from the purchases ledger was £8,670 at the same date. The following errors were discovered:

(1)   The total from the discounts received day book of £980 was omitted from the purchases ledger control account.

(2)   A page in the purchases day book totalling £3,592 was omitted from the general ledger.

(3)   A purchases invoice of £660 was entered on the wrong side of the subsidiary purchases ledger account.

(4)   A credit note of £1,210 was omitted from the subsidiary purchases ledger account.

(5)   The total of a page in the cash book – credit side relating to payments to suppliers was undercast by £320.

(6)   Purchases credit notes totalling £620 had incorrectly been entered on the credit side of the subsidiary purchases ledger account.

Use the following table to show the THREE adjustments required to the listing of subsidiary purchases ledger balances.

Adjustment	Amount £	Debit ✓	Credit ✓
▼			
▼			
▼			

Picklist:

Adjustment (1)
Adjustment (2)
Adjustment (3)
Adjustment (4)
Adjustment (5)
Adjustment (6)

Task 10.7

This task is about period end routines.

You are preparing the reconciliation between a credit supplier's statement of account and the supplier's account as shown in the purchases ledger of Magenta at the end of June 20X6.

Gerry Green
Garden Industrial Estate
Westham WM2 3FS

To: Magenta
14 Manor Road
Eastham
EM3 4NJ

Statement of account

Date 20X6	Details	Transaction amount	Outstanding amount
01 June	Opening balance		500
02 June	Cheque	420	80
10 June	Invoice 147	1,750	1,830
17 June	Credit note 23	530	1,300
22 June	Invoice 178	925	2,225
29 June	Invoice 195	1,250	3,475

Purchases ledger account – Gerry Green

Date 20XX	Details	Amount £	Date 20XX	Details	Amount £
02 June	Cheque	420	01 June	Balance b/f	500
17 June	Purchases returns – credit note 23	530	10 June	Purchases – invoice 147	1,750
			22 June	Purchases – invoice 178	925

(a) **Calculate the balance on the supplier's account in Magenta's purchases ledger and reconcile this with the balance showing on the supplier's statement of account.**

	£
Balance on supplier's statement of account	3,475
Balance on supplier's account in purchases ledger	
Difference	

(b) **Which item on the supplier's statement of account has not yet been entered in the supplier's account in Magenta's purchases ledger?**

Items	✓
Cheque for £420	
Invoice number 147	
Credit note number 23	
Invoice number 178	
Invoice number 195	

Task 10.8

This task is about accounting for payroll.

Marten Trading pays its employees by bank transfer every month and maintains a wages control account (also known as the 'net pay control account'). A summary of last month's payroll transactions is shown below.

Item	Amount £
Gross pay	120,000
Employees' NI	4,000
Income tax	16,000
Employer's NI	8,000

In the general ledger:

(a)   Record the wages expense

Account name	Amount £	Debit ✓	Credit ✓
▼			
▼			

(b)   Record the HM Revenue and Customs liability

Account name	Amount £	Debit ✓	Credit ✓
▼			
▼			

(c)   Record the net wages paid to the employees

Account name	Amount £	Debit ✓	Credit ✓
▼			
▼			

Picklist:

Bank
HM Revenue and Customs
Wages control account
Wages expense

Chapter 11 – The trial balance, errors and the suspense account

Task 11.1

In the 'type of error' column, show the error being described in the 'Description' column.

In the 'balancing trial balance' column, indicate whether the error will permit the trial balance to balance or not.

Description	Type of error	Balancing trial balance
A debit entry has been posted with no corresponding credit made.	▼	▼
An entry has been made so that debits equal credits but the amount is incorrect.	▼	▼
A transaction has been recorded at the correct amount but the debit and credit entries have been reversed.	▼	▼
Debits equal credits; however, one of the entries has been made to the wrong type of account.	▼	▼

Picklist for type of error:

Error of original entry
Error of principle
Reversal of entries
Single entry error

Picklist for balancing trial balance:

No
Yes

Task 11.2

For each of the following errors indicate whether there is an imbalance in the trial balance or not.

Error	Imbalance ✓	No imbalance ✓
The payment of the telephone bill was posted to the cash book – credit side and then credited to the telephone account.		
The depreciation expense was debited to the accumulated depreciation account and credited to the depreciation charges account.		
The electricity account balance of £750 was taken to the trial balance as £570.		
The motor expenses were debited to the motor vehicles at cost account. The credit entry is correct.		
Discounts received were not posted to the general ledger.		

Task 11.3

A trial balance has been prepared for a business and the total of the debit balances is £228,678 and the total of the credits is £220,374.

What is the balance on the suspense account?

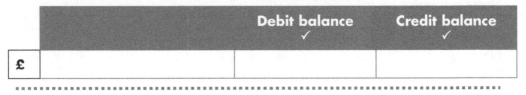

	Debit balance ✓	Credit balance ✓
£		

Task 11.4

Show the journal entries required to correct each of the following errors.

Narratives are not required. Ignore VAT.

(a) Telephone expenses of £236 were debited to the electricity account.

Account name	Debit £	Credit £
▼		
▼		

(b) A sales invoice for £645 was entered into the sales day book as £465.

Account name	Debit £	Credit £
▼		
▼		

(c) A credit note received from a supplier for £38 was omitted from the purchases returns day book.

Account name	Debit £	Credit £
▼		
▼		

Picklist:

Electricity
Purchases ledger control account
Purchases returns
Sales
Sales ledger control account
Telephone

Task 11.5

Show the journal entries required to correct each of the following errors.

Narratives are not required. Ignore VAT.

(a) The increase in allowance for doubtful debts of £127 was debited to the allowance for doubtful debts account and credited to the allowance for doubtful debts adjustment account.

Account name		Debit £	Credit £
	▼		
	▼		

(b) A contra entry of £200 was debited to the sales ledger control account and credited to the purchases ledger control account.

Account name		Debit £	Credit £
	▼		
	▼		

(c) The irrecoverable debts expense of £680 was omitted from the general ledger.

Account name		Debit £	Credit £
	▼		
	▼		

Picklist:

Allowance for doubtful debts
Allowance for doubtful debts – adjustments
Irrecoverable debts
Purchases ledger control account
Sales ledger control account

Task 11.6

This task is about accounting adjustments.

You are a trainee accounting technician reporting to a managing partner in an accounting practice. You are working on the accounting records of a business client.

A trial balance has been drawn up and balanced using a suspense account. You now need to make some corrections and adjustments for the year ended 31 December 20X7.

You may ignore VAT in this task.

Depreciation on the plant must be calculated. Plant is depreciated at 20% per year on a straight line basis assuming no residual value.

(a)   Calculate the depreciation charge on plant for the year.

£	

(b)   (i)   Record this adjustment into the extract from the extended trial balance below.

(ii)   Make the following further adjustments.

You will NOT need to enter adjustments on every line. Do NOT enter zeros into unused cells.

*   The carriage outwards balance of £460 was omitted from the trial balance. The corresponding entry (a cheque payment) is correctly included in the cash book.

*   The purchases balance was incorrectly transferred to the trial balance. The balance should be £88,540 and not £89,430.

*   The payment of office expenses of £70 has been reversed in both general ledger accounts.

Extract from the extended trial balance

Ledger account	Ledger balances		Adjustments	
	Debit £	Credit £	Debit £	Credit £
Bank	5,321			
Carriage outwards				
Depreciation charges				
Irrecoverable debts	632			
Office expenses	52,832			
Plant at cost	32,400			
Plant accumulated depreciation		6,480		
Prepaid expenses	305			
Purchases	89,430			
Purchases ledger control account		11,230		
Rent	12,520			
Sales		104,502		
Sales ledger control account	16,230			
Suspense		430		
VAT		9,320		

Task 11.7

This task is about accounting adjustments.

You are a trainee accounting technician reporting to a managing partner in an accounting practice. You are working on the accounting records of a business client.

A trial balance has been drawn up and balanced using a suspense account. You now need to make some corrections and adjustments for the year ended 30 April 20X9.

You may ignore VAT in this task.

The allowance for doubtful debts needs to be adjusted to 2% of the outstanding trade receivables.

(a) **Calculate the value of the adjustment required.**

£	

(b) **(i)** **Record this adjustment into the extract from the extended trial balance below.**

(ii) **Make the following further adjustments.**

You will NOT need to enter adjustments on every line. Do NOT enter zeros into unused cells.

- Closing inventory has been valued at £8,430.

- The bank balance has been included on the wrong side of the trial balance.

- Purchases returns of £560 have been correctly included in the purchases ledger control account. The other entry was omitted.

Extract from the extended trial balance

Ledger account	Ledger balances		Adjustments	
	Debit £	Credit £	Debit £	Credit £
Allowance for doubtful debts		350		
Allowance for doubtful debts – adjustments				
Accrued expenses		750		
Bank		6,320		
Carriage inwards	219			
Closing inventory				
Depreciation charges	6,625			
Discounts allowed	620			
Office expenses	488			
Opening inventory	4,420			
Prepaid expenses	305			
Purchases	89,430			
Purchases returns				
Purchases ledger control account		11,230		
Sales		104,502		
Sales ledger control account	18,200			
Suspense	12,080			

Task 11.8

You are a trainee accounting technician working in an accounting practice. You are working on the accounting records of a business known as SYH Trading for the year ended 30 September 20X6. The proprietor of SYH Trading is trying to obtain a bank loan for the business and is keen to maximise the profit for the year to encourage the bank to lend. Your line manager is concerned that the proprietor might propose year end adjustments with the deliberate intent of maximising profit. Therefore, she has asked you to look out for period end adjustments which would result in an increase to profit for the year.

Which of the following period end adjustments would result in an increase to profit for the year?

Choose ONE.

	✓
A decrease in the allowance for doubtful debts from 3% of outstanding trade receivables to 2% of outstanding trade receivables	
The write down of an item of inventory which cost £1,500 and had a selling price of £1,350 and expected selling costs of £200	
Recognising an accrual for vehicle running expenses for September 20X6 but not invoiced and paid until October 20X6	
Decreasing the useful life of a computer with effect from the start of the year (1 October 20X5)	

Task 11.9

You are a trainee accounting technician reporting to a managing partner in an accounting practice. You are working on the accounting records of a business known as KSB Trading for the year ended 31 December 20X6. The proprietor is KSB Trading is a great friend of the managing partner in your accounting practice. KSB Trading is trying to increase its bank overdraft limit and a meeting is set up with the bank next week. The proprietor is convinced that the current year's profit should persuade the bank to increase the overdraft limit and has asked the managing partner not to amend the draft profit figure. The managing partner has asked you to respect the proprietor's wishes.

As part of your preparation of the year end accounts, you have discovered a letter from one of KSB Trading's customers explain that they have gone into liquidation and are unable to pay the amount owing to KSB Trading. No adjustment has been made in respect of this.

What should you do next and why?

Choose ONE.

	✓
Complete the accounts without any further adjustment, as any change could affect the outcome of the meeting with the bank.	
Complete the accounts without any further adjustment because the client's needs must take priority.	
Explain to the managing partner that you have discovered an irrecoverable debt which needs writing off because the accounts must be prepared in accordance with International Financial Reporting Standards.	
Write off the irrecoverable debt without telling your managing partner as you want to make sure that you get the pay rise that he's promised you.	

Task 11.10

You are a trainee accounting technician reporting to a managing partner in an accounting practice. You are working on the accounting records of a business known as TWG Trading for the year ended 30 June 20X3. Whilst you are preparing the accounts for the year ended 30 June 20X3, you come across some cash sales recorded on 30 June 20X3 which are then reversed out as sales returns on 1 July 20X3.

What should you do next and why?

Choose ONE.

	✓
Do nothing because the cash sales were accurately recorded in the cash book.	
Seek advice from the managing partner as it is possible that these sales were deliberately created with the intention of increasing profit for the year ended 30 June 20X3 and are not a genuine business transaction.	
Ignore the discovery because the client is a good friend and you trust him implicitly.	
Insist that the client reverses these sales and threaten to resign because it is clear that there has deliberately overstated the profit.	

Task 11.11

Which of the following statements about the trial balance is correct?

Choose ONE.

	✓
It is a memorandum account to keep track of amounts owing from individual customers and owed to individual suppliers.	
It will detect all bookkeeping errors.	
It is prepared after closing off the general ledger accounts and before preparing the final accounts.	
It will always include a suspense account.	

Task 11.12

This task is about accounting adjustments.

You are working as an accounting technician for a sole trader business with a year end of 30 September. A trial balance has been drawn up and a suspense account opened. You now need to make some corrections and adjustments for the year ended 30 September 20X6.

You may ignore VAT for this task.

Record the journal entries needed in the general ledger to deal with the items below.

You should:

- **Remove any incorrect entries where appropriate**
- **Post the correct entries**

Do NOT enter zeros into unused column cells.

Note. **You do NOT need to give narratives.**

(a) **Depreciation of £1,056 on fixtures and fittings has not yet been accounted for.**

Account		Debit £	Credit £
▼			
▼			

Picklist:

Depreciation expense
Fixtures and fittings cost
Fixtures and fittings accumulated depreciation
Suspense

(b) **An accrual for a telephone bill of £120 has been made correctly to the telephone expenses account but the other side of the entry has not been posted.**

Account		Debit £	Credit £
▼			
▼			

Picklist:

Accruals
Telephone expense
Prepayments
Purchases
Suspense

(c) **Closing inventory for the year end 30 September 20X6 has not yet been recorded. Its value at cost is £8,450. Included in this figure are some items costing £445 that will be sold for £250.**

Account		Debit £	Credit £
	▼		
	▼		

Picklist:

Closing inventory – statement of financial position
Closing inventory – statement of profit or loss

(d) **Credit notes of £887 have been posted to the correct side of the purchases ledger control account, but have been made to the same side of the purchases returns account.**

Account		Debit £	Credit £
	▼		
	▼		

Picklist:

Purchase ledger control account
Sales ledger control account
Purchase returns
Suspense
Sales returns

Now that you have posted the journals, you are pleased to see that the suspense account is clear and the trial balance totals agree.

(e)   Complete the following sentences:

▼

conclude that the balances included are now free from all errors.

▼

conclude that the debt and credit sides of the trial balance will be equal.

Picklist:

I can
I cannot

Chapter 12 – The extended trial balance

Task 12.1

(a) **Complete the following sentence.**

An extended trial balance is an accounting technique of moving from the [▼   ] trial balance, through the year end adjustments, to the figures for the [▼   ] accounts.

Picklist:

final
initial

(b) **Complete the following sentence.**

When an extended trial balance is extended and a business has made a profit, this figure for profit will be in the [▼   ] column of the statement of profit or loss.

Picklist:

credit
debit

Task 12.2

In respect of the extended trial balance, show which ONE of the following statements is correct.

Statements	✓
The balance on the suspense account should appear on the debit side of the statement of profit or loss columns.	
The balance on the suspense account should appear on the credit side of the statement of financial position columns.	
The balance on the suspense account should not appear in the statement of profit or loss or the statement of financial position columns in the extended trial balance.	

Task 12.3

Enter a tick in the relevant place to show where the following ledger accounts are usually included in the extended trial balance.

Where necessary, enter more than one tick on a row.

Extended trial balance

Ledger account	Statement of profit or loss		Statement of financial position	
	Debit ✓	Credit ✓	Debit ✓	Credit ✓
Allowance for doubtful debts				
Allowance for doubtful debts – adjustment (increase in allowance)				
Bank overdraft				
Capital				
Closing inventory				
Depreciation charges				
Purchases returns				
Opening inventory				
VAT owed from HMRC				

Task 12.4

Extend the figures into the statement of profit or loss and statement of financial position columns.

Do NOT enter zeros into unused column cells.

Complete the extended trial balance by entering figures and a label in the correct places.

Extended trial balance

Ledger account	Ledger balances		Adjustments		Statement of profit or loss		Statement of financial position	
	Debit £	Credit £	Debit £	Credit £	Debit £	Credit £	Debit £	Credit £
Allowance for doubtful debts		2,380	420					
Allowance for doubtful debts – adjustment	1,600			420				
Bank	2,400		230					
Capital		25,800						
Closing inventory			13,500	13,500				
Depreciation charges	9,203		4,000					
Office expenses	600							
Opening inventory	2,560							
Payroll expenses	16,400							
Purchases	22,400							
Purchases ledger control account		8,900	300					
Sales		45,150		60				
Sales ledger control account	11,205			300				
Selling expenses	1,700							
Suspense	170		60	230				
VAT		12,000						
Vehicles at cost	64,192							
Vehicles accumulated depreciation		38,200		4,000				
▼								
Total	132,430	132,430	18,510	18,510				

Picklist:

Balance b/d
Balance c/d
Gross loss for the year
Gross profit for the year
Loss for the year
Profit for the year
Suspense

....

Task 12.5

Extend the figures into the statement of profit or loss and statement of financial position columns.

Do NOT enter zeros into unused column cells.

Complete the extended trial balance by entering figures and a label in the correct places.

Extended trial balance

Ledger account	Ledger balances		Adjustments		Statement of profit or loss		Statement of financial position	
	Debit £	Credit £	Debit £	Credit £	Debit £	Credit £	Debit £	Credit £
Bank		4,123		4,235				
Capital		20,000						
Closing inventory			3,414	3,414				
Depreciation charges	2,415		1,352					
Irrecoverable debts	124							
Loan		10,000						
Machine at cost	51,600							
Machine accumulated depreciation		13,210		1,352				
Opening inventory	6,116							
Prepaid expenses	215		352					
Purchases	39,321		519					
Purchases ledger control account		13,421						
Purchases returns		299		519				
Sales		72,032		511				
Sales ledger control account	38,597			3,770				
Sales returns	2,057		511					
Suspense		3,418	3,770	352				
VAT		3,942	4,235					
▼								
Total	140,445	140,445	14,153	14,153				

Picklist:

Balance b/d
Balance c/d
Gross loss for the year
Gross profit for the year
Loss for the year
Profit for the year
Suspense

Answer Bank

Chapter 1

Task 1.1

The sales returns day book lists	credit notes sent to customers
The purchases day book lists	invoices received from suppliers
The purchases returns day book lists	credit notes received from suppliers
The sales day book lists	invoices sent to customers

Explanation:

Remember, the books of prime entry are the records in which transactions are initially recorded. Postings will then be made from the books of prime entry to the ledgers.

Task 1.2

(a)

Account	Debit £	Credit £
Bank	15,000	
Capital		15,000

(b)

Account	Debit £	Credit £
Rent	2,000	
Bank		2,000

(c)

Account	Debit £	Credit £
Purchases	6,200	
Bank		6,200

(d)

Account	Debit £	Credit £
Electricity	150	
Bank		150

Explanation:

For every transactions, there is a dual effect on the general ledger (ie a debit entry and a corresponding credit entry).

....

Task 1.3

Bank

	£		£
Capital (1)	20,000	Purchases (2)	2,100
Sales (3)	870	Purchases ledger control account (6)	1,500
Sales ledger control account (7)	1,600	Balance c/d	18,870
	22,470		22,470
Balance b/d	18,870		

Capital

	£		£
Balance c/d	20,000	Bank (1)	20,000
	20,000		20,000
		Balance b/d	20,000

Purchases

	£		£
Bank (2)	2,100	Profit or loss account	4,900
Purchases ledger control account (4)	2,800		
	4,900		4,900

Purchases ledger control account

	£		£
Bank (6)	1,500	Purchases (4)	2,800
Balance c/d	1,300		
	2,800		2,800
		Balance b/d	1,300

Sales

	£		£
Profit or loss account	4,270	Bank (3)	870
		Sales ledger control account (5)	3,400
	4,270		4,270

Sales ledger control account

	£		£
Sales (5)	3,400	Bank (7)	1,600
		Balance c/d	1,800
	3,400		3,400
Balance b/d	1,800		

Explanation:

The statement of financial position accounts (bank, capital, purchases ledger control account and sales ledger control account) are totalled at the period end. For each account a balance c/d and balance b/d is calculated.

The statement of profit or loss accounts (purchases and sales) are totalled at the year end. The balancing figures are taken to the profit or loss account.

Task 1.4

Trial balance	Amount £	Debit £	Credit £
Bank (positive balance)	11,000	**11,000**	
Capital	14,000		**14,000**
Electricity	2,000	**2,000**	
Purchases	4,500	**4,500**	
Purchases ledger control account	3,000		**3,000**
Rent expense	2,500	**2,500**	
Sales	9,000		**9,000**
Sales ledger control account	12,000	**12,000**	
VAT control account (due to HMRC)	6,000		**6,000**
		32,000	**32,000**

Explanation:

In accordance with the principles of double entry bookkeeping, assets and expenses are entered on the debit side of the trial balance. Liabilities, income and capital are recorded on the credit side of the trial balance.

Task 1.5

(a)

Ledger account	Amount £	Debit ✓	Credit ✓
Sales	13,000		✓
Sales returns	1,000	✓	
Purchases	8,000	✓	
Purchases returns	2,000		✓
Bank	3,500	✓	

(b)

Amount owed at the end of the period: £	2,500
Asset or liability	Liability

Explanation:

The amount owed at the end of the period is calculated as sales £13,000 plus purchases returns £2,000 less sales returns £1,000 less purchases £8,000 less bank £3,500 = £2,500.

The credit entries exceed the debit entries. This shows that there is an amount owed to HMRC at the end of the period, and therefore a liability.

Chapter 2

Task 2.1

Description	Term
Assets which do not have a physical substance, for example licences and brands	Intangible assets
Assets which have a physical substance, for example property, plant and equipment	Tangible assets

Task 2.2

Description	Term
This shows what the business owes back to its owner.	Capital
These relate to liabilities owed by the business due to its day-to-day activities and include trade payables, accruals, VAT owed to the tax authorities and bank overdrafts.	Current liabilities
These are costs that a business has incurred over the accounting period.	Expenses
These relate to assets used by the business on a day-to-day basis and include inventory, trade receivables and bank balances.	Current assets
Tangible or intangible assets held and used in the business over the long term (ie more than one year).	Non-current assets
These are amounts that the business has earned over the accounting period.	Income
These relate to the long-term debts of the business and include items such as long-term bank loans.	Non-current liabilities

Task 2.3

Item	Asset, liability, income, expense or capital
A laptop used in the accounts department of a retail store	Asset
Equity interest	Capital
A bank loan	Liability

Explanation:

The classifications reflect the principles of double entry bookkeeping.

Task 2.4

	✓
an asset, capital or an expense	
a liability or an expense	
an amount owing to the organisation	
a liability, capital or income	✓

Explanation:

Statement 1: This is incorrect as assets and expenses are debit balances, not credit balances.

Statement 2: This is incorrect as an expense is a debit balance, not a credit balance.

Statement 3: This is incorrect as an amount owing to the organisation is an asset. An asset is a debit balance, not a credit balance.

Task 2.5

Scenarios	Fundamental principle
Employees who may receive a bonus depending on the financial performance of the accounting practice do not prepare the accounting practice's financial statements.	Objectivity
The new trainee accounting technician is supervised by her manager and receives the necessary training.	Professional competence and due care

Task 2.6

Control procedures	✓
Physical controls	✓
Segregation of duties	
Authorisation of transactions	
Written record of procedures	

Explanation:

Businesses should ensure physical restrictions are in place to limit access to assets such as inventory.

Task 2.7

	✓
To ensure that the accounting policies selected maximise the business's profits	
To ensure the accounting records truly reflect the transactions and financial results of the business	✓
To ensure that the business acts in the owner's best interests	
To minimise the tax payable on the business's profits	

Explanation:

Accounting policies should result in information that is relevant and reliable to users of financial statements rather than with the aim of maximising the business's profits.

The business should act in the business's and its stakeholders' best interests rather than the owner's own personal interests.

As explained above, accounting policies should be designed around making the information relevant and reliable rather than specifically to minimise the tax liability on the business's profits.

Task 2.8

	✓
Reviews	
Written record of procedures	
Physical controls	✓
Authorisation of transactions	

Explanation:

Physical controls are most appropriate here. The checkout operation and store manager should count the cash float together at the beginning and end of the day and a written record of the amount should be made. The physical cash amount should then be reconciled to the expected amount of cash from the till receipts by the store manager and any discrepancies investigated.

Task 2.9

	Acceptable reason ✓	Not acceptable reason ✓
The business has high value desirable inventory making the risk of theft high which could be covered up by unauthorised alteration of accounting records.	✓	
Only the accounts department are likely to have the necessary skills and knowledge to maintain the accounting records.	✓	
The password will prevent anyone in the accounts department deliberately manipulating accounting records.		✓
The password will prevent theft of inventory and cash from the business.		✓

Explanation:

Technological products typically have a high retail price and are very popular making the risk of theft high. If a member of warehouse staff for example, had access to both the accounting records and the inventory in the warehouse, he/she could steal inventory and cover it up by altering the accounting records. Limiting access to the accounting records to the accounting department would prevent other members of staff covering up their theft.

The accounts department are likely to be made up of trainee and qualified accountants so best placed to maintain the accounting records.

However, the password would not prevent deliberate manipulation of accounting records by the accounts department as all members of the department have access to it. Nor will it prevent physical theft of inventory or cash – physical controls, such as needing a keycard to access the warehouse, would be appropriate here.

Task 2.10

	✓
A write down of a line of inventory at the year end from cost to NRV is it was sold at a loss in July 20X6	✓
A decrease in the allowance for doubtful debts because of a rise in the average number of days credit customers are taking to pay	
An increase in the useful life of plant and machinery to reduce the depreciation charge	
Posting a cash payment to the suspense account	

Explanation:

IAS 2 requires inventory to be valued at the lower of cost and net realisable value (NRV). Sale of goods at a loss post year end is an indication that NRV is lower than cost and therefore that the inventory must be written down. So this transaction appears genuine.

A rise in the average number of days credit customers are taking to pay would indication that the allowance for doubtful debts should be increased not decreased.

The useful life of plant and machinery should be increased if a business believes that it will be able to use the asset for longer than originally anticipated. Evidence of a useful life being too short would be a large profit on disposal. However, changing the useful life of an asset purely to reduce depreciation and increase profit is not acceptable.

The suspense account should only be used as a temporary account – for example, when an accountant is unsure where to post a double entry or to make a trial balance balance. However, it should never appear in the final accounts.

Task 2.11

	Appropriate ✓	Not appropriate ✓
Allowing the manager partner to review the year end accounts that you have prepared	✓	
Emailing the accounts to your friend who is thinking of applying for a job with the client		✓
Allowing the client's bank to access the accounts with the proprietor's permission	✓	
Allowing a credit supplier of your client access to the accounts when deciding whether or not to increase credit terms without authorisation from the proprietor		✓

Explanation:

Under the AAT's *Code of Professional Ethics*, following the fundamental principle of confidentiality means that client information should only be disclosed to third parties with permission from the client. The managing partner of your accounting practice does not qualify as a third party as your firm as a whole has been engaged to prepare the accounts of your client and in fact, the client would expect sign off from the managing partner.

Task 2.12

	Valid ✓	Not valid ✓
The accounting treatment is correct so there has been no breach of the AAT's *Code of Professional Ethics.*		✓
If this treatment was deliberate, there has been a breach of the fundamental principle of integrity.	✓	
If this treatment was a genuine error, there has been a breach of the fundamental principle of professional competence and due care.	✓	
There is a clear breach of confidentiality here requiring your firm to resign as accountants for this client.		✓

Explanation:

When an owner takes money out of the business, it is classified as drawings not an expense. Therefore, the client's accounting treatment is incorrect. As he is a trainee accounting technician, he is bound by the AAT's *Code of Professional Ethics.* If he knowingly and deliberately classified the drawings incorrectly as an expense, he appears to be trying to hide money that he is taking out of the business for personal use which would be a breach of the fundamental principle of integrity. However, if the treatment was a genuine error, there has been a breach of the fundamental principle of professional competence and due care as he has not followed the accounting treatment required by accounting standards.

There is no issue with confidentiality here. That would occur if we had disclosed client information to a third party without client consent.

....

Task 2.13

	✓
Self-interest	
Self-review	
Advocacy	
Familiarity	✓
Intimidation	

BPP
LEARNING MEDIA

Explanation:

The client's close friendship with the managing partner introduces a familiarity threat because there is a risk of a breach of the fundamental principle of integrity when the managing partner reviews your work on the client's accounts. It is possible that the managing partner may put the client's personal interests before the business's best interests.

....

Task 2.14

£	155,300

Explanation:

Use the accounting equation to calculate capital.

Capital = Assets – Liabilities

Capital = £120,000 + £43,000 + £65,000 + £16,400 – £57,100 – £32,000

= £155,300

....

Task 2.15

£	294,800

Explanation:

The accounting equation is:

Capital = Assets – Liabilities

Closing capital = Opening capital + New capital introduced + Profit – Drawings

Closing capital = £250,000 + £12,000 + £37,500 – £4,700

= £294,800

....

Task 2.16

	✓
Capital – Liabilities = Assets	
Double entry bookkeeping is based on the accounting equation	✓
All elements of the accounting equation can be found in the statement of profit or loss	
Closing capital = Opening capital – Profit + Drawings	

Explanation:

The accounting equation is: Capital = Assets – Liabilities. This can also be stated as: Capital + Liabilities = Assets which makes the first option incorrect.

All elements of the accounting equation can be found in the statement of financial position but not the statement of profit or loss. This makes the third statement incorrect.

Closing capital = Opening capital + New capital introduced + Profit – Drawings. This makes the last option incorrect as the signs for profit and drawings are the wrong way round.

Double entry bookkeeping is based on the accounting equation as the fundamental concept of debits = credits is reflected with the equation Assets = Capital + Liabilities.

Task 2.17

	Increase ✓	Decrease ✓	No change ✓
Assets	✓		
Liabilities			✓
Capital	✓		

Task 2.18

	✓
To ensure that you understand your responsibilities	
To ensure that the company meets all of its legal responsibilities	✓
To make it easy for you to complete your day-to-day tasks	
To improve your technical knowledge	

....

Task 2.19

	✓
You have been asked to account for a provision but you are unsure how to do this, so you make a guess at the appropriate treatment.	
A client has given you tickets to a high profile football match. The next day they ask you to ignore the liquidation of a customer that owes the client a substantial amount of money.	
Your firm needs to meet its deadline in preparing the accounts. Your supervisor tells you to save time by just repeating the depreciation entry from last year, rather than recalculating it.	
The bank statement for your firm shows that an insurance bill covering the next accounting period has been paid in the current accounting period. Your manager asks you to make a prepayment for the cost of the insurance.	✓

....

Chapter 3

Task 3.1

Expenditure	Capital expenditure £	Revenue expenditure £
A machine has been purchased at a cost of £12,000. The delivery charge was £400.	12,400	0
A building has been purchased at a cost of £120,000. The building is subsequently re-decorated at a cost of £13,000.	120,000	13,000
A new main server has been purchased at a cost of £10,000. Professional fees of £200 were also incurred, as a result of this expenditure.	10,200	0

Explanation:

Expenditure on the machine exceeds the threshold for capitalisation. The cost of the machine (£12,000) and the associated delivery charges (£400) meet the definition of non-current asset expenditure and are therefore capitalised as a non-current asset.

Expenditure on the building is also capital in nature and exceeds the threshold for capitalisation. Again, it is classified as capital expenditure. However, costs of redecorating the building constitute revenue expenditure. Therefore, the £13,000 is excluded from the cost of the non-current asset and instead expensed to the profit or loss account.

Expenditure on the main server (£10,000) is capital expenditure. The professional fees of £200 are also capitalised as part of the cost of the asset. At £200, in themselves they are below the capitalisation threshold for this business. However, they contribute to the cost of the main server which exceeds the level at which assets are capitalised and therefore are recorded as a non-current asset.

Task 3.2

£	48,000

Explanation:

The non-current asset is capitalised at the VAT-inclusive amount of £48,000. The business is not VAT registered and is therefore is unable to reclaim the VAT on this purchase from the tax authorities. Consequently, the VAT is added to the cost of the asset.

Task 3.3

Description	Method
The vending machines in a business's premises were financed by paying an initial deposit to the finance company followed by a fixed number of instalments. After all instalments have been paid, the vending machines will be owned by the business.	Hire purchase
When a business purchases a new motor vehicle, the old vehicle is given to the dealer to cover part of the cost of the new vehicle.	Part-exchange
Factory equipment is acquired as part of a major refurbishment. The bank provides the funding, which is then paid back in instalments over an agreed period of time, together with interest.	Loan

Task 3.4

Details	Acquisition date	Cost £	Funding method
HF405	01/06/X4	13,550.00	Finance lease

Explanation:

Item HF405 is capitalised at a cost of £13,550.00. It was acquired on 01/06/X4 and funded through a finance lease. The boardroom table, table fittings and delivery costs are all part of this non-current asset and therefore included as part of the total cost.

In particular, although the delivery costs (£450) are below the level of capitalisation (£500), they contribute to the part of the cost of the boardroom table which is greater than the capitalisation threshold. Therefore, the delivery costs are capitalised as part of the cost of this non-current asset.

The chairs (details PN2948) are below the level for capitalisation and therefore are not recorded in the solution above. For this reason, no entries are made in the second row of the data entry table.

Task 3.5

Account	Debit £	Credit £
Machine at cost	19,200	
Bank		19,200

Working:

VAT: £16,000 × 20% = £3,200

Cost of the machine: £16,000 plus £3,200 = £19,200

As the business is not registered for VAT, the VAT cannot be reclaimed from the tax authorities. Therefore, it is added to the cost of the asset.

Task 3.6

Machine at cost

	£		£
Balance b/d	24,500	**Balance c/d**	**38,000**
Bank	**13,500**		
	38,000		**38,000**

Bank

	£		£	
Balance b/d	32,000	**Machine at cost**	**13,500**	Gross:
		VAT control account	**2,700**	16,200
		Balance c/d	**15,800**	
	32,000		**32,000**	

VAT control account

	£		£
Bank	**2,700**	Balance b/d	5,000
Balance c/d	**2,300**		
	5,000		**5,000**

Explanation:

This business is registered for VAT and therefore can generally reclaim VAT on purchases from the tax authorities. For this reason, the VAT levied on the asset it is not capitalised as part of its cost. Instead it is debited to the VAT control account. The VAT on the new machine is calculated as: £13,500 × 20% = £2,700. The amount paid from Bank is the amount gross of VAT: £13,500 + £2,700 = £16,200 (alternatively calculated as £13,500 × 1.2 = £16,200).

Task 3.7

	✓
On non-current assets, including repairs and maintenance	
On expensive assets	
Relating to the acquisition or improvement of non-current assets	✓

Explanation:

Expenditure relating to the acquisition or improvement of non-current assets constitutes capital expenditure. Repairs and maintenance expenditure qualifies as revenue rather than capital expenditure.

Whilst non-current assets may be expensive, 'expensive assets' is not a criteria for capitalisation.

Task 3.8

Description	Term
Expenditure for the trade of the business or to repair, maintain and service non-current assets.	Revenue expenditure
Expenditure for the acquisition, replacement or improvement of non-current assets.	Capital expenditure

Explanation:

It is important to distinguish between capital and revenue expenditure.

Capital expenditure results in a non-current asset in the statement of financial position. Revenue expenditure results in an expense in the statement of profit or loss and therefore a reduction in profit.

Task 3.9

Description	Impact	Amount £
Statement of financial position	**Increase non-current assets**	**517,300**
Statement of profit or loss	**Reduce profit**	**8,700**

Explanation:

When a business buys a non-current asset, the purchase price plus directly attributable costs are capitalised. At £500,000, the property is well in excess of the capitalisation threshold. The amount to be capitalised as a non-current asset in the statement of financial position is £517,300 (£500,000 + £15,000 + £2,300).

The repairs are revenue rather than capital expenditure and therefore, the £8,700 should be recorded as an expense in the statement of profit or loss. This will have the effect of reducing profit.

Task 3.10

It is important to obtain prior authority for capital expenditure in order to ensure that: | the assets are necessary to the business and purchased at the best price. |

The business's solicitor | would not | be the most

appropriate person to give this authority.

Explanation:

Authorising capital expenditure does not ensure that the assets are correctly recorded in either the non-current assets register or the general ledger. An accounts department supervisor reviewing the bookkeeper's entries would, for example, be in a better position to check that non-current asset purchases are recorded accurately.

The purpose of authorisation is to ensure that the business as a whole will benefit from the purchase.

A person internal to the business rather than the external solicitor would be the most appropriate person to authorise the expenditure. For a small business, the owner might wish to authorise all capital expenditure. For a larger business, a department supervisor or manager might be more appropriate.

Task 3.11

	✓
Bank loan	✓
Cash purchase	
Finance lease	
Hire purchase	

Explanation:

A cash purchase would not be appropriate here because the business only has a cash balance of £750 yet the asset costs well in excess of that amount at £100,000. As the business wishes to become legal owner with immediate effect, neither a finance lease or hire purchase agreement would be appropriate. Therefore, a bank loan would be the best option here.

Task 3.12

Account	Amount £	Debit ✓	Credit ✓
Bank	10,000	✓	
Loan	10,000		✓

Account	Amount £	Debit ✓	Credit ✓
Motor vehicles at cost	9,800	✓	
Bank	9,800		✓

Explanation:

The receipt of the loan results in an increase in the bank account. Bank is an asset and therefore a debit is required. The corresponding credit is to the loan account which is a liability as the business now owes money to the bank.

Then the actual purchase of the asset is recorded by debiting the motor vehicles at cost account, being an increase in non-current assets. The corresponding credit entry is to bank, as this asset is now decreasing.

Chapter 4

Task 4.1

	✓
To spread the cost of a non-current asset over its useful life in order to match the cost of the asset with the consumption of the asset's economic benefits	✓
To ensure that funds are available for the eventual replacement of the asset	
To reduce the cost of the asset to its estimated market value	
To recognise the fact that assets lose their value over time	

Task 4.2

Depreciation is an application of the │accruals│ basis of accounting.

Task 4.3

(a)

Depreciation charge £	Carrying amount £
3,480	6,960

Working:

Depreciation charge: £17,400/5 years = £3,480

Carrying amount: £17,400 – (3 × £3,480) = £6,960

(b)

Depreciation charge £	Carrying amount £
2,700	7,400

Working:

Depreciation charge:

$$\frac{12,800 - 2,000}{4 \text{ years}} = £2,700$$

Carrying amount: £12,800 − (2 × £2,700) = £7,400

(c)

Depreciation charge £	Carrying amount £
1,300	3,300

Working:

Depreciation charge:

$$\frac{4,600 - 700}{3 \text{ years}} = £1,300$$

Carrying amount: £4,600 − £1,300 = £3,300

Task 4.4

(a)

Depreciation charge £	Carrying amount £
4,920	19,680

Workings:

Depreciation charge for the year end 31 March 20X9: £24,600 × 20% = £4,920

Carrying amount as at 31 March 20X9: £24,600 − £4,920 = £19,680

(b)

Depreciation charge £	Carrying amount £
608	2,432

Workings:

Depreciation charge for the year end 31 March 20X8: £3,800 × 20% = £760 (even though the motor vehicle was only owned for 5 months of the year, the accounting policy is to charge a full year's depreciation in the year of acquisition and so no pro-rating is required)

Carrying amount as at 31 March 20X8: £3,800 – £760 = £3,040

Depreciation charge for the year end 31 March 20X9: £3,040 × 20% = £608

Carrying amount as at 31 March 20X9: £3,040 – £608 = £2,432

Task 4.5

(a)

Depreciation charge £	Accumulated depreciation £
7,200	7,200

Working:

Depreciation charge for the year end 31 March 20X9: £24,000 × 30% = £7,200

Accumulated depreciation at 31 March 20X9 = £7,200 (as the business has only owned the asset for one year)

(b)

Depreciation charge £	Accumulated depreciation £
3,927	9,537

Working:

Depreciation charge for the year end 31 March 20X8: £18,700 × 30% = £5,610 (even though the asset was only owned for 8 months in the year, no pro-rating is required as the accounting policy is to charge a full year in the year of acquisition)

Accumulated depreciation at 31 March 20X8 = £5,610

Depreciation charge for the year end 31 March 20X9: (£18,700 – £5,610) × 30% = £3,927

Accumulated depreciation at 31 March 20X9: £5,610 + £3,927 = £9,537

Task 4.6

(a)

Depreciation charge £	Carrying amount £
2,000	13,000

Working:

Depreciation charge for the year end 31 December 20X8: £15,000 × 20% × 8/12 = £2,000

Carrying amount for the year end 31 December 20X8: £15,000 – £2,000 = £13,000

(b)

Depreciation charge £	Carrying amount £
280	3,920

Working:

Depreciation charge for the year end 31 December 20X8: £4,200 × 40% × 2/12 = £280

Carrying amount for the year end 31 December 20X8: £4,200 – £280 = £3,920

Task 4.7

Year	Number of units produced	Carrying amount b/d £	Depreciation charges £	Accumulated depreciation £	Carrying amount c/d £
1	90,000	120,000	36,000	36,000	84,000
2	72,000	84,000	28,800	64,800	55,200
3	30,000	55,200	12,000	76,800	43,200

Workings:

Year	Working	Depreciation charge
1	90,000 / 300,000 × 120,000	36,000
2	72,000 / 300,000 × 120,000	28,800
3	30,000 / 300,000 × 120,000	12,000

Task 4.8

	Account
Debit	Depreciation charges
Credit	Vehicles accumulated depreciation

Explanation:

This is the journal to record depreciation in the general ledger. Depreciation charges are a debit entry being an increase in expenses. Vehicles accumulated depreciation is a credit entry being a reduction in the carrying amount of the asset.

Task 4.9

Vehicles at cost

	£		£
Balance b/d	50,600	**Balance c/d**	**58,800**
Bank	**8,200**		
	58,800		**58,800**

Depreciation charges

	£		£
Balance b/d	12,300	**Profit or loss account**	**13,850**
Vehicles accumulated depreciation	**1,550**		
	13,850		**13,850**

Vehicles accumulated depreciation

	£		£
Balance c/d	**25,950**	Balance b/d	24,400
		Depreciation charges	**1,550**
	25,950		**25,950**

Working:

Depreciation on new vehicle = (Cost £8,200 less residual value £2,000) / 4 = £1,550 (even though the asset was only owned for 9 months in the year, no pro-rating is required as the accounting policy is that a full year's depreciation is applied in the year of acquisition)

Task 4.10

(a)

Depreciation method	✓
Diminishing balance method	
Straight line method	
Units of production method	✓

(b)

Depreciation method	✓
Diminishing balance method	
Straight line method	✓
Units of production method	

(c)

Depreciation method	✓
Diminishing balance method	✓
Straight line method	
Units of production method	

Task 4.11

Percentage: [2] %

Apply to: [Cost]

Explanation:

The percentage is calculated as: $1/50 \times 100\% = 2\%$

As the straight line method is used, it is applied to the cost of the asset rather than the carrying amount.

Chapter 5

Task 5.1

		Gain	Loss
£	125		✓

Workings:

Gain or loss on disposal working	£
Proceeds	6,000
Less carrying amount at date of disposal*	(6,125)
Loss on disposal	(125)
Carrying amount at date of disposal:	
Cost	12,500
Less depreciation for year ended 31 March 20X7 (£12,500 × 30%)	(3,750)
Carrying amount at end of year 1	8,750
Less depreciation for year ended 31 March 20X8 (£8,750 × 30%)	(2,625)
Carrying amount at date of disposal	6,125*

Explanation:

Even though the machine was sold six months into the current year end of 31 March 20X9, there is no depreciation charge for the year as the business's policy is to charge a full year's depreciation in the year of acquisition and none in the year of disposal.

Task 5.2

		Gain	Loss
£	132	✓	

Workings:

Gain or loss on disposal working	£
Proceeds	5,100
Less carrying amount at date of disposal *	(4,968)
Gain on disposal	132
Carrying amount at date of disposal:	
Cost	13,800
Less depreciation for year ended 31 March 20X5 (£13,800 × 40%)	(5,520)
Carrying amount at end of year 1	8,280
Less depreciation for year ended 31 March 20X6 (£8,280 × 40%)	(3,312)
Carrying amount at date of disposal	4,968*

Explanation:

Even though the machine was sold three months into the current year end of 31 March 20X7, there is no depreciation charge for the year as the business's policy is to charge a full year's depreciation in the year of acquisition and none in the year of disposal.

••

Task 5.3

	Answer
The gain or loss arising on disposal of a non-current asset is recorded in the	statement of profit or loss
In the business's accounts, the carrying amount of non-current assets is entered in the	statement of financial position
The carrying amount of a non-current asset is calculated as the cost of the asset less the	accumulated depreciation

Task 5.4

(a)

£	10,000

Working:

Annual depreciation charge: (25,000 /5) = £5,000

Accumulated depreciation at 31 December 20X4 = £5,000 for year ended 31 December 20X3 + £5,000 for the year ended 31 December 20X4 = £10,000.

No depreciation is charged in the year ended 31 December 20X5, the year of disposal.

(b)

Machine at cost

	£		£
Balance b/d	60,000	**Disposals**	25,000
		Balance c/d	35,000
	60,000		**60,000**

Bank

	£		£
Balance b/d	22,000	**Balance c/d**	**34,000**
Disposals	**12,000**		
	34,000		**34,000**

Machine accumulated depreciation

	£		£
Disposals	**10,000**	Balance b/d	26,000
Balance c/d	**16,000**		
	26,000		**26,000**

Disposals

	£		£
Machine at cost	**25,000**	**Machine accumulated depreciation**	**10,000**
		Bank	**12,000**
		Profit or loss account	**3,000**
	25,000		**25,000**

(c)

The business has made a | **loss** | on disposal of the machine.

Explanation:

The carrying amount of £15,000 (cost £25,000 less accumulated depreciation £10,000) exceeds the sale proceeds of £12,000. Therefore, a loss on disposal of £3,000 arises.

The loss is credited to the disposals account. In the general ledger, the corresponding debit is to the profit or loss account, being an increase in expenses and therefore a reduction in profit for the year.

Task 5.5

(a)

Account	Amount £	Debit ✓	Credit ✓
Bank	4,500	✓	
Disposals	4,500		✓

(b)

Account	Amount £	Debit	Credit
Disposals	20,000	✓	
Office equipment at cost	20,000		✓

Explanation:

When a non-current asset is disposed of, all financial transactions relating to that asset will be transferred to the disposals account.

Where bank proceeds are received on sale of a non-current asset, there is a debit to the bank general ledger account, being an increase in the bank asset and a corresponding credit the disposals account.

Removing the original cost of the equipment from the general ledger requires a credit to the office equipment at cost account, being a decrease in the asset and a corresponding debit to the disposals account.

Task 5.6

Disposal account

	£		£
Machine at cost	15,600	Machine accumulated depreciation	9,425
		Bank	6,000
		Profit or loss account	175
	15,600		15,600

Explanation:

On disposal the machine must be removed from the general ledger. Therefore, the cost of the machine and the machine accumulated depreciation are transferred to the disposals account.

Having included the sales proceeds in the disposals account, the disposals account can be totalled. The balancing figure is the gain or loss arising on disposal of the asset.

In this scenario, a loss has arisen on disposal of the non-current asset as the carrying amount at the date of disposal (machine at cost £15,600 less machine accumulated depreciation £9,425 = carrying amount £6,175) is less than the sales proceeds (£6,000).

Workings:

Accumulated depreciation at the date of disposal:

Depreciation period	Calculation	£
01.07.X6 to 31.12.X6	15,600 × 25% × 6/12	1,950
01.01.X7 to 31.12.X7	15,600 × 25%	3,900
01.01.X8 to 30.11.X8	15,600 × 25% × 11/12	3,575
		9,425

Task 5.7

	✓
To record non-current assets in the general ledger	
To assist in the physical verification of non-current assets and check the accuracy of the general ledger entries relating to tangible non-current assets	✓
To list all intangible non-current assets of the business	
To authorise capital expenditure	

Explanation:

The non-current assets register is a list of all the tangible non-current assets owned by the business. It is part of the business's internal control system rather than its double entry system.

It helps with the physical verification of the assets as it can be checked that tangible assets are recorded in the register and that the assets in the register actually exist. Also, the accuracy of the non-current asset general ledger entries can be checked by reconciling the general ledger entries with the non-current asset register.

The non-current asset register does not include intangible non-current assets. The authorisation of capital expenditure is typically shown on authorisation forms rather than in the non-current assets register.

Task 5.8

Extract from non-current assets register

Description	Acquisition date	Cost £	Depreciation charges £	Carrying amount £	Funding method	Disposal proceeds £	Disposal date
Plant and machinery							
Plant PM672	01/04/X6	3,300.00			Cash		
Year end 30/06/X6			165.00	3,135.00			

Explanation:

The purchase price of plant PM672 of £3,000.00 plus any directly attributable costs which include the testing costs of £300.00 must be capitalised. Even though the testing costs are below the capitalisation threshold of £400.00, they relate to an asset which has met the capitalisation threshold (with its purchase price of £3,000.00). Therefore, they must also be capitalised as part of the cost. This means the item is capitalised at a total cost of £3,300.00.

The maintenance contract qualifies as revenue expenditure and therefore the £550.00 is not capitalised. As the business is VAT registered, it may reclaim VAT on purchases so the VAT should not be included in the cost of the asset.

Depreciation = £3,300.00 × 1/5 × 3/12 = £165.00.

Task 5.9

Extract from non-current assets register

Description	Acquisition date	Cost £	Depreciation charges £	Carrying amount £	Funding method	Disposal proceeds £	Disposal date
Office equipment							
Desk DSK452	01/06/X5	2,500.00			Loan		
Year end 31/12/X5			625.00	1,875.00			
Year end 31/12/X6			468.75	1,406.25			
Year end 31/12/X7			**0.00**	**0.00**		**800.00**	**30/09/X7**

Explanation:

The policy here is no depreciation in the year of disposal. On disposal, the carrying amount is zero as the item is effectively removed both from both the business and the accounting records.

The disposal proceeds and disposal date must be recorded in the non-current assets register.

....

Task 5.10

Extract from the non-current assets register

Description	Acquisition date	Cost £	Depreciation charges £	Carrying amount £	Funding method	Disposal proceeds £	Disposal date
Office equipment							
Computer COM987	01/04/X1	5,700.00			Part exchange		
Year end 31/03/X2			1,140.00	4,560.00			
Year end 31/03/X3			1,140.00	3,420.00			
Year end 31/12/X4			**855.00**	**0.00**		**1,300.00**	**01/01/X4**

Explanation:

As the policy is to charge depreciation on a monthly pro-rata basis, depreciation in the year ended 31 March 20X4 is: £5,700.00 × 20% × 9/12 = £855.00. As the asset has been sold, the carrying amount is now zero. Finally, the proceeds and disposal date must also be recorded.

Task 5.11

Description/ Serial number	Acquisition date	Cost £	Depreciation charges £	Carrying amount £	Funding method	Disposal proceeds £	Disposal date
Furniture and fittings							
Filing racks	31/10/X5	832.60			Cash		
Year end 31/03/X6			124.89	707.71			
Year end 31/03/X7			**124.89**	**582.82**			
Oak boardroom table	**24/06/X6**	**925.00**			**Loan**		
Year end 31/03/X7			**138.75**	**786.25**			
Motor vehicles							
1.6 litre car AF05 LKR	01/09/X4	10,600.00			Part-exchange		
Year end 31/03/X5			2,650.00	7,950.00			
Year end 31/03/X6			1,987.50	5,962.50			
Year end 31/03/X7			**0.00**	**0.00**		**5,340.00**	**23/09/X6**
1.8 litre van AD05 ACT	01/03/X5	10,400.00			Part-exchange		
Year end 31/03/X5			2,600.00	7,800.00			
Year end 31/03/X6			1,950.00	5,850.00			
Year end 31/03/X7			**1,462.50**	**4,387.50**			

Explanation:

Depreciation for filing racks = £832.60 × 15% = £124.89

Oak boardroom table: Capitalise purchase price £850.00 + Direct costs £75.00 = £925.00. Depreciation = £925.00 × 15% = £138.75 (a full year's depreciation is charged in the year of acquisition). The maintenance and repair kit is revenue expenditure and therefore is not capitalised.

Each refurbished operator chair at £60 each is below the £350 capitalisation threshold and so these chairs are not capitalised.

1.6 litre car AF05 LKR: No depreciation is charged in the year of disposal and on disposal, the carrying amount is reduced to £0.00. The sales proceeds and disposal date are then recorded.

1.8 litre van AD05 ACT: Depreciation = £5,850.00 × 25% = £1,462.50.

....

Task 5.12

Description/ Serial number	Acquisition date	Cost £	Depreciation charges £	Carrying amount £	Funding method	Disposal Proceeds £	Disposal date
Office equipment							
Copier 4	01/04/X5	3,200.00			Finance lease		
Year end 31/03/X6			400.00	2,800.00			
Year end 31/03/X7			**400.00**	**2,400.00**			
Reception desk – FaradyR	01/01/X5	1,200.00			Cash		
Year end 31/03/X5			37.50	1,162.50			
Year end 31/03/X6			150.00	1,012.50			
Year end 31/03/X7			**75.00**	**0.00**		**600.00**	**30/09/X6**

Description/ Serial number	Acquisition date	Cost £	Depreciation charges £	Carrying amount £	Funding method	Disposal Proceeds £	Disposal date
Machinery							
CNC machine CNC3491	01/04/X4	16,400.00			Part-exchange		
Year end 31/03/X5			4,100.00	12,300.00			
Year end 31/03/X6			3,075.00	9,225.00			
Year end 31/03/X7			**2,306.25**	**6,918.75**			
Power lathe PM892	**01/04/X6**	**10,189.80**			**Hire purchase**		
Year end 31/03/X7			**2,547.45**	**7,642.35**			

Explanation:

Copier 4: Depreciation = £3,200 × 1/8 = £400.00

Reception desk – FaradyR: Depreciation = £1,200 × 1/8 × 6/12 = £75.00 (as depreciation is charged on a monthly pro-rata basis). On disposal, the carrying amount is reduced to £0.00 and the disposal proceeds and date are recorded.

CNC machine CNC3491: Depreciation = £9,225.00 × 25% = £2,306.25

Power lather PM892: The purchase price of £9,930.00 + direct costs £259.80 = £10,189.80 are capitalised. The maintenance contract is revenue expenditure so is not capitalised. QW Trading is VAT registered and therefore can recover the VAT on this purchase from HMRC. For this reason, VAT is not included as part of the cost of the asset.

Depreciation = £10,189.80 × 25% = £2,547.45.

Task 5.13

(a)

(i) £ | 1,350

Working:

	£
1 January 20X3: Cost	3,500
Depreciation (15% × 3,500)	(525)
31 July 20X3	2,975
Depreciation (15% × 2,975)	(446)
31 July 20X4	2,529
Depreciation (15% × 2,529)	(379)
31 July 20X5	2,150

Accumulated depreciation at disposal = £525 + £446 + £379 = £1,350

(ii) Disposals

	£		£
Machinery at cost	**3,500**	**Machinery accumulated depreciation**	**1,350**
		Machinery at cost	**575**
		Profit or loss account	**1,575**
	3,500		**3,500**

(b)

(i) £ | 2,725.00

Working

Cost of new machinery = Part exchange value £575 + cash paid £2,150 = £2,725

(ii) The machinery at cost account will have a final balance carried down

of   £   25,045   when the ledger accounts are closed

for the year.

Working

Machines at cost

	£		£
Balance b/d	25,820	Disposals	3,500
Disposals	575		
Bank	2,150	Balance c/d	25,045
	28,545		28,545

Task 6.1

(a) Telephone expenses

	£		£
Bank	845	Profit or loss account	1,015
Accrued expenses	170		
	1,015		1,015

(b)

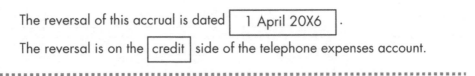

The reversal of this accrual is dated ⌊ 1 April 20X6 ⌋ .

The reversal is on the ⌊ credit ⌋ side of the telephone expenses account.

Task 6.2

Electricity expense

	£		£
Bank	**2,300**	**Accrued expenses (reversal)**	**370**
Accrued expenses (2/3 × £900)	**600**	**Profit or loss account**	**2,530**
	2,900		**2,900**

Accrued expenses (SOFP)

	£		£
Electricity expense	**370**	Balance b/d	370
Balance c/d	**600**	**Electricity expense**	**600**
	970		**970**

Task 6.3

Insurance expense

	£		£
Prepaid expenses (reversal)	180	Prepaid expenses	250
Bank	2,300	Profit or loss account	2,230
	2,480		2,480

Task 6.4

Prepaid expenses

	£		£
Balance b/d	300	**Rent expense**	**300**
Rent expense (3/6 × £800)	**400**	**Balance c/d**	**400**
	700		**700**

Task 6.5

(a)

£	5,610

Explanation:

This is calculated as the cash book receipts of £5,600 less the £490 received in relation to the prior year plus the amount outstanding for June 20X3 at the year end (1/3 × £1,500 = £500). This comes to £5,610 (£5,600 – £490 + £500).

Alternatively, you could have drawn up the ledger account for rental income:

Rental income

	£		£
Accrued income (reversal)	490	Bank	5,600
Profit or loss account	5,610	Accrued income (1/3 × £1,500)	500
	6,100		6,100

(b)

Reason for considering the receipt dated 10 September 20X3	Acceptable reason	Not acceptable reason
The accruals concept requires income to be recorded in the financial statements in the period in which it is earned.	✓	
The proprietor of the business has asked you to increase the profit for the year to maximise his chances of increasing the business' overdraft limit.		✓
The transaction results in a current liability for June's rental income as at 30 June 20X3.		✓

Explanation:

Under the AAT's *Code of Professional Ethics*, as an accountant, we are required to act with Professional Competence and Care which means that when preparing accounts, we should follow International Financial Reporting Standards and concepts. This makes the first option acceptable. However, we should not act purely on the motivation of self-interest of the proprietor which makes the second option not acceptable. Finally, the transaction results in a current asset not a current liability at 30 June 20X3, making the final option not acceptable.

Task 6.6

	✓
Overstated by £375	
Overstated by £750	
Understated by £375	
Understated by £750	✓

Explanation:

An accrual of £375 should have been set up, which would have increased the electricity expense for the year by £375 and resulted in accrued expenses of £375 (a current liability). Instead a prepayment was set up, decreasing the expense by £375 and resulting in prepaid expenses of £375 (a current asset). Setting up the prepayment instead of an accrual has therefore understated the expense for the year by £750 (2 × £375). The correcting journal would be:

Debit Electricity expense	£750
Credit Prepaid expenses	£375
Credit Accrued expenses	£375

Task 6.7

£	20,388.23

Working:

	£
Paid in year (£7,279.47 + £4,663.80 + £4,117.28)	16,060.55
Accrual (2/3 × £6,491.52)	4,327.68
	20,388.23

Task 6.8

£	900

Working:

Rent expense

	£		£
Bank	1,275	Accrued expenses (reversal)	250
		Prepaid expenses (1/3 × £375)	125
		Profit or loss account	900
	1,275		1,275

Task 6.9

	✓
£4,000	
£4,500	✓
£5,000	
£5,500	

Working:

Commission income

	£		£
Accrued income (reversal)	1,000	Bank	5,000
Profit or loss account	4,500	Accrued income	500
	5,500		5,500

Task 6.10

(a)

	Amount £	Debit	Credit
Prepaid income	850	✓	
Maintenance services income	850		✓

(b) **Maintenance services income**

	£		£
Prepaid income (6/12 × £3,000)	1,500	Prepaid income (reversal)	850
Profit or loss account	12,100	Bank	12,750
	13,600		13,600

Task 6.11

(a) **Service income**

	£		£
Accrued income (reversal)	210	**Bank**	**1,680**
Profit or loss account	**1,655**	**Accrued income**	**185**
	1,865		**1,865**

(b)

(i)

	Increase ✓	Decrease ✓	No change ✓
Assets			✓
Liabilities		✓	
Equity	✓		

(ii)

	✓
1 April 20X5	✓
31 March 20X5	
31 March 20X6	

(c)

Prepaid expenses	of	£15	dated	**31 March 20X6**

(d)

£	**577**

Working:

Insurance

	£		£
		Accrued insurance (reversal)	78
		Prepaid expenses	**15**
Bank	**670**	**Profit or loss account**	**577**
	670		**670**

Chapter 7

Task 7.1

(a)

£	25.10

Working: £24.60 + £0.50

(b)

£	24.80

Working: £25.80 – £1.00

(c)

£	3,100

Working: 125 units × £24.80

Explanation:

Inventory is recorded at the lower of cost and net realisable value, hence being valued at £24.80 unit in this scenario.

....

Task 7.2

	✓
Selling costs	
Cost of purchase, including delivery	✓
Storage costs of finished goods	
Costs of conversion, including direct labour	✓

Explanation:

Under IAS 2 *Inventories*, selling costs and storage costs of finished goods cannot be included in the cost of inventory.

....

Task 7.3

	✓
The expected selling price of the inventory	
The expected selling price of the inventory less costs to completion and selling costs	✓
The replacement cost of the inventory	
The market price of the inventory	

Explanation:

Net realisable value is the amount that can be obtained, less any further future expenses to be incurred to bring the inventory to a condition in which it can be sold.

....

Task 7.4

The rule for inventory is that it should be valued at the | **lower**

of | **cost** | and | **net realisable value**

....

Task 7.5

(a) and (b)

Inventory line	Quantity (units)	Cost £	Selling price £	Selling costs £	Net realisable value £	Value per unit £	Total value £
A	180	12.50	20.40	0.50	19.90	12.50	2,250
B	240	10.90	12.60	1.80	10.80	10.80	2,592
C	300	15.40	22.70	1.20	21.50	15.40	4,620
D	80	16.50	17.80	1.50	16.30	16.30	1,304
E	130	10.60	18.00	1.00	17.00	10.60	1,378
Total							12,144

Explanation:

Inventory is valued at the lower of cost and net realisable value on a line by line basis. Therefore, inventory lines A, C and E are valued at cost. Inventory lines B and D are valued at net realisable value.

....

Task 7.6

(a)

Description	Method of estimating cost
Under this method a simple average cost can be calculated whereby the cost of all purchases/production during the year is divided by the total number of units purchased.	Average cost
Under this method it is assumed that the last goods to be purchased/produced will be the first to be sold.	Last in first out
Under this method it is assumed that the first goods purchased/produced will be the first to be sold.	First in first out

(b)

Question	Answer
Is LIFO permitted by International Financial Reporting Standards?	No

Explanation:

The Last in first out (LIFO) method is prohibited by international International Financial Reporting Standards because it is unlikely to produce a cost figure which is a close approximation to actual costs.

....

Task 7.7

Account	Debit £	Credit £
Closing inventory (SOFP)	20,000	
Closing inventory (SPL)		20,000

Explanation:

Inventory is an asset in the statement of financial position, and therefore a debit balance in the general ledger.

Inventory is a reduction in expenses in the statement of profit or loss, and therefore a credit entry in the general ledger.

Task 7.8

Statement	Term
Closing inventory in the statement of financial position is best described as	an asset
Closing inventory in the statement of profit or loss is best described as	a reduction in expenses

Explanation:

Closing inventory is owned by the business at the year end. It can be sold in the next accounting period and will generate economic benefits for the business. Therefore, it is an asset in the statement of financial position.

In the statement or profit or loss closing inventory is included under the 'cost of goods sold' heading. It is a reduction in the cost of goods sold expense, as the items have not been sold in the current accounting period.

Task 7.9

Statement	True or false
In the statement of profit or loss, carriage inwards must be included within cost of goods sold.	True
In the statement of profit or loss, carriage outwards must be included within cost of goods sold.	False

Explanation:

Statement 1: Carriage inwards (ie the cost of transporting inventory to the businesses premises) forms part of cost of goods sold, along with opening inventory and purchases.

Statement 2: Carriage outwards (ie the cost of transporting inventory to customers) is part of selling expenses which sit below the gross profit line.

Task 7.10

Statement	True or false
The main purpose of an inventory count is to value inventory at the end of the accounting period.	False
On a regular basis an inventory reconciliation should be performed, comparing the warehouse's record of the quantity of each item held with the actual quantity counted.	True

Explanation:

Statement 1: The main purpose of an inventory count is to ascertain the quantity of inventory on hand at the end of the accounting period.

Statement 2: An inventory reconciliation must be performed on a regular basis, so that the business can confirm that its inventory records are accurate.

Task 7.11

Accounting for inventory as a deduction from cost of goods sold in the statement profit or loss is an application of the ⎥ accruals ⎥ basis of accounting.

Explanation:

In cost of goods sold, we only want to show the purchase price of goods actually sold in the period to match to the sales price of goods sold which is included in revenue. This is why we remove from purchases any goods that have not been sold in the year with the closing inventory adjustment in the statement of profit or loss at the year end.

Task 7.12

£	6,000

Working:

Selling price (net of VAT) = £12,000 × 100/120 = £10,000
Cost = Selling price £10,000 – Profit £4,000 = £6,000

As the business is VAT-registered, it must charge VAT on its sales and then pass this VAT onto HMRC.

However, when calculating the cost of the inventory, VAT is excluded from the selling price because it does not belong to the business. Then, to calculate the cost of the inventory, the profit is deducted from the net selling price.

Chapter 8

Task 8.1

Account	Debit £	Credit £
Irrecoverable debts	4,500	
Sales ledger control account		4,500

Explanation:

If a debt is irrecoverable it must be removed from the sales ledger control account as it is no longer an asset. It is written off as an expense in the irrecoverable debts account.

....

Task 8.2

(a)

Account	Debit £	Credit £
Irrecoverable debts	6,900	
Sales ledger control account		6,900

(b)

Sales ledger control account

	£		£
Balance b/d	45,000	**Irrecoverable debts**	**6,900**
		Balance c/d	**38,100**
	45,000		**45,000**

Irrecoverable debts

	£		£
Sales ledger control account	**6,900**	**Profit or loss account**	**6,900**
	6,900		**6,900**

(c)

ZX – Sales ledger account

	£		£
Balance b/d	6,900	**Irrecoverable debts**	**6,900**
	6,900		**6,900**

Task 8.3

Account	Debit £	Credit £
Bank	9,500	
Irrecoverable debts		9,500

Explanation:

As the debt has already been written off, it is no longer listed in the sales ledger and so the cash received cannot be offset against it in the usual way. Therefore, the cash received is offset against the irrecoverable debt expense in the current accounting period. In other words, it is a reduction in the current period irrecoverable debt expense.

Task 8.4

(a)

£	1,720

Working:

Trade receivables £86,000 × 2% = £1,720

(b)

£	560	Increase in expenses

Working:

	£
Opening allowance (per scenario)	1,160
Adjustment	560
Closing allowance	1,720

Explanation:

The closing allowance of £1,720 is higher than the opening allowance of £1,160. Therefore, expenses are increased as a result of the allowance for doubtful debts adjustment.

....

Task 8.5

Sales ledger control account

	£		£
Balance b/d	90,000	**Irrecoverable debts**	**4,400**
		Balance c/d	**85,600**
	90,000		**90,000**

Irrecoverable debts

	£		£
Sales ledger control account	**4,400**	**Profit or loss account**	**4,400**
	4,400		**4,400**

Allowance for doubtful debts

	£		£
Balance c/d	**4,672**	Balance b/d	1,600
		Allowance for doubtful debts – adjustments	**3,072**
	4,672		**4,672**

Allowance for doubtful debts – adjustments

	£		£
Allowance for doubtful debts	3,072	Profit or loss account	3,072
	3,072		3,072

Working:

	£
Opening balance per sales ledger control account	90,000
Less Irrecoverable debts	(4,400)
Adjusted balance per sales ledger control account	85,600
Less specific allowance	(1,300)
	84,300
General allowance (£84,300 × 4%)	3,372
∴ Total allowance:	
Specific	1,300
General	3,372
Total closing allowance	4,672
Calculating the allowance for doubtful debts – adjustments	
Opening allowance (per scenario)	1,600
Adjustment (to TB – SPL)	3,072
Closing allowance (to TB – SOFP)	4,672

Explanation:

The closing allowance (£4,672) is higher than the opening allowance (£1,600). Therefore, the allowance for doubtful debts – adjustment is an expense in the profit or loss account (£3,072) and would be a debit entry in the trial balance.

Task 8.6

Trial balance (extract)

Ledger account	Ledger balance	
	Debit £	Credit £
Sales ledger control account	184,000	
Irrecoverable debts	16,000	
Allowance for doubtful debts		6,620
Allowance for doubtful debts – adjustments		980

Working:

	£
Opening balance per sales ledger control account	200,000
Less Irrecoverable debts	(16,000)
Adjusted balance per sales ledger control account	184,000
Less specific allowance	(3,000)
	181,000
General allowance (£181,000 × 2%)	3,620
∴ **Total allowance:**	
Specific	3,000
General	3,620
Total closing allowance	6,620
Calculating the allowance for doubtful debts – adjustments	
Opening allowance (per scenario)	7,600
Adjustment (to TB – SPL)	(980)
Closing allowance (to TB – SOFP)	6,620

Explanation:

The closing allowance (£6,620) is lower than the opening allowance (£7,600). Therefore, the allowance for doubtful debts – adjustment (£980) is a reduction in expenses in the profit or loss account and a credit entry in the trial balance.

Task 8.7

	✓
Depreciation	
Inventory	
Accruals	✓
Prudence	

Explanation:

The allowance for doubtful debts is offset against the trade receivables balance in the statement of financial position, thereby achieving matching under the accruals basis of accounting.

Chapter 9

Task 9.1

	Answer
A credit balance on the bank statement indicates a	**positive cash balance**
A credit balance on the cash book indicates a	**negative cash balance**

Explanation:

Statement 1: The bank statement is prepared from the bank's point of view. So if a customer has money in their account, the money is held by the bank but does not belong to the bank. Effectively, from the bank's perspective, it represents a liability to the customer. Therefore, a credit balance on the bank statement indicates a positive cash balance for the customer.

Statement 2: The cash book is prepared from the business's point of view. In accordance with the rules of double entry bookkeeping, a credit balance indicates a liability and therefore a negative cash balance.

··

Task 9.2

A positive cash balance is a ⬚ **debit** ⬚ entry in the cash book.

A negative cash balance is shown on the bank statement as a ⬚ **debit** ⬚ entry.

Explanation:

When a business has a negative cash balance, the bank shows this as a debit balance (D) on the bank statement. This is because from the bank's point of view, the business owes the bank money so the business is effectively the bank's receivable.

··

BPP LEARNING MEDIA

Task 9.3

Cash book as at 31 July

Date 20X2	Details	Bank £	Date 20X2	Cheque number	Details	Bank £
01 July	Balance b/d	8,751	11 July	103122	ENG	1,100
03 July	LKI	2,875	18 July	103123	JHP	158
14 July	ABW	6,351	27 July	103125	MWY	7,565
17 July	WNY	3,560	29 July	103126	YMN	4,320
28 July	**OKM**	**8,590**	**13 July**		**Direct debit – Gas**	**4,895**
			31 July		**Balance c/d**	**12,089**
		30,127				**30,127**
1 August	**Balance b/d**	**12,089**				

Bank reconciliation statement	£
Balance per bank statement	**12,849**
WNY	**3,560**
Total to add	
YMN	**4,320**
Total to subtract	
Balance as per cash book	**12,089**

Task 9.4

Adjustment	Amount £	Debit ✓	Credit ✓
Adjustment (1)	25		✓
Adjustment (3)	9	✓	
Adjustment (4)	2,827		✓

Explanation – cash book:

Narrative	Amount £
Unadjusted balance per cash book	3,851
Adjustment (1)	(25)
Adjustment (3)	9
Adjustment (4)	(2,827)
Adjusted balance per cash book	1,008

Explanation – bank statement:

Narrative	Amount £
Balance per bank statement	(778)
Outstanding lodgements (note 2)	1,738
Payment to supplier (note 5)	(452)
Bank error (note 6)	500
Balance as per the adjusted cash book	1,008

Task 9.5

Adjustment	Amount £	Debit ✓	Credit ✓
Adjustment (3)	996	✓	
Adjustment (4)	2,827		✓
Adjustment (6)	440		✓

Explanation – cash book:

Narrative	Amount £
Unadjusted balance per cash book	11,442
Adjustment (3)	996
Adjustment (4)	(2,827)
Adjustment (6)	(440)
Adjusted balance per cash book	9,171

Explanation – bank statement:

Narrative	Amount £
Balance per bank statement	7,377
Payment to supplier (note 1)	(990)
Outstanding lodgements (note 2)	3,560
Payment to supplier (note 5)	(776)
	9,171

Chapter 10

Task 10.1

Sales ledger control account

	£		£
Balance b/d	4,268	Sales returns	995
Sales	15,487	Irrecoverable debts	210
		Bank	13,486
		Discounts allowed	408
		Purchases ledger control account	150
		Balance c/d	4,506
	19,755		19,755

Task 10.2

Purchases ledger control account

	£		£
Bank	10,379	Balance b/d	3,299
Purchases returns	1,074	Purchases	12,376
Discounts received	302		
Sales ledger control account	230		
Balance c/d	3,690		
	15,675		15,675

Task 10.3

Adjustment	Amount £	Debit ✓	Credit ✓
Adjustment (3)	3,300		✓
Adjustment (4)	1,000	✓	
Adjustment (6)	840		✓

Explanation – subsidiary sales ledger balances:

Narrative	Amount £
Per scenario:	6,310
Adjustment (1)	(460)
Adjustment (2)	(250)
Adjustment (5) (£680 × 2)	(1,360)
Adjusted subsidiary sales ledger balance:	4,240

Explanation – sales ledger control account:

Narrative	Amount £
Per scenario:	7,380
Adjustment (3) (£1,650 × 2)	(3,300)
Adjustment (4)	1,000
Adjustment (6)	(840)
Adjusted sales ledger control account balance:	4,240

Task 10.4

Adjustment	Amount £	Debit ✓	Credit ✓
Adjustment (1)	100	✓	
Adjustment (4)	1,140	✓	
Adjustment (5)	1,360		✓

Explanation – subsidiary sales ledger balances:

Narrative	Amount £
Per scenario:	6,100
Adjustment (1)	100
Adjustment (4) (£570 × 2)	1,140
Adjustment (5) (£680 × 2)	(1,360)
Adjusted subsidiary sales ledger balance:	5,980

Explanation – sales ledger control account:

Narrative	Amount £
Per scenario:	11,840
Adjustment (2)	(3,000)
Adjustment (3)	(2,400)
Adjustment (6)	(460)
Adjusted sales ledger control account balance:	5,980

Task 10.5

Adjustment	Amount £	Debit ✓	Credit ✓
Adjustment (2)	850	✓	
Adjustment (3)	72	✓	
Adjustment (6)	1,329	✓	

Explanation – subsidiary purchases ledger balances:

Narrative	Amount £
Per scenario:	2,219
Adjustment (4)	(214)
Adjustment (5) (£403 × 2)	(806)
Adjusted subsidiary purchases ledger balance:	1,199

Note. Adjustment 1 does not change the total of the subsidiary purchases ledger balances.

Explanation – purchases ledger control account:

Narrative	Amount £
Per scenario:	3,450
Adjustment (2)	(850)
Adjustment (3) (£791 – £719)	(72)
Adjustment (6)	(1,329)
Adjusted purchases ledger control account balance:	1,199

Task 10.6

Adjustment	Amount £	Debit ✓	Credit ✓
Adjustment (3)	1,320		✓
Adjustment (4)	1,210	✓	
Adjustment (6)	1,240	✓	

Explanation – subsidiary purchases ledger balances:

Narrative	Amount £
Per scenario:	8,670
Adjustment (3) (£660 × 2)	1,320
Adjustment (4)	(1,210)
Adjustment (6) (£620 × 2)	(1,240)
Adjusted subsidiary purchases ledger balance:	7,540

Explanation – purchases ledger control account:

Narrative	Amount £
Per scenario:	5,248
Adjustment (1)	(980)
Adjustment (2)	3,592
Adjustment (5)	(320)
Adjusted purchases ledger control account balance:	7,540

Task 10.7

(a)

	£
Balance on supplier's statement of account	3,475
Balance on supplier's account in Magenta's purchases ledger *(£500 + £1,750 + £925) – (£420 + £530)	2,225
Difference (£3,475 – £2,225) *	1,250

* Calculations are included for tutorial purposes and do not form part of the answer.

Explanation:

To work out the balance on the supplier's account in the purchases ledger, add up the amounts on each side of the supplier's account and find the balance as a missing figure on the side with the lower total. Remember that everything on the left side of the account reduces the total owed to the supplier, and everything on the right side of the account increases the total owed to the supplier.

(b)

	✓
Cheque for £420	
Invoice number 147	
Credit note number 23	
Invoice number 178	
Invoice number 195	✓

Explanation:

The best way to approach part (b) is to work through the statement of account and tick off each item that also appears in the purchases ledger. The unticked items remaining will enable you to answer part (b). Ignore the brought forward balance on the statement of account for the purposes of the ticking exercise.

Note that the difference identified in part (a) of £1,250 is the amount of the missing invoice 195 identified in part (b). This is a good way to check that the reconciliation is accurate.

Task 10.8

(a)

Account name	Amount £	Debit ✓	Credit ✓
Wages expense	128,000	✓	
Wages control account	128,000		✓

Working: £120,000 + £8,000 = £128,000

(b)

Account name	Amount £	Debit ✓	Credit ✓
Wages control account	28,000	✓	
HM Revenue and Customs	28,000		✓

Working: £4,000 + £16,000 + £8,000 = £28,000

(c)

Account name	Amount £	Debit ✓	Credit ✓
Wages control account	100,000	✓	
Bank	100,000		✓

Working: £120,000 – £16,000 – £4,000 = £100,000

Remember, the employer's NI of £8,000 is not deducted from the gross pay. It is an additional amount paid by the employer to HMRC.

Chapter 11

Task 11.1

Description	Type of error	Balancing trial balance?
A debit entry has been posted with no corresponding credit made.	Single entry error	No
An entry has been made so that debits equal credits but the amount is incorrect.	Error of original entry	Yes
A transaction has been recorded at the correct amount but the debit and credit entries have been reversed.	Reversal of entries	Yes
Debits equal credits; however, one of the entries has been made to the wrong type of account.	Error of principle	Yes

Task 11.2

Error	Imbalance ✓	No imbalance ✓
The payment of the telephone bill was posted to the cash book – credit side and then credited to the telephone account.	✓	
The depreciation expense was debited to the accumulated depreciation account and credited to the depreciation charges account.		✓
The electricity account balance of £750 was taken to the trial balance as £570.	✓	
The motor expenses were debited to the motor vehicles at cost account. The credit entry is correct.		✓
Discounts received were not posted to the general ledger.		✓

Task 11.3

		Debit balance ✓	Credit balance ✓
£	8,304		✓

Task 11.4

(a)

Account name	Debit £	Credit £
Telephone	236	
Electricity		236

(b)

Account name	Debit £	Credit £
Sales ledger control account	180	
Sales		180

(c)

Account name	Debit £	Credit £
Purchases ledger control account	38	
Purchases returns		38

Task 11.5

(a)

Account name	Debit £	Credit £
Allowance for doubtful debts – adjustments	254	
Allowance for doubtful debts		254

Explanation:

The correction is twice the original error (£127 × 2 = £254)

(b)

Account name	Debit £	Credit £
Purchases ledger control account	400	
Sales ledger control account		400

Explanation:

The correction is twice the original error (£200 × 2 = £400)

(c)

Account name	Debit £	Credit £
Irrecoverable debts	680	
Sales ledger control account		680

Task 11.6

(a)

£	6,480

Working:

£32,400 (from the trial balance) × 20% = £6,480.

(b) Extract from the extended trial balance

Ledger account	Ledger balances		Adjustments	
	Debit £	Credit £	Debit £	Credit £
Bank	5,321			**140**
Carriage outwards			**460**	
Depreciation charges			**6,480**	
Irrecoverable debts	632			
Office expenses	52,832		**140**	
Plant at cost	32,400			
Plant accumulated depreciation		6,480		**6,480**
Prepaid expenses	305			
Purchases	89,430			**890**
Purchases ledger control account		11,230		
Rent	12,520			
Sales		104,502		
Sales ledger control account	16,230			
Suspense		430	**890**	**460**
VAT		9,320		

Workings:

Offices expenses: £70 × 2 = £140

Purchases balance: £89,430 – £88,540 = £890

Task 11.7

(a)

£	14

Working:

	£
Balance per the sales ledger control account	18,200
Closing allowance for doubtful debts (£18,200 × 2%)	364
Opening allowance for doubtful debts (per TB)	(350)
Allowance for doubtful debts adjustment	14

Extract from the extended trial balance

Ledger account	Ledger balances		Adjustments	
	Debit £	Credit £	Debit £	Credit £
Allowance for doubtful debts		350		**14**
Allowance for doubtful debts – adjustments			**14**	
Accrued expenses		750		
Bank		6,320	**12,640**	
Carriage inwards	219			
Closing inventory			**8,430**	**8,430**
Depreciation charges	6,625			
Discounts allowed	620			
Office expenses	488			
Opening inventory	4,420			
Prepaid expenses	305			
Purchases	89,430			
Purchases returns				**560**
Purchases ledger control account		11,230		
Sales		104,502		
Sales ledger control account	18,200			
Suspense	12,080		**560**	**12,640**

Explanation:

Bank entry: £6,320 × 2 = £12,640

£6,320 removes the error and then £6,320 includes bank on the correct side of the extended trial balance. In respect of the bank error, this removes the suspense account entry.

•••

Task 11.8

	✓
A decrease in the allowance for doubtful debts from 3% of outstanding trade receivables to 2% of outstanding trade receivables	✓
The write down of an item of inventory which cost £1,500 and had a selling price of £1,350 and expected selling costs of £200	
Recognising an accrual for vehicle running expenses for September 20X6 but not invoiced and paid until October 20X6	
Decreasing the useful life of a computer with effect from the start of the year (1 October 20X5)	

Explanation:

The double entry to record a decrease in allowance for doubtful debts is:

Debit Allowance for doubtful debts (SOFP)

Credit Allowance for doubtful debts – adjustments (SPL)

The credit of this double entry results in an increase in profit, making this the correct answer. All of the other adjustments result in a decrease in profit:

Write down of inventory of £350 (£1,500 – [£1,350 – £200]):

Debit Closing inventory – statement of profit or loss   £350
Credit Closing inventory – statement of financial position   £350

Recognising an accrual:

Debit Vehicle running expenses (SPL)

Credit Accrued expenses (SOFP)

Decreasing the useful life of a computer would increase the depreciation expense and therefore reduce the profit:

Debit Depreciation charges (SPL)

Credit Accumulated depreciation (SOFP)

....

Task 11.9

	✓
Complete the accounts without any further adjustment, as any change could affect the outcome of the meeting with the bank.	
Complete the accounts without any further adjustment because the client's needs must take priority.	
Explain to the managing partner that you have discovered an irrecoverable debt which needs writing off because the accounts must be prepared in accordance with International Financial Reporting Standards.	✓
Write off the irrecoverable debt without telling your managing partner as you want to make sure that you get the pay rise that he's promised you.	

Explanation:

As a trainee accounting technician, we are bound by the *AAT's Code of Professional Ethics.* If we were to ignore the potential adjustment for the irrecoverable debt, we would not be complying with the fundamental principle of professional competence as the accounts would not be prepared in accordance with accounting standards.

There is a familiarity threat here due to the relationship between the proprietor and the managing partner and a potential intimidation threat arising from the possible loss of pay rise if the managing partner's wishes are not followed. So the only acceptable treatment is to try and persuade the managing partner of the need to adjust for the irrecoverable debt.

....

Task 11.10

	✓
Do nothing because the cash sales were accurately recorded in the cash book.	
Seek advice from the managing partner as it is possible that these sales were deliberately created with the intention of increasing profit for the year ended 30 June 20X3 and are not a genuine business transaction.	✓
Ignore the discovery because the client is a good friend and you trust him implicitly.	
Insist that the client reverses these sales and threaten to resign because it is clear that there has deliberately overstated the profit.	

Explanation:

As an AAT trainee accounting technician, we need to be aware of the effects including misleading period end adjustments. They could, for example, result in misinformed decision-making by users of the final accounts. These sales look suspicious because they were created on the last day of the year and then reversed on the first day of the following accounting period. Therefore, even if the client is a good friend, we have a duty to investigate this and as a trainee, it would be best to approach the managing partner for advice on how to proceed.

....

Task 11.11

	✓
It is a memorandum account to keep track of amounts owing from individual customers and owed to individual suppliers.	
It will detect all bookkeeping errors.	
It is prepared after closing off the general ledger accounts and before preparing the final accounts.	✓
It will always include a suspense account.	

Explanation:

The trial balance lists the closing balances on each general ledger account. The balances are listed on the debit or credit side as appropriate. It is an important step in the preparation of the final accounts.

It is not a memorandum account showing amounts owing from individual customers or owed to individual suppliers; this is a description of the purchases and sales ledgers.

It will not detect every error as some errors allow the trial balance to balance.

It only includes a suspense account if it does not initially balance; it will not always include a suspense account.

Task 11.12

(a)

Account	Debit £	Credit £
Depreciation expense	1,056	
Fixtures and fittings accumulated depreciation		1,056

(b)

Account	Debit £	Credit £
Suspense	120	
Accruals		120

(c)

Account	Debit £	Credit £
Closing inventory – statement of financial position	8,255	
Closing inventory – statement of profit or loss		8,255

Workings:

Inventory should be valued at the lower of cost (£445) and NRV (£250) so a write down of £195 is required (£445 – £250).

This reduces total closing inventory to £8,255 (£8,450 – £195).

(d)

Account	Debit £	Credit £
Suspense	1,774	
Purchase returns		1,774

Workings:

Should have done		Did do		Correction	
DR PLCA	£887	DR PLCA	£887	DR Suspense	£1,774
CR Purchases returns	£887	DR Purchases returns	£887	CR Purchase returns	£1,774
		CR Suspense	£1,774		

(e) Complete the following sentence:

I cannot conclude that the balances included are now free from all errors.

I can conclude that the debit and credit sides of the trial balance will be equal.

Chapter 12

Task 12.1

(a) An extended trial balance is an accounting technique of moving from the
$\boxed{\text{initial}}$ trial balance, through the year end adjustments, to
the figures for the $\boxed{\text{final}}$ accounts.

(b) When an extended trial balance is extended and a business has made a
profit, this figure for profit will be in the $\boxed{\text{debit}}$ column of the
statement of profit or loss.

Task 12.2

Statements	✓
The balance on the suspense account should appear on the debit side of the statement of profit or loss columns.	
The balance on the suspense account should appear on the credit side of the statement of financial position columns.	
The balance on the suspense account should not appear in the statement of profit or loss or the statement of financial position columns in the extended trial balance.	✓

Task 12.3

Extended trial balance

Ledger account	Statement of profit or loss		Statement of financial position	
	Debit ✓	Credit ✓	Debit ✓	Credit ✓
Allowance for doubtful debts				✓
Allowance for doubtful debts – adjustment (increase in allowance)	✓			
Bank overdraft				✓
Capital				✓
Closing inventory		✓	✓	
Depreciation charges	✓			
Purchases returns		✓		
Opening inventory	✓			
VAT owed from HMRC			✓	

Explanation:

In this task, the following should be noted:

- The allowance for doubtful debts – adjustment is an increase in the allowance. This results in an expense. Therefore, it is shown on the debit side of the statement of profit or loss columns.

- The bank has an overdraft and therefore is a liability. For this reason, it is included in the statement of financial position credit column.

- The VAT is owed from HMRC. This means it is an asset and so it is shown in the statement of financial position debit column.

Task 12.4

Extended trial balance

Ledger account	Ledger balances		Adjustments		Statement of profit or loss		Statement of financial position	
	Debit £	Credit £	Debit £	Credit £	Debit £	Credit £	Debit £	Credit £
Allowance for doubtful debts		2,380	420					1,960
Allowance for doubtful debts – adjustment	1,600			420	1,180			
Bank	2,400			230			2,630	
Capital		25,800						25,800
Closing inventory			13,500	13,500			13,500	13,500
Depreciation charges	9,203		4,000		13,203			
Office expenses	600				600			
Opening inventory	2,560				2,560			
Payroll expenses	16,400				16,400			
Purchases	22,400				22,400			
Purchases ledger control account		8,900	300					8,600
Sales		45,150		60		45,210		
Sales ledger control account	11,205			300			10,905	
Selling expenses	1,700				1,700			
Suspense	170		60	230				
VAT		12,000						12,000
Vehicles at cost	64,192						64,192	
Vehicles accumulated depreciation		38,200		4,000				42,200
Profit for the year					667			667
Total	132,430	132,430	18,510	18,510	**58,710**	**58,710**	**91,227**	**91,227**

Explanation:

In this task, the following should be noted:

The allowance for doubtful debts – adjustment is in the statement of profit or loss debit column. This shows that the allowance for doubtful debts is higher at the end of this year than at the end of the previous period.

The VAT balance of £12,000 is entered in the credit column of the statement of financial position. This shows it is an amount due to HMRC and a liability.

By adding across the suspense account row, this account is cleared to zero, as is expected after all year end adjustments have been posted.

Having extended the figures into the statement of profit or loss columns, adding down, the credit side is the higher of the two columns (£58,710). Before adjustment the statement of profit or loss debit column is only £58,043. Therefore, by including a 'Profit for the year' figure of £667 in the final row of the debit column, the two columns balance. To complete the double entry, £667 is recorded in the statement of financial position credit column.

All pairs of columns now balance. As the £667 is in the statement of profit or loss debit column and statement of financial position credit column, this shows that the business has generated a profit for the year.

Task 12.5

Extended trial balance

Ledger account	Ledger balances		Adjustments		Statement of profit or loss		Statement of financial position	
	Debit £	Credit £	Debit £	Credit £	Debit £	Credit £	Debit £	Credit £
Bank		4,123		4,235				8,358
Capital		20,000						20,000
Closing inventory			3,414	3,414		3,414	3,414	
Depreciation charges	2,415		1,352		3,767			
Irrecoverable debts	124				124			
Loan		10,000						10,000
Machine at cost	51,600						51,600	
Machine accumulated depreciation		13,210		1,352				14,562
Opening inventory	6,116				6,116			
Prepaid expenses	215			352			567	
Purchases	39,321			519	39,840			
Purchases ledger control account		13,421						13,421
Purchases returns		299		519		818		
Sales		72,032		511		72,543		
Sales ledger control account	38,597			3,770			34,827	
Sales returns	2,057		511		2,568			
Suspense		3,418	3,770	352				
VAT		3,942	4,235				293	
Profit for the year					24,360			24,360
Total	140,445	140,445	14,153	14,153	**76,775**	**76,775**	**90,701**	**90,701**

Explanation:

In this task, the following should be noted:

The bank balance of £8,358 is an overdraft and therefore in the statement of financial position credit column.

The VAT balance of £293 is money owed from HMRC (being the difference between a credit balance £3,942 and a debit balance of £4,235). It is entered in the debit column of the statement of financial position.

By adding across the suspense account row, this account is cleared to zero, as is expected after all year end adjustments have been posted.

Having extended the figures into the statement of profit or loss columns, adding down, the credit side is the higher of the two columns (£76,775). Before adjustment the statement of profit or loss debit column is only £52,415. Therefore, by including a 'Profit for the year' figure of £24,360 in the final row of the debit column, the two columns balance. To complete the double entry, £24,360 is recorded in the statement of financial position credit column.

All pairs of columns now balance. As the £24,360 is in the statement of profit or loss debit column and statement of financial position credit column, this shows that the business has generated a profit for the year.

AAT AQ2016 SAMPLE ASSESSMENT 1
ADVANCED BOOKKEEPING

Time allowed: 2 hours

Advanced Bookkeeping (AVBK)
AAT sample assessment 1

Task 1 (21 marks)

This task is about non-current assets.

You are working on the accounting records of a business known as AMBR Trading.

You may ignore VAT in this task.

The following is an extract from a purchase invoice received by AMBR Trading relating to new equipment for its commercial kitchen:

To: AMBR Trading Unit 6, East End Trading Estate Southgrove HS14 6PW	Invoice 965270 Katerkit Ltd Cator Way Gatebury TY6 5VB	Date: 01 April 20X6
Item	**Details**	**£**
Electric combi-steam oven	CSO31	5,565.00
Colour touch control display	For CSO31	999.00
Floor stand	For CSO31	224.00
Electric portable pasta boiler	PSB69	245.00
Net total		7,033.00

The acquisition has been made under a finance lease agreement.

The following information relates to the sale of some computer equipment no longer used by the business:

Item description	Desktop DTC3
Date of sale	31 December 20X6
Selling price	£180.00

- AMBR Trading has a policy of capitalising expenditure over £500.

- Kitchen equipment is depreciated at 20% per year on a diminishing balance basis.

- Computer equipment is depreciated over four years on a straight line basis assuming no residual value.

- Depreciation is calculated on an annual basis and charged in equal instalments for each full month an asset is owned in the year.

(a) **For the year ended 31 March 20X7, record the following in the extract from the non-current assets register below:**

- **Any acquisition of non-current assets**
- **Any disposals of non-current assets**
- **Depreciation.**

Note. **Not every cell will acquire an entry.**

Show your numerical answers to TWO decimal places.

Use the DD/MM/YY format for any dates.

Use the drop-down list below to select your answers where indicated, otherwise enter the number or date into the relevant cell.

Extract from non-current assets register

Description/ Serial number	Acquisition date	Cost £	Depreciation charges £	Carrying amount £	Funding method	Disposal proceeds £	Disposal date
Kitchen equipment							
Double-door freezer DDF4	01/04/X4	1,995.00			Part-exchange		
Year end 31/03/X5			399.00	1,596.00			
Year end 31/03/X6			319.20	1,276.80			
Year end 31/03/X7							
▼					▼		
Year end 31/03/X7							
Computer equipment							
Restaurant POS tablet bundle	01/10/X4	1,380.00			Hire purchase		
Year end 31/03/X5			172.50	1,207.50			
Year end 31/03/X6			345.00	862.50			

Description/ Serial number	Acquisition date	Cost £	Depreciation charges £	Carrying amount £	Funding method	Disposal proceeds £	Disposal date
Year end 31/03/X7				517.50			
Desktop DTC3	01/01/X5	579.84			Cash		
Year end 31/03/X5			36.24	543.60			
Year end 31/03/X6			144.96	398.64			
Year end 31/03/X7			▼	▼			

Drop-down list:

Desktop DTC3	0.00	0.00	Cash
Freezer DDF4	99.66	253.68	Finance lease
Electric oven CSO31	108.72	289.92	Hire purchase
Pasta boiler PSB69	144.96	298.98	

(b) Complete the following sentences.

It is important to obtain prior authority for capital expenditure in order

▼

The bank manager [▼] be the appropriate person to give this authority.

Drop-down list:

to achieve the appropriate level of materiality.
to comply with international financial reporting standards.
to ensure that the business as a whole will benefit from the purchase.

would
would not

··

Task 2 (17 marks)

This task is about ledger accounting for non-current assets.

* You are working on the accounting records of a business for the year ended 31 March 20X7. VAT can be ignored.

* A new vehicle has been acquired. It is estimated it will be used for four years.

* The cost was £12,448; this was paid from the bank.

- The business plans to sell the vehicle after four years when its residual value is expected to be £4,000.

- Vehicles are depreciated on a straight line basis. A full year's depreciation is applied in the year of acquisition.

- Depreciation has already been entered into the accounting records for existing vehicles.

(a) **Calculate the depreciation charge for the year on the new vehicle.**

£	

Make entries in the accounts below for:

- **The acquisition of the new vehicle**
- **The depreciation charge on the new vehicle**

On each account, show clearly the balance to be carried down or transferred to the statement of profit or loss, as appropriate.

Vehicle at cost

	£		£
Balance b/d	46,300	▼	
▼		▼	
▼		▼	

Depreciation charges

	£		£
Balance b/d	7,575	▼	
▼		▼	
▼			

Vehicles accumulated depreciation

	£		£
▼		Balance c/d	15,150
▼		▼	
▼		▼	

Drop-down list:

Balance b/d
Balance c/d
Bank
Depreciation charges
Disposals
Profit or loss account
Purchases
Purchases ledger control account
Sales
Sales ledger control account
Vehicle running expenses
Vehicle accumulated depreciation
Vehicles at cost
Empty

The business sold an item of office equipment which originally cost £1,800. The proceeds of £600 were paid into the bank:

(b) Insert the account names to the debit and credit columns to show where the entries for the proceeds will be made.

Debit	Credit

Disposals

Office equipment at cost

Bank

(c) **Show the journal entries required to remove the original cost of the equipment for the general ledger.**

Account		Amount £	Debit	Credit
	▼			
	▼			

Drop-down list:

Bank
Depreciation charges
Disposals
Office equipment accumulated depreciation
Office equipment at cost
Profit and loss account
Purchases
Purchases ledger control account
Sales
Sales ledger control account
Sales returns
Suspense
Vehicles accumulated depreciation
Vehicles at cost
Empty

··

Task 3 (19 marks)

This task is about ledger accounting, including accruals and prepayments, and applying ethical principles.

(a) **Enter the figures given in the table below in the appropriate trial balance columns.**

Do not enter zeros in unused column cells. Do not enter any figures as negatives.

Extract from the trial balance as at 31 March 20X7

Account	Ledger balance	Trial balance	
	£	Debit £	Credit £
Accrued expenses	850		
Carriage inwards	2,240		
Discounts allowed	1,420		
Prepaid income	975		

You are working on the accounting records of a business for the year ended 31 March 20X7.

In this task, you can ignore VAT.

Business policy: accounting accruals and prepayments

An entry is made into the income or expense account and an opposite entry into the relevant asset or liability account. In the following period, this entry is removed.

You are looking at vehicle running expenses for the year.

- The cash book for the year shows payments for vehicle running expenses of £9,468.

- This includes the following payments for road fund licenses.

Road fund licenses for the period:	£
1 January – 31 December 20X7	516
1 April 20X7 – 31 March 20X8	405

(b) **Calculate the value of the adjustment required for vehicle running expenses as at 31 March 20X7.**

£	

Update the vehicles running expenses account. Show clearly:
- **the cash book figure**
- **the year end adjustment**
- **the transfer to the statement of profit or loss for the year**

Vehicle running expenses

	£			£
Prepaid expenses (reversal)	840		▼	
▼			▼	
▼			▼	

Drop-down list:

Accrued expenses
Accrued income
Balance b/d
Balance c/d
Bank
Commission income
Prepaid expenses
Prepaid income
Profit or loss account
Purchases
Purchases ledger control account
Sales
Sales ledger control account
Statement of financial position
Vehicle running expenses
Empty

You are now looking at commission income for the year.

Commission income of £2,070 was accrued on 31 March 20X6.

(c)   Complete the following statements:

The reversal of this accrual is dated [▼] .

The reversal is on the [▼] side of the commission income account.

Drop-down list:

31 March 20X6
1 April 20X6
1 April 20X7

credit
debit

- The cash book for the year shows receipts for commission income of £42,805.

- Commission of £1,960 for the month ended 31 March 20X7 was received into the bank on 15 April 20X7.

(d)   Taking into account all the information you have, calculate the commission income for the year ended 31 March 20X7.

£ [   ]

Your junior colleague asks why you are considering the receipt dated 15 April.

She is confused as the financial year ended on 31 March.

(e)   Which of the following can you use in your explanation to her?

You must choose ONE answer for each row.

Reason for considering the receipt dated 15 April	Acceptable reason	Not acceptable reason
The proprietor of the business asked you to increase the profit for the year ended 31 March 20X7.		
The transaction is an expense relevant to the period ended 31 March 20X7.		
The figure is a current asset as at 31 March 20X7.		

Task 4 (23 marks)

This task is about accounting adjustments.

You are a trainee accounting technician reporting to a managing partner in an accounting practice. You are working on the accounting records of a business client.

A trial balance has been drawn up and balanced using a suspense account. You now need to make some corrections and adjustments for the year ended 31 March 20X7.

You may ignore VAT in this task.

The allowance for doubtful debts needs to be adjusted to 1% of the outstanding trade receivables.

(a)   Calculate the value of the adjustment required.

£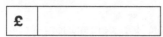

(b)   (i)   Record this adjustment into the extract from the extended trial balance below.

(ii)   Make the following further adjustments.

You will NOT need to enter adjustments on every line. Do NOT enter zeros into unused cells.

- Purchases of £984 have been posted to the office expenses account in error.

- A prepayment of £450 for airfares has been posted correctly on the credit side. There was no corresponding debit entry. These costs are classified as sales expenses.

- The plant as cost account in the general ledger correctly shows a balance of £24,500. This has been incorrectly transferred to the final balances as £25,400.

Extract from the extended trial balance

Ledger account	Ledger balances		Adjustments	
	Debit £	Credit £	Debit £	Credit £
Allowance for doubtful debts		225		
Allowance for doubtful debts – adjustments				
Bank	2,815			
Irrecoverable debts	390			
Office expenses	116,310			
Plant at cost	25,400			
Plant accumulated depreciation		12,250		
Prepaid expenses	505			
Purchases	108,265			
Purchases ledger control account		9,622		
Rent	14,800			
Sales		188,748		
Sales expenses	8,606			
Sales ledger control account	17,900			
Suspense		450		

(c) **Show the journal entries that will be required to close off the rent account for the financial year end and select an appropriate narrative.**

Journal

		Dr £	Cr £
	▼		
	▼		

Narrative:

▼

Drop-down list:

Allowance for doubtful debts
Allowance for doubtful debts – adjustment
Bank
Irrecoverable debts
Office expenses
Plant accumulated depreciation
Plant at cost
Prepaid expenses
Profit of loss account
Purchases ledger control account
Rent
Sales
Sales expenses
Sales ledger control account
Statement of financial position
Suspense
Empty

Closure of general ledger for the year ended 31 March 20X7
Closure of rent account to the suspense account
Transfer of rent for year ended 31 March 20X7 to the statement of financial position
Transfer of rent for year ended 31 March 20X7 to the profit or loss account

Your manager has now reviewed the resulting figures in the draft accounts. He is concerned that the client may have significantly understated the irrecoverable debt figures and this will need further investigation. You know that the client is pressuring to get the final accounts completed for what she describes as an important meeting for the future of the business. Any further investigation will mean her deadline cannot be met.

(d) **What should you and your manager do next, and why? Choose ONE.**

	✓
Investigate the collectability of debts and delay completion of the accounts, as any adjustment could affect the outcome of the meeting.	
Investigate the collectability of debts and delay completion of the accounts because the client will have overstated the importance of the meeting.	
Complete the accounts by the deadline without any further adjustment, as any change is unlikely to be relevant to the meeting.	
Complete the accounts by the deadline without any further adjustment because the client's needs must take priority.	

Task 5 (20 marks)

This task is about period end routines using accounting, records and the extended trial balance.

You are preparing the bank reconciliation for a sole trader.

The balance showing on the bank statement is a debt of £1,930 and the balance in the cash book is a debit of £2,407.

The bank statement has been compared with the cash book at 31 March and the following points noted.

1. A remittance advice from a customer has been received and an entry made in the cash book for the correct amount of £734. This is not yet showing on the bank statement.

2. A cheque from a customer for £367 for a debt outstanding at the year end was received in April 20X7.

3. A faster payment of £2,174 for the purchase of a non-current asset is showing on the bank statement but has not been entered in the accounting records.

4. The bank has made an error. On the last day of the month, a payment of £1,087 on the statement was duplicated.

5. A direct debit payment of £422 has been recorded in the accounts as £222.

6. Interest charges of £142 have not been entered in the cash book.

(a) Use the following table to show the THREE items that should appear on the cash book side of the reconciliation. Enter only ONE figure for each line. Do not enter zeros in unused cells.

Adjustment		Debit £	Credit £
	▼		
	▼		
	▼		

Drop-down list:

Adjustment 1
Adjustment 2
Adjustment 3
Adjustment 4
Adjustment 5
Adjustment 6
Empty

(b) Which of the following statements about the net pay control account is TRUE? Choose ONE.

The net pay control account...

	✓
...is a summary of memorandum accounts for each employee.	
...should have a balance of zero when all relevant entries have been correctly made.	
...will always be accurate when the bank reconciliation has been completed.	
...should include individual entries for gross pay due to each employee.	

You are now working on the accounting records of a different business.

You have the following extended trial balance. The adjustments have already been correctly entered.

(c) **Extend the figures into the statement of profit or loss and statement of financial position columns.**

Do NOT enter zeros into unused column cells.

Complete the extended trial balance by entering figures and a label in the correct places.

Drop-down list:

Profit/loss for the year
Suspense
Balance b/d
Balance c/d
Gross profit/loss for the year

Extended trial balance

Ledger account	Ledger balances		Adjustments		Statement of profit or loss		Statement of financial position	
	Debit £	Credit £	Debit £	Credit £	Debit £	Credit £	Debit £	Credit £
Bank		958		75				
Capital		11,000						
Closing inventory			9,930	9,930				
Depreciation charges	3,895							
Equipment at cost	20,162			689				
Equipment accumulated depreciation		15,579						
Interest paid	63		75					
Loan		6,566	1,085					
Office expenses	22,495		689	290				
Opening inventory	10,058							
Payroll expenses	20,825							
Prepayments			290					
Purchases	79,454							
Purchases ledger control account		13,167						
Sales		126,139		485				
Sales ledger control account	16,979							
Suspense	600		485	1,085				
VAT		1,122						
▼								
Total	174,531	174,531	12,554	12,554				

AAT AQ2016 SAMPLE ASSESSMENT 1 ADVANCED BOOKKEEPING

ANSWERS

Advanced Bookkeeping (AVBK)
AAT sample assessment 1

Task 1 (21 marks)

(a) For the year ended 31 March 20X7, record the following in the extract from the non-current assets register below:

- Any acquisitions of non-current assets
- Any disposals of non-current assets
- Depreciation

Description/ Serial number	Acquisition date	Cost £	Depreciation charges £	Carrying amount £	Funding method	Disposal proceeds £	Disposal date
Kitchen equipment							
Double door freezer DDF4	01/04/X4	1,995.00			Part-exchange		
Year end 31/03/X5			399.00	1,596.00			
Year end 31/03/X6			319.20	1,276.80			
Year end 31/03/X7			**255.36**	**1,021.44**			
Electric oven CSO31	**01/04/X6**	**6,788.00**			**Finance lease**		
Year end 31/03/X7			**1,357.60**	**5,430.40**			
Computer equipment							
Restaurant POS tablet bundle	01/10/X4	1,380.00			Hire purchase		
Year end 31/03/X5			172.50	1,207.50			
Year end 31/03/X6			345.00	862.50			
Year end 31/03/X7			**345.00**	517.50			

Description/ Serial number	Acquisition date	Cost £	Depreciation charges £	Carrying amount £	Funding method	Disposal proceeds £	Disposal date
Desktop DTC3	01/01/X5	579.84			Cash		
Year end 31/03/X5			36.24	543.60			
Year end 31/03/X6			144.96	398.64			
Year end 31/03/X7			**108.72**	**0.00**		**180.00**	**31/12/X6**

Workings:

Kitchen Equipment depreciation

1276.80 × 20% = 255.36 (carrying value multiplied by the rate of depreciation) = 255.36

Electric oven CSO31

The cost is calculated as 5,565.00 (the oven) + 999.00 (the control display) + 224.00 (the floor stand) = 6.788. This is because all of these costs relate to the oven. The pasta boiler is a separate asset and falls below the £500 capitalisation threshold so should be recorded as an expense rather than an asset.

Depreciation = 6,788 × 20% = 1,357.60

Computer equipment (Restaurant POS tablet bundle) is depreciated on a straight line basis, therefore, the charge for year ended 31/3/07 is the same as the previous year (1380/4 = 345). The first year's depreciation was apportioned for the number of months of ownership in the year of acquisition.

Desktop DTC3 was disposed of in year ended 31/3/X7, so the depreciation in that final year has been apportioned accordingly:

579.84/4 = 144.96 (full year depreciation)

144.96/12 months × 9 months (disposed of 31 December) = 108.72

(b) Complete the following sentences.

It is important to obtain prior authority for capital expenditure in order

to ensure that the business as a whole will benefit from the purchase .

The bank manager would not be the appropriate person to give this authority.

Explanation:

Capital purchases should be considered as to whether they will benefit the company, in terms of generating revenues, improving efficiencies or supporting the production of new product lines.

The decision to buy a new capital asset would not be affected by the international reporting standards (although how the purchase is recorded in the financial statements **would** be considered) and the question of materiality would only arise when the auditors look at the financial statements.

The bank manager is not an official within the company and therefore would not be the most appropriate person to approve the purchase.

Task 2 (17 marks)

(a) Calculate the depreciation charge for the year on the new vehicle.

£	2,112

Workings:

$$\frac{£12,448 - £4,000}{4 \text{ years}} = £2,112$$

No apportionment as a full year charge in year of acquisition.

Make entries in the accounts below for:

- **The acquisition of the new vehicle**
- **The depreciation charge on the new vehicle**

Vehicle at cost

	£		£
Balance b/d	46,300	Balance c/d	58,748
Bank	12,448		
	58,748		58,748

BPP
LEARNING MEDIA

Depreciation charges

	£		£
Balance b/d	7,575	Profit or loss account	9,687
Vehicles accumulated depreciation	2,112		
	9,687		9,687

Vehicles accumulated depreciation

	£		£
Balance c/d	17,262	Balance b/d	15,150
		Depreciation charges	2,112
	17,262		17,262

(b) **Insert the account names to the debit and credit columns to show where the entries for the proceeds will be made.**

Debit	Credit
Bank	Disposals

(c) **Show the journal entries required to remove the original cost of the equipment from the general ledger.**

Account	Amount £	Debit	Credit
Disposals	1,800	✓	
Office equipment at cost	1,800		✓

Task 3 (19 marks)

(a) **Enter the figures given in the table below in the appropriate trial balance columns.**

Do not enter zeros in unused column cells. Do not enter any figures as negatives.

Extract from the trial balance as at 31 March 20X7

Account	Ledger balance	Trial balance	
	£	£ Dr	£ Cr
Accrued expenses	850		850
Carriage inwards	2,240	2,240	
Discounts allowed	1,420	1,420	
Prepaid income	975		975

(b) **Calculate the value of the adjustment required for vehicle running expenses as at 31 March 20X7.**

£	–792

Workings:

Year end is 31 March 20X7

Apportion the road licences to cover any period after 1 April X7 as being prepaid for the next period (needs to be removed from current year's expenses):

1 Jan-31 Dec 20X7= £516 × 9/12	=	387	
1 Apr 20X7 – 31 March 20X8	=	405	(100% next period cost)
Adjustment		792	

Update the vehicles running expenses account. Show clearly:

- **The cash book figure**
- **The year end adjustment**
- **The transfer to the statement of profit or loss for the year**

Vehicle running expenses

	£		£
Prepaid expenses (reversal)	840	Prepaid expenses	792
Bank	9,468	Profit or loss account	9,516
	10,308		10,308

(c)   Complete the following statements:

The reversal of this accrual is dated ☐ 1 April 20X6 ☐ .

The reversal is on the ☐ debit ☐ side of the commission income account.

(d)   Taking into account all the information you have, calculate the commission income for the year ended 31 March 20X7.

£ | 42,695

Workings:

	£
Accrual brought forward at 1 April 20X7	(2,070)
Commission income received during year	42,805
Income received post year end	1,960
Total commission income for the year	42,695

The commission income received during the year in the cash book of £42,805 is reduced by the amount which related to the prior year (the accrual of £2,070). The income received in the cash book in April 20X7 of £1,960 related to the year ended 31 March 20X7 therefore needs to be accrued at 31 March 20X7.

(e) **Which of the following can you use in your explanation to her?**

You must choose ONE answer for each row.

Reason for considering the receipt dated 15 April	Acceptable reason	Not acceptable reason
The proprietor of the business asked you to increase the profit for the year ended 31 March 20X7.		✓
The transaction is an expense relevant to the period ended 31 March 20X7.		✓
The figure is a current asset as at 31 March 20X7.	✓	

Explanation:

The figure is a genuine current asset (accrued income) as at 31 March 20X7. The asset is genuine (the cash has been fully received post year end) and the invoices confirm the service was supplied in the year ended 31 March 20X7, therefore it should be accrued at year end.

The transaction is income not expense.

It would be unethical for an accountant to make an adjustment to the financial statements to adjust profit for the proprietor to achieve a particular aim. Under the *AAT Code of Professional Ethics* should follow the principle of professional competence by preparing accounts in accordance with accounting standards rather than the proprietor's wishes.

Task 4 (23 marks)

(a) **Calculate the value of the adjustment required.**

£	– 46

Working:

The closing allowance for doubtful debts is calculated as 1% of the trade receivables (sales ledger control account) balance of £17,900 giving a figure of £179. There an opening allowance of £225, therefore a decrease of £46 (£225 – £179) is required.

(b) (i) Record this adjustment into the extract from the extended trial balance below.

(ii) Make the following further adjustments. You will **NOT** need to enter adjustments on every line. Do **NOT** enter zeros into unused cells.

Extract from the extended trial balance

Ledger account	Ledger balances		Adjustments	
	Dr £	Cr £	Dr £	Cr £
Allowance for doubtful debts		225	46	
Allowance for doubtful debts – adjustments				46
Bank	2,815			
Irrecoverable debts	390			
Office expenses	116,310			984
Plant at cost	25,400			900
Plant accumulated depreciation		12,250		
Prepaid expenses	505		450	
Purchases	108,265		984	
Purchases ledger control account		9,622		
Rent	14,800			
Sales		188,748		
Sales expenses	8,606			
Sales ledger control account	17,900			
Suspense		450	900	450

Working:

Purchases:

Should have done		Did do		Correction	
DR Purchases	984	DR Office expenses	984	DR Purchases	984
CR Cash	984	CR Cash	984	CR Office expenses	984

228

Prepayment:

Should have done	Did do	Correction
DR Prepaid expenses 450	DR Suspense 450	DR Prepaid expenses 450
CR Sales expenses 450	CR Sales expenses 450	CR Suspense 450

Plant:

This was posted to the trial balance as a debit of £25,400 instead of a debit of £24,500. This would have made the debits in the trial balance £900 (£25,400 – £24,500) higher than the credits, giving rise to a credit to the suspense account of £900 to make the TB balance. Therefore, the correction is:

DR Suspense   £900
CR Plant at cost   £900

(c) **Show the journal entries that will be required to close off the rent account for the financial year end and select an appropriate narrative.**

Journal

	Dr £	Cr £
Profit or loss account	14,800	
Rent		14,800

Narrative:

Transfer of rent for year ended 31 March 20X7 to the profit or loss account

(d) **What should you and your manager do next, and why? Choose ONE.**

	✓
Investigate the collectability of debts and delay completion of the accounts, as any adjustment could affect the outcome of the meeting.	✓
Investigate the collectability of debts and delay completion of the accounts because the client will have overstated the importance of the meeting.	
Complete the accounts by the deadline without any further adjustment, as any change is unlikely to be relevant to the meeting.	
Complete the accounts by the deadline without any further adjustment because the client's needs must take priority.	

Explanation:

It is important to ensure that all of the necessary work has been completed. By agreeing to complete the accounts at the insistence of the client, this is a threat to the fundamental principle of advocacy (whereby the client's position has been unduly promoted by the lack of work by the accountant) or even intimidation (undue pressure placed on them by the client). This goes against the *AAT Code of Professional Ethics.*

Task 5 (20 marks)

(a) **Use the following table to show the THREE items that should appear on the cash book side of the reconciliation. Enter only ONE figure for each line. Do not enter zeros in unused cells.**

Adjustment	Dr £	Cr £
Adjustment 3		2,174
Adjustment 5		200
Adjustment 6		142

Explanation:

Adjustment 3 is the payment which needs to be reflected in the cashbook of £2,174. As the cash is leaving the bank account, it is a credit in the business' general ledger. Adjustment 5 is an understatement of the payment in the cashbook by £200 (£422 – £222), therefore a credit entry to decrease the cashbook balance is required. Adjustment 6 reflects the interest paid at the bank of £142, and therefore the cashbook balance needs to be reduced with a credit.

(b) **Which of the following statements about the net pay control account is TRUE? Choose ONE.**

The net pay control account...

	✓
...is a summary of memorandum accounts for each employee.	
...should have a balance of zero when all relevant entries have been correctly made.	✓
...will always be accurate when the bank reconciliation has been completed.	
...should include individual entries for gross pay due to each employee.	

(c) **Extend the figures into the statement of profit or loss and statement of financial position columns.**

Do NOT enter zeros into unused column cells.

Complete the extended trial balance by entering figures and a label in the correct places.

Extended trial balance

Ledger account	Ledger balances		Adjustments		Statement of profit or loss		Statement of financial position	
	Dr £	Cr £	Dr £	Cr £	Dr £	Cr £	Dr £	Cr £
Bank		958		75				**1,033**
Capital		11,000						**11,000**
Closing inventory			9,930	9,930		**9,930**	**9,930**	
Depreciation charges	3,895				**3,895**			
Equipment at cost	20,162			689			**19,473**	
Equipment accumulated depreciation		15,579						**15,579**
Interest paid	63		75		**138**			
Loan		6,566	1,085					**5,481**
Office expenses	22,495		689	290	**22,894**			
Opening inventory	10,058				**10,058**			
Payroll expenses	20,825				**20,825**			
Prepayments			290				**290**	
Purchases	79,454				**79,454**			
Purchases ledger control account		13,167						**13,167**
Sales		126,139		485		**126,624**		
Sales ledger control account	16,979						**16,979**	
Suspense	600		485	1,085				
VAT		1,122						**1,122**
Profit/loss for the year						**710**	**710**	
Total	174,531	174,531	12,554	12,554	**137,264**	**137,264**	**47,382**	**47,382**

AAT AQ2016 SAMPLE ASSESSMENT 2 ADVANCED BOOKKEEPING

You are advised to attempt sample assessment 2 online from the AAT website. This will ensure you are prepared for how the assessment will be presented on the AAT's system when you attempt the real assessment. Please access the assessment using the address below:

https://www.aat.org.uk/training/study-support/search

AAT AQ2016 SAMPLE ASSESSMENT 2

BPP PRACTICE ASSESSMENT 1
ADVANCED BOOKKEEPING

Time allowed: 2 hours

Advanced Bookkeeping (AVBK)
BPP practice assessment 1

Task 1

This task is about non-current assets.

You are working on the accounting records of a business known as RTL Trading.

You may ignore VAT in this task.

The following is an extract from a purchase invoice received by RTL Trading:

Fittings Supplies plc Unit 76 East Trading Estate Mendlesham ME2 9FG	Invoice 9032	Date:	20 June 20X5
To:	RTL Trading 14 Larkmead Road Mendlesham ME6 2PO		
Description	**Item number**	**Quantity**	**£**
Warehouse racking system	WR617	1	2,000.00
Delivery and set-up charges		1	200.00
Specialist oil for racking @ £15.00 per litre		3 litres	45.00
Net total			2,245.00

The acquisition has been made under a hire purchase agreement.

The following information relates to the sale of an item of machinery:

Identification number	MC5267
Date of sale	22 June 20X5
Selling price	£3,250.00

- RTL Trading has a policy of capitalising expenditure over £200.

- Furniture and fittings are depreciated at 25% using the straight line method. There are no residual values.

- Machinery is depreciated at 40% using the diminishing balance method.
- A full year's depreciation is charged in the year of acquisition and none in the year of sale.

(a) **For the year ended 30 September 20X5, record the following in the non-current assets register below:**

- **Any acquisitions of non-current assets**
- **Any disposals of non-current assets**
- **Depreciation**

Extract from non-current assets register

Description	Acquisition date	Cost £	Depreciation charges £	Carrying amount £	Funding method	Disposal proceeds £	Disposal date
Furniture and fittings							
Racking system WR290	01/12/X2	6,000.00			Loan		
Year end 30/09/X3			1,500.00	4,500.00			
Year end 30/09/X4			1,500.00	3,000.00			
Year end 30/09/X5							
▼1	▼2				▼3		
Year end 30/09/X5							
Machinery							
Machine MC5267	01/10/X2	7,500.00			Cash		
Year end 30/09/X3			3,000.00	4,500.00			
Year end 30/09/X4			1,800.00	2,700.00			
Year end 30/09/X5			▼4	▼5			▼2
Machine MC5298	31/01/X4	8,800.00			Part exchange		
Year end 30/09/X4			3,520.00	5,280.00			
Year end 30/09/X5							

Picklist 1:

Machine MC5267
Machine MC5298
Racking system WR290
Racking system WR617

Picklist 2:

01/12/X2
01/10/X2
31/01/X4
20/06/X5
22/06/X4

Picklist 3:

Cash
Finance lease
Hire purchase
Loan

Picklist 4:

0.00
810.00
1,080.00
1,875.00

Picklist 5:

0.00
825.00
1,620.00
1,890.00

RTL Trading is planning its non-current asset purchases for the next year. The business currently has a large bank overdraft and very high borrowings. All existing bank loans are secured on non-current assets and no further assets are available to offer as security. All non-current assets are currently in working order and needed for the business. The business wishes to become the legal owner of the asset.

(b) **Which one of the following would be the most suitable funding method for the next purchase of non-current assets?**

	✓
Cash	
Bank loan	
Hire purchase	
Finance lease	

Task 2

This task is about accounting for non-current assets.

- You are working on the accounting records of a business for the year ended 31 December 20X7. The business is registered for VAT.

- On 1 September 20X7 the business bought a new machine for the business.

- The machine cost £14,640 including VAT; this was paid from the bank.

- The machine's residual value is expected to be £2,300, excluding VAT.

- The business's depreciation policy for machines is 10% per annum on a straight line basis. A full year's depreciation is charged in the year of acquisition and none in the year of disposal.

- Depreciation has already been entered into the accounts for the business's existing machines.

(a) **Calculate the depreciation charge for the year on the new machine.**

£	

Make entries to account for:

- **The acquisition of the new machine**
- **The depreciation on the new machine**

On each account, show clearly the balance carried down or transferred to the statement of profit or loss.

Machines at cost

	£		£
Balance b/d	20,000	▼	
▼		▼	

Depreciation charges

	£		£
Balance b/d	5,700	▼	
▼		▼	

Machines accumulated depreciation

	£		£
▼		Balance b/d	8,600
▼		▼	

VAT control account

	£		£
▼		Balance b/d	4,200
▼		▼	

Picklist:

Balance b/d
Balance c/d
Bank
Depreciation charges
Disposals
Machines accumulated depreciation
Machines at cost
Machines running expenses
Profit or loss account
Purchases

Purchases ledger control account
Sales
Sales ledger control account
VAT control account

The business sold a vehicle which originally cost £15,000, net of VAT. At the date of disposal, accumulated depreciation amounted to £10,000. The selling price of the vehicle was £7,500, net of VAT.

(b) **What is the gain or loss on disposal?**

	Amount £
▼	

Picklist:

Gain
Loss

(c) **Show the journal entry required to remove the accumulated depreciation of the vehicle from the general ledger.**

	Amount £	Debit ✓	Credit ✓
▼			
▼			

Picklist:

Bank
Depreciation charges
Disposals
Machines accumulated depreciation
Machines at cost
Machines running expenses
Profit or loss account
Purchases
Purchases ledger control account
Sales
Sales ledger control account
Vehicles accumulated depreciation
Vehicles at cost
VAT control account

Task 3

This task is about ledger accounting, including accruals and prepayments, and applying ethical principles.

(a) **Enter the figures given in the table below in the appropriate trial balance columns.**

Do not enter zeros in unused column cells.

Do not enter any figures as negatives.

Extract from trial balance as at 30 June 20X4

Account	Ledger balance £	Trial balance Debit £	Credit £
Capital	10,000		
Discounts received	1,209		
Interest expense	201		
Irrecoverable debts	780		

You are working on the final accounts of a business for the year ended 30 June 20X4. In this task, you can ignore VAT.

Business policy: accounting for accruals and prepayments

An entry is made into the income or expense account and an opposite entry into the relevant asset or liability account. In the following period, this entry is removed.

You are now looking at rental income for the year. There was a prepayment of rental income at 30 June 20X3.

The cash book for the year shows receipts of rental income of £5,000. Included in this figure is £270 for the quarter ended 31 July 20X4.

(b) **Calculate the value of the adjustment required for rental income as at 30 June 20X4.**

Enter an increase to rental income as a positive number and a decrease as a negative number.

£	

Update the rental income account. Show clearly:

- **The cash book figure**
- **The year end adjustment**
- **The transfer to the statement of profit or loss for the year**

Rental income

	£			£
▼		Prepaid income (reversal)		250
▼			▼	
▼			▼	

Picklist:

Accrued income
Accrued income (reversal)
Balance c/d
Bank
Capital
Discounts received
Irrecoverable debts
Interest expense
Prepaid income
Prepaid income (reversal)
Profit or loss account
Statement of financial position

You are now looking at selling expense for the year.

Selling expenses of £87 were accrued on 30 June 20X3.

(c)   Complete the following statements:

The reversal of the accrual is dated [▼] .

The reversal is on the [▼] side of the selling expenses account.

Picklist:

30 June 20X3
1 July 20X3
1 July 20X4

credit
debit

The cash book for the year shows payments for selling expenses of £2,850.

In July 20X4, an invoice for £63 was received for costs incurred in June 20X4.

(d) **Taking into account all the information you have, calculate the selling expenses for the year ended 30 June 20X4.**

£	

A trainee colleague asks you why you are making adjustments for accruals and prepayments at the year end.

(e) **Which of the following can you use in your explanation to her?**

You must choose ONE answer for each row.

Reason for considering accruals and prepayments	Acceptable reason ✓	Not acceptable reason ✓
Adjustments are a way of manipulating profits to give a favourable impression of the business.		
Income and expenditure must be matched to the accounting period to which they relate.		
The timing of receipts and payments does not always align with the business's accounting periods.		

Task 4

This task is about accounting adjustments.

You are a trainee accountant reporting to a managing partner in an accounting practice. You are working on the accounting records of a business client.

A trial balance has been drawn up and balanced using a suspense account. You now need to make some corrections and adjustments for the year ended 31 December 20X4.

You may ignore VAT in this task.

Closing inventory has been recorded in the trial balance. However, one item of inventory which has been included at its cost of £750 has a selling price of £680 and a further £90 must be spent to complete the inventory before it can be sold. Selling costs are expected to amount to 5% of the selling price.

BPP
LEARNING MEDIA

(a) **Calculate the value of the adjustment required to closing inventory.**

Enter an increase to inventory as a positive number and a decrease to inventory as a negative number.

£ [   ]

(b) (i) **Record this adjustment into the extract from the extended trial balance below.**

(ii) **Make the following further adjustments.**

You will NOT need to enter adjustments on every line. Do NOT enter zeros into unused cells.

- The allowance for doubtful debts needs to be adjusted to 3% of the outstanding trade receivables.

- Discounts received of £257 have only been entered into the purchases ledger control account from the discounts received day book.

- The office expenses account in the general ledger correctly shows a balance of £38,430. This has been incorrectly transferred to the trial balance as £34,830.

Extract from the extended trial balance

Ledger account	Ledger balances		Adjustments	
	Debit £	Credit £	Debit £	Credit £
Allowance for doubtful debts		900		
Allowance for doubtful debts – adjustments				
Bank	8,445			
Closing inventory – statement of financial position	22,600			
Closing inventory – statement of profit or loss		22,600		
Discounts received				
Irrecoverable debts	1,170			
Office expenses	34,830			
Plant accumulated depreciation		36,750		
Plant at cost	76,200			
Prepaid expenses	1,515			
Purchases	324,795			
Purchases ledger control account		28,866		
Sales		566,244		
Sales expenses	25,818			
Sales ledger control account	53,700			
Suspense	3,343			

(c) Show the journal entries that will be required to close off the sales account for the financial year end and select an appropriate narrative.

Journal

		Debit £	Credit £
	▼		
	▼		

Narrative:

	▼

Picklist:

Allowance for doubtful debts
Allowance for doubtful debts – adjustment
Bank
Closing inventory – statement of financial position
Closing inventory – statement of profit or loss
Discounts received
Irrecoverable debts
Office expenses
Plant accumulated depreciation
Plant at cost
Prepaid expenses
Profit of loss account
Purchases ledger control account
Rent
Sales
Sales expenses
Sales ledger control account
Statement of financial position
Suspense

Closure of general ledger for the year ended 31 December 20X4
Closure of sales account to the suspense account
Transfer of sales for year ended 31 December 20X4 to the profit or loss account
Transfer of sales for year ended 31 December 20X4 to the statement of financial position

Your manager has now reviewed the resulting figures in the draft accounts. He is concerned that the client may have significantly overstated the profit for the year ended 31 December 20X4 as it is much higher than both the budgeted and prior year figures. You are aware that the client is trying to persuade his friend to invest in the business and that he has already passed the draft accounts on to his friend to review.

(d)   What should you and your manager do next, and why? Choose ONE.

		✓
Take no action because if the profit figure is amended, the client could lose out on the investment from his friend		
Take no action because the client is a longstanding one and the fee our firm earns from him is substantial		
Request a meeting with the client to discuss why the profit is higher than budget and prior year to try and ascertain whether it is due to genuine business transactions		
Email the client's friend to warn him not to invest because the profit might be overstated		

Task 5

This task is about period end routines, using accounting records and the extended trial balance.

You are preparing the sales ledger control account reconciliation for a sole trader.

The balance showing on the sales ledger control account is £5,097 and the total of the list of sales ledger balances is £4,144.

The sales ledger control account has been compared with the total of the list of balances from the sales ledger and the following points noted.

1. The sales ledger column in the cash book – debit side was undercast by £100.

2. A contra for £76 was only recorded in the sales ledger.

3. An invoice for £536 in the sales day book was not posted to the sales ledger.

4. A total in the sales returns day book of £489 was recorded in the general ledger as £498.

5. A balance of £250 was omitted for the sales ledger listing.

6. A cash receipt of £95 from A Smith was accidentally posted to the sales ledger account of J Smith.

(a) **Use the following table to show the THREE adjustments you need to make to the sales ledger control account.**

Adjustment		Amount £	Debit ✓	Credit ✓
	▼			
	▼			
	▼			

Picklist:

Adjustment 1
Adjustment 2
Adjustment 3
Adjustment 4
Adjustment 5
Adjustment 6

(b) **Which of the following statements about bank reconciliations are TRUE?**

Select ONE answer for each row.

	True ✓	False ✓
A bank reconciliation helps identify items missing from the cash book		
A bank reconciliation forms part of the general ledger		
The balance on the bank statement is the balance that should be posted to the trial balance		
Items in the cash book but not in the bank statement may relate to timing differences		

(c) Extend the figures into the statement of profit or loss and statement of financial position columns.

Do NOT enter zeros into unused column cells.

Make the columns balance by entering figures and a label in the correct places.

Extended trial balance

Ledger account	Ledger balances		Adjustments		Statement of profit or loss		Statement of financial position	
	Dr £	Cr £	Dr £	Cr £	Dr £	Cr £	Dr £	Cr £
Administration expenses	6,739			569				
Allowance for doubtful debts		1,347		203				
Allowance for doubtful debts adjustment			203					
Bank		5,290						
Capital		9,460						
Closing inventory			7,234	7,234				
Depreciation charges			7,800					
Machinery accumulated depreciation		62,400		7,800				
Machinery at cost	115,000		750					
Marketing	7,365							
Opening inventory	9,933							
Purchases	34,289							
Purchases ledger control account		5,096						
Sales		112,015		3,000				
Sales ledger control account	8,023							
Suspense		8,819	9,569	750				
VAT		6,300						
Wages and salaries	29,378			6,000				
▼								
	210,727	210,727	25,556	25,556				

Picklist:

Balance b/d
Balance c/d
Gross profit/loss for the year
Profit/loss for the year
Suspense

BPP PRACTICE ASSESSMENT 1
ADVANCED BOOKKEEPING

ANSWERS

Advanced Bookkeeping (AVBK)
BPP practice assessment 1

Task 1

(a) Non-current assets register

Description	Acquisition date	Cost £	Depreciation charges £	Carrying amount £	Funding method	Disposal proceeds £	Disposal date
Furniture and fittings							
Racking system WR290	01/12/X2	6,000.00			Loan		
Year end 30/09/X3			1,500.00	4,500.00			
Year end 30/09/X4			1,500.00	3,000.00			
Year end 30/09/X5			**1,500.00**	**1,500.00**			
Racking system WR617	**20/06/X5**	**2,200.00**			**Hire purchase**		
Year end 30/09/X5			**550.00**	**1,650.00**			
Machinery							
Machine MC5267	01/10/X2	7,500.00			Cash		
Year end 30/09/X3			3,000.00	4,500.00			
Year end 30/09/X4			1,800.00	2,700.00			
Year end 30/09/X5			**0.00**	**0.00**		**3,250.00**	**22/06/X5**
Machine MC5298	31/01/X4	8,800.00			Part exchange		
Year end 30/09/X4			3,520.00	5,280.00			
Year end 30/09/X5			**2,112.00**	**3,168.00**			

Explanations:

For the new racking system (WR617), the purchase price (£2,000.00) and directly attributable costs (£200.00 delivery and set up) are capitalised but the specialist oil is revenue expenditure and as such, should be expensed in profit or loss which is why it is not recorded in the non-current asset register. Depreciation is calculated at 25% of cost using the straight line basis and is not pro-rated as the policy is to charge a full year in the year of acquisition: £2,200.00 × 25% = £550.00.

For machine MC5267 which is sold in the year, no depreciation should be charged as the accounting policy is a full year in the year of acquisition and none in the year of sale. The carrying amount is cleared to zero as the asset has been sold.

For machine MC5298, as the depreciation is charged at 40% using the diminishing balance method, depreciation is calculated as £5,280.00 × 40% = £2,112.00.

(b)

	✓
Cash	
Bank loan	
Hire purchase	✓
Finance lease	

Explanation:

Cash is not appropriate as the business currently has a large overdraft. Nor is a bank loan suitable as the business currently has very high borrowings so a bank is unlikely to lend particularly as no non-current assets are available to offer as security. Of the remaining two options, hire purchase is more suitable as under a hire purchase agreement, the business always becomes the legal owner of the asset which is not necessarily the case with a finance lease.

Task 2

(a)

£	990

Working:

As the business is VAT registered, it can recover the VAT on the new machine from HMRC. Therefore, the cost to the business is the amount excluding VAT which is calculated as £14,640 × 100/120 = £12,200. When the business sells the machine, VAT on the sales price will be payable to HMRC, therefore, the residual value excludes VAT when calculating depreciation.

VAT on the new machine is: £12,200 × 20% = £2,440.

Depreciation = (£12,200 – £2,300) × 10% = £990

Machines at cost

	£		£
Balance b/d	20,000	**Balance c/d**	**32,200**
Bank	**12,200**		
	32,200		**32,200**

Depreciation charges

	£		£
Balance b/d	5,700	**Profit or loss account**	**6,690**
Machines accumulated depreciation	**990**		
	6,690		**6,690**

Machines accumulated depreciation

	£		£
Balance c/d	**9,590**	Balance b/d	8,600
		Depreciation charges	**990**
	9,590		**9,590**

VAT control account

	£		£
Bank	**2,440**	Balance b/d	4,200
Balance c/d	**1,760**		
	4,200		**4,200**

(b) **Gain or loss on disposal**

	Amount £
Gain	2,500

Working:

	£
Sales proceeds (net of VAT)	7,500
Carrying amount (£15,000 – £10,000)	(5,000)
Gain	2,500

Note. When calculating the gain or loss on disposal, VAT is excluded from the sales price as it is payable to HMRC and it is also excluded from the purchase price as that VAT would have been reclaimed from the HMRC. This is because the business is VAT registered.

(c) **Journal entry**

	Amount £	Debit ✓	Credit ✓
Vehicles accumulated depreciation	10,000	✓	
Disposals	10,000		✓

Task 3

(a) **Extract from trial balance as at 30 June 20X4**

Account	Ledger balance £	Trial balance Debit £	Trial balance Credit £
Capital	10,000		10,000
Discounts received	1,209		1,209
Interest expense	201	201	
Irrecoverable debts	780	780	

(b)

£	– 90

Working:

Prepaid income = 1/3 × £270 = £90

This needs to be removed from income as it relates to next year (July 20X4).

Rental income

	£		£
Prepaid Income	90	Prepaid income (reversal)	250
Profit and loss account	5,160	Bank	5,000
	5,250		5,250

(c)

The reversal of the accrual is dated | 1 July 20X3 | .

The reversal is on the | credit | side of the selling expenses account.

(d)

£	2,826

Working:

The expense for the year is calculated as:

£2,850 cash paid – £87 paid in relation to prior year + £63 owing at the year end

Alternatively you can use a ledger account to help you work out your answer.

Selling expenses

	£		£
Bank	2,850	Accrued expenses (reversal)	87
Accrual	63	Profit or loss account	2,826
	2,913		2,913

(e) **Explanation:**

Reason for considering accruals and prepayments	Acceptable reason ✓	Not acceptable reason ✓
Adjustments are a way of manipulating profits to give a favourable impression of the business.		✓
Income and expenditure must be matched to the accounting period to which they relate.	✓	
The timing of receipts and payments does not always align with the business's accounting periods.	✓	

Task 4

(a)

£	– 194

Working:

Inventory should be valued at the lower of its cost of £750 and net realisable value of £556 (£680 – £90 – [5% × £680]). Therefore, a write down of £194 (£750 – £556) is required:

DR Closing inventory – statement of profit or loss £194
CR Closing inventory – statement of financial position £194

(b) **Extract from the extended trial balance**

Ledger account	Ledger balances Debit £	Ledger balances Credit £	Adjustments Debit £	Adjustments Credit £
Allowance for doubtful debts		900		**711**
Allowance for doubtful debts – adjustments			**711**	
Bank	8,115			
Closing inventory – statement of financial position	22,600			**194**
Closing inventory – statement of profit or loss		22,600	**194**	
Discounts received				**257**
Irrecoverable debts	1,170			
Office expenses	34,830		**3,600**	
Plant accumulated depreciation		36,750		
Plant at cost	76,200			
Prepaid expenses	1,515			
Purchases	324,795			
Purchases ledger control account		28,866		
Sales		566,244		
Sales expenses	25,818			
Sales ledger control account	53,700			
Suspense	3,343		**257**	**3,600**

Explanation:

Allowance for doubtful debts

This needs to be increased to 3% of the outstanding trade receivables (sales ledger control account) balance of £53,700. This comes to £1,611. The current allowance per the TB is £900, so an increase of £711 (£1,611 - £900) is required.

DR Allowance for doubtful debts – adjustments   £711
CR Allowance for doubtful debts   £711

Discounts received

Should have done	Did do	Correction
DR PLCA £257	DR PLCA £257	DR Suspense £257
CR Discounts received £257	CR Suspense £257	CR Discounts received £257

Office expenses

The balance in the TB needs to be increased from £34,830 to £38,430 – resulting in an increase of £3,600. As the balance was initially incorrectly listed in the TB as too small a debit balance (as expenses are a debit balance), it would have resulted in an imbalance and the need for a debit to suspense to make the TB balance. Therefore, the correcting entry is:

DR Office expenses   £3,600
CR Suspense   £3,600

(c) Journal

	Debit £	Credit £
Sales	566,244	
Profit and loss account		566,244

Narrative:

Transfer of sales for year ended 31 December 20X4 to the profit or loss account

(d)

	✓
Take no action because if the profit figure is amended, the client could lose out on the investment from his friend	
Take no action because the client is a longstanding one and the fee our firm earns from him is substantial	
Request a meeting with the client to discuss why the profit is higher than budget and prior year to try and ascertain whether it is due to genuine business transactions	✓
Email the client's friend to warn him not to invest because the profit might be overstated	

Explanation:

As an AAT accounting technician, you are bound by the AAT's Code of Professional Ethics and to comply with the fundamental principle of professional competence and due care, you need to respond appropriately to period end pressures and ensure that the accounts do not contain misleading or inaccurate information. Therefore, taking no action is not an option. Emailing the client's friend would be a breach of the fundamental principle of confidentiality so is not an acceptable option. The correct action to take here is to try and understand why the profit is higher than expected by having a direct discussion with the client because there might be genuine business reasons.

Task 5

(a)

Adjustment	Amount £	Debit ✓	Credit ✓
Adjustment for 1	100		✓
Adjustment for 2	76		✓
Adjustment for 4	9	✓	

Explanation:

Adjustments 3 and 5 only affect the total of the list of sales ledger accounts. Although adjustment 6 affects the individual sales ledger accounts of A Smith and J Smith, it will not affect the total of the list of balances.

(b)

	True ✓	False ✓
A bank reconciliation helps identify items missing from the cash book	✓	
A bank reconciliation forms part of the general ledger		✓
The balance on the bank statement is the balance that should be posted to the trial balance		✓
Items in the cash book but not in the bank statement may relate to timing differences	✓	

(c)

Ledger account	Ledger balances		Adjustments		Statement of profit or loss		Statement of financial position	
	Dr £	Cr £	Dr £	Cr £	Dr £	Cr £	Dr £	Cr £
Administration expenses	6,739			569	**6,170**			
Allowance for doubtful debts		1,347		203				**1,550**
Allowance for doubtful debts – adjustment			203		**203**			
Bank		5,290						**5,290**
Capital		9,460						**9,460**
Closing inventory			7,234	7,234		**7,234**	**7,234**	
Depreciation charges			7,800		**7,800**			
Machinery accumulated depreciation		62,400		7,800				**70,200**
Machinery at cost	115,000		750				**115,750**	
Marketing	7,365				**7,365**			
Opening inventory	9,933				**9,933**			
Purchases	34,289				**34,289**			
Purchases ledger control account		5,096						**5,096**
Sales		112,015		3,000		**115,015**		
Sales ledger control account	8,023						**8,023**	
Suspense		8,819	9,569	750				
VAT		6,300						**6,300**
Wages and salaries	29,378			6,000	**23,378**			
Profit/loss for the year					**33,111**			**33,111**
	210,727	210,727	25,556	25,556	**122,249**	**122,249**	**131,007**	**131,007**

BPP PRACTICE ASSESSMENT 2
ADVANCED BOOKKEEPING

Time allowed: 2 hours

PRACTICE ASSESSMENT 2

Advanced Bookkeeping (AVBK)
BPP practice assessment 2

Task 1

This task is about non-current assets.

You are working on the accounting records of a business known as Hagbourne.

Hagbourne is registered for VAT and its year end is 31 March.

The business has part exchanged an item of machinery used in its workshop.

The following is the relevant purchase invoice:

Office Supplies Ltd 28 High Street Cridley CR4 6AS	Invoice 198233	Date:	1 December 20X5
To:	Hagbourne & Co 67 Foggarty Street Cridley CR9 0TT		
Description	**Item number**	**Quantity**	**£**
Modular office workstation system	OFF783	1	6,500.00
Delivery and assembly charges		1	295.00
Printer paper		75 reams	200.00
Net			6,995.00
VAT @ 20%			1,399.00
Total			8,394.00

Part exchange with workstation GT551. Balance £6,048 settled by hire purchase agreement.

VAT can be reclaimed on the purchase of these items.

The following information relates to the workstation replaced:

Identification number	GT551
Date of purchase	1 July 20X3
Date of sale	1 December 20X5
Part exchange value	£1955.00 + VAT

- Hagbourne's policy is to recognise items of capital expenditure over £100 as non-current assets.

- Office equipment is depreciated over a useful life of five years on a straight line basis. A residual value of 25% of cost is assumed.

- Motor vehicles are depreciated at 40% per annum using the diminishing balance method.

- Depreciation is calculated on an annual basis and charged in equal instalments for each full month an asset is owned.

(a) **For the year ended 31 March 20X6, record the following in extract from the non-current assets register below:**

- **Any acquisitions of non-current assets**
- **Any disposals of non-current assets**
- **Depreciation**

Show your numerical answers to TWO decimal places.

Use the DD/MM/YY format for any dates.

Note. **Not every cell will require an entry, and not all cells will accept entries.**

Extract from Non-current assets register

Description	Acquisition date	Cost £	Depreciation charges £	Carrying amount £	Funding method	Disposal proceeds £	Disposal date
Motor vehicles							
Car CR04 YTR	01/04/X3	18,000.00			Cash		
Year end 31/03/X4			7,200.00	10,800.00			
Year end 31/03/X5			4,320.00	6,480.00			
Year end 31/03/X6							
Office equipment							
Desk OFF253	01/01/X4	10,000.00			Finance lease		
Year end 31/03/X4			375.00	9,625.00			
Year end 31/03/X5			1,500.00	8,125.00			
Year end 31/03/X6							
▼ (1)	▼ (2)				▼ (3)		
Year end 31/03/X6							
Workstation GT551	01/07/X3	5,210.00			Cash		
Year end 31/03/X4			586.00	4,624.00			
Year end 31/03/X4			782.00	3,842.00			
Year end 31/03/X4			▼ (4)	▼ (5)			▼ (6)

(1) Picklist for description:

Car CR04 YTR
Desk OFF253
Workstation GT551
Workstation OFF783

(2) Picklist for acquisition date:

01/07/X3
01/04/X5
01/12/X5
31/03/X6

(3) Picklist for funding method:

Cash
Finance lease
Hire purchase
Loan

(4) Picklist for depreciation charges:

0.00
391.00
586.00
782.00

(5) Picklist for carrying amount:

0.00
3,060.00
3,256.00
3,842.00

(6) Picklist for disposal date:

01/07/X3
01/04/X5
01/12/X5
31/03/X6

(b)   **Which ONE of the following best describes the residual value of a non-current asset?**

	✓
Expected market value at the estimated date of its disposal	
Difference between its carrying amount and the estimated scrap proceeds	
Original cost less its depreciation to date	
Carrying amount plus its accumulated depreciation at any given time	

Task 2

This task is about ledger accounting for non-current assets.

- You are working on the accounts of a business which is not registered for VAT. The business's year end is 31 December 20X6.

- An item of machinery was part exchanged for a newer model on 1 January 20X6.

- The original machinery cost £2,000 on 1 January 20X3.

- The business's depreciation policy for machinery is 20% using the diminishing balance method.

- A full year's depreciation is applied in the year of acquisition and none in the year of disposal.

- A part exchange allowance of £350 was given.

- £950 was paid from the bank to complete the purchase.

(a) **Complete the following tasks relating to the original machinery:**

(i) **Calculate the accumulated depreciation at 31 December 20X5.**

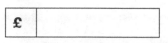

£	

(ii) **Complete the disposals account. Show clearly the balance to be carried down or transferred to the statement of profit or loss, as appropriate.**

Disposals

	£		£
▼		▼	
▼		▼	
▼		▼	

Picklist:

Bank
Machinery accumulated depreciation
Machinery at cost
Profit or loss account

(b) **Complete the tasks below:**

(i) **Calculate the purchase cost of the new machinery from the information above.**

£ [   ]

Before the part-exchange entries were posted, the balance on the machinery at cost account was £18,050.

The entries have now been correctly made.

(ii) **Complete the sentence:**

The machinery at cost account will have a final balance carried down

of £ [   ] when the ledger accounts are closed

for the year.

On 1 November 20X6, new fixtures and fittings were purchased. These were bought with a loan from the bank. You are given the following information:

- Purhase cost: £1,985
- Depreciation charged for the year ended 31/12/X6: £97

(c) **Complete the journal below.**

Account	Amount £	Debit ✓	Credit ✓
▼			
▼			
Narrative:			
Depreciation charged for the year ended 31 December 20X6 for fixtures and fittings purchased 1 November 20X6			

Picklist:

Depreciation charges
Bank
Fixture and fittings accumulated depreciation

Task 3

This task is about ledger accounting, including accruals and prepayments.

You are working on the final accounts of a business for the year ended 30 September 20X6. In this task, you can ignore VAT.

Business policy: accounting for accruals and prepayments

An entry is made into the income or expense account and an opposite entry into the relevant asset or liability account. In the following period, this entry is removed.

You are looking at commission income:

The cash book for the year shows receipts of commission income of £496. Commission of £63 is still due for September 20X6 at the year end.

(a) **Update the rental income account. Show clearly:**
- **The cash book figure**
- **The year end adjustment**
- **The transfer to the statement of profit or loss for the year**

Commission income

	£		£
Accrued income (reversal)	175	▼	
▼		▼	

Picklist:

Accrued expenses
Accrued income
Balance b/d
Balance c/d
Bank
Commission income
Prepaid expenses
Prepaid income
Profit or loss account
Sales
Sales ledger control account

(b) **Answer the following regarding the accrued income reversal of £175 in the commission income account above.**

(i) **How were the elements of the accounting equation affected by this transaction?**

Tick ONE box for each row.

	Increase ✓	Decrease ✓	No change ✓
Assets			
Liabilities			
Equity			

(ii) **Which ONE of the following dates should be entered for this transaction in the ledger account? Tick the appropriate box.**

	✓
1 October 20X5	
30 September 20X5	
30 September 20X6	

You are now looking at stationary expenses for the year.

There is an opening prepayment of £134 for the year ended 30 September 20X6.

The cash book for the year shows payments for stationery of £798. In September 20X6, £48 was paid for items delivered and used in October 20X6.

(c) **Complete the following statement:**

The stationery expenses account needs an adjustment for

☐ ▼ of £ ☐ dated ☐ ▼ .

Picklist:

Description:
Accrued expenses
Prepaid expenses
Amount:
£798
£48
Date:
30 September 20X6
1 October 20X7

(d) **Taking into account all the information you have, calculate the stationary expense for the year ended 30 September 20X6.**

£	

. . . .

Task 4

This task is about accounting adjustments.

You are working as an accounting technician for a sole trader business with a year end of 31 December. A trial balance has been drawn up and a suspense account opened with a credit balance of £1,826. You now need to make some corrections and adjustments for the year ended 31 December 20X6.

You may ignore VAT for this task.

Record the journal entries needed in the general ledger to deal with the items below.

You should:

- **Remove any incorrect entries where appropriate**
- **Post the correct entries**

Do NOT enter zeros into unused column cells.

Note. **You do NOT need to give narratives.**

(a) **No entries have been made for an irrecoverable debt of £672.**

Account	Debit £	Credit £
▼		
▼		

Picklist:

Allowance for doubtful debts
Allowance for doubtful debts – adjustments
Irrecoverable debts
Profit or loss account
Sales ledger control account
Suspense

(b) **Drawings of £850 have been made. The correct entry was made in the cash book but no other entries were made.**

Account		Debit £	Credit £
	▼		
	▼		

Picklist:

Drawings
Bank
Suspense account

(c) **Closing inventory for the year end 31 December 20X6 has not yet been recorded. Its value at cost is £9,350. Included in this figure are some items costing £345 that will be sold for £200.**

Account		Debit £	Credit £
	▼		
	▼		

Picklist:

Closing inventory – statement of financial position
Closing inventory – statement of profit or loss

(d) **Credit notes of £1,338 have been posted to the correct side of the purchases ledger control account, but have been made to the same side of the purchases returns account.**

Account		Debit £	Credit £
	▼		
	▼		

Picklist:

Purchase ledger control account
Sales ledger control account
Purchase returns
Suspense
Sales returns

Now that you have posted the journals, you are pleased to see that the suspense account is clear and the trial balance totals agree.

(e) **Complete the following sentence:**

▼

conclude that the balances included are now free from all errors.

▼

conclude that the inventory valuation as at 31 December 20X6 is included in the trial balance.

Picklist:

I can
I cannot

(f) **Which ONE of the these would be acceptable professional behaviour if actioned by you?**

	✓
A client's sales manager wants you to accrue for a bonus based on the current year sales. The bank statement shows that the bonus was paid in the next financial year.	
A client wants to improve his profit figure. She asks you to delay recording a liability until after the year end.	
One of the client's credit customers is going out of business. You feel this news can be disregarded as the effective date of the business closure is after the year end date.	
Your firm needs to meet its deadline for preparing the final accounts. Your supervisor tells you to save time by using net realisable value for all items in the inventory valuation.	

Task 5

This task is about period end routines, using accounting records and the extended trial balance.

You are preparing a purchase ledger control account reconciliation for a sole trader.

The balance showing on the purchases ledger control account is £7,092 and the total of the list of purchases ledger balances is £3,309.

The purchase ledger control account and the purchase ledger have been compared and the following items noted:

1. Total discounts received of £1,489 were only recorded in the discounts received account.

2. A purchases ledger column of £1,267 in the cash book – credit side was not posted to the purchases ledger control account.

3. A contra for £123 was recorded in the purchases ledger control account but not in the individual supplier account.

4. The total column in the purchases returns day book was overcast by £180.

5. A supplier account with a credit balance of £580 was omitted from the total.

6. A purchase invoice of £375 was posted to the supplier account as a credit note.

(a) **Use the following table to show the THREE adjustments you need to make to the purchases ledger control account.**

Adjustment		Amount £	Debit ✓	Credit ✓
	▼			
	▼			
	▼			

Picklist:

Adjustment 1
Adjustment 2
Adjustment 3
Adjustment 4
Adjustment 5
Adjustment 6

(b) **To reduce the allowance for doubtful debts we must:**

Choose ONE.

	✓
Credit the allowance for doubtful debts account	
Debit the irrecoverable debts account	
Credit the allowance for doubtful debts adjustment account	
Credit the sales ledger control account	
None of the above	

You are now working on the accounting records of a different business.

You have the following extended trial balance. The adjustments have already been correctly entered.

(c) **Extend the figures into the statement of profit or loss and statement of financial position columns.**

Do NOT enter zeros into unused column cells.

Make the columns balance by entering figures and a label in the correct places.

Extended trial balance

Ledger account	Ledger balances		Adjustments		Statement of profit or loss		Statement of financial position	
	Dr £	Cr £	Dr £	Cr £	Dr £	Cr £	Dr £	Cr £
Bank	5,246							
Capital		19,600						
Closing inventory			6,712	6,712				
Depreciation charges	4,298		4,000					
Discounts received		2,291		1,325				
Drawings	11,712		9,826					
Irrecoverable debts	627							
Motor expenses	2,065							
Motor vehicles accumulated depreciation		12,500		4,000				
Motor vehicles at cost	20,000							
Office expenses	7,219							
Opening inventory	4,820							
Purchases	91,289							
Purchases ledger control account		7,109	786					
Salaries	32,781		3,484					
Sales		156,782						
Sales ledger control account	11,092							
Suspense	12,771		1,325	14,096				
VAT		5,638						
▼								
	203,920	203,920	26,133	26,133				

Picklist:

Balance b/d
Balance c/d
Gross profit/loss for the year
Profit/loss for the year
Suspense

BPP PRACTICE ASSESSMENT 2
ADVANCED BOOKKEEPING

ANSWERS

Advanced Bookkeeping (AVBK)
BPP practice assessment 2

Task 1

(a) Non-current assets register

Description	Acquisition date	Cost £	Depreciation charges £	Carrying amount £	Funding method	Disposal proceeds £	Disposal date
Motor vehicles							
Car CR04 YTR	01/04/X3	18,000.00			Cash		
Year end 31/03/X4			7,200.00	10,800.00	Cash		
Year end 31/03/X5			4,320.00	6,480.00			
Year end 31/03/X6			**2,592.00**	**3,888.00**			
Office equipment							
Desk OFF253	01/01/X4	10,000.00			Finance lease		
Year end 31/03/X4			375.00	9,625.00			
Year end 31/03/X5			1,500.00	8,125.00			
Year end 31/03/X6			**1,500.00**	**6,625.00**			
Workstation OFF783	**01/12/X5**	**6,795.00**			**Hire purchase**		
Year end 31/03/X6			**340.00**	**6,455.00**			
Workstation GT551	01/07/X3	5,210.00			Cash		
Year end 31/03/X4			586.00	4,624.00			
Year end 31/03/X4			782.00	3,842.00			
Year end 31/03/X4			**586.00**	**0.00**		1,955.00	01/12/X3

Working:

Depreciation on car CR04 YTR = £6,480.00 × 40% = £2,592.00.

Depreciation on desk OFF253 = £10,000.00 × 1/5 × 75% (to remove residual value) = £1.500.00.

Cost of workstation OFF783: Purchase price £6,500.00 + directly attributable costs £295 = £6,795.00 (as the company is VAT registered, VAT is not included in the cost of the asset as it can be recovered from HMRC).

Note. The printer paper is revenue expenditure so is not capitalised.

Depreciation of workstation OFF783 = £6,795.00 × 1/5 × 75% × 4/12 = £340.00 (as depreciation is charged on a monthly pro-rata basis).

Depreciation of workstation GT551 to date of disposal = £5,210 × 1/5 × 75% × 9/12 = £586.00 (as depreciation is charged on a monthly pro-rata basis).

Carrying amount of workstation GT551: this is cleared to 0.00 as the workstation has been sold.

(b)

	✓
Expected market value at the estimated date of its disposal	✓
Difference between its carrying amount and the estimated scrap proceeds	
Original cost less its depreciation to date	
Carrying amount plus its accumulated depreciation at any given time	

Task 2

(a)

(i) £ | 976.00

Working:

	£
1 January 20X3: Cost	2,000
Depreciation (20% × 2,000)	(400)
31 December 20X3	1,600
Depreciation (20% × 1,600)	(320)
31 December 20X4	1,280
Depreciation (20% × 1,280)	(256)
31 December 20X5	1,024

Accumulated depreciation at disposal = £400 + £320 + £256 = £976

(ii) Disposals

	£		£
Machinery at cost	**2,000**	**Machinery accumulated depreciation**	**976**
		Machines at cost	**350**
		Profit or loss account	**674**
	2,000		**2,000**

(b)

(i) £ | 1,300.00

Working

Cost of new machinery = Part exchange value £350 + cash paid £950 = £1,300

(ii) The machinery at cost account will have a final balance carried down

of $£$ | 17,350 | when the ledger accounts are closed

for the year.

Working

Machines at cost

	£		£
Balance b/d	18,050	Disposals	2,000
Disposals	350		
Bank	950	Balance c/d	17,350
	19,350		19,350

(c)

Account	Amount £	Debit ✓	Credit ✓
Depreciation charges	97	✓	
Fixtures and fittings accumulated depreciation	97		✓
Narrative:			
Depreciation charged for the year ended 31 December 20X6 for fixtures and fittings purchased 1 November 20X6			

Task 3

(a) Commission income

	£		£
Accrued income (reversal)	175	**Bank**	496
Profit or loss account	384	**Accrued income**	63
	559		559

(b)

(i)

	Increase ✓	Decrease ✓	No change ✓
Assets			✓
Liabilities		✓	
Equity	✓		

(ii)

	✓
1 October 20X5	✓
30 September 20X5	
30 September 20X6	

(c)

| Prepaid expenses | of | £48 | dated | **30 September 20X6** | . |

(d) £ | 884

Working

Stationery

	£		£
Prepaid expenses (reversal)	134	**Prepaid expenses**	48
Bank	798	**Profit or loss account**	884
	932		932

Task 4

(a)

Account	Debit £	Credit £
Irrecoverable debts	672	
Sales ledge control account		672

(b)

Account	Debit £	Credit £
Drawings	850	
Suspense		850

Workings:

Should have done	Did do	Correction
DR Drawings £850	DR Suspense £850	DR Drawings £850
CR Bank £850	CR Bank £850	CR Suspense £850

(c)

Account	Debit £	Credit £
Closing inventory – statement of financial position	9,205	
Closing inventory – statement of profit or loss		9,205

Workings:

Inventory should be valued at the lower of cost (£345) and NRV (£200) so a write down of £145 is required (£345 – £200).

This reduces total closing inventory to £9,205 (£9,350 – £145).

(d)

Account	Debit £	Credit £
Suspense	2,676	
Purchase returns		2,676

Workings:

Should have done	Did do	Correction
DR PLCA £1,338	DR PLCA £1,338	DR Suspense £2,676
CR Purchases returns £1,338	DR Purchases returns £1,338	CR Purchase returns £2,676
	CR Suspense £2,676	

(e) **Complete the following sentence:**

| I cannot | conclude that the balances included are now free from all errors.

| I can | conclude that the inventory valuation as at 31 December 20X6 is included in the trial balance.

(f)

	✓
A client's sales manager wants you to accrue for a bonus based on the current year sales. The bank statement shows that the bonus was paid in the next financial year.	✓
A client wants to improve his profit figure. She asks you to delay recording a liability until after the year end.	
One of the client's credit customers is going out of business. You feel this news can be disregarded as the effective date of the business closure is after the year end date.	
Your firm needs to meet its deadline for preparing the final accounts. Your supervisor tells you to save time by using net realisable value for all items in the inventory valuation.	

Task 5

(a)

Adjustment	Amount £	Debit ✓	Credit ✓
Adjustment 1	1,489	✓	
Adjustment 2	1,267	✓	
Adjustment 4	180		✓

Explanation:

Discounts received reduce the amounts owed to our suppliers so are a debit balance. Cash payments again reduce what we owe our suppliers so are also a debit. Purchases returns are debited to the purchase ledger control account (PLCA) but here as the total was overcast, the PLCA has been debited by too much so a credit is required.

Adjustments 3, 5 and 6 require adjustments to the individual purchase ledger accounts rather than the PLCA.

(b)

	✓
Credit the allowance for doubtful debts account	
Debit the irrecoverable debts account	
Credit the allowance for doubtful debts adjustment account	✓
Credit the sales ledger control account	
None of the above	

(c) Extended trial balance

Ledger account	Ledger balances		Adjustments		Statement of profit or loss		Statement of financial position	
	Dr £	Cr £	Dr £	Cr £	Dr £	Cr £	Dr £	Cr £
Bank	5,246						5,246	
Capital		19,600						19,600
Closing inventory			6,712	6,712		6,712	6,712	
Depreciation charges	4,298		4,000		8,298			
Discounts received		2,291		1,325		3,616		
Drawings	11,712		9,826				21,538	
Irrecoverable debts	627				627			
Motor expenses	2,065				2,065			
Motor vehicles accumulated depreciation		12,500		4,000				16,500
Motor vehicles at cost	20,000						20,000	
Office expenses	7,219				7,219			
Opening inventory	4,820				4,820			
Purchases	91,289				91,289			
Purchases ledger control account		7,109	786					6,323
Salaries	32,781		3,484		36,265			
Sales		156,782				156,782		
Sales ledger control account	11,092						11,092	
Suspense	12,771		1,325	14,096				
VAT		5,638						5,638
Profit/loss for the year					16,527			16,527
	203,920	203,920	26,133	26,133	**167,110**	**167,110**	**64,588**	**64,588**

BPP PRACTICE ASSESSMENT 3
ADVANCED BOOKKEEPING

Time allowed: 2 hours

PRACTICE ASSESSMENT 3

Advanced Bookkeeping (AVBK)
BPP practice assessment 3

Task 1

This task is about recording information for non-current assets for a business known as Tilling Brothers. The business is registered for VAT and its year end is 31 December.

The following is a purchase invoice received by Tilling Brothers:

Prestatyn Machinery Ltd 82 Main Road Perwith PE5 9LA	Invoice 654723	Date:	1 May 20X3
To:	Tilling Brothers 56 Kerrick Street Perwith PE4 7PA		
Description	Item number	Quantity	£
Press machine	MAC637	1	8,640.00
Delivery and set-up charges		1	300.00
Maintenance pack (1 year)		1	184.00
Net			9,124.00
VAT @ 20%			1,824.80
Total			10,948.80

This invoice was paid in full out of the business's bank account.

The following information relates to the sale of a desktop computer:

Identification number	COM265
Date of sale	1 January 20X3
Selling price excluding VAT	£850.00

- Tilling Brothers' policy is to recognise items of capital expenditure over £200 as non-current assets.

- Machinery is depreciated at 25% using the straight line method with a full year's charge in the year of purchase and none in the year of sale.

- Computer equipment is depreciated at 30% per annum using the diminishing balance method.

For the year ended 31 December 20X3, record the following in the extract from the non-current assets register below:

- **Any acquisitions of non-current assets**
- **Any disposals of non-current assets**
- **Depreciation for the year**

Show your numerical answers to TWO decimal places.

Use the DD/MM/YY format for any dates.

Note. **Not every cell will required an entry, and not all cells will accept entries.**

Extract from the non-current assets register

Description	Acquisition date	Cost £	Depreciation charges £	Carrying amount £	Funding method	Disposal proceeds £	Disposal date
Computer equipment							
Desktop COM265	01/01/X1	5,600.00			Loan		
Year end 31/12/X1			1,680.00	3,920.00			
Year end 31/12/X2			1,176.00	2,744.00			
Year end 31/12/X3			▼(1)	▼(2)			▼(3)
Laptop COM399	01/01/X2	7,200.00			Finance lease		
Year end 31/12/X2			2,160.00	5,040.00			
Year end 31/12/X3							

Description	Acquisition date	Cost £	Depreciation charges £	Carrying amount £	Funding method	Disposal proceeds £	Disposal date
Machinery							
Machine MAC434	01/07/X1	12,940.00			Part exchange		
Year end 31/12/X1			3,235.00	9,705.00			
Year end 31/12/X2			3,235.00	6,470.00			
Year end 31/12/X3							
▼(4)	▼(5)				▼(6)		
Year end 31/12/X3							

(1) Picklist for depreciation charges:

0.00
823.20
1,400.00
1,680.00

(2) Picklist for carrying amount:

0.00
1,064.00
1,344.00
1,920.80

(3) Picklist for date:

31/12/X2
01/01/X3
01/05/X3
31/12/X3

(4) Picklist for description:

Desktop COM265
Laptop COM399
Machine MAC434
Machine MAC637

(5) Picklist for date:

31/12/X2
01/01/X3
01/05/X3
31/12/X3

(6) Picklist for funding method:

Cash
Finance lease
Hire purchase
Loan

....

Task 2

This task is about recording non-current asset information in the general ledger and other non-current asset matters.

- You are working on the accounts of a business which is not registered for VAT. The business's year end is 31 December 20X3.

- On 1 January 20X3 the business part exchanged an old machine for a new one with a list price of £3,500. A cheque for £1,000 was paid in full and final settlement and this amount has already been entered in the cash book.

- The old machine cost £4,000 on 1 January 20X1.

- The business's depreciation policy for machinery is 20% using the diminishing balance method.

(a) **Make entries to account for the disposal of the old machine and acquisition of the new one.**

On each account, show clearly the balance carried down or transferred to the statement of profit or loss.

Machines at cost

	£		£
Balance b/d	12,500	▼	
▼		▼	
▼		▼	

Machines accumulated depreciation

	£			£
▼		Balance b/d		4,500
▼			▼	

Disposals

	£			£
▼			▼	
▼			▼	
▼			▼	

Picklist:

Balance b/d
Balance c/d
Bank
Depreciation charges
Disposals
Machines accumulated depreciation
Machines at cost
Machines running expenses
Profit or loss account
Purchases
Purchases ledger control account
Sales
Sales ledger control account

(b) **When a non-current asset is acquired by paying a regular monthly amount over a set period and then having ownership transferred at the end of that period, the funding method is described as:**

		✓
Cash purchase		
Hire purchase		
Loan		
Part exchange		

Task 3

This task is about ledger accounting including accruals and prepayments and ethical principles.

(a) **Enter the figures given in the table below in the appropriate trial balance columns.**

Do not enter zeros in unused column cells.

Do not enter any figures as negatives.

Extract from trial balance as at 30 June 20X4

Account	Ledger balance £	Trial balance Debit £	Credit £
Administration costs	6,940		
Capital	7,300		
Sales returns	456		
Sundry income	1,050		

You are working on the final accounts of a business for the year ended 31 December 20X3. In this task, you can ignore VAT.

> **Business policy: accounting for accruals and prepayments**
>
> An entry is made into the income or expense account and an opposite entry into the relevant asset or liability account. In the following period, this entry is removed.

You are looking at rental income and heat and light.

Balances as at 1 January 20X3	£
Accrual of rental income	1,000
Accrual of heat and light	345

The cash book for the year shows receipts of rental income of £3,750. In January 20X4, the business received £500 in respect of rent for the month of December 20X3.

(b)   Prepare the rental income account for the year ended 31 December 20X3 and close it off by showing the transfer to the statement of profit or loss.

Rental income

Details	£	Details	£
Accrued income (reversal)	1,000	▼	
▼		▼	

The cash book for the year shows payments for heat and light of £4,670. In February 20X4, an invoice for £1,290 was received in respect of the quarter ended 31 January 20X4.

(c)   Prepare the heat and light account for the year ended 31 December 20X3 and close it off by showing the transfer to the statement of profit or loss.

Heat and light

	£		£
▼		Accrued expenses (reversal)	345
▼		▼	

Picklist for (b) and (c):

Accrued expenses
Accrued income
Balance b/d
Balance c/d
Bank
Heat and light
Prepaid expenses
Prepaid income
Profit or loss account
Purchases
Purchases ledger control account
Rental income
Sales
Sales ledger control account
Statement of financial position

You are preparing the year end accounts for another client. The client's bank calls you up and asks you to email them the draft accounts as they are trying to decide whether to extend the client's overdraft.

(d) **If you respond to the bank's request without permission from your client, which of the fundamental principles from the AAT's *Code of Professional Ethics* are you at risk of breaching?**

	✓
Integrity	
Objectivity	
Professional competence and due care	
Confidentiality	

Task 4

This task is about recording adjustments.

You are a trainee accounting technician reporting to a managing partner in an accounting practice.

You are working on the final accounts of a business with a year end of 31 December 20X3. A trial balance has been drawn up and a suspense account opened with a debit balance of £1,772. You now need to make some corrections and adjustments for the year ended 31 December 20X3.

You may ignore VAT in this task.

(a) **Record the adjustments needed on the extract from the extended trial balance to deal with the items below.**

You will not need to enter adjustments on every line. Do NOT enter zeros into unused cells.

(i) An allowance for doubtful debts of £2,420 is required at the year end.

(ii) A total column of £1,560 in the purchases returns day book was credited to the purchases ledger control account. All the other entries were made correctly.

(iii) Closing inventory for the year end 31 December 20X3 has not yet been recorded. Its value at cost is £12,860. Included in this figure are some items costing £1,250 that will be sold for £1,140.

(iv) A contra for £674 was debited to both the sales ledger control account and the purchases ledger control account.

Extract from extended trial balance

| | Ledger balances | | Adjustments | |
	Debit £	Credit £	Debit £	Credit £
Allowance for doubtful debts		2,563		
Allowance for doubtful debts – adjustments				
Bank overdraft		265		
Closing inventory – statement of financial position				
Closing inventory – statement of profit or loss				
Irrecoverable debts				
Purchases	567,239			
Purchases ledger control account		81,272		
Purchases returns		8,922		
Sales		926,573		
Sales ledger control account	109,282			
Sales returns	4,982			
Suspense	1,772			

The ledgers are ready to be closed off for the year ended 31 December 20X3.

(b) **Show the correct entries to close off the sales returns account and insert an appropriate narrative.**

Account		Debit ✓	Credit ✓
	▼		
	▼		

Narrative:

	▼

Picklist for account:

Allowance for doubtful debts
Allowance for doubtful debts – adjustments
Bank overdraft
Closing inventory – statement of financial position
Closing inventory – statement of profit or loss
Irrecoverable debts
Profit or loss account
Purchases ledger control account
Purchases returns
Sales
Sales ledger control account
Sales returns
Statement of financial position
Suspense

Picklist for narrative:

Closure of general ledger for the year ended 31 December 20X3

Closure of sales returns account to the suspense account

Transfer of sales returns for the year ended 31 December 20X3 to the profit or loss account

Transfer of sales returns for the year ended 31 December 20X3 to the statement of financial position

You are now in the process of finalising the figures for the draft accounts. Your manager is concerned because there are no accrued expenses at 31 December 20X3 whereas at 31 December 20X2, accrued expenses amounted to £7,800. You are aware that the client is looking to retire and that a potential buyer has made a generous offer for the business.

(c) **Which of the following statements are appropriate in light of the above situation?**

Choose TWO.

	✓
The client may have deliberately omitted accrued expenses to maximise the offer from the potential buyer	
It is your duty as the client's accountant to maximise the sales price of his business	
Your manager should request a meeting with the client to discuss why there are no accrued expenses in the current year	
You should report the possible missing accrued expenses to the potential buyer of the business	

Task 5

This task is about period end routines and the extended trial balance.

You are preparing the bank reconciliation for a sole trader.

The balance showing on the bank statement is a debit of £800 and the balance in the cash book is a credit of £374.

The bank statement has been compared to the cash book and the following points noted.

1. Bank charges of £121 were not entered in the cash book.

2. A cheque received from a customer for £280 has been recorded in the cash book but it has been dishonoured and this has not yet been entered in the records.

3. A cheque for £765 to a supplier has not yet been presented for payment at the bank.

4. A direct debit of £650 to the local council appears only on the bank statement.

5. Cash sales receipts of £90 have been entered into the cash book but are not yet banked.

6. The bank has deducted a payment of £50 in error.

BPP
LEARNING MEDIA

(a) **Use the following table to show the THREE adjustments you need to make to the cash book.**

Adjustment	Amount £	Debit ✓	Credit ✓
▼			
▼			
▼			

Picklist:

Adjustment 1
Adjustment 2
Adjustment 3
Adjustment 4
Adjustment 5
Adjustment 6

(b) **Which of the following statements about the sales ledger control account (SLCA) is TRUE?**

Choose ONE.

	✓
It is a record of amounts owed from individual customers	
Totals from the sales day book and cash book – debit side are posted to the sales ledger control account	
Sales returns will be recorded on the debit side of the SLCA	
Discounts received will be recorded on the credit side of the SLCA	

You are now working on the accounting records of a different business.

You have the following extended trial balance. The adjustments have already been correctly entered.

(c) **Extend the figures into the statement of profit or loss and statement of financial position columns.**

Do NOT enter zeros into unused column cells.

Complete the extended trial balance by entering figures and a label in the correct places.

Extended trial balance

Ledger account	Ledger balances		Adjustments		Statement of profit or loss		Statement of financial position	
	Dr £	Cr £	Dr £	Cr £	Dr £	Cr £	Dr £	Cr £
Accrued income			3,825					
Bank	7,281							
Capital		152,600						
Closing inventory			15,729	15,729				
Commission income		18,272		3,825				
Depreciation charges			27,600					
Drawings	40,000							
General expenses	67,298			1,427				
Motor vehicles accumulated depreciation		88,900		27,600				
Motor vehicles at cost	170,000		4,300					
Opening inventory	17,268							
Prepaid expenses			1,427					
Purchases	98,245			726				
Purchases ledger control account		14,681	710					
Salaries	69,256							
Sales		201,675						
Sales ledger control account	17,504			710				
Suspense	3,574		726	4,300				
VAT		14,298						
▼								
	490,426	490,426	54,317	54,317				

Picklist:

Balance b/d
Balance c/d
Gross profit/loss for the year
Profit/loss for the year
Suspense

BPP PRACTICE ASSESSMENT 3 ADVANCED BOOKKEEPING

ANSWERS

Advanced Bookkeeping (AVBK)
BPP practice assessment 3

Task 1

Non-current assets register

Description	Acquisition date	Cost £	Depreciation charges £	Carrying amount £	Funding method	Disposal proceeds £	Disposal date
Computer equipment							
Desktop COM265	01/01/X1	5,600.00			Loan		
Year end 31/12/X1			1,680.00	3,920.00			
Year end 31/12/X2			1,176.00	2,744.00			
Year end 31/12/X3			**0.00**	**0.00**		**850.00**	**01/01/X3**
Laptop COM399	01/01/X2	7,200.00			Finance lease		
Year end 31/12/X2			2,160.00	5,040.00			
Year end 31/12/X3			**1,512.00**	**3,528.00**			
Machinery							
Machine MAC434	01/07/X1	12,940.00			Part exchange		
Year end 31/12/X1			3,235.00	9,705.00			
Year end 31/12/X2			3,235.00	6,470.00			
Year end 31/12/X3			**3,235.00**	**3,235.00**			
Machine MAC637	**01/05/X3**	**8,940.00**			**Cash**		
Year end 31/12/X3			**2,235.00**	**6,705.00**			

Workings:

Desktop COM265

The accounting policy is no depreciation in the year of disposal hence the depreciation charge of 0.00. On disposal, the carrying amount is cleared to 0.00 and the disposal proceeds and date are recorded. The sales price is recorded net of VAT because the VAT must be passed on to HMRC.

Laptop COM399

Depreciation = 30% × £5,040.00 carrying amount = £1,512.00

Machine MAC434

Depreciation = 25% × £12,940.00 cost = £3,235.00

Machine MAC637

This is capitalised at its purchase price of £8,640.00 plus the directly attributable costs of £300.00 coming to a total of £8,940.00. The maintenance pack is revenue expenditure and as such should be expensed to profit or loss rather than capitalised. The asset is recorded net of VAT because as the business is VAT registered, it can reclaim the VAT from HMRC.

Depreciation = 25% × £8,940.00 = £2,235.00 as a full year is charged in the year of acquisition.

Task 2

(a) Machines at cost

	£		£
Balance b/d	12,500	**Disposals**	**4,000**
Bank	**1,000**	**Balance c/d**	**12,000**
Disposals	**2,500**		
	16,000		**16,000**

Machines accumulated depreciation

	£		£
Disposals	**1,440**	Balance b/d	4,500
Balance c/d	**3,060**		
	4,500		**4,500**

Disposals

	£		£
Machines at cost	**4,000**	**Machines at cost**	**2,500**
		Machines accumulated depreciation	**1,440**
		Profit or loss account	**60**
	4,000		**4,000**

Workings:

	£
1 January 20X1: Cost	4,000
Depreciation (20% × 4,000)	(800)
31 December 20X1	3,200
Depreciation (20% × 3,200)	(640)
31 December 20X2	2,560

Accumulated depreciation at disposal = £800 + £640 = £1,440

Part exchange allowance = List price £3,500 – Cash paid £1,000 = £2,500

(b)

	✓
Cash purchase	
Hire purchase	✓
Loan	
Part exchange	

Task 3

(a) Extract from trial balance as at 30 June 20X4

Account	Ledger balance	Trial balance Debit	Trial balance Credit
	£	Debit £	Credit £
Administration costs	6,940	**6,940**	
Capital	7,300		**7,300**
Sales returns	456	**456**	
Sundry income	1,050		**1,050**

(b) Rental income

	£		£
Accrued income (reversal)	1,000	**Bank**	**3,750**
Profit or loss account	**3,250**	**Accrued income**	**500**
	4,250		**4,250**

(c) Heat and light

	£		£
Bank	**4,670**	Accrued expenses (reversal)	345
Accrued expenses (2/3 × £1,290)	**860**	**Profit or loss account**	**5,185**
	5,530		**5,530**

(d)

	✓
Integrity	
Objectivity	
Professional competence and due care	
Confidentiality	✓

Task 4

(a) Extract from extended trial balance

	Ledger balances		Adjustments	
	Debit £	Credit £	Debit £	Credit £
Allowance for doubtful debts		2,563	**143**	
Allowance for doubtful debts – adjustments				**143**
Bank overdraft		265		
Closing inventory – statement of financial position			**12,750**	
Closing inventory – statement of profit or loss				**12,750**
Irrecoverable debts				
Purchases	567,239			
Purchases ledger control account		81,272	**3,120**	
Purchases returns		8,922		
Sales		926,573		
Sales ledger control account	109,282			**1,348**
Sales returns	4,982			
Suspense	1,772		**1,348**	**3,120**

Workings:

Allowance for doubtful debts

The balance per the TB is £2,563. Therefore, a reduction of £143 (£2,563 – £2,420) is required. The necessary double entry is:

DR Allowance for doubtful debts   £143
CR Allowance for doubtful debts – adjustments   £143

Purchases returns

Should have done		Did do		Correction	
DR PLCA	£1,560	DR Suspense	£3,120	DR PLCA	£3,120
CR Purchases returns	£1,560	CR PLCA	£1,560	CR Suspense	£3,120
		CR Purchases returns	£1,560		

Closing inventory

Inventory should be valued the lower of cost (£1,250) and net realisable value (£1,140). Therefore, a write down of £110 (£1,250 – £1,140) is required. This brings closing inventory in total down to £12,750 (£12,860 – £110). The double entry to post this is:

DR Closing inventory – statement of financial position   £12,750
CR Closing inventory – statement of profit or loss   £12,750

Contra

Should have done		Did do		Correction	
DR PLCA	£674	DR PLCA	£674	DR Suspense	£1,348
CR SLCA	£674	DR SLCA	£674	CR SLCA	£1,348
		CR Suspense	£1,348		

(b)

Account	Debit ✓	Credit ✓
Profit or loss account	✓	
Sales returns		✓

Narrative:

Transfer of sales returns for year ended 31 December 20X3 to the profit or loss account

(c)

	✓
The client may have deliberately omitted accrued expenses to maximise the offer from the potential buyer	✓
It is your duty as the client's accountant to maximise the sales price of his business	
Your manager should request a meeting with the client to discuss why there are no accrued expenses in the current year	✓
You should report the possible missing accrued expenses to the potential buyer of the business	

Explanation:

As a trainee accounting technician, you should be acting in the business's best interests rather than the client's personal interests. If you were to disclose the possible missing accrued expenses to the potential buyer, you would be breaching the fundamental principle of confidentiality from the AAT's *Code of Professional Ethics*. It is possible here that the client has deliberately omitted the accrued expenses in order to overstate the profit and maximise the selling price of the business. Therefore, as this is a delicate situation, it would be appropriate for your manager to arrange a meeting to discuss the matter with the client.

Task 5

(a)

Adjustment	Amount £	Debit ✓	Credit ✓
Adjustment 1	121		✓
Adjustment 2	280		✓
Adjustment 4	650		✓

Explanation:

Bank charges missing from the cash book will increase the overdraft with a credit. A dishonoured cheque from a customer needs to be removed from the cash book with a credit. A direct debit is a payment so results in a credit to the cash book.

Adjustments 3, 5 and 6 only affect the balance per the bank statement. Adjustment 3 will result increase the overdraft in the bank as it's a missing payment. Adjustment 5 relates to missing receipts so will reduce the overdraft. Adjustment 6 requires the reversal of a payment made in error so again will reduce the overdraft.

(b)

	✓
It is a record of amounts owed from individual customers	
Totals from the sales day book and cash book – debit side are posted to the sales ledger control account	✓
Sales returns will be recorded on the debit side of the SLCA	
Discounts received will be recorded on the credit side of the SLCA	

Explanation:

The amounts for individual customers are recorded in the sales ledger memorandum accounts. Sales returns will be recorded on the credit side of the SLCA rather than the debit side. Discounts are received from suppliers not customers so should be recorded in the PLCA not the SLCA.

Individual invoices and receipts in the day books are posted to the sales ledger memorandum accounts. Totals from the day books are posted to the sales ledger control account.

(c) Extended trial balance

Ledger account	Ledger balances		Adjustments		Statement of profit or loss		Statement of financial position	
	Dr £	Cr £	Dr £	Cr £	Dr £	Cr £	Dr £	Cr £
Accrued income			3,825				3,825	
Bank	7,281						7,281	
Capital		152,600						152,600
Closing inventory			15,729	15,729		15,729	15,729	
Commission income		18,272		3,825		22,097		
Depreciation charges			27,600		27,600			
Drawings	40,000						40,000	
General expenses	67,298			1,427	65,871			
Motor vehicles accumulated depreciation		88,900		27,600				116,500
Motor vehicles at cost	170,000		4,300				174,300	
Opening inventory	17,268				17,268			
Prepaid expenses			1,427				1,427	
Purchases	98,245			726	97,519			
Purchases ledger control account		14,681	710					13,971
Salaries	69,256				69,256			
Sales		201,675				201,675		
Sales ledger control account	17,504			710			16,794	
Suspense	3,574		726	4,300				
VAT		14,298						14,298
Profit/loss for the year						38,013	38,013	
	490,426	490,426	54,317	54,317	**277,514**	**277,514**	**297,369**	**297,369**

BPP PRACTICE ASSESSMENT 4
ADVANCED BOOKKEEPING

Time allowed: 2 hours

PRACTICE ASSESSMENT 4

Advanced Bookkeeping (AVBK)
BPP practice assessment 4

Task 1

This task is about non-current assets.

You are working on the accounting records of a business known as Markham.

You may ignore VAT in this task.

The following is an extract from a purchase invoice received by Markham:

Office Solutions Ltd Unit 7 Tenton Industrial Estate TN14 5YJ	Invoice 9746	Date:	1 March 20X3
To:	Markham 14 The Green Tenton TN3 4ZX		
Description	Item number	Quantity	£
Corner office suite	OF477	1	1,950.00
Delivery and assembly charges	For OF477	1	150.00
Printer ink cartridges		20	160.00
Desk lamp	DL234		110.00
Net total			2,370.00

The acquisition has been made under a finance lease agreement.

The following information relates to the sale of an item of factory machinery:

Identification number	MN864
Date of sale	1 July 20X2
Selling price	£1,050.00

- Markham's policy is to recognise items of capital expenditure over £500 as non-current assets.

- Office equipment and furniture is depreciated at 20% per annum using the straight line method. There are no residual values.

327

- Factory machinery is depreciated at 25% per annum using the diminishing balance method.

- Depreciation is calculated on an annual basis and charged in equal instalments for each full month the asset is owned in the year.

(a) **For the year ended 30 June 20X3, record the following in the extract from the non-current assets register below:**

- **Any acquisitions of non-current assets**
- **Any disposals of non-current assets**
- **Depreciation for the year ended 30 June 20X3**

Extract from non-current assets register

Description	Acquisition date	Cost £	Depreciation charges £	Carrying amount £	Funding method	Disposal proceeds £	Disposal date
Factory machinery							
Machine MN864	01/07/X0	15,600.00			Cash		
Year end 30/06/X1			3,900.00	11,700.00			
Year end 30/06/X2			2,925.00	8,775.00			
Year end 30/06/X3			▼(1)	▼(2)			▼(3)
Machine MN982	01/07/X1	9,400.00			Loan		
Year end 30/06/X2			2,350.00	7,050.00			
Year end 30/06/X3							

328

Description	Acquisition date	Cost £	Depreciation charges £	Carrying amount £	Funding method	Disposal proceeds £	Disposal date
Office equipment							
Server OF025	01/04/X1	12,940.00			Part exchange		
Year end 30/06/X1			647.00	12,293.00			
Year end 30/06/X2			2,588.00	9,705.00			
Year end 30/06/X3							
▼(4)	▼(5)				▼(6)		
Year end 30/06/X3							

(1) Picklist for depreciation charge for machine MN864:

0.00
2,193.75
3,120.00
3,900.00

(2) Picklist for carrying amount for machine MN864:

0.00
4,875.00
5,655.00
6,581.25

(3) Picklist for date:

30/06/X2
01/07/X2
01/03/X3
30/06/X3

(4) Picklist for description:

Corner office suite OF477
Desk lamp DL234
Machine MN864
Machine MN982
Server OF025

(5) Picklist for date:

30/06/X2
01/07/X2
01/03/X3
30/06/X3

(6) Picklist for funding method:

Cash
Finance lease
Hire purchase
Part exchange

(b) **Complete the following sentences.**

The non-current assets register is [▼] .

Checking physical non-current assets to entries in the non-current asset

register will enable the business to [▼] .

Picklist 1:

part of the general ledger
a list of the business's intangible non-current assets
part of the business's internal control systems
recorded in the statement of financial position

Picklist 2:

ensure that depreciation has been calculated correctly

verify that the double entries in the general ledger are correct

identify non-current assets not in the register or in the register but that do not exist

ensure all revenue expenditure has been correctly recorded

Task 2

This task is about recording non-current asset information in the general ledger and other non-current asset matters.

- You are working on the accounts of a business that is registered for VAT. The business's year end is 31 December 20X5.

- On 1 September 20X5 the business bought a new motor vehicle costing £15,000 excluding VAT. This was paid from the bank.

- The vehicle's residual value is expected to be £3,000 excluding VAT.

- The business's depreciation policy for motor vehicles is 20% per annum on a straight line basis. A full year's depreciation is charged in the year of acquisition and none in the year of disposal.

- Depreciation has already been entered into the accounts for the business's existing motor vehicles.

(a) **Calculate the depreciation charge for the year on the new motor vehicle.**

£	

Make entries to account for:

- **The purchase of the new motor vehicle**
- **The depreciation on the new motor vehicle**

On each account, show clearly the balance carried down or transferred to the statement of profit or loss.

Motor vehicles at cost

	£			£
Balance b/d	35,000		▾	
	▾			▾	

Motor vehicles accumulated depreciation

	▾	£			£
	▾		Balance b/d	9,400
	▾			▾	

Depreciation charges

	£			£
Balance b/d	6,300		▾	
	▾			▾	

(b) **When non-current assets are depreciated using the straight line method, an equal amount is charged for each year of the asset's life.**

	✓
True	
False	

A business sells a motor vehicle and receives a part exchange allowance of £5,000 on a replacement vehicle costing £20,000.

(c) **Ignoring VAT, show the journal entry required to record the part exchange allowance.**

Account		Amount £	Debit ✓	Credit ✓
	▾			
	▾			

Profit or loss account
Purchases
Purchases ledger control account
Sales
Sales ledger control account
Empty

Task 3

This task is about ledger accounting, including accruals and prepayments, and applying ethical principles.

(a) **Enter the figures given in the table below in the appropriate trial balance columns.**

Do not enter zeros in unused column cells.

Do not enter any figures as negatives.

Extract from trial balance as at 30 June 20X4

Account	Ledger balance	Trial balance	
		Debit	Credit
	£	£	£
Purchases returns	8,400		
Discounts allowed	1,556		
Discounts received	2,027		
Office costs	2,950		

You are working on the final accounts of a business for the year ended 31 December 20X3. In this task, you can ignore VAT.

Business policy: accounting for accruals and prepayments

An entry is made into the income or expense account and an opposite entry into the relevant asset or liability account. In the following period, this entry is removed.

You are looking at interest income for the year.

- As at 31 December 20X2, there was an accrual for interest income of £750.

- The cash book for the year shows receipts of interest income income of £4,850.

- On 31 January 20X4, the business receives £900 of interest income for the quarter ended 31 January 20X4.

(b) **Prepare the interest income account for the year ended 31 December 20X3 and close it off by showing the transfer to the statement of profit or loss.**

Interest income

	£			£
Accrued income (reversal)	750		▼	
	▼		▼	

Picklist:

Accrued expenses
Accrued income
Balance b/d
Balance c/d
Bank
Prepaid expenses
Prepaid income
Profit or loss account
Purchases
Purchases ledger control account
Rental income
Sales
Sales ledger control account
Selling expenses
Statement of financial position

You are now looking at selling expenses for the year.

Selling expenses of £1,445 were accrued on 31 December 20X2.

(c) **Complete the following statements:**

The reversal of this accrual is dated [▼] .

The reversal is on the [▼] side of the selling expenses account.

Picklist:

31 December 20X2
31 December 20X3
1 January 20X2
1 January 20X3

credit
debit

- The cash book for the year shows payments for selling expenses of £5,770.

- In April 20X4, an invoice of £3,180 was paid for selling expenses for the six months ended 31 March 20X4.

(d) Taking into account all the information you have, calculate the selling expenses for the year ended 31 December 20X3.

£	

This is your first year of preparing the accounts for this client. The owner of the business asks you not to record the accrued interest income in the accounts for the year ended 31 December 20X3 as she is trying to reduce her tax liability. She offers you a free week in her holiday cottage if you do as she asks. You are very tempted as you have not had a holiday for a long time.

(e) Which threat to the fundamental principles of the AAT's *Code of Professional Ethics* is most significant here?

	✓
Self-interest	
Self-review	
Intimidation	
Familiarity	

Task 4

This task is about preparing accounting adjustments.

You are the accountant preparing the final accounts of a business with a year end of 31 December 20X5. A trial balance has been drawn up and a suspense account opened with a credit balance of £2,098. You now need to make some corrections and adjustments for the year ended 31 December 20X5.

(a) Record the adjustments needed on the extract from the extended trial balance to deal with the items below.

You will not need to enter adjustments on every line. Do NOT enter zeros into unused cells.

(i)   An allowance for doubtful debts of £3,200 is required at the year end.

(ii) A total column of £1,885 in the sales returns day book was debited to the sales ledger control account. All the other entries were made correctly.

(iii)   Closing inventory for the year end 31 December 20X5 has not yet been recorded. Its value at cost is £13,185. Included in this figure are some items costing £1,575 that will be sold for £1,400.

(iv)   A discount received for £836 was credited to both the purchases ledger control account and the discounts received account.

Extract from extended trial balance

	Ledger balances		Adjustments	
	Debit £	Credit £	Debit £	Credit £
Allowance for doubtful debts – adjustments				
Allowance for doubtful debts		2,888		
Bank overdraft		590		
Closing inventory – statement of financial position				
Closing inventory – statement of profit or loss				
Discounts received		2,300		
Irrecoverable debts	790			
Purchases	675,564			
Purchases returns		9,247		
Purchases ledger control account		92,597		
Sales		843,898		
Sales returns	5,307			
Sales ledger control account	98,607			
Suspense		2,098		

The ledgers are ready to be closed off for the year ended 31 December 20X5.

(b) **Show the correct entries to close off the irrecoverable debts account and insert an appropriate narrative.**

Account		Debit £	Credit £
	▼		
	▼		

Narrative:

	▼

Picklist for account:

Allowance for doubtful debts
Allowance for doubtful debts – adjustments
Bank overdraft
Closing inventory – statement of financial position
Closing inventory – statement of profit or loss
Discounts received
Irrecoverable debts
Profit or loss account
Purchases
Purchases ledger control account
Purchases returns
Sales
Sales ledger control account
Sales returns
Statement of financial position
Suspense

Picklist for narrative:

Carrying down the balance on the irrecoverable debts account

Closure of general ledger for the year ended 31 December 20X5

Transfer of irrecoverable debts for the year ended 31 December 20X5 to the profit or loss account

Transfer of irrecoverable debts for the year ended 31 December 20X5 to the statement of financial position

You are now in the process of preparing the final accounts from the trial balance. Normally you have three days to do this but as you are about to go on holiday, you need to complete work in one day.

(c) **What type of period end pressure are you most exposed to in this situation?**

Choose ONE.

	✓
Pressure from authority	
Pressure to report favourable results	
Time pressure	
Pressure from stakeholders	

Task 5

This task is about period end routines, using accounting records and the extended trial balance.

You are preparing a bank reconciliation for a sole trader.

The balance showing on the bank statement is a credit of £3,050 and the balance in the cash book is a debit of £3,554.

The bank statement has been compared with the cash book and the following differences identified:

1. A standing order of £269 has not been entered in the cash book.

2. A cheque received from a customer for £500 has been recorded in the cash book but the bank has informed us that the cheque was subsequently dishonoured.

3. A cheque for £940 to a supplier has not yet been presented for payment at the bank.

4. A direct debit of £485 to an utility company appears only on the bank statement.

5. Cash sales of £330 have been recorded in the cash book but not yet banked.

6. The bank has credited interest of £140 to our account in error.

(a) Use the following table to show the THREE adjustments you need to make to the cash book. Enter only ONE figure for each line. Do not enter zeros in unused cells.

Adjustment	Amount £	Debit ✓	Credit ✓
▼			
▼			
▼			

Picklist:

Adjustment 1
Adjustment 2
Adjustment 3
Adjustment 4
Adjustment 5
Adjustment 6

(b) A debit balance on the cash book means that the business has funds available.

	✓
True	
False	

This task is about completing an extended trial balance and showing your accounting knowledge.

You have the following extended trial balance. The adjustments have already been correctly entered.

(c) Extend the figures into the statement of profit or loss and statement of financial position columns.

Do NOT enter zeros into unused column cells.

Complete the extended trial balance by entering figures and a label in the correct places.

Extended trial balance

Ledger account	Ledger balances Dr £	Cr £	Adjustments Dr £	Cr £	Statement of profit or loss Dr £	Cr £	Statement of financial position Dr £	Cr £
Accrued income			249					
Bank	7,281							
Capital		150,000						
Closing inventory			9,433	9,433				
Commission income		7,893		249				
Depreciation charges			14,600					
Drawings	10,000							
General expenses	42,932			765				
Machinery at cost	200,000		3,400					
Machinery accumulated depreciation		125,000		14,600				
Opening inventory	13,254							
Prepaid expenses			765					
Purchases	128,994			2,458				
Purchases ledger control account		17,493	399					
Salaries	75,606							
Sales		195,433						
Sales ledger control account	25,775			399				
Suspense	942		2,458	3,400				
VAT		8,965						
▼								
	504,784	504,784	31,304	31,304				

Picklist:

Gross loss for the year
Gross profit for the year
Profit for the year
Loss for the year

BPP PRACTICE ASSESSMENT 4
ADVANCED BOOKKEEPING

ANSWERS

Advanced Bookkeeping (AVBK)
BPP practice assessment 4

Task 1

(a)

Non-current assets register

Description	Acquisition date	Cost £	Depreciation charges £	Carrying amount £	Funding method	Disposal proceeds £	Disposal date
Factory machinery							
Machine MN864	01/07/X0	15,600.00			Cash		
Year end 30/06/X1			3,900.00	11,700.00			
Year end 30/06/X2			2,925.00	8,775.00			
Year end 30/06/X3			**0.00**	**0.00**		**1,050.00**	**01/07/X2**
Machine MN982	01/07/X1	9,400.00			Loan		
Year end 30/06/X2			2,350.00	7,050.00			
Year end 30/06/X3			**1,762.50**	**5,287.50**			
Office equipment							
Server OF025	01/04/X1	12,940.00			Part exchange		
Year end 30/06/X1			647.00	12,293.00			
Year end 30/06/X2			2,588.00	9,705.00			
Year end 30/06/X3			**2,588.00**	**7,117.00**			
Corner office suite OF477	**01/03/X3**	**2,100.00**			**Finance lease**		
Year end 30/06/X3			**140.00**	**1,960.00**			

Workings:

Machine MN864

This machine was sold on the first day of the year so there is no depreciation charge. The carrying amount is reduced to 0.00 on disposal. Then the sales proceeds and disposal date must be recorded.

Machine MN982

Depreciation = 25% × £7,050.00 carrying amount = £1,762.50

Office equipment OF477

Depreciation = 20% × £12,940.00 cost = £2,588.00

Office equipment OF477

The amount capitalised is the purchase price (which is over the capitalisation threshold of £500) of the corner off suite of £1,950.00 plus directly attributable costs of £150.00, coming to a total of £2,100.00. The printer ink cartridges are revenue expenditure so should be expensed to profit or loss. The desk lamp is not capitalised as it is below the capitalisation threshold of £500.

Depreciation = 20% × £2,100.00 × 4/12 (as asset was owned for 4 months of year) = £140.00.

(b) The non-current assets register is | part of the business's internal control systems | .

Checking physical non-current assets to entries in the non-current asset register will enable the business to

| identify non-current assets not in the register or in the register that the do not exist |

.

Explanation:

The other answers are incorrect because:

The non-current assets register is a list of tangible non-current assets (not intangible) and forms part of the internal controls system rather than the general ledger. As it is not part of the general ledger, it is not posted directly into the statement of financial position.

A physical verification of assets in the register will not verify whether depreciation has been calculated nor the correctness of the double entries (as it is not part of the general ledger) nor will it help with revenue expenditure as this is not capitalised as a non-current asset.

Task 2

(a)

£	2,400

Working:

(£15,000 – £3,000) × 20% = £2,400

Motor vehicles at cost

	£		£
Balance b/d	35,000	**Balance c/d**	**50,000**
Bank	**15,000**		
	50,000		**50,000**

Motor vehicles accumulated depreciation

	£		£
Balance c/d	**11,800**	Balance b/d	9,400
		Depreciation charges	**2,400**
	11,800		**11,800**

Depreciation charges

	£		£
Balance b/d	6,300	**Profit or loss account**	**8,700**
Motor vehicles accumulated depreciation	**2,400**		
	8,700		**8,700**

(b)

	✓
True	✓
False	

(c)

Account	Amount £	Debit ✓	Credit ✓
Motor vehicles at cost	5,000	✓	
Disposals	5,000		✓

Task 3

(a) Extract from the trial balance as at 30 June 20X4

Account	Ledger balance £	Trial balance Debit £	Trial balance Credit £
Purchases returns	8,400		**8,400**
Discounts allowed	1,556	**1,556**	
Discounts received	2,027		**2,027**
Office costs	2,950	**2,950**	

(b) Interest income

	£		£
Accrued income (reversal)	750	**Bank**	**4,850**
Profit or loss account	**4,700**	**Accrued income (2/3 × £900)**	**600**
	5,450		**5,450**

(c) The reversal of this accrual is dated [**1 January**] .

The reversal is on the [**credit**] side of the selling expenses account.

(d)

£	5,915

Working:

Cash paid £5,770 – Accrual from prior year £1,445 + Accrual from current year £1,590 (3/6 × £3,180) = £5,915

Alternatively you could have prepared a ledger account:

Selling expenses

	£		£
Bank	5,770	Accrued expenses (reversal)	1,445
Accrued expenses (3/6 × £3,180)	1,590	Profit or loss account	5,915
	7,360		7,360

(e)

	✓
Self-interest	✓
Self-review	
Intimidation	
Familiarity	

Explanation:

Self-interest is the biggest threat here as you will personally benefit if you do as the client wishes. Self-review is not relevant as you are not reviewing any of your own work here. Intimidation is not relevant either as the client has not threatened you. Familiarity is unlikely to be an issue here as this is your first year working for this client.

Task 4

(a) Extract from extended trial balance

	Ledger balances		Adjustments	
	Debit £	Credit £	Debit £	Credit £
Allowance for doubtful debts – adjustment			312	
Allowance for doubtful debts		2,888		312
Bank overdraft		590		
Closing inventory – SOFP			13,010	
Closing inventory – SPL				13,010
Discounts received		2,300		
Irrecoverable debts	790			
Purchases	675,564			
Purchases returns		9,247		
Purchases ledger control account		92,597	1,672	
Sales		843,898		
Sales returns	5,307			
Sales ledger control account	98,607			3,770
Suspense		2,098	3,770	1,672

Workings:

Allowance for doubtful debts

An increase of £312 is required (£3,200 – £2,888 in the TB). The journal needed is:

DR Allowance for doubtful debts – adjustments   £312
CR Allowance for doubtful debts   £312

Sales returns

Should have done	Did do	Correction
DR Sales returns £1,885	DR Sales returns £1,885	DR Suspense £3,770
CR SLCA £1,885	DR SLCA £1,885	CR SLCA £3,770
	CR Suspense £3,770	

Closing inventory

Inventory should be valued at the lower of cost (£1,575) and NRV (£1,400). As NRV is lower, a write down of £175 (£1,575 – £1,400) is required. This brings closing inventory to £13,185 – £175 = £13,010.

The double entry required is:

DR Closing inventory – statement of financial position £13,010
CR Closing inventory – statement of profit or loss £13,010

Discount received

Should have done	Did do	Correction
DR PLCA £836	DR Suspense £1,672	DR PLCA £1,672
CR Discounts received £836	CR PLCA £836	CR Suspense £1,672
	CR Discounts received £836	

(b)

Account	Debit £	Credit £
Profit or loss account	**790**	
Irrecoverable debts		**790**

Narrative:

Transfer of irrecoverable debts for year ended 31 December 20X5 to the profit or loss account

(c)

	✓
Pressure from authority	
Pressure to report favourable results	
Time pressure	✓
Pressure from stakeholders	

Task 5

(a)

Adjustment	Amount £	Debit ✓	Credit ✓
Adjustment 1	269		✓
Adjustment 2	500		✓
Adjustment 4	485		✓

Explanation:

Adjustments 3, 5 and 6 are all to the balance per the bank statement – adjustment 3 will decrease the balance by £940, adjustment 5 will increase the balance by £330 and adjustment 6 will reduce the balance by £140.

(b)

	✓
True	✓
False	

(c) Extended trial balance

Ledger account	Ledger balances		Adjustments		Statement of profit or loss		Statement of financial position	
	Dr £	Cr £	Dr £	Cr £	Dr £	Cr £	Dr £	Cr £
Accrued income			249				249	
Bank	7,281						7,281	
Capital		150,000						150,000
Closing inventory			9,433	9,433		9,433	9,433	
Commission income		7,893		249		8,142		
Depreciation charges			14,600		14,600			
Drawings	10,000						10,000	
General expenses	42,932			765	42,167			
Machinery at cost	200,000		3,400				203,400	
Machinery accumulated depreciation		125,000		14,600				139,600
Opening inventory	13,254				13,254			
Prepaid expenses			765				765	
Purchases	128,994			2,458	126,536			
Purchases ledger control account		17,493	399					17,094
Salaries	75,606				75,606			
Sales		195,433				195,433		
Sales ledger control account	25,775			399			25,376	
Suspense	942		2,458	3,400				
VAT		8,965						8,965
Loss for the year						59,155	59,155	
	504,784	504,784	31,304	31,304	**272,163**	**272,163**	**315,659**	**315,659**

Notes

BPP
LEARNING MEDIA